Once Upon a Crown

ALSO BY LEANÉ GILIOMEE

THE TWISTED CROWN TRILOGY
Book 1: If the Crown Fits
Book 2: Crown of Hearts
Book 3: Once Upon a Crown

ONCE UPON A CROWN

LEANÉ GILIOMEE

The Twisted Crown Trilogy, Book 3

JOFFE BOOKS

Joffe Books, London
www.joffebooks.com

First published in Great Britain in 2025

We love to hear from our readers!
Please email any feedback you have to: feedback@joffebooks.com

Cover design by SeventhStar Art

ISBN: 978-1-80573-146-7

To all the girls who long for a happily ever after.
It's out there somewhere. I promise.

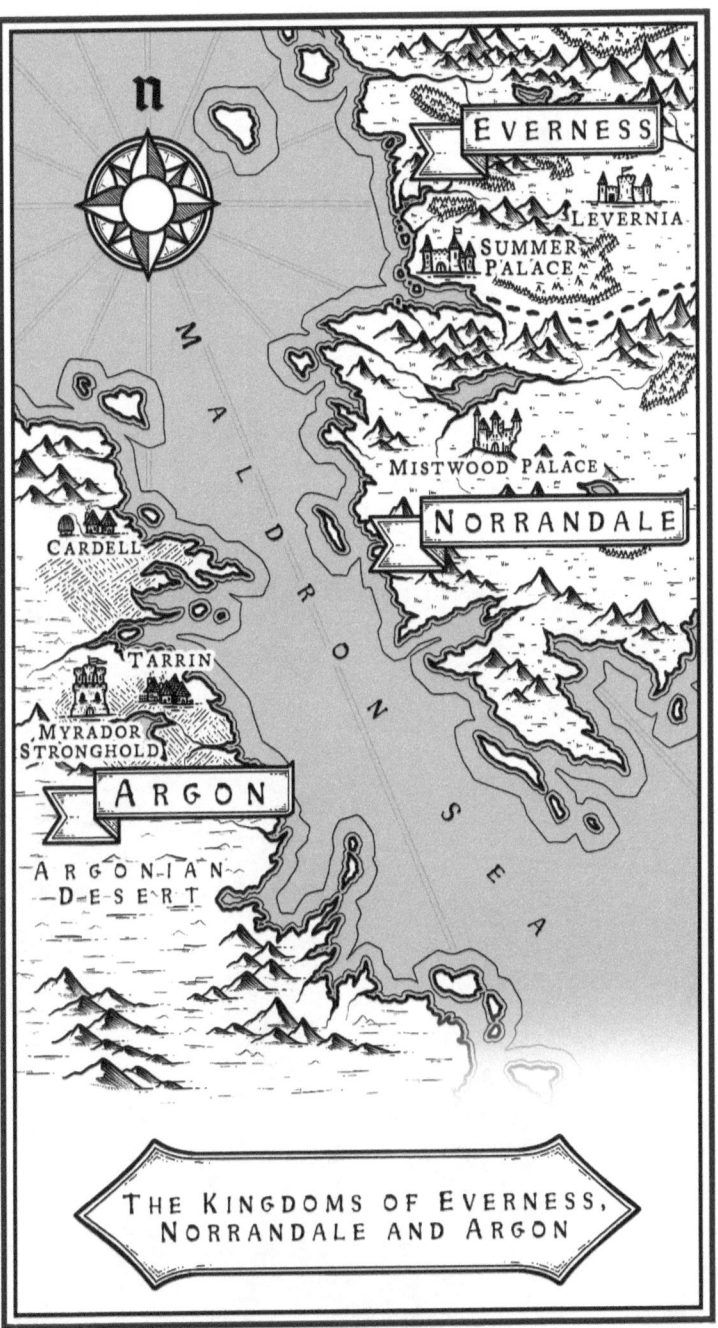

THE KINGDOMS OF EVERNESS,
NORRANDALE AND ARGON

Chapter 1

Elara

The forest beckoned me towards it.

Hands on the windowsill, I stared at the vast emerald landscape of broadleaved trees from my bedroom in the Palace of Levernia.

"Come," the forest whispered. *"Come back where you belong."*

Dark clouds clustered in the sky, casting Everness in a blanket of grey. The mountain ranges in the distance had yet to be tipped with snow but winter was here, and it wouldn't be long before the fields of green became a bleak map of brown hues, drenched in mud and fallen leaves.

"Which crown will it be today, Your Majesty?" Anesta, my lady-in-waiting, jerked me from my thoughts. I turned to face the cabinet that housed some of my jewellery. There was a vast selection to choose from, pieces that had been in the royal family for many generations, including the crown I'd inherited from Lance. According to Rhen, that specific crown had been around since Evrin's time, the first king of Everness. It was almost strange to think that an object with so much history had become an accessory that I wore most days. That

I was somehow part of something greater, a long line of kings and queens of this kingdom.

"Today's council meeting is very important," I reminded myself more than her. "Which do you think would be most appropriate?" The truth was, even after all these months of being queen, I still hadn't the slightest idea what was fashionable and which colours complemented each other. I didn't have the time or the interest to keep up with these sorts of things. Which was one of the many reasons I was grateful to have Anesta. If I wanted to present myself as a strong leader to my people, then it was important that I looked the part.

When our group arrived in Norrandale from Argon, Cordelia and Anesta had stayed in the harbour and taken the ship back to Everness, wanting to bring my sister, Eloisa, home. I could not have been more relieved when they arrived here unharmed. Especially after what happened with Jack, and Cai's family. Every time I relived Thatcher driving his sword through Jack, shivers ran down my spine. Not to mention the fact that he'd murdered Cai's mother and grand-mother. We'd been living with a monster that whole time, unknowing, believing we could trust him. It was sobering to realise, once again, that you could know someone your entire life and still know nothing about them.

"I think this one will go well with your dress, Your Majesty." Anesta held up a delicate crown of silver leaves, garnished with small green jewels.

"Good." I pulled the window shut so hard it made the glass rattle. "We'd better hurry up." I took it from her and stepped in front of the mirror before placing the crown atop my head. "I can't afford to be late today." Turning from side to side, I looked at the reflection in the mirror. My dress was light blue with long sleeves and hints of green in the patterns and stitching, and while it was beautiful, there were dark circles under my eyes, and I could no longer see any colour in my cheeks. The lack of sun these days did nothing for my pale complexion. I suppressed a frown when a knock sounded on my bedroom door.

"Come in."

Rhen, the captain of my guard, stepped inside the room, his eyes landing on me. "Don't tell me I'm late." His gaze lingered for a moment before he cleared his throat.

"No, Your Majesty. There are still a few minutes left to spare."

"Well, we'd better get a move on, then. It takes twice as long to reach the other side of the palace with these shoes." I wished I was joking. "Thanks for the help, Anesta."

"Of course, Your Majesty," she replied, but she wasn't looking at me. Her eyes were on Rhen, in his dashing guard's uniform. Anesta wasn't the only person at court whose gaze tended to linger on Rhen. His strong facial features and dark eyes often made him the subject of whispers and giggles shared by the female servants.

Rhen held the door open for me, and we left the room. I lifted the hems of my dress, keeping my hands from clenching into fists. Without meaning to, I let out a loud breath.

"Are you all right, Your Majesty?"

"Just glad I haven't had breakfast yet." My stomach was in a knot at the thought of walking into that council room.

"Everything will be fine," Rhen tried to reassure me. Something that had become a major part of his duties.

"Since when do you lie?" I gave him a side glance.

"I'm not lying."

"Cai's kingdom has been taken from him. His family was murdered by his best friend. I have yet to solidify my claim to the throne without a husband or an heir, and it's just a matter of time before Aries comes for Everness." Not even to mention what would happen if he discovered the mines with the Myrgonite stones. The thought of it all really made me feel sick now.

"Which is exactly why this council meeting is taking place. We need to come up with a plan," Rhen replied.

I just didn't know if I had any plans left in me. I was all out of ideas.

We hurried through the palace, and I readjusted my crown. Then I picked invisible pieces of lint from the sleeve of my dress, each step bringing me closer to a meeting I'd rather not attend.

"Stop fidgeting," Rhen whispered. I could see two guards standing at the council-room doors. "You're the queen, remember?"

Yes, but for how long? I didn't say it out loud. Rhen was right — the best thing I could do was keep my head up and act like I could still have them all executed if I wanted to. Technically I could, but that would only create more chaos than it was worth. And I didn't exactly feel like overseeing any hangings.

We stopped in front of the council-room doors, and I avoided eye contact with the guards. They were everywhere these days. But even the increased security didn't put me at ease. I took another deep breath.

"Are you ready?"

No. "Ready as I'll ever be."

Rhen stepped inside the room and announced me. The guards opened both doors, allowing me to make an entrance, and the council stood up from the central table as I entered. My older brother was at the opposite end of the table from where I would be sitting. In some

4

strange way, it brought me a little comfort to know Lance was there. At the very least I could trust he wanted to keep me on the throne.

Next to him were the dukes of Dalloway and Wells, as well as Brimsey. I'd taken a liking to him from the moment we'd met. He was a sweet man but serious when it mattered. His spectacles always sat very low on his nose, looking like they would fall off at any second. As far as I knew, I could trust all of them.

Levington had also been brought to my side. There were a few trays of sandwiches and desserts on the table, and Levington had already filled his plate more than was appropriate. The grand dukes of Brett and Creston were less eager to have me there. They did little to hide their disapproval of my reign.

On Lance's right stood Lady Gwen, her hands fisted at her side. I'd asked her to join us today because it was her brother, after all, who had played a big part in this. Not that I believed her to be connected to Thatcher's treachery in any way. She looked just as traumatised as the rest of us. But she was the only person, beside Cai, who knew Thatcher very well. She could give us some insight into what he might do next.

Alastor was there too. No one verbally confirmed it, but we all knew he'd taken Jack's place as Cai's new right-hand man, the head of his guard. It was a daunting task, and I admired him for stepping up to the role. Then again, he probably didn't have any more of a choice than the rest of us here, all forced into our new circumstances.

I took my seat at the head of the table and everyone else in the council room sat down.

"Good morning, gentlemen." I nodded towards them. "Lady Gwen." She hid behind a smile, but I could tell she was just as uncomfortable as I was.

"Your Majesty." There were a few murmurs of greeting.

The only person not present in the room, and perhaps the one I wanted there more than anyone else, was Cai. He hadn't left his rooms much since we'd arrived in Everness. He didn't attend meetings or dinners or really talk to anyone at all.

But he'd been deeper through hell than any of us. His family had been killed. His best friend betrayed him. His throne had been taken, and his enemy was invading his kingdom. I was trying to give him all the space he needed. But I was worried. This couldn't go on for ever. I wasn't willing to give up and let Aries win. Not without a fight.

"What's the latest news?" I asked no one in particular. Everyone seemed to have spies just about everywhere these days, something I'd grown to appreciate to an extent in the past few weeks.

"Lord Thatcher has been working with King Aries these past months, letting his spies into Norrandale and the palace, aiding in multiple assassination attempts on King Cai and eventually murdering the royal family of Norrandale. He was also in charge of the coup, along with Aries' soldiers, allowing him to take control of the palace in Norrandale and give Aries passage into the kingdom." Alastor decided to speak up first. He wasn't a man of many words, so every time I heard him talk, the sound was unfamiliar. His dark hair had grown even longer in the past few months, and he kept it tied up most of the time.

"We know all this," Wells replied, sounding somewhat bored. He was a tall man, well into his later years, and his long grey hair was tied neatly with a ribbon. His eyes looked similar to those of many of the people in the paintings in the palace. Evidence that his family had been close to the monarchy for a very long time.

"I was just making sure everyone was aware of the current situation." Alastor was quick to bite back without changing the tone of his voice. "The latest news suggests that Aries has sailed a large number of men to Norrandale. Just short of two thousand."

"His army, you mean?" Brimsey asked.

"Some are soldiers, yes, but many of them appear to be labourers. Aries plundered a few towns near the coast, but they've been moving inland, closer to the mountains."

The council members frowned at Alastor's response.

"Why the hell would Aries bring a few thousand labourers to the mountains of Norrandale?" This time, it was the Duke of Brett who asked the question. He always appeared tired, regardless of the time of day, and I wondered what kept him up at night. Based on the rumours circulating at court, it sounded like Brett spent many of his evenings in establishments of ill repute. He had sharp facial features, and I could imagine him being quite handsome in his younger years. I might have liked him had it not been for the fact that he had never truly supported my claim to the throne.

"Maybe he's looking for something." It was the first time Lance had spoken. His dark hair looked slightly ruffled. Almost as if he'd just rolled out of bed. My brother's icy-blue eyes fell on me, his gaze suggesting I knew exactly what he was talking about.

"What could he be looking for? Norrandale's mines have been abandoned for years. There's nothing out there."

"And why would Aries go through all that trouble and invade the kingdom for a few worthless mines?" Creston questioned, the tone of his voice matching his harsh expression. He was a close confidant of Brett, and if any two members of my council were ever to conspire against me, they would be my first suspects.

One of my first orders of business as queen was to restore land to some of the aristocracy, but also to the common folk, who could have their own plots of land to sustain themselves instead of paying the wealthy landowners. Brett and Creston never approved of my order, but it did not surprise me, considering how much tax money they collected from those who lived on their land.

"Maybe he was misinformed. Perhaps he believes there to be a lot of undiscovered gold," the Duke of Dalloway suggested.

"I thought Aries had some kind of personal vendetta against King Cai for killing his brother. Now, all of a sudden, he wants to mine gold that may or may not be there?" It was Wells's turn to interject.

"Surely, if there were gold, Norrandale would already have been mining it?" Brett said.

"Gentlemen." The sound of my voice made them all pipe down and turn to look at me. "Perhaps we are getting a little sidetracked about what exactly Aries is doing in Norrandale and forgetting that he has still invaded the kingdom, broken the peace treaty, and is now posing a potential threat to Everness." There was a part of me that was relieved that Aries' first order of business was not coming after me or Cai or taking over the kingdom. But that didn't ease the worrying idea of the Argonians heading for the mountains. Aries was looking for the Myrgonite mines, and if he didn't find them, how long until he came after the Myrgonite objects? Three stones forged into objects using ancient magic, now reduced to myth and legend. I didn't know the extent of Aries' knowledge about the stones, but he knew enough to break a peace treaty and invade Norrandale.

"Everness isn't ready for a war." The Grand Duke of Creston had a disapproving look on his face. "It's winter and the treasury is near empty because of all the money the Crown owed the aristocracy." I gave him a slight warning look, and then he added, "Which you so graciously repaid, Your Majesty." I could tell by his tone that he was not sincere.

"Don't forget the fact that you haven't been collecting taxes as often, either," Brett added.

"As long as King Aries doesn't have his entire army here and isn't trying to conquer Norrandish cities, we might stand a chance," Alastor said.

"The only reason Aries managed to invade Norrandale so quickly was because he had Thatcher working for him on the inside. If His Majesty is only mining in Norrandale then it doesn't appear to be an Evernean problem to me," Creston retorted.

"The King of Norrandale was forced into exile, yes. So where are his supporters who would fight with him for his throne?" Dalloway asked.

"Cai has many loyalists all over the kingdom, but it would take months to gather all his forces and secure the proper funds," Alastor replied.

"We might not have months," I interjected. How long before Aries couldn't find what he was looking for and decided he wanted to confront Cai? Who knew what he would do to Cai to get information out of him. "Aries can turn any second. We need to be prepared. And Cai needs to take back Mistwood Palace if he wants to reclaim his throne."

"Speaking of which, where is His Majesty? Shouldn't he be joining us for meetings that regard him and his kingdom?" Brett's question made my stomach coil with nerves. I didn't know how much longer I could keep making excuses for Cai.

"The King is currently indisposed." Alastor, thankfully, answered for me. "He will join us as soon as he is feeling well."

Brimsey spoke up. "His Majesty cannot go to Norrandale and try to win back his throne with no support on the ground. He needs soldiers."

"And what if we send our soldiers to Norrandale and they all get slaughtered?" Creston raised his voice. "Who will be left to protect Everness?"

"The King and Queen were still engaged the last time I checked." I was surprised by Lance's words, and apparently so was everyone else, because there was a moment of silence in the room.

"They are not married yet and Everness has signed nothing to agree to aid Norrandale in the event of war against Argon," Creston shot back.

The tension in the room was high, everyone on edge. This meeting was not going well.

"You are right, Your Grace." I raised my own voice. "We have not agreed to send soldiers to Norrandale." I looked about the room, eyeing my council — the rich aristocrats whom I barely knew, half of whom didn't even want me on the throne and would most likely use this as an opportunity to have me removed. I had to watch my back like never before. "But Aries is coming one way or another. So, I suggest we start to gather an army and ready our forces. We must be prepared if he decides to attack or if we should march to Norrandale in the spring."

"Will there have been a royal wedding by then?" the Duke of Wells asked carefully. I felt my cheeks tint slightly. I could barely get Cai to speak to me or leave his room. There hadn't exactly been the right moment for us to discuss our engagement or the uniting of the two kingdoms.

"The wedding is not the most important topic that needs to be discussed." I attempted to change the subject and shifted my gaze to Gwen.

"Lady Gwen." Her eyes found mine, her expression filled with uncertainty. She'd been more quiet during this meeting than ever before. Usually she was the lively, bubbly sort, but ever since the betrayal by her brother, something had changed about her.

"Yes, Your Majesty?"

"I think it is safe to say you know the man currently in charge of Mistwood Palace very well."

"Yes, Your Majesty," she said again.

"If, for whatever reason, Cai should decide to go to Norrandale, your brother would be his first immediate threat. I must admit, though I've met Lord Thatcher, I don't feel that well acquainted with him. Especially in the context of warfare."

"My brother has always been very determined, Your Majesty. But I never knew him to be capable of such violence." With every word, she was trying to hold herself together. I hadn't meant to sabotage Gwen by asking her to the council meeting. I only wanted to get a better understanding of our new enemy.

"Say we were to attack the palace — how would he go about defending himself?" I folded my hands on the table. The whole council room was quiet, listening to our exchange, Aries and the mines temporarily forgotten.

"Thatcher might be able to prey on those weaker than him, but I think he's always been threatened by Cai. You were taken by surprise last time, but should you be on the offensive now, I don't think my brother would be in the front row to fight. He'll be looking for a way to protect himself."

"How do we know that anything she says is true?" Creston said. "For all we know, she is here on Thatcher's behalf, spying on all of us."

"I assure you I am not," Gwen replied, her tone a little firmer now. She wasn't the sort of person to take kindly to being falsely accused.

"Of course, there are means of extracting information should it be necessary." A sickening feeling washed over me at the thought of these men hurting Gwen. Based on Creston's expression, he looked like he might enjoy it.

"I can assure you that Lady Gwen is not working with her brother and that she can be trusted," I said quickly, placing my palm flat on the table.

Brett interrupted the conversation. "Perhaps we should consider how Lady Gwen could aid us in relation to her brother, then."

"What do you mean?"

"Thatcher doesn't have many reasons to distrust his sister. She could be valuable to us when it comes to getting information."

I was at the end of my wits with the men in this room. A hanging suddenly didn't seem like such a bad idea anymore.

"I will not use Lady Gwen as a pawn and put her life in danger. She grew up in Mistwood and she's very familiar with the layout of the palace as well as the territory of the kingdom. Combined with the knowledge of her brother, this makes her valuable to us." Gwen and I had known each other for some time now, and while we'd yet to have deep and very meaningful discussions, I liked her company very much. I could see some relief in her expression at my words.

"I would never suggest such a thing, Your Majesty," Brett responded, unable to tell his opinion was unwanted. "I understand her value as an ally. But we do need to take all our options into consideration."

"Aries has not given us a reason to believe he is coming after Everness yet. But once he has conquered Norrandale, there is nothing stopping him from coming here. I would like to increase our defences by stationing more men at the border."

"That can be arranged, Your Majesty," Brimsey said.

"Since Norrandale wasn't taken by war, Aries will use the towns and farms to keep his army sustained. I want to be ready should he decide to invade."

"If Aries should decide to come to Everness, before his men could make it to the towns and villages, they would have to cross the Evernean Forest and this would slow them down drastically." Wells made a good point. We could find a way to use the forest to our advantage.

"If the Argonians should make it through the forest, the small towns and villages would be hit first. The people need to gather provisions and start making their own weapons. We must also ready the palace in the event that a siege takes place." I didn't want to be taken by surprise again.

"We all have plenty to think about," I continued. "Our soldiers need to be readied, and we must prepare for any possibility." I stood up from the table, indicating that this meeting had come to its end.

"If we were to send an army, we might have to raise a tax, Your Majesty." Dalloway, though appearing to be on my side thus far, raised a valid concern. "Wars and armies are expensive to fund."

"In this season? The people will revolt." Levington was also right. He'd kept rather quiet during most of the meeting, indulging in the complimentary sandwiches and biscuits while he listened to us bicker back and forth. Little did they all know that should Aries' "mining" expedition be successful, we would have much bigger problems than taxes and revolts.

Chapter 2

Gwen

I tightened the girth around the horse's stomach, making sure the saddle wouldn't slide around. The grey mare chewed on some hay while I tacked her up. Apart from a few small spots on her legs, her coat was pristine. Combined with her sweet temperament, you had yourself a very fine horse. I'd only been riding her the past week or two but one could easily tell that every other horse in the royal stables had been selected with just as much care. Whoever was in charge clearly took their duty seriously.

I adjusted the stirrups while the stable boy pretended to be busy in a far-off corner. I hoped I hadn't insulted him by insisting that I tack up the horse myself. It was not that I thought him incapable. The truth was I enjoyed the grooming and tacking part just as much as I enjoyed the riding part. There was something about being in the presence of these animals that soothed me.

I took the reins and led the mare away from the hay and towards a nearby mounting block. She was momentarily hesitant to leave her food but quickly obeyed. "Good girl, Bessie."

It seemed like an odd name for a horse but somehow it suited her sweet personality.

I mounted and pulled the reins between my fingers, nudging the horse into a walk. The morning air was crisp, and I wondered how long the weather would allow me these early-morning rides. Every day the sun rose later and later. These rides had become my solace and comfort in a time where I felt as though I was at my wits' end. It was a chance to be alone with my thoughts. And while I often found myself without company in the palace, there was something about the fresh air and the movement of the horse's steps that brought a sense of calm over me. I found the sounds of nature to be soothing in comparison to the daily hustle and bustle of Levernia's palace.

The two of us crossed the path from the stables to the palace gardens. I pushed the mare into a brisk walk on the path between the lawns. Soon, some of the guards would come out to start training, but for now, I was alone.

I preferred it this way. The quiet, lonesome palace grounds with nothing but the sound of horse hooves relaxed me a little. The grey mare twitched under me, and I realised how my body had tensed up in the saddle. I forced myself to let out a long breath.

Finally, I made it out of the gardens, through a gate. The flowers and hedges turned to trees and tall uncut grass.

Tightening my grip on the reins, I nudged the horse into a slow trot, and she lowered her head.

"Good girl." I wasn't the most experienced of riders, but this was clearly a very well-trained horse. "I wonder why no one rides you more often?" The mare continued to trot through the grass. "Were you perhaps the late king's horse?" I had a hard time imagining a man as hardened as him could have had an animal so sweet. The mare would require a kind owner with a gentle spirit. Someone just as calm as she was.

Grey clouds darkened the sky but there was no breeze in the air. Still, I pulled the mare back into a walk while trying to cover more of my body with my cloak.

My nerves were shaken by the council meeting a few days earlier. And I wasn't really the type of girl to have her nerves shaken about anything. I was thankful that Queen Elara hadn't asked me to join them because she was suspicious of me in any way, but because she wanted a better understanding of my brother.

The thought brought a sting to my chest. The very idea that someone who'd been so close to me could do such a thing ... But when I truly thought on it, if there was anyone, I knew capable of doing something so abhorrent, it would be Thatcher. We were the kind of siblings to mess with each other a lot, despite both of us being young adults, and for the most part, it was all in good fun. But I knew my brother better than anyone and he had a dark side lurking underneath that cool exterior. And maybe, as his sister, I'd always suspected as much. But perhaps I'd just wanted to ignore it. Didn't want to believe that the person I was closest to in the world would partake in such cruelty. Thatcher could be cunning, even sometimes selfish and despicable, but this ... this was unforgiveable. He'd hurt everyone I cared about. He betrayed me too. My mind drifted to the day he left Everness. It was after Cai and Elara had gone to Argon for Eloisa and to see if it would be possible to negotiate peace between Norrandale and Argon once again. Thatcher and I had stayed at the Palace of Levernia, awaiting their return ...

"Where are you going?" I walked into the foyer of the palace, surprised to have stumbled upon all of Thatcher's belongings being carried out by the servants. I noticed a carriage waiting through the open doors.

Thatcher spun around. "You're up early." He looked surprised to see me, which was odd.

"I'm going for a walk." As was evident by my outdoor attire. The weather wasn't bound to stay decent for much longer, so I wanted to make the most of the palace grounds while I could.

"I was going to leave you this." There was a folded piece of paper in his hand with my name scribbled in his handwriting. He quickly tucked it away. "But I suppose it doesn't matter now."

"Are you leaving?" I had a hard time believing my brother would just pack up his things and go, especially without telling me.

"Yes, I have to go back home, I'm afraid."

"What for? We haven't even been here that long." His whole posture looked uncomfortable. He was on edge, which wasn't normal for Thatcher, who was laid-back, with a "couldn't care less" attitude most of the time.

"I have a few loose ends to tie up. Besides" — he looked around the foyer of the palace — "I think I prefer Norrandale." Levernia wasn't home, to be certain. Norrandale's towns were much more vibrant, with their endless shops and quaint little markets and the taverns from which music often spilled out onto the streets. But with the recent rebellion and the people being so divided, I supposed it would take time for Levernia to regain its liveliness.

Thatcher loved his life at court in Norrandale. But did he honestly plan on leaving me alone here with no one but Prince Lance to keep me company? Something didn't feel right.

"Is it Mother and Father? Is everything all right?" Our parents hadn't been to court for quite some time. Perhaps something had gone awfully wrong with Father's businesses and we'd lost all our money. I could think of few other things that would get Thatcher rattled like this.

"Mother and Father are fine," he assured me, but I wasn't sure what to believe.

"What about Cai?" The King and Queen had just left for Argon, hoping to sort out matters with King Aries.

Thatcher put his hands in his pockets. Took them out again. *"I'll meet him at Mistwood. They'll probably stop there on their way back. Who knows what Aries is planning. Cai might need my support that side."* He did have a point there. But it didn't settle the uneasy feeling in my stomach.

"Do you want me to come with you?" I wasn't sure which answer I wanted. Part of me feared I would feel alone here but the other part of me wasn't ready to return home yet, to face my duties that side. Mother was not pleased that I had come here with Thatcher, and she would see me married off as soon as possible.

"I think it's better if you stay for now. I'll be back soon."

It was the last thing my brother had said to me. And now I didn't know if I would ever see him again. I knew something was wrong that day. I should have stopped him or done something. In a way I felt responsible for letting him go, unknowing of the atrocities he was about to commit.

Everyone here had been treating me kindly, but how long before they turned and decided I was a traitor too? I looked at the thick Evernean Forest in the distance and thought about all the stories and myths I'd heard. I remembered Elara briefly mentioning, once, that the woods contained some kind of magic. I'd heard some of the fairy tales as a kid and wondered now if they had any merit to them.

"Come on." I lightly pulled at the rein, coaxing the mare to turn around. "Let's go back."

My brother's words followed me as I made my way along the wooded track: "*I'll be back soon …*"

Chapter 3

Cai

The fire was dying in the hearth. I couldn't remember falling asleep in my clothes. My body was splayed in the chair in front of the fireplace in my room. The curtains were still unopened, leaving the room dark. The only light was from the embers that were slowly burning out.

I rubbed my eyes. My neck was stiff from the position I'd been lying in.

What time of day was it? *What* day was it?

Most of the time it felt like they were all merging into each other.

I was unsure how long I'd been sleeping. There were noises coming from outside my bedroom door. It sounded like people talking, or arguing was more like it. Pulling myself into a better sitting position, I ran my fingers through my messy hair. It was longer than it had been in many years, but I couldn't find the motivation to cut it.

"I just want to talk to him. No one has seen him for days." The voice on the other side of the door was familiar — Elara.

"The King has asked us that he not be disturbed, Your Majesty," the guard outside my door responded.

"Well, the *queen* of this kingdom is going to have your head if you do not open this door immediately."

There was an uncomfortable clearing of a throat before the door hinges squeaked. My back was to the door, and I didn't turn as she stepped inside the room.

"Cai?" Elara sounded a lot more uncertain than she had a few seconds ago. I heard a rustle behind me and suddenly a bright light bathed the room as Elara pulled open one of the curtains I squinted in discomfort.

"Cai, when did you last eat?" I looked around me but there were no signs of empty plates or cups. Perhaps the servants had taken them away while I was sleeping, I didn't know. I still couldn't recall what day it was, much less when I had had my last meal.

Finally, she came into my line of sight and took a seat on the chair next to me. I kept my gaze intently fixed on the last of the fire.

The scent of her was like a breath of fresh air, sweet with a warm undertone. She looked dazzling in her dark red dress, the cuffs and collar made of animal fur. It complemented her dark red lips, along with her golden crown. I quickly looked away, too ashamed to meet her eyes.

She had to pull me away that day. Had to force me to get on a horse and flee as I was exiled from my own kingdom. I couldn't protect Elara … or anyone for that matter. And I hated myself for failing her. I knew if I looked into her eyes, it would shatter me.

"There was a council meeting a few days ago." She tried to start up a conversation again. "Everyone was there, even Alastor and Gwen."

What would Gwen be doing in a council meeting? I hadn't seen much of her after confining myself to my rooms, but I imagined she must be just as distraught over her brother.

"How many cities has Aries sacked?" I forced the words out of my mouth. My throat was dry and scratchy. I needed something to drink.

"He hasn't really been attacking the cities." The hesitation in her voice told me I wasn't going to like what she was about to say. "He's been making his way to the mountains." Of course he had. Our biggest fear was coming into being and I didn't know how to stop it. How would we go up against the entire Argonian army? How would I reclaim my throne?

"The council wants to meet with you as well. I want Everness to prepare for war." She'd expected me to be at that meeting and I felt bad for not having shown up. Truthfully, I couldn't remember being told about it. Sometimes my dreams and reality blended into one and I had a hard time knowing what was real.

I couldn't imagine meeting with the council. Not until I could pull myself together. They would look to me for wisdom and answers and I felt lost. What good was a king who couldn't even get into his own kingdom? I wanted my father. The sound of his reassuring voice, his hand on my shoulder. I needed him to tell me what to do.

"Is Everness ready for that kind of battle?"

"I doubt it." She sighed. "Some of my people don't even want me on the throne." She hadn't been queen for long enough. They might view her sending Evernean armies to Norrandale as impulsive and naive.

When I didn't respond, she placed her hand on mine, where it rested on the arm of the chair. It was warm and soft and part of me so desperately wanted to reach for her, but I found myself unable to. "We need allies in Norrandale. We need to take back Mistwood."

I could imagine Thatcher in the throne room, seated on a throne that had hosted my family for generations, making a mockery of my legacy. The court would have fled, Aries' guards stationed everywhere.

Who knew how many more people he had killed after he had murdered my family, after he had murdered one of my closest friends.

"Walking into that palace would be like walking into a deathtrap." I pulled my hand away from hers and tried not to picture her expression, no doubt full of hurt or disappointment.

There was a moment of silence, another sigh from her. "Well, we have to do something, Cai."

"So that more people we care about can die?" I knew she was right and that we needed to take action. I just didn't know where to begin. Not when I was still so consumed by my own grief.

Elara stood up and I thought she was about to leave, put off by my words, but instead she crouched down in front of me. My eyes remained focused on the fireplace.

"I'm so sorry about your mother and your grandmother. And I'm sorry about Jack." Her voice cracked a little in sincerity, and a wave of sadness and loss washed over me once more. "But we cannot let Aries see this through. We cannot let him win."

"Aries has already won," I replied.

"Look at me, Cai." I couldn't. She was so much stronger and braver than I could ever be, and I couldn't protect her.

I couldn't protect her.

I couldn't protect any of them.

They were all dead because of me.

Because I failed them.

"Look at me," Elara said, more determined this time. Her hands reached for my stubbled cheeks and forced my head to turn. I met her eyes. Where they once smouldered with fire, I could only see pain behind them now. They were searching me for answers I did not possess.

"I cannot imagine how difficult this must be for you. But please don't push me away."

I didn't want to, but everything we had done to protect Norrandale had been in vain, and I couldn't change it. Too many people had died because of me. I wasn't ready for war and yet it was here anyway.

I gently took her hands and lowered them, turning my head away. "I don't want to put more people's lives at risk."

"Our lives are already at risk." There was anger in her voice now. Or maybe desperation. She stood up abruptly. "Aries is a monster, and I will not allow him to trample over more innocent people. But I cannot do this on my own."

"I'm sorry, Elara." It was all I could get out. *Please forgive me.*

"So that's it? You're just going to sit up here alone and wait for death to come and get you? You're just going to give up on everything, on all of us?" No, I just didn't know how to fight when all I could see and feel was pain and anger.

"I'm sorry," I said again, my voice barely above a whisper.

"I'll see you in the morning, okay?" she said, a bit more gently. I heard the door shut behind her.

Chapter 4

Lance

I stared at the chessboard in front of me.

I'd been purposely trying to give white the advantage and yet black was about to corner the king. My eyes wandered to the glass of whisky on the table next to the chessboard. Perhaps it wasn't the wisest idea to be drinking while playing chess with myself.

Oh well.

Leaning back in my chair, I intertwined my fingers, inspecting the board and possible moves for white. I could always take the bishop with the white knight but that would leave the queen exposed.

The door to the library suddenly opened and I nearly jumped in my seat at the interruption. I was about to scold whatever servant didn't knock before entering rooms when, to my surprise, Lady Gwen came into view.

Her eyes immediately landed on me and the chessboard, and I watched her cheeks flush as her expression settled into slight discomfort. "Oh," she said, as if surprised to find me in my own home. "My apologies for intruding."

"There's no need to apologise." I took a sip from my drink, the liquid burning all the way down my throat. Maybe I should have had breakfast before this and then perhaps everything would be clearer. "Are you looking for something, Lady Gwen?"

She didn't move from her position at the door. "I was looking for His Majesty, actually. Have you seen him?"

"I believe Cai is still confined to his rooms." Whatever the hell that was supposed to mean. At least that was the excuse Elara had been giving, but I could see the worry behind her eyes every time it was mentioned.

"Oh."

"How long have you known Cai?" I tilted my head, swirling the ice in my glass.

"My whole life," Gwen replied, brows furrowed as if I'd just asked the most idiotic question in the world.

"So why on earth do you refer to him as 'His Majesty'?" I knew she was just trying to be respectful, but I couldn't help myself from seeing if I could press her buttons.

"Because he is my king." There was a tone of distaste in her voice.

"Well, thanks to your brother, we're playing fast and loose with the term *king*."

My response must have sparked something inside her because she stepped into the room and swung the door shut behind her, still keeping a considerable distance between us.

"Just because Cai isn't currently sitting on his throne in Norrandale, doesn't mean he's not my king." She wouldn't take the bait. How unfortunate.

"You're very loyal," I said, and while it was intended as a partial compliment, Gwen looked as if I'd just insulted her.

"Why wouldn't I be? Cai is like a brother to me."

"Family can be tough sometimes, especially brothers." I never did like Thatcher much. Was even relatively happy to see him go back to Norrandale, obviously without knowing what his intentions were. I mean, *I* could be a prick, and though I couldn't exactly put my finger on it, something about him just ticked me off.

"Well, Her Majesty would know." She crossed her arms, her eyes daring a response out of me.

"Elara would know what?"

"What it's like to have a brother with no regard for others."

Though I was surprised by her blunt words, I forced my expression to stay neutral — perhaps even a little amused. Gwen's lips pressed together, as if she too realised how inappropriate her comment was to someone of a much higher station than herself. For someone so eager to use titles, she certainly didn't seem interested in using mine.

Gwen had changed in the years since I last saw her when Father and I had gone to visit Norrandale. We'd only met once but her face wasn't the sort you were likely to forget. Gone were the traces of girlhood. Gone was the shyness and blushing cheeks. The young lady who stood before me might as well have been a stranger. Her light hair fell in slight curls over her shoulders. My eyes travelled to her collarbone that peeked out from the neckline of her dress and then back to her eyes, caught somewhere between the shades of blue and green.

"My, my, Lady Gwen. You've certainly grown bold since I've last seen you."

"Would you prefer false flattery?" Few people made a habit of speaking their minds to me. Which was probably a wise thing in most cases. I didn't appreciate being made to look foolish. But there was something refreshing about her honesty. She didn't want anything from me. In fact, her expression appeared as though she'd rather be anywhere else in the world than talking to me in the library.

"Never," I replied, unable to keep myself from grinning. "I only want honest confessions from your mouth." The words slipped out before I could think better of it. Both of our eyes travelled to the almost empty glass of whisky on the table.

"Are you drunk before eleven o'clock in the morning?"

"I believe that's 'are you drunk before eleven o'clock in the morning, *Your Highness*?'" I drawled out the title, unable to help myself.

After what happened in Norrandale, the past few months in the palace had been dreary and depressing at best. There were no social events, no parties or revelry of any kind. Most days I spent in utter boredom. In fact, this was the most exciting conversation I'd had in weeks.

Gwen did not think I was being funny at all. Her face held nothing but annoyance at me. When she didn't respond, I gestured to the glass. "Would you like a drink?"

"No, thank you," she said quickly.

"You don't drink?"

Gwen shrugged. "My father and brother are both fond of the bottle. No good ever came from it." Clearly not.

"You know—" I took a sip, returning to my comfortably reclined position — "I do feel as though I'm being judged here somehow."

"And what right would I have to judge a prince?" Gwen's tone brimmed with sarcasm.

"You tell me. What gives you the moral high ground, Lady Gwen?"

She scoffed, looking away from me to shake her head. "You haven't changed one bit, have you?"

"Well, you know what they say." I gestured to myself. "You can't improve perfection."

Gwen clenched her jaw to prevent herself from saying whatever it was she felt impelled to say. She took a step back.

"Of course not, Your Highness." Gwen disguised her mocking with polite words. "I'd better be on my way, then."

"Do send my regards to my future brother-in-law." I knew that she would do no such thing.

Gwen was halfway out the door when I called her name. She looked over her shoulder.

"I hope you'll change your mind and join me for a drink sometime."

"I wouldn't hold my breath if I were you."

Chapter 5

Elara

A crow shrieked in the distance, and I crossed my arms to keep from shivering, despite all my warm layers of clothing. The air was cold enough that I could see my own breath. I stared at the gravestone that was inscribed with Ray's name. Members of the royal family were usually buried in the crypts beneath the palace and there was a cemetery in town, but I knew if Ray could choose, he wouldn't want to be buried in any of those places.

Ray loved the forest. His life was the forest.

I never got the chance to give my friend a proper funeral. But I was grateful that, at the very least, his body now rested in a place he would have wanted.

I had arranged for a grave to be dug on the outskirts of the forest with a heavy marble gravestone resting on top.

Ray would have probably said it was too extravagant. I smiled at the thought.

With my gloved hands, I placed a bunch of daisies on top of the grave. Part of me was reluctant to believe that it was my oldest friend lying there beneath the earth. It didn't feel real. None of what we were going through felt real. So much had changed in so little time.

"Oh, Ray." Just saying his name out loud created a pang in my chest. "How did we find ourselves here?"

I brushed a few stray leaves away from the gravestone. "Everything is such a mess and it feels like I have nobody to talk to," I confessed. "The situation is so dire, and everyone is looking at me for answers." The council was rushing me for a decision — all while, in the back of my mind, I knew I could be expendable as well.

"I need Cai more than ever and he can't even look at me." My voice cracked a little and I sniffed in the cold winter air. My eyes wandered to the trees around me and into the distance where the forest grew deeper. It was entering its annual slumber — I could feel it. I couldn't even hear the birds singing anymore.

I looked back to the grave with melancholy when a cool breeze rose up and slithered past me.

Come. The wind whispered against my skin.

You belong here in the forest.

If I hadn't known better, I might have thought it to be my imagination. But I wasn't afraid. Though this place could be dangerous, it had been my home for so long. I'd started to realise, quite some time ago, that it may have protected me in many ways, from a young age.

I looked to where my horse was tied to a nearby tree. A year ago, or even six months ago, I would not have hesitated. I would have run away from everything and everyone. I would have ridden deep into the forest and never looked back. But Cai was right about one thing: I wasn't that girl anymore — and I didn't think I could ever go back to her.

"I wish you were here to give me some advice." I turned my gaze back to the grave and a sad smile crept onto my face. "You would probably say that I should tell them all to go to hell." I sniffed again, the cold air pinching my cheeks.

"I don't know what I'm going to do, Ray. I don't know how I'm going to do this."

The crunching of footsteps on the forest floor drew my attention. Someone wanted me to know they were coming. I looked over my shoulder to see Rhen making his way towards me while leading his horse.

I'd told him I would be coming out here so that no one would worry but I'd also given specific instructions that I wanted to be left alone.

"I haven't been gone that long," I called out as he neared me. "Surely war hasn't broken out already."

Rhen stopped close to my mare. "Thankfully not." He sounded a little out of breath. "I do have some other important news, though."

"What could be so important that you had to ride all this way to tell me?" A list of possibilities popped into my mind and none of them were good.

"It's your sister," Rhen replied. "She's awake."

Eloisa had been in a sleeping state since Cordelia and Anesta had arrived with her at the palace. We were all surprised to find out she'd been in Argon all those months, and I had no doubt King Aries had had something to do with it. Eloisa was in no state to talk about her stay in Argon, and then she had taken ill on the journey back to Norrandale.

It got so bad that the physician told us she might never wake from her sleep.

I was nervous to see her again. Especially after our initial encounters had been less than comfortable. There was no telling what she would do.

Lance seemed unaffected by all of this. According to him, this behaviour was completely normal. It was clear why Princess Eloisa had stayed out of the public eye for most of her life. She was in no way able to perform any of her royal duties.

Maybe it was the warmth of the palace interior or my ever-growing nerves, but I was starting to feel too hot. With my gloved hands, I yanked on the ties of my cloak but only managed to tangle them further. I let out a groan of frustration and Rhen, who had been walking next to me this whole time, stepped in front of me. "May I, Your Majesty?" He gestured to the knot around my neck.

I hesitated for a moment, not wanting to admit defeat.

"Very well." I sighed and dropped my hands. Rhen started working on the knot, his eyes focused on the task at hand.

"Would it make me the worst person in the world if I'm not overcome with joy to see my sister?"

"Your situation is …" He searched for the right word. "Complex."

"Perhaps things would be different if we could actually get to know each other but with Eloisa's illness …" I trailed off.

"I know," Rhen replied, managing to pull the ties of my cloak free. He helped me take it off and draped the heavy piece of material over his arm.

"According to Lance, she wasn't always as …" I searched for the right word. "… ill as she is now. It's got worse, slowly, over the years. But he doesn't seem overly concerned."

"That's because Lance is too hungover every morning to care."

A slightly less significant problem in a very long list of problems. Rhen and I made our way up the white marble stairs and towards the east wing of the palace. Eloisa's sleeping quarters had been set up in one of the rooms furthest away from any possible commotion. She also had a nurse looking after her.

"We'll cross that bridge when we get there," I responded. "One royal problem at a time."

"Fair enough." Though there was no need for it, Rhen made a habit of avoiding Lance since he'd imprisoned Rhen all that time ago. In all fairness, Rhen did commit treason by aiding the rebellion, and I doubted Lance had ever truly moved on from that betrayal.

The maroon-wallpapered corridors grew smaller the further we walked. Rhen trailed a good distance behind me now, as was probably more appropriate.

I didn't realise I was holding my breath until we stopped in front of Eloisa's doors.

Rhen knocked for me, and Eloisa's nurse, Agatha, opened the door. She was a sweet older lady with a wrinkled smile and a few grey hairs peeking out from her bun.

"Your Majesty." She quickly bowed.

"I heard our patient is awake." I forced an optimistic smile.

"She is, Your Majesty." Agatha stepped aside to let us in. "But I'm afraid she's not very talkative yet."

Fine by me. Though Eloisa's room had many windows, most of the curtains were shut, allowing only a little bit of light to creep in. On the far side of the room, her figure was enveloped in layers of blankets, beneath the canopy of her bed.

Eloisa sat upright but she made no eye contact as we entered.

"Should I wait outside?" Rhen offered but I shook my head.

"No, I want you to stay." I wasn't ready to face her alone and I wished more than anything that Cai was here with me. Rhen nodded and resumed a soldier-like stance as I turned and approached the bed.

"Hello, Eloisa." She was staring at the bedding as if there was something terribly interesting about it. I stopped next to the bed. "We're glad to see you're awake."

She made no attempt to acknowledge me.

"Are you feeling better?"

Her pale face turned to the window, which gave her a view of the stables and part of the training grounds.

"Would you like me to open the window?" Even though she didn't respond, I walked over and unlatched it, allowing fresh winter air to creep into the room. We wouldn't be able to keep it open for very long or we'd be putting Eloisa's health at risk all over again.

"Eloisa, do you remember me?" I dared to ask, hoping to elicit some reaction out of her. But she kept staring at the window, seemingly listening to the sounds of the servants bustling outside.

"We went to Argon to come and get you. I'm your sister. Do you remember?" Nothing in her face shifted to hint at any recognition.

I turned to her nurse. "How's her fever?"

"It seems to have come down, Your Majesty," Agatha responded.

"Good. Keep an eye on it for me and make sure she is eating, please." Eloisa was already so frail as it was.

"Of course, Your Majesty."

"Where's Lance?" A croaky voice piped up from the bed, causing us all to turn our heads.

"Where's Lance?" Eloisa asked again, softer this time, her eyes wide.

"Uhm, I don't know," I replied honestly. "I haven't seen him this morning."

"I want my brother." The idea that anyone ill would want Lance at their bedside as soon as they woke up was far-fetched. I wondered if Lance was capable of caring for Eloisa in a way he never could for anyone else.

"All right." I looked at Agatha. "Have a servant call Lance, please." She curtsied and scurried off.

"I want my brother," Eloisa said once more and pulled her knees up to her chest. She was looking out the window again, rocking slightly back and forth.

I made eye contact with Rhen, who looked just about as confused as I felt. Agatha returned after a minute.

"I must leave. I have many commitments today, I'm afraid."

"Of course, Your Majesty." The nurse gave a small bow.

I started making my way towards the door but looked back over my shoulder before I walked out of the room. Eloisa continued to rock herself while humming softly. I considered waiting until Lance arrived, to see if she would act any differently towards him but then decided I'd rather not. Shutting the door softly, I stood outside the room for a moment, unsure what to think.

"Are you all right, Your Majesty?" Rhen asked.

"Of course." I shrugged it off. "Why wouldn't I be?"

Chapter 6

Cai

The silver cutlery practically sparkled on the dining table.

Dinner was laid out on a white tablecloth with a cup of wine next to each plate. There were slices of roasted pork glazed in a honey sauce, along with some vegetables, and some fruit on the side. I stared at the food in front of me but didn't have much of an appetite.

Elara had requested I join them for dinner this evening. So far, I had mostly dined in my rooms. I wondered how many nights Elara had sat at this dining table alone. The thought created a pang in my chest.

I knew she'd been doing everything alone these days, running the palace, going to council meetings. I couldn't recall the last time I'd left my rooms. I didn't really want to come down tonight either, but Elara's eyes were so pleading that I didn't have it in me to break her heart any further.

Instead of taking her seat at the head of the table, she'd walked into the dining room and taken a seat next to me.

Elara was looking beautiful again. The upper part of her hair was pulled back, and she wore a dark blue dress, one of my favourite colours on her.

Gwen and Anesta sat next to each other while Lance took a seat on the other side of Elara. It was strange to think that, despite everything he'd done to me and his sister, he was not the person I despised most in the world.

My eyes travelled to Gwen. She took a sip from her cup and met my gaze across the table.

"It's good to see you out and about, Cai. I'm glad you're feeling better."

I forced a small smile for her sake. While Thatcher had been like a brother to me, he was actually Gwen's older sibling. She must have been equally, if not more, devastated, though she did a much better job of hiding it than I did.

"Yes, Your Majesty." Lance spoke up, meeting my gaze. "We haven't seen you for quite some time. I do hope you're feeling better." There was no sincerity in his tone, but I gave him a nod anyway. I didn't have the will or the energy to deal with Lance's games tonight.

Gwen shifted her attention to Elara. "This supper is delicious, Your Majesty. Thank you for inviting me to join you."

"Of course. You are always welcome to join us. I hope you know that."

I used my knife to cut a piece of meat. It was warm and juicy, but everything tasted bland in my mouth.

The table was awkwardly silent until Anesta spoke up. "I must say, I adore your dress, Lady Gwen." Gwen often wore green or teal dresses, which complemented the colour of her eyes. Tonight's dress was forest green with gold trim on the bodice and sleeves.

"Thank you." Gwen used a napkin to wipe the corners of her mouth. "There was a wonderful seamstress back home." Her expression grew sad suddenly and she must have been wondering if she was ever going to go back. But Gwen quickly recomposed herself. "She always knew exactly what I liked."

"Perhaps, one day, the three of us should go into town," Elara suggested. "We could look at materials and dresses and make a whole day of it."

"That sounds lovely, Your Majesty," Gwen said.

Lance cut in. "As long as I don't have to tag along on this little day trip." He grabbed a nearby jug and refilled his cup. "It sounds positively dreadful."

Elara opened her mouth to respond but Gwen beat her to it.

"Very well. But then we won't bring you any cakes or tarts from the bakery either." Lance shifted his gaze to Gwen and his expression changed to intrigue. I couldn't remember them interacting much when Lance had come to Norrandale a few years ago, but since we'd arrived, it looked like Gwen wasn't overly fond of him. And she appeared in no hurry to change her mind. Not that I was complaining. She should stay as far away from Lance as possible, as far as I was concerned.

"Lucky for me, I don't like cakes," Lance responded, and Gwen's brows lowered into a near glare.

"I don't know how we're related," Elara muttered under her breath.

"You know, there's a new bakery in town that just makes the most exquisite desserts, Your Majesty." Anesta attempted to prevent the tension in the room from growing.

I took a sip of wine and sat back in my chair. There was a tiredness creeping onto my eyelids. I wasn't sure why — I spent most of my time sleeping the day away.

"Then we shall add it to our list of places to visit." Elara sent a smile in Anesta's direction, but I could tell it wasn't fully sincere. Not like the way she used to smile at me. Her thoughts were running away with her again and I saw the worry hidden beneath her expression.

She doesn't deserve this.

"What do you mean you don't like cakes?" Gwen clearly wasn't ready to let the subject go.

Lance thought about it for a moment. "I don't know. They're too ... sweet."

She looked at him like he'd just said the most ridiculous thing in the world.

"Maybe you're just too dark and depressing to enjoy anything good and worthwhile," Gwen threw back. If I hadn't been so caught up in my own thoughts, I might have raised my eyebrows. Gwen had always been feisty, and most people didn't like Lance, but I wondered what her particular reason was.

Lance surprised us all by responding, "Maybe I am." His face didn't give anything away, but he lifted his cup as if making a toast before taking a sip.

"That's not something to be proud of." She continued to prod the bear, and I expected Lance to grow annoyed, but it was quite the opposite. The Prince of Everness appeared rather entertained by the conversation. That made one of them.

"Perhaps not. But I have a reputation to uphold." For Lance to suggest that he was anything other than a heartless prick was almost laughable.

"Any desserts you have a preference for, Lady Gwen?" Anesta attempted to draw her attention again, but it was almost as if Gwen hadn't heard her.

"Is that really all you care about? Your reputation?"

"Touchy subject for you, is it? Considering you are now known as the sister of the man who betrayed his kingdom."

Elara tensed up next to me and Anesta's eyes widened a little. A momentary silence fell over the room, as if nobody knew quite what to say.

"Enough." I found the word escaping my mouth, but my tone remained calm. "Gwen is not her brother." And just because Lance always seemed to get a thrill out of pushing people, and because my temper and patience were not at their best, I added, "And neither is Elara."

"Of course not, Your Majesty," Lance responded after a second. "No one would make the mistake of believing such a thing."

I nearly flinched when Elara's hand carefully took hold of mine under the table. Her hands were a little softer in comparison to when we first met, but the calluses were still there. There was a slight comfort in knowing that some things didn't change.

I didn't pull away, nor did I look at her. But I heard Elara release a breath as if she was relieved.

My mind drowned out the sound as Gwen and Anesta continued their earlier conversation. I wanted to turn my head and look at her, but I was afraid of the expression I would see.

I feared the pain and anxiety that probably hid in her eyes, and I couldn't face her knowing I was the cause of most of it.

Her thumb brushed back and forth in a caressing manner, and we continued to sit like that throughout dinner.

After dinner, I decided to go to the library to have a drink and find something to read for the evening. I would welcome the distraction of a work of fiction. Perhaps the story would infiltrate my dreams, and I wouldn't wake in the middle of the night from another nightmare. One of the servants had lit a fire, warming up the room. I poured myself a drink and started walking along the shelves, scanning through the titles, hoping to find something of interest.

The Levernian palace had a very large collection of books, some old and dusty, while others still had bright covers and unworn spines.

My mother had encouraged me to read from a young age. Not just because it was important that I was literate as I would be king one day but because she believed it would open up my mind to new words and ideas. She used to say that books sat on shelves waiting every day to be read, hoping to be picked up so that they could tell their story.

As a little boy, I used to think books contained some kind of magic. I couldn't understand how ink on paper had the ability to create places and people that you could see in your mind. As I'd grown older, that magic slowly began to fade, until the only things I had time for reading were letters and ledgers.

I picked up one of the books, scanned the first few pages and put it back on the shelf. This I did repeatedly, making my way through the fiction section of the library. I couldn't find anything to catch my interest, so I decided to move along to the next section.

I discovered the shelves where the much older books were kept, and the further I walked, the older the books got. Some of their covers were so worn that it was difficult to make out the titles. If I had to guess, I would have said that a few of the books were at least two hundred years old, if not older.

I put my glass down on a nearby reading table and picked up one of the books. As I paged through it, I quickly realised it was a romance novel, which was not something I was particularly in the mood for, so I put it back on the shelf.

The one next to it didn't have a title, which I thought was a little odd, but it did have a crown on the spine.

When I looked for the name of the author, I could find none.

The first page began to tell the story of a wicked queen who craved power. She was cruel and fierce, and the people hated her. One day, she went to a sorcerer and asked him to make her three powerful objects that would protect her and help her rule without opposition. The sorcerer warned her that there would be a price for using such magic, but the queen did not care. She threatened him that if he did not make her the objects, she would kill his family.

The story had now caught my attention. It reminded me of the legend of Queen Riona and the Myrgonite objects. The book was clearly inspired by the tale, but considering how old the writing was, I wondered if the book contained anything about the history of Queen Riona and King Evrin that might have been lost to time.

I took a seat in one of the big reading chairs, the fire crackling in the hearth.

Once the evil queen had her objects, her greed for power grew. The king wanted to stop her, but he didn't know what all of the objects were. The kingdom grew to despise her even more, but despite all the attempts on her life, no one managed to kill her. It was almost as if she'd become immortal. But the magic started to consume her. The woman that the king had married was gone and she was replaced by a monster.

The king knew he had to find the objects before the magic killed her. He began to struggle with his mind and, fearing he would grow mad, he kept a journal of his discoveries. He was afraid the queen would try to kill him if he took the objects away from her. He learned that the magic could not be destroyed, but he did not want to give up. Then the queen died in mysterious circumstances, but the king knew it had to do with the power of the objects. He had discovered what two of the objects were and decided to hide them, but the third was never found.

I ran a hand through my hair before taking a sip from my glass. This was just a story based on true events that took place during the reign of King Evrin, but what if the writer's work had some truth to it? What if King Evrin truly had kept a diary that held the answers to what the objects were? If there was a chance it could help us, then it was worth looking into.

Chapter 7

Elara

I braced myself to knock on my friend's door. Everyone had gone their own way after dinner, and while I still wanted to talk to Cai, I thought it would be a good time to see Cordelia before she went to bed.

My hand rapped against the white wooden door and a hesitant voice said, "Come in."

I'd made sure Cordelia was situated in one of the nicest guest rooms in the palace. I wished there was more that I could do to try to ease her pain.

Cordelia was gazing out the window, seated on the wide ledge. She was still in her black dress. "I just wanted to come and see how you were doing." Of course she wasn't doing well. The person she had planned to spend the rest of her life with had been taken from her.

"It's getting late." I felt a chill sweep through the room. "Can I ask one of the servants to light a fire?"

She shrugged. "I don't care."

Cordelia didn't seem to care about most things these days. Not that I could blame her. She was in mourning. But I didn't know how to help.

Instead of calling a servant, I decided to light a fire myself. Something I hadn't done in a while, but the room was freezing. I didn't understand how Cordelia wasn't shivering.

"I wish you'd joined us for dinner. Everyone was there."

"I know." She didn't look at me, so I continued to stack the wood in the fireplace.

"Anesta and Gwen were there as well. I'm sure they would have loved to see you." I got a small fire going, and when she didn't answer, I turned to look at her. "Why didn't you come?"

"Wasn't hungry."

"Have you eaten today?" I looked around the room for plates or remnants of food but there was nothing. Rhen and I tried to check up on her as much as possible, but she didn't always want to see us.

"Don't remember."

This conversation was going nowhere. I hated seeing my friend in so much pain, knowing there wasn't anything I could do to change the circumstances. Despite having just made a fire, I looked at the bedroom door. "Would you like to go for a stroll?"

She shook her head. "Not now."

I sighed. "You need to get out of your rooms, Cordelia. You can't stay cooped up in here for ever."

Now she looked at me. "I'll do whatever the hell I want," she responded, and then she turned back to the window. It was dark outside, so I wasn't sure exactly what she was looking at.

"You're right. I'm sorry." And I was sorry. My heart broke for her. I couldn't imagine what I would have done if I'd lost Cai. "I'm sorry," I said again.

When she didn't respond, I continued. "But I do think it would be good for you to get out a bit more. I know I haven't seen you as much as I would have liked in the past few days with the council being here and everything, but I am here for you and I would like for us to do things together."

"You're queen. You're too busy to have friends. I understand."

"That's not fair," I responded. I didn't want her to think I didn't care when I'd been tearing myself apart in the last week, trying to get to everyone and everything.

Cordelia's head swivelled in my direction. "Not fair? You want to talk to me about what's not fair?"

In hindsight, it might not have been my best choice of words.

"Not fair is the fact that I made a home for myself in Norrandale and now I can't go back. Not fair is the life I've lived to get here, only to have it taken away." She stood up from the windowsill. "Not fair is the fact that you and everybody else still have the people they care about, and I lost the one person I cared most about in the world," she cried out. "That's what's not fair."

"I know. I'm … sorry." I was repeating myself now.

She wiped a tear from her cheek and turned away from me. "It doesn't matter anymore."

"Of course it matters." I walked over to her and put my arms around her frail frame. Cordelia only hesitated for a moment before allowing herself to be hugged.

"I wish I could go back and change things for you," I said softly, and then Cordelia began to cry onto my shoulder.

"I'm sorry for being mean." Her body shook as she sobbed. "I just miss him so much." She cried for a little while longer, and I continued to hold her until she pulled back. "Maybe I need to get away from court for a while. Go and stay somewhere in the country."

I would miss her terribly if she decided to leave but Cordelia had to do what was best for herself now.

"You just say the word and I'll make the arrangements for you."

"Thank you." She sniffed, using her hands to wipe the tears off her face. "And thanks for checking up on me."

I added another log to the fire. "I'll have one of the servants bring you up some dinner." And I hoped she would eat it.

"Thanks."

"I know it doesn't feel like it right now, but you're the strongest person I know. And I know you'll get through this somehow. Maybe not today or tomorrow, but someday it will be better." All of us had taken our own knocks with this coming war, but I had to believe we would get through it. Or die trying.

After making sure Cordelia was settled and looked after for the evening, I headed straight for Cai's rooms. I wasn't sure where he'd gone after dinner but the fact that he'd held my hand without pulling away gave me hope that perhaps he was closer to opening up, closer to being his old self again. Maybe he just needed some more time to process everything.

Cai looked up as I entered the room. He was standing by his dressing table, undoing the buttons of his shirt. I wondered why there was no servant around, though the candles and fireplace were already lit.

"Sorry, I didn't mean to intrude."

He looked worn out from the evening's events.

"You're not intruding." He rolled up the sleeves of his shirt as I became momentarily distracted by his strong forearms.

"Are you sure? I can come back tomorrow." He probably didn't want company if he was tired. My hand was already reaching for the door.

"No, stay." It was the best thing he'd said to me in weeks. I didn't move away from the door, and he remained standing by the dressing table.

"Thank you for coming to dinner. I really appreciated it."

He nodded, his eyes travelling over the furniture in the room, anywhere but me.

"Should I call for some wine or something?"

"I'm good, thanks."

That was too bad. I could have definitely used the alcohol to calm my nerves.

I stepped a little further into the room, contemplating whether or not I should take a seat on one of the chairs. Cai was making no attempt to move.

"I just wanted to come and ask if you would like to do something together tomorrow morning?" Maybe I was pushing my luck. Just because I'd finally managed to get him to leave his rooms didn't mean I was going to get him frolicking about the palace grounds.

Cai always tried to be the strongest person but everything that had happened had broken something inside him. He was never good at communicating his feelings, especially not when it came to his own weaknesses, because he was always so hard on himself. I didn't know how to be there for him if he couldn't tell me what he needed from me.

"Like what?"

I placed my hands behind my back so that he couldn't see I was wringing my fingers.

"Well, we could go for a walk, or ride through the woods. Maybe I'll let you give me another archery lesson." It was a poor attempt at humour, but I was so desperate to see him smile again. I had no such luck.

"I'm not sure that's a good idea."

"The archery lesson? Yeah, you're probably right. I might accidentally miss the target and hit one of the groundskeepers in the process, considering how terrible I am."

"I don't mean the archery," he said softly, still not looking at me.

"Well, we don't have to go outside." I was stumbling over my words now, hating every moment of this awkward tension between us. *Tell me how to help you.*

"I could ask the cook to make your favourite blueberry tarts and we can have them with tea."

Cai's lips pressed together and he let out a sigh. "I'm sorry but I'm not sure I'm feeling up to it."

"Is it me? Did I do something?"

His forehead creased. "Of course not."

I walked over until I was standing in front of him. "Then why won't you talk to me? Why won't you leave your rooms?" I placed my hands on his cheeks and turned his face to me. "You hardly even look at me." Those once vibrant emerald eyes were now filled with sadness. "And I don't know what I'm doing wrong," I cried out, not realising how much all of this had bothered me until I confessed it out loud. I'd been trying for so long to keep it together. To be the strong queen and leader that everyone needed. But Cai used to be my anchor, keeping me steady, and now I felt lost at sea.

"You're not ... it's not—" He looked for the right words.

"Then why do you keep pushing me away?" I asked and Cai pulled away from me.

He pressed his palms to his face and said, "I'm not pushing you away. I just don't know how to do this." His voice was laced with desperation.

"Don't know how to do what?" I asked more gently.

"I don't know how to make this right."

I stepped up to him again and took his hands in mine. "I don't know what I'm doing either. But your kingdom needs you."

"My kingdom?" he said. "I am no longer king."

"Cai, a throne and a crown don't make a king. You know that."

"But I failed them." He looked away again and I placed my hand on his face.

"You didn't deserve any of the things that happened to you, and you are not the one to blame. And *I* still need you. I'll always need you," I said firmly, so he could know how much I meant it.

When the words left my mouth, Cai pressed his lips to mine. I was a little surprised at first, considering it had been a while since we'd kissed. But I welcomed the feeling of his mouth and the familiarity of him. I had missed being this close to him. Had missed his warm, caressing hands and the taste of him.

He took my wrists and wrapped my hands around his neck before grabbing my hips. I pressed myself up against his broad chest, fingers twisting into the hair at the nape of his neck. There was a desperation in the way his mouth moved against mine.

Cai turned us, so that I was leaning against the dressing table. I savoured the heat of him against me, having missed his affection more than I realised.

The air around us grew hot and Cai's hands snaked up my back, allowing me to lean further into his touch. I suppressed a gasp when he gently took my bottom lip between his teeth. We were both breathing hard. His lips trailed to my jaw and then slowly down my neck.

"I need to confront you more often if this is how the conversation is going to end," I said through heavy breaths. And then Cai did something I had feared he might never do again. I felt the smallest hint of a smile against my skin.

"I actually needed to tell you something important, but I got momentarily distracted."

If we didn't have the threat of war hanging over our heads, I might have ignored what he said and kissed him again. But Cai wouldn't say something was important unless it really mattered.

I pulled back a little to look him in the eye. "What's going on?"

He took a second to regulate his breath again.

"Alastor came and spoke to me earlier today. He'd met with one of his spies who had finally returned from Norrandale."

I didn't know how many spies Alastor had working for him, but they always managed to find valuable information in the end, and I was thankful that there were people who were willing to risk their lives for such important knowledge.

"As we know, Aries is in Norrandale looking for the Myrgonite mines."

"Well, he does have a thing for power and greed."

"But Alastor's spy found out that Aries was also looking for something he labelled 'archaic treasures'. Objects from hundreds of years ago that the old kings used to believe contained magic."

My stomach twisted into a knot. "You mean Aries is actively looking for the Myrgonite objects?" There was so little known about them apart from the stories that had been told through the generations.

"I'm afraid so."

"But we don't know for certain what these objects are. Only that we have been warned against their magic."

"I think I might have found something on it."

"Oh?" I said with surprise. The old Cai hadn't wanted anything to do with the objects or any kind of magic. I supposed what happened in Norrandale had changed him in more ways than one.

"After dinner I went to the library to look for something to read, you know, to try and get my mind off things a little." Not my idea of a distraction, but fair enough. "And I found this really old book with a story inspired by Queen Riona and the Myrgonite objects."

My brows furrowed. "Someone wrote a story about it?"

"It was strange, the book had no title and no author. But it did mention that King Evrin had a diary where he wrote about the queen and the objects."

This was interesting. "Do you think there's a chance that the diary is real?"

"I'm not sure." Cai shrugged. "The chances are pretty slim. But if it does exist, then maybe it would have some answers about the objects."

"Maybe." I thought about it. There was so little known about those magical objects, and the stories had become too distorted over the centuries. It was hard to know what was true and what had simply been made up. But if we had a trusted source like King Evrin's diary, it might tell us everything we needed to know. Based on the conversation I had had with Aries in Argon, I knew he wasn't only coming after the Myrgonite mines in Norrandale. The gemstones would make him rich beyond compare, yes. But there was no end to Aries' greed. It had always been a matter of time before he came after the objects.

"We need to find some more writing that confirms the existence of the diary."

"I'll go and see if I can find anything in the library tomorrow," Cai replied

Even if nothing came of it, at the very least Cai was leaving his rooms again.

"That's a good idea. I'll see if I can find anything in the royal study."

It was a long shot. If the diary existed, we didn't know what was written inside and where we would find it. It could be a complete waste of time, or it could be the answer to everything.

Chapter 8

Gwen

I tied my hair into a braid, though a few stray strands still managed to fall in front of my eyes.

My grey mare was already saddled up and ready for our early-morning ride. The air was ice cold — I could see every breath I exhaled — but snow had yet to fall.

I pulled on my riding gloves, my fingers already numb.

"You ready, girl?"

Bessie looked slightly unimpressed that I'd dragged her away from her breakfast, but she followed as I led her out of the stables. Her hooves clacked on the cobblestones until we reached the grass, where I used an old tree stump to mount.

We started on our usual route away from the palace gardens and towards the line of trees in the distance.

I'd woken up this morning not planning to go on a ride. It was almost too cold to get out of bed. But much as I wanted to stay snuggled within the warmth of my sheets, my mind was running rampant with the events of the past few days. I couldn't stop thinking about the way Cai looked at dinner last night. Not only did he look pale and exhausted, but he'd barely said a word during the meal. I'd known Cai for as long as I could remember but I'd never seen him like this. He'd looked so distraught, like he no longer possessed the will to live. To say I was worried would be an understatement.

Elara said that she was going to talk to him after dinner. I had no idea what the results of the conversation were, but I hoped she managed to get something out of him because we could not go on like this. If someone didn't do something, Cai was going to lose his kingdom. And after he'd already lost everything else … I couldn't bear the thought.

I nudged the mare into a slow trot.

Just the thought of all of it practically made me sick to my stomach. Especially knowing it was my very brother that had caused most, if not all, of it. I was thankful that, so far, nobody seemed to be blaming me for any of it. At least Elara looked happy to have me in her company, inviting me to dinner and to go out into town. It was a massive weight off my shoulders. I knew I wasn't guilty of anything. Hell, I was just as betrayed as everyone else. But somehow, I couldn't help feeling remorse.

I would never admit it to anyone, but I sometimes wondered if I should write to Thatcher. Not because I missed him or wanted to hear from him but because I didn't have the opportunity to scream at him in person — to ask him how he had it in his heart to stab his friends and family in the back … and for what? He betrayed Cai, who was as good as his brother. He murdered Jack, who was the head of Cai's guard, and perhaps worst of all, he killed Cai's mother and grandmother, who were like family to me. It was hard and painful to imagine him doing it. I wished I could have begged him for some explanation that would prove he wasn't as horrid as everyone believed that he was, just the annoying older brother that I adored. But after everything he'd done, even I was not that naive.

There was a sickening feeling in my gut. Or maybe I was just hungry. I would get breakfast once I was back at the palace. Many of the trees that were not evergreen had lost their leaves by now, allowing the grey sky to cast some lights in the forest. The ground had turned brown and quite muddy in some places.

I wondered if my horse could sense my distress. She felt tense under me. Father had always said that horses could tell what you were feeling. I never knew if it was true, but he was the one who'd taught me to ride as a child. I had never been particularly close to my parents, which was probably why I'd always been so close to Thatcher. But now, I didn't even know if I would ever see my mother again.

The mare and I disrupted the silence of the forest as I urged her into a canter. She obeyed and I tightened my grip on the reins, forcing myself to sit back in the saddle so that I could keep my balance.

I turned her so that we wouldn't be heading too deep into the forest, forcing my mind away from Cai and my brother. Unfortunately, it moved to the only other thing that irked me impossibly. Lance's smug face from last night appeared in my head. Had my behaviour not been of importance, all things concerned, I might have thrown the nearest piece of cutlery at his head. Everything he said was like a trigger to my brain. Even more so because I could tell he was doing it on purpose. The rich prince was bored in his huge palace and had found an unwilling victim to torment with what he must have falsely assumed was humour.

"Hmph," I scoffed out loud. "He couldn't be funny if he tried." I told the mare, who had no choice but to listen. She was cantering quite fast now but I held on to her with my thighs. The trees became more spread out and I decided to push her a little faster.

"I don't like cakes." I repeated Lance's words in a mocking tone, despite knowing how childish I sounded. "What an ass." I shook my head. "You have never met such a pompous, self-absorbed man in your life. And then he wants to talk about his reputation? I mean, I honestly don't know if I can trust someone who doesn't like cakes." I knew Lance's remarks were often made for the purpose of annoying me. And I was letting him.

One moment I was still properly seated on Bessie and the next I was lying on the cold, wet ground, gasping for breath. She'd reared. Luckily, she hadn't run away or I would have had to go after her, and out in the open, that could have been a very tiresome task. I sat up and placed a hand on my chest. I hated feeling like the air had been sucked out of my lungs. I tried to feel for any injuries. My arms and ribs weren't in pain, which was a good sign. I looked at the mare standing a few feet away, wondering if something had frightened her.

"What was that for?" I asked, somewhat annoyed. She tended to be a relaxed mare, so this certainly wasn't normal behaviour for her.

When I tried to stand up, a pain shot through my ankle, and I groaned. That wasn't good.

I slowly tried to roll it, confirming that at least it wasn't broken. Manoeuvring myself awkwardly, I managed to get into a standing position. I hobbled over to the mare and I looked for any sign that she might have hurt herself. It didn't take long to spot the lone horseshoe lying on the ground. I picked up her feet one by one until I saw that she had, in fact, lost her left front iron shoe. My guess was that whoever had done it hadn't done their job properly, and it must have been fiercely uncomfortable for her. No wonder she'd reared.

"Poor girl." I rubbed her shoulder. "I'm sorry." She looked fairly content now, nibbling a few stray blades of grass.

I looked at the palace in the distance. It was a long walk back, but I wouldn't be able to mount her with my ankle. Nor did I think it was a good idea to ride her until I was certain her hoof wasn't in any pain.

"Well, come on, then." I pulled at her reins and we slowly started making our way back to the stables. The royal gardens eventually came into sight and so did a figure riding a horse. The man trotted into the treeline until he came close enough that I could recognise his face.

Prince Lance wore casual riding attire with a black cape draped across the dark horse.

"Lady Gwen?" He looked equally surprised to find me here. As a prince, of course, he had been taught to ride from a young age, but in all my morning outings, I had never come across him before.

Lance dismounted as I bowed my head in greeting. "Your Highness."

"What are you doing here?"

The question should have been what was *he* doing there?

He stopped in front of me, still holding his horse by the reins, and gave Bessie's nose a little rub.

"Oh, you know, just took old Bessie here out for a morning walk."

Lance's gaze travelled from my face towards my hair. I watched in surprise as he picked a leaf out of my braids, raising his eyebrow in confusion.

"Did you have a fall?"

I looked over his shoulder at the palace. The stables were so close and yet so far.

"Of course not." I let out an involuntary snort as if he'd just suggested the most ridiculous thing, when, in truth, I was too embarrassed to admit that I'd fallen off a horse. I didn't have any interest in continuing this conversation. I just needed to find a way to get past him.

I placed my hand on Bessie's neck so that I could keep my balance, but I knew if I attempted to walk, he would see that I was injured.

"Are you heading back?"

"Yes." I cleared my throat. "I am, actually."

"Well, don't let me get in your way, Lady Gwen." He stepped out of the way, pulling his horse along with him and leaving a clear path ahead of me. Suddenly the stables felt miles off and I didn't know how I was going to get myself out of this compromising position.

"Thank you. Good day then." I hoped he would mount his horse and leave me in peace, but Lance remained just where he was, a curious expression on his face.

I was going to have to force myself to walk as normally as possible and hope I didn't injure myself further in the process.

I braced myself for the pain that was to come. Just as I took my first step, Lance spoke up. "Gwen?"

"Mh?" I pressed my lips together, looking at him quizzically.

"Do you want to tell me why there's blood on your head?"

"What blood?" I hadn't the faintest idea what he was talking about.

"There's blood on your forehead." He reached up to show me but thought better of it and pulled his hand back. I touched my fingers to my hairline, and sure enough, there were small traces of blood. I'd been so focused on my ankle, I didn't even realise I must have scratched it on a branch or something.

"Oh, that's odd."

"Gwen," he said again, stretching out my name. "Did you get hurt?"

"No, why would you think that?"

"Because there's blood on your face and you're clearly not able to walk properly."

"It's nothing, I'm fine." I looked towards the stables again.

"Of course you're not fine. I can tell you're in pain." For a moment Lance almost looked concerned, but I knew I must have read his expression wrong.

"Fine," I said curtly. "I fell off the horse, all right?"

"Come on," he replied without hesitation. "I'll take you back to the palace and we'll get a physician to look at you."

"I'll be fine, thank you. You go ahead and enjoy your morning ride."

Lance tilted his head a little and a hint of amusement danced on his face.

"Could you just stop being so stubborn and let me help you?"

I didn't take pleasure in the thought, but I also didn't have many options. When I didn't protest, Lance pulled his horse towards me and placed his hands on my hips to help me into the saddle.

He got on behind me and I straightened my back, not wanting to lean into him. Lance's arm came around my waist to take hold of the reins, while his other hand held Bessie's reins so that he could lead her behind us. I prayed for this ride to be over as soon as possible.

"I didn't know you liked to ride," Lance said after a few minutes. We had almost reached the gardens. I tried to ignore the feeling of his chest pressing into my back.

"Of course I do. And I'll have you know, I'm actually very good."

"Clearly not, if you're falling off."

My mouth fell a little bit open. "It wasn't my fault. Whoever is responsible for shoeing your horses clearly isn't doing their job because the horse lost a shoe and injured her hoof, which is why she threw me off."

"Oh well, that makes a lot more sense."

I shook my head at his sarcasm. My ankle was in too much pain for me to care about defending my riding skills.

"I'm just teasing you," he said after a second. "I'll have someone take a look at Bessie's hoof."

We made our way to the stables, where the stable boy took the horses, and Lance helped me inside the palace. I didn't want to be carried by the Prince of Everness, but I could barely walk on my own. We reached my room, and he placed me on the bed.

"I'll call for a physician."

"That really isn't necessary." I just needed a warm bath and for one of the servants to wrap my ankle.

"Yes," Lance insisted. "It is."

His eyes remained on me until I couldn't take it any longer and finally asked, "What?"

"Nothing." The prince gave me his most devilish smile. "It's just that you've still got dirt on your face."

Chapter 9

Cai

I was in the forest.

Moss covered the earth in a quilt of green while my ears took in the cheerful melody of a bird somewhere high up in the branches.

The air was filled with warmth. Winter had not yet clawed its way to wherever I was. My surroundings were unfamiliar to me.

"Oh, how the mighty have fallen." A voice rose from behind me. One I could easily recognise anywhere.

I turned to face Thatcher, immediately reaching for my sword, but I was surprised to find nothing there.

Thatcher carried a smug expression. It was one I'd often seen him with, but never thought it would be in reaction to my downfall.

My oldest friend had betrayed me.

"Too bad you have nothing to protect you now." He was right. I had no weapon but at least I was not outmanned.

My hands clenched into fists. Although I had no recollection of how or why I was there, I had only one thought — I had to stop him.

I ran forward without hesitance, but Thatcher made no attempt to move. I was about to tackle him to the ground when my arms wrapped around nothing but air, and Thatcher disappeared.

My eyes searched the trees for a trace of him. Thatcher stood a few feet away, his expression unchanged.

"Why don't you just give up, Cai? We both knew you were never going to make it as a king anyway."

Every word that left his mouth increased my anger.

"How could you?" I shouted, my voice echoing through the forest. "You were like my brother. How could you betray your family?"

He shrugged. "I had to do what was best for the kingdom. Gwen will learn to forgive me. She will see that you would have driven Norrandale to the ground."

I was going to kill him.

"Here." Thatcher pulled out a knife and tossed it on the ground before me. "I'll make it easier on you."

I stepped over the knife towards him. "This has to end, Thatcher." I need you to stop haunting me, was what I didn't say.

"Does it?"

Once more I ran at him, but he vanished into thin air just before I could reach him. This time, when I turned, Thatcher was no longer alone.

My mother was on her knees next to him as he held her by her hair. My blood ran cold. Some part of my mind knew she was already dead, that Thatcher had already killed her, but seeing her in front of me, alive and breathing, caused all rationality to escape me.

"Let her go." I put my hands up in surrender. "Let her go and you can have anything you want."

Thatcher let out a menacing laugh. "Don't you get it? I already have your kingdom."

I moved towards the two of them, but the knife was back in Thatcher's hand.

"Ah ah," he warned me. "Not a step closer."

"Don't worry, Cai, I'm fine," my mother said. Thatcher yanked at her hair, and she let out a cry of pain.

"What do you want from me?" I asked in defeat, my eyes never leaving my mother's pale face.

"Well, let's see." He played with the knife in his hands. "Why don't we start with you admitting that I make a better king than you?"

My breathing was heavy. I felt caught between a rock and a hard place. How could I say out loud the one thing I never wanted to believe but perhaps always secretly did?

"Or how about the Evernean queen who's probably going to leave you anyway. Do you think you deserve her?" I had once believed I could live up to the man she needed me to be. Now I wasn't so sure.

"Please just let her go. Do you want me to beg?"

Thatcher toyed with the idea for a quick moment. "Though it might have been fun to see you on your knees, I believe I'm going to enjoy this a lot more." Before I could move, Thatcher slit my mother's throat.

I screamed myself awake, my voice raspy.

It wasn't real. My eyes took in the surroundings of my bedroom.

Except it was.

Thatcher had murdered my family and taken my kingdom from me. And I couldn't stop him. Sweat coated the skin on my back despite the fact it was winter. I brushed the sheets away from my legs. The room was pitch-black, so I assumed it was still the middle of the night.

I got up from the bed, feeling disoriented. The floor was cold beneath my feet and my stomach twisted with nausea. I'd woken up every night this past week with the exact same dream. And every time I had to watch as Thatcher killed my mother.

I tried to push the image from my mind. I would never see her face again. Never get to hear her laugh or see her smile at me.

My body shook and I was unsure if it was from the cold or the nightmare. Knowing better than to believe I was going to fall back asleep, I decided to put on some clothes.

There was a guard outside my chambers, but he pretended not to see me, and I gave him a grateful smile. I wondered if he'd heard my screaming.

The palace was dark, with only a few lamps here and there to illuminate the hallways. I wasn't sure exactly where I was going, but it was better than rolling around in my bed. With everyone asleep, it was deathly quiet, and my steps created an annoying pitter-patter on the tiled floor, though I doubted I would wake anyone. I passed a few more guards, standing quietly at their posts as they attempted to remain awake.

I made my way down the main flight of stairs. It was almost eerie to be walking in this place at night. The moonlight shone through the windows of the hallway to the right, illuminating the way. I ventured past the portraits, stopping occasionally to inspect one. After what felt like an hour, I made my way back towards my chambers.

When I passed the study close to Elara's rooms, light creeping under the door caught my attention.

I listened for who could be inside, but it was quiet.

Who would be in the study at this hour?

I pushed the door open, and Elara looked up with surprise.

"You scared me." She placed a hand on her chest. "I didn't think anyone was awake."

"Nor did I," I admitted, somewhat sheepishly.

I closed the door behind me and stepped into the room. Elara stood behind a large, dark oak desk with papers strewn from edge to edge.

The entire room was lit with candles, a few of them already burnt out. How long had she been here?

"What are you still doing up?"

"I couldn't sleep." She shrugged. "I figured I might as well get some work done." I watched as Elara tucked a strand of hair behind her ear. I could almost smell the sweet scent of her hair, remembering kissing her on that sensitive spot beneath her ear.

"What about you?"

"I couldn't sleep either." I didn't feel like bringing up the nightmare. I just wanted to forget it.

We both looked at the many papers on her desk filled with paragraphs and paragraphs of ink. Most of the pages looked old and worn.

"Are you looking for something?"

"I don't even know." She sighed. "I've been going through old ledgers of the royal family and some of the historical archives of the kingdom. I'm hoping that maybe there's some more information somewhere about that diary you read about. I'm not sure there's actually anything of value but …" She hesitated. "I can't sit still and wait until something happens."

"You're not," I reassured her. "You're doing everything you can to protect your kingdom." I wished I could say the same. I'd let my pain consume me in these past months and I feared failing everyone again. What if I'd done more before it was too late? Now we could only try to salvage what was left.

I walked closer to the desk and picked up one of the pages. It was a record of the kingdom's produce from all the farmlands fifty years ago. That definitely wasn't going to help anyone with anything.

"I see what you mean." I put the piece of paper back down. "Where did you even get all this?"

"In here." She gestured to the room around us. "And Rhen got some of it from the library." If there was any mention of the king's diary, these old documents were a good start, but none of them appeared to have any information of value.

"Would you like me to call a servant and ask them to bring us something?"

"No," I said quickly. "No, please don't wake anyone."

Elara looked at me curiously before she said, "All right."

At the fear of saying or doing something stupid, I turned away from her and started looking through some of the books near the fireplace. I'd gone back to the library to see if there were any more books on that period but my search had come up empty.

Apart from the sound of Elara shuffling through the papers, the air was quiet and almost peaceful.

I should apologise to her. For locking myself away from the world and from her. But where would I even begin?

"Are you sure you're all right, Cai?" she said after a minute.

"Yes." I sighed. "I just haven't been sleeping well these past few days."

"Me neither," she said very softly. There was no point in asking her if she was all right. Of course she wasn't all right. None of this was all right.

"Did you hear about Gwen?"

I looked over my shoulder. "What about Gwen?"

Elara seemed surprised at my response. "She had a riding accident."

"A what?" My eyes widened. "Is she okay?"

"Yes, I believe she only sprained her ankle. I'm sure she'll be healed in no time."

I hadn't spoken much to Gwen in the past few weeks. It didn't surprise me that she'd been out riding. Gwen was always a very good rider. But the fact that I didn't even know that she'd had an accident and injured herself made me feel terrible. I used to be like a brother to her and now I had no idea how she was really doing and how she was dealing with all of this.

"I'll go and check on her in the morning," I said, my gaze on the books.

"I think she'd appreciate that." She began ruffling through the papers again.

"You were right, you know." I thought back to our conversation a few nights earlier. Though Elara and I were on good terms, I knew I should be more open with her instead of isolating myself. She still needed me and I very much needed her.

Elara didn't look up once as I spoke, and for a moment, I thought she was purposely ignoring me, until I realised something had caught her attention and she hadn't heard me.

"Elara." I took a step closer, and she looked up from the page she'd been reading.

"Mmhh?" Her gaze had intensified, something curious behind those eyes.

"Is something wrong?"

She looked at the page and then back to me.

"I think I've found something."

She carefully slid the old piece of paper across the desk.

"It's a letter." I quickly scanned the page.

"Yes." Elara nodded. "And it's addressed to King Evrin."

The ink had faded in some parts and I had to squint to make out the writing.

"It's from a man called Finnegan. I think he was a friend of the king's."

I write to inform you that I have safely returned to Norran, where my estates are well kept, and the town is constantly growing and expanding.

"Norran?" Elara questioned. "As in Norrandale?"

I nodded. "That was the name of the town before it became a separate kingdom, expanding to the entire south."

I heard news that you plan to close down the mines in the mountains north from here, though I must confess, I do not understand why. Is that not what we came all this way for? Have you entirely lost interest in growing the Evernean kingdom? I wish you would reconsider, but if not, perhaps you would think about selling the land. I would be happy to fund the mining project for the foreseeable future.

"Rhen once told me that Everness and Norrandale came into conflict over the mountains with the Myrgonite stones. Do you think this is where it started?" Elara asked.

"It would make sense. Maybe Finnegan eventually decided that he would take the mountains by force, severing his friendship with King Evrin."

"Greed will make people do horrible things," Elara agreed. "But here, look at this part." She pointed to one of the middle paragraphs. Finnegan wrote about a conversation he and King Evrin had on his visit to Levernia. Apparently, King Evrin confided in him about Queen Riona and his growing concerns.

I must admit that you do not seem yourself, old friend. I fear whatever dark magic Riona has got herself entangled with is starting to sink its claws into you. You must find whatever it is that is giving Riona her power. I suggest you keep a journal of your discoveries. It will keep your thoughts in order and help to ease your mind. I've been keeping one for years and writing in it has always brought me a sense of calm. You can use it to collect information until you find a way to free Riona from this spell. I hope to hear from you soon.

Your friend,

Finnegan

"Where did you find this?" I asked Elara.

"It was stashed in between the pages of an old ledger in this cupboard." She pointed to the small wooden cupboard in her desk. The desk that belonged to the rulers of Everness.

"Any chance there is another letter in there?" I had managed to forget about the nightmare and why I was there. This was the first piece of information to suggest that the king's diary truly existed.

"Only one way to find out." Elara got down on her knees, her nightgown splayed over the floor around her. She pulled all the ledgers from the cupboard and flipped through the pages. I picked up one of the old books, careful not to damage it as I searched for loose pieces of paper.

"I've got it."

"Another letter from Finnegan?" I asked as she carefully unfolded the paper.

"Even better."

I moved so that I could sit next to her, our shoulders touching.

"It's written by King Evrin."

For the first time, it felt as though luck might be on our side and there was a flicker of hope in my chest.

"This is his response," Elara said.

The page was only half written, the letter incomplete. "He never finished it."

I am glad to hear you are well and safely returned to your home. I assure you that I have not forgotten that our search for the Myrgonite stones is what led us here. But I fear it has become more of a threat to our kingdom than an aid. Everness is flourishing well now, and I believe it is in the best interest of the kingdom if we do not meddle any further with this stone. The less people know, the better. As there are some who might be willing to kill for it.

I have taken your advice and started a journal, though it is an effort to keep it hidden. No one must discover what is written inside. I think I know what one of the objects is, but I cannot be certain yet. Riona is a clever woman, and with each day that goes by, I lose more of her. I don't know how this will end but I fear it will not end well.

The letter ended abruptly, and Elara and I looked at each other with widened eyes.

"This means the diary must be real."

"And that the answers to the Myrgonite objects are in there," I added, and Elara looked at the letter again.

"We have to find that diary."

Chapter 10

Elara

My foot tapped on the floor of the council room.

After my discovery in the study last night, I knew I needed to call a meeting as soon as possible. But not with the council. If my guesses were correct, this information could be too valuable to share with people I wasn't sure I could trust.

I'd asked Rhen to call everyone here first thing this morning and now I was waiting for them to make their way to the council room.

I rubbed my hands together. A servant had yet to come and light a fire and the room was freezing.

My head jerked up as the door opened and Cai walked inside, and a little bit of relief settled over me.

"You're here," I said, trying not to sound too surprised. He looked tired and I wondered if he'd managed to fall back to sleep after the two of us had retired to our rooms.

Cai gave me a small smile and took a seat next to me at the table. "You doing okay?"

I nodded and he placed his hand atop mine on the table, and I immediately felt better.

"Cordelia left for the country today."

Cai gave a slow nod, and I knew he was thinking about Jack.

"It's probably the best decision for her."

"I know." I sighed. "I'm just going to miss her. But hopefully we can visit her once this is all over."

"Yes, hopefully," he said but his expression suggested we probably wouldn't live to see the end of the war.

I squeezed his hand.

Anesta arrived next.

As a lady of the court, she didn't really have much to do with the political situation of the kingdom. But this was about more than armies and land. If the diary truly contained knowledge about what the Myrgonite objects were, we needed to find it as soon as possible, before someone else did.

Anesta looked uncertain and I couldn't blame her. But she was my friend. And this affected all of us.

Rhen entered next, looking slightly out of breath. Alastor followed shortly behind, and I gestured for them to take a seat at the table. Gwen and Lance were the last to enter the room. Poor Gwen hobbled in with a walking stick to support her injured ankle.

Cai wasn't too happy about allowing Lance to join the meeting, but I convinced him that Lance knew more about Everness and its history than any of us. He'd grown up in this palace. If anyone knew something that could be valuable to us, it was him.

Though, after what Lance had put us through, I didn't blame Cai for his hesitance. Lance was once almost as eager as Aries to get hold of those stone objects. His motivations were never entirely clear, as Lance was also a fantastic liar. I had to tread carefully in how much we chose to involve him.

Once everyone was seated, a servant had lit a fire and the room was starting to heat up a little, I motioned for Rhen to close the door for privacy.

"Thank you for meeting me here on such short notice," I said, somewhat nervously folding my hands together. Everyone looked at me expectantly.

"I know we've all been on edge with everything going on lately." And rightfully so. "But I've been doing some research, and I think Cai and I may have found something that could help us."

I unfolded a map of Norrandale and Everness, placing it in the centre of the table. "What I'm about to tell you must not leave this room," I said sternly. "I don't want the court or the public to know anything about this." But I knew they, my inner circle, were the only people I could rely on for help.

I looked at Cai for approval. He hesitated for a moment but gave me a small nod. We had nothing to lose at this point. This knowledge was dangerous, but the situation required risk.

"Aries isn't only trying to conquer Norrandale for power." I pointed to the mountain ranges of Norrandale on the map. The mountains that had been part of Everness a very, very long time ago. "He's after something much more valuable."

Lance gave a bit of a snort, catching my attention.

"Is there something you'd like to say?" I called him out, slightly annoyed.

"Don't tell me you're caught up in this fairy-tale nonsense now." Had the situation not been so serious, I could have laughed at the irony. There was a time, not too long ago, that Lance had tortured

Cai over that fairy-tale nonsense. I decided to keep my voice calm and proceed as diplomatically as possible.

"I'm not, but regardless of whether or not it's true, Aries believes it, and this could be a way to stop him."

"I'm sorry," Gwen interrupted. "But could someone please tell me what the hell we're talking about?"

"Myrgonite stones," Rhen said. "The valuable gemstones our kingdoms fought over centuries ago."

"Are we to receive a history lesson now?" Lance queried and Rhen pressed his mouth into a line of disapproval. But he knew better than to try to correct the prince.

"Long ago, people believed these gemstones to be in the mountains that are now in Norrandale. For some reason, King Aries seems to have committed to this belief and that's why he's gone on his expedition through Norrandale," I continued.

Which was half true. Aries knew the stones could make him wealthy, and if he couldn't find the objects, at least it wouldn't have been a lost cause. But based on my brief encounter with the King of Argon, I doubted he would ever stop looking for those three magical objects.

"I remember hearing stories about lost treasure in Norrandale as a child but surely King Aries isn't risking all of this on some childhood story," Gwen said.

"Oh, Aries is a crazy bastard," Lance replied. "That's exactly the kind of thing he would do." I didn't know how much knowledge Lance had on the Argonian king, but his tone sounded a little sarcastic.

"The point is—" I tried to bring everyone's attention back to the topic — "if anyone knew anything about this, it would be the first king of Everness."

"Really?" Lance said, and I reined in my annoyance at his repeated interruptions. "I would think that if anyone knew anything about this, it would be the King of Norrandale himself." He looked at Cai and slowly everyone else turned to the exiled king.

My heart rate increased along with the tension in the room. Why did Lance have to choose this moment to pick on Cai?

I watched his face change as he contemplated how to respond to Lance or perhaps if he should punch him in the face.

"Why should His Majesty care about some old legend?" Gwen asked before Cai could respond. "It has nothing to do with running a kingdom."

Lance's eyes glinted with amusement as he looked at Gwen. "I only mean to say that if His Majesty knows anything about this, it would be kind of him to indulge us."

Cai's expression told of all the things he could imagine doing to Lance, none of them indulging.

"I was doing some reading in the study last night when I came across some important information." I was starting to think that calling this meeting was a mistake. Perhaps we were in over our heads, with no way out of this mess.

"It is believed that King Evrin, the first king of Everness, had a diary. I found some documents that refer to it. If there's any information that could tell us more about this, it would be in there."

"Your Majesty?" Rhen said. "How can we be certain that the diary still exists?"

"We can't," I admitted. "But if it does, then there's a chance it could still be in the palace."

"You have no way of knowing that," Lance replied.

"If you have any better ideas, I would love to hear them." Brother or not, if he did not pipe down, I would seriously reconsider that prison cell he spent a few months in.

"Not at all." Lance put his hands up defensively. "I'm merely suggesting we don't put all our faith in this."

"Of course not. The rest will be for me and the council to worry about. But if I may ask a favour of all of you, it would be to start looking for anything you can find about that diary. The more of us working on this, the quicker we will find something."

"Your Majesty, if I may." Anesta spoke up with uncertainty. She'd been very quiet thus far. "What do you think we'll find in the diary?"

"Hopefully some answers as to what went down in the kingdom during the reign of our first king." I had a gut feeling that a lot of history was about to be unravelled.

Chapter 11

Gwen

I stepped into the stables, the sound of my walking stick loud on the cobbled floor. As much as I'd wanted to avoid a physician, when the swelling in my ankle only got worse, I knew I didn't have much of a choice. It had taken me a few days to get used to my new walking aid and my wrist was hurting terribly from carrying most of my weight, but at least the pressure was off my ankle, which helped a little.

It was quite annoying that I wouldn't be able to ride for a while, though. But at the very least I could come and see how the mare was doing. She did, after all, get just as big a fright as I did.

Hobbling through the stables, I didn't notice the stable boy anywhere, and I wondered if he was out training one of the other horses.

Luckily, I knew my way around pretty well by now. The air smelled of fresh hay and leather. It took me a while, especially considering the size of the royal stables, but I eventually managed to reach the stall of the grey mare. I hadn't seen her in one of the paddocks outside, which had to mean she was still in here, recovering.

Huffing out a breath, I peeked over the heavy, dark wood door. The sweet little mare happily grazed on a bale of lucerne, appearing unbothered. I also found the stable boy, with his back towards me, bent over the horse's hoof.

My arm reached just far enough over the door to pet the horse's head.

"I was wondering where you were," I told the shy boy, who had to be quite a few years younger than me. He had a stable master who oversaw him, but most of the time he did a pretty good job of taking care of all these horses. I hoped they treated him well.

The boy with the dark hair stilled, obviously startled by my sudden presence behind him, though I was sure, with my walking stick, he could have heard me coming for miles.

"It's really not fair that I won't be able to ride her for a while now. I hope whatever farrier did her shoes got into big trouble for not doing them properly," I said earnestly. I felt quite sorry for the mare despite how happy she looked to be staying in the warm stables with the extra food and attention.

"He definitely did," the stable boy said, with a voice that did not belong to him. He stood up, taller than he'd been before, and it took me a moment to realise that it was, in fact, not the stable boy standing there, covered in hay and dust.

Prince Lance turned to face me. "We'll have to find something else for you to ride then."

He was dressed unlike I'd ever seen him before. Gone were his lavish clothes made of expensive fabrics. Instead, the prince before me wore a plain white shirt with the sleeves rolled up to his elbows and a pair of well-worn riding breeches. No wonder I'd momentarily mistaken him for the stable boy.

"What?" I blurted out.

"One of the other horses." He cleared his throat. "You can pick any of the other horses to ride when your ankle is better."

"What are you doing here?" A piece of hay had got caught in his hair. He looked so unlike the prince I knew.

"I came to take a look at Bessie's hoof." Lance gestured to the mare standing behind him.

"I can see that. But why? Don't you have servants for this kind of thing?"

"Well, yes," he said almost hesitantly. "But I wanted to see for myself. She is my horse, after all."

My throat had gone dry. His horse?

All this time, I'd been riding his horse.

My face scrunched up in anger at the stable boy, who'd apparently forgotten to inform me of this very important detail.

"Your horse?"

Lance nodded. "Bessie's been in the family for quite some time, haven't you, girl?" He patted her neck, and I almost started looking around in case the prince also had a twin, because this definitely wasn't Lance.

"Are you all right?" He must have seen my shocked expression.

"Yes." I cleared my throat. "Yes, I am. It's just … I'm surprised to see you here."

"I used to come here a lot when I was younger. Haven't been riding much in the past few years, though."

I decided to steer the conversation quickly away from him. "How's she doing?"

Lance looked at Bessie's hoof and then back to me. "It's getting better. She should be fine soon."

"Well, I …" I wasn't sure how to approach this. "I apologise for injuring your horse." I disliked every word that left my mouth. I wouldn't want to apologise to him for anything if I could help it. But I did feel bad for Bessie.

"It's not your fault." Lance shrugged. "Just getting a new farrier."

I took a step back with my walking stick. "I'd better get going." I didn't know what was going on with Lance but he was acting weird.

"Your Highness!" the stable boy called out, running towards us. *There you are, you little rat*, I thought. He stopped in front of Bessie's stall, out of breath. "It's happening, Your Highness."

"All right, I'll be there in a moment."

The boy gave a small bow, running back in the direction he'd come from.

Lance opened Bessie's stall door and stepped out.

"What's happening?" I asked, not being able to curb my curiosity.

"One of the mares is having a foal."

"Really?"

Lance seemed to ponder for a moment before he asked, "Do you want to see?"

"Uhm." I hesitated. I'd never seen a foal being born before. "Uhm, okay."

I hobbled on after him, trying not to take note of the fact that his lean chest was visible through the thin material of his shirt.

We reached one of the stalls at the end and I looked over the door to see a light bay mare lying in the straw.

Lance went in, then looked back and held the door for me. "Come on."

"Oh, I don't know."

"It'll be fine."

I didn't want to come across as some kind of coward, so I stepped inside.

He knelt down next to the horse and stroked her head. "Hey, girl," Lance said in a voice that was almost gentle, and I once again contemplated who this man was and what had happened to the real Lance. His hand moved to her big belly and lingered there.

"Everything all right?" I asked, nervously.

"Think so."

"Do you deliver baby horses often, then?"

Lance met my gaze with an expression I couldn't quite read. "Not really."

Well, okay then.

"Here you go, Your Highness." The stable boy entered and handed Lance a bucket of water and a sponge.

"Thanks, lad." The boy scurried off to whatever duty he had to perform next, and I watched as Lance soaked the sponge and patted it on the horse's neck, which glistened with sweat.

"How do you know what to do?" I made myself comfortable, leaning back against the stable wall.

"I don't really," Lance replied honestly, and my worry grew for the poor mare, who appeared to be in pain. I wondered if we should call someone who might actually know what they were supposed to do. But then I had to remind myself that horses probably didn't require all the help that humans tend to.

Lance continued trying to cool down the mare with the wet sponge. Part of me wanted to pet her as well, if only to reassure her. But that would require a very awkward manoeuvre with my injured ankle and then I would unfortunately be much closer to Lance. So, I chose to remain standing.

"Bessie's a very sweet horse." Almost too sweet for a person like him. It was a wonder she hadn't bucked him off repeatedly. I couldn't stop myself from smiling at the mental image of Lance being thrown off a horse.

"She's an old horse now but she was a gift from my mother. Bessie's the least temperamental horse I've ever come across. She's always had a lot of patience with me. My mother once said that she reminded her of an old milk cow that she had while growing up. The cow's name was Bessie, and I guess it just kind of stuck." I knew Lance's mother died when the twin princesses were born. He must have been very young, but it must be hard for anyone to lose a mother at that age. Crazy as my mother could drive me sometimes, she was still my mother. Thatcher was never very close to our mother, and I wondered what she made of all of this. She must have been shattered to find out what he'd done.

I was unsure how to respond to Lance, the conversation suddenly feeling more personal than I would like.

"If I'd known she was your horse, I wouldn't have taken her out riding every day."

"It's good that you did," he said, surprising me. "Someone should be riding her."

I knew I shouldn't be getting attached to horses that weren't mine. But now, knowing she was Lance's horse, and probably one of the last things his mother had ever given him, I didn't think I'd have the courage to get on her again.

The horse let out a whinny and tossed her head. Surely it wouldn't be much longer now.

Lance and I waited for what felt like hours but was probably only minutes. I felt my anxiety grow, hoping the mare and the foal would both be okay.

The mare started making grunting noises and my heartbeat quickened.

"It's time." Lance continued stroking her head and neck as the light bay mare started pushing out the little foal. With each noise she made, I cringed in pain for her, until finally the baby horse emerged, and I felt myself breathe for the first time in minutes. It was certainly not the most pleasant thing I'd ever seen, but the mother and foal were both alive at least. Lance stood back and allowed the mare to get up and reach for her baby.

"It's a boy," Lance noted after the two of us had stood there staring at them for a few minutes.

"What are you going to name him?"

Lance looked over at me with those icy eyes. "You should name him."

"Me?"

"It'll probably be a hell of a lot better than whatever I can come up with. Poor Bessie is stuck with a cow's name for the rest of her life."

I suppressed a chuckle, thinking about it for a moment.

"He looks like he's going to be fast when he grows up. What about Windchaser?"

He looked at the foal, tilting his head. "That could work." He kept his face neutral, but somewhere underneath that cold exterior, I swore I could see a hint of a smile.

Chapter 12

Elara

I rummaged through a drawer filled with books.

After going through the library, the study and the books that lined the parlour walls, I had yet to find anything resembling an old diary.

I'd never once thought this was going to be easy, but the more I looked, the more I doubted the diary even existed at all. It was a long shot to begin with, but for the first time in what seemed like months, I felt something other than overwhelming fear or anger. I felt hope, and it was difficult not to cling to it with every morsel of my being.

After signing a few documents and doing my correspondence that morning, I decided it was time to explore a room I'd purposely avoided since moving into the palace.

King Magnus's sleeping chambers. The monarch's rooms.

I'd grown up hating the man who I later discovered was my father. I'd been taught to hate him by my uncle, who believed his brother was not fit for the throne. And while many people suffered under Magnus's rule, I'd never taken the time or spared the effort to get to know more about the man who'd spent years looking for me.

Maybe it was because I was afraid that I would discover something that would change my mind about him, and I wasn't sure if I was ready for that.

But desperation does funny things to people sometimes and so I found myself venturing to the locked rooms of the old king. It was much like I'd expected — expensive furnishings now covered in white sheets. Large tapestries by fine artists, with long golden candlesticks placed about the room, gathering dust.

I'd opened one of the curtains, allowing just enough light to creep in so that I could see what I was doing. Then, I started looking through everything. There was a chest at the foot of the bed, another next to the fireplace, and a small desk in which I found nothing but some writing quills and blank pages. No drawer or cupboard would escape my search, but so far, I'd yet to turn up anything worthwhile.

There was a knock at the door, causing me to jump and drop one of the books.

"Sorry." Cai stepped into the room.

"You keep doing that." I bent down to pick up the book.

"Doing what?" He closed the door behind him.

"Scaring me." I started placing all the books back in the drawer.

"I don't mean to."

"I know. I guess I just don't expect you to show up outside your rooms so out of the blue."

After all, it had taken weeks just to get him to come out of his chambers in the first place.

Cai's face contorted a little. "You're right," he said sheepishly.

"What are you doing here?" I pulled open the next drawer.

"I heard a ruckus, so I thought I'd come take a look." Gosh, then I really must have been quite loud.

"I've been looking for the diary," I informed him, inspecting the next drawer. It had a few hunting knives and some other knick-knacks inside.

"Any luck?"

I let out a sigh. "It would appear not."

"Do you mind if I help you look?"

I turned to meet his eyes. "Of course not." Ever since the kiss we'd had in his room, I felt like something in Cai had changed. Nothing extraordinary, but I could see him trying, and I knew it must have taken a lot for him to get to that point. I just wasn't sure how to let him know that I appreciated it.

"What have you checked so far?"

"The chests, that desk." I pointed to it. "That cupboard and these drawers."

Cai made his way to another little side table that had a small drawer in it.

I shoved the drawer shut with some frustration, unsure of where to look next, when I noticed Cai running his hands along the fireplace.

"What are you doing?"

"Looking for secret doors."

"Secret doors?" I replied. "Do you really think there are secret doors in here?"

"Why wouldn't there be?" He moved away from the fireplace and to the wall panels.

I knew about the passage in Norrandale's palace that led away from the throne room. It was built for the safety of the kings and queens. But I couldn't believe I hadn't considered any other passageways in the palace.

"Wait, do you have a secret door in your rooms in Norrandale?" I asked, temporarily forgetting about my search for the diary.

Cai hesitated. "Not in my room, no, but there is a hidden passage from the king's rooms, yes." I'd forgotten that Cai had never moved into King Erik's chambers, even long after he'd been crowned.

"And where does it lead?" I questioned, somewhat idiotically.

Cai looked over his shoulder for a moment before continuing his search. "The queen's rooms," he said softly.

Right.

"Any other secret hallways or rooms I should know about?" If we made it out of this mess alive, then Mistwood would be my home as well.

"There are a few in the palace but not many. Most of them just lead to the catacombs or the servants use it for ... other activities."

He cleared his throat, and I felt myself grow a little red. Being alone with him now, having this conversation, had my head running wild with ideas that were not going to help either of us in the moment.

"Well, let me know if you find something." I walked to the other side of the room, when suddenly the wood underneath my feet made an odd sound. Almost like the panel was loose.

I stopped walking, taking a step back to see if it made the sound again, and it definitely did.

Cai looked at my little back-and-forth dance questioningly.

"What is it?"

"I think this piece of wood can be removed."

I quickly bent down, and Cai hurried over, dropping onto his knees next to me. It took some effort but eventually we wiggled the wooden panel out of place and lifted it away from the floor.

Sure enough, hidden beneath the floor of the king's room were many envelopes and folded letters.

"It's not a diary," Cai admitted with some defeat.

"But if he's hidden it, it has to be valuable."

We each picked up a piece of paper and I started scanning through.

To His Majesty, the King of Everness
I will not forget what happened last night. I can still
feel your—

I quickly folded the letter, wishing I could unread what I just saw.

"This is not—"

"Political correspondence, no," Cai said, going through one of the other papers. "These are letters between your father and his apparent mistress. Quite explicit letters, if I may say so."

"Well, stop reading it." I was so embarrassed I could bury myself under one of the floorboards.

"It's not bad actually. Some of it is even quite poetic."

"Put it away!" I hit him over the head with one of the envelopes I had in my hand and felt a chill crawl over me. This was something I'd really not like to think about. Much less read about in so much detail.

Cai let out a chuckle and it practically made me freeze. It had been months since I'd heard him laugh. I'd almost forgotten what it sounded like. I managed to forget my morbid embarrassment. After what we'd been through, I'd have given anything to keep seeing him smile.

Cai helped me put the letters back before returning the floorboard to its rightful position.

"I could have lived without knowing that. And we're not at all closer to finding the diary."

He looked around the room. "It has to be here somewhere in the palace."

"Do you really think so?" I asked earnestly.

"I want to believe it but I'm afraid to …" He trailed off.

"Hope?" I asked and Cai nodded.

"I know. I'm afraid of getting disappointed again. But I know I have to try and do something. Even if it's looking for some old diary that may or may not still exist." While Everness was preparing its defences, I couldn't sit and wait.

"Beating Aries on a battlefield won't be enough. Not if he finds what he's looking for."

"He's not going to stop until he finds the Myrgonite objects — just the thought of what he'll do with them absolutely terrifies me. Aries doesn't have a morsel of sympathy or mercy in his heart. He thrives on greed and power." And there had been nothing but warnings regarding the magic used on the objects. I feared what Aries might do with it.

"I wonder what made him like that." Based on my life experience, I had the tendency to believe monsters were made and not born.

"Do you know how Aries inherited his throne?" Cai asked and I shook my head. "From what I heard, his father was a horribly cruel man. Apparently, he would beat Aries and his brother often." The thought made me feel sympathy for Aries as a child, but that did not in any way justify the choices he'd made since.

"The pride in the kingdom of Argon lies in their army, in their men being the strongest warriors one could ever come across. So, when the heir to the throne turns eighteen, he is to fight the current king to prove his strength." I had a bad feeling about where this was going.

"But Aries decided to kill his father that day, proving he was the stronger leader."

I'd been betrayed by the people I cared about the most but never had it crossed my mind to end their lives. As if Cai could read my mind he said, "Hate makes people do desperate things sometimes."

"We're not beating Aries on a battlefield as long as we don't have the numbers he does." Just admitting it aloud sent a spiral of fear through my body. "We have to find those objects before he does, Cai. We need to make sure he never gets them."

"In the story that I read about the king and queen, it said that the gemstones protected her, through assassination attempts and other attacks. In a way, it was like she'd become immortal. Until, of course, the very same stones killed her."

"Aries wants to become undefeatable."

Cai's expression told me he knew I was right. "We have everything to lose. This is dangerous."

"Yes, we do, but it's like you said, Aries is not going to stop and we owe it to the people who have given their lives for us to be here." I reached for where he sat on the floor next to me, and placed my hand atop his.

"For Jack?"

"For Jack."

Chapter 13

Cai

The palace grounds provided a decent walk for the first time in days. Though not warm, the weather was more pleasant than before, allowing the cool morning to turn into an almost pleasant afternoon.

Alastor walked next to me — his sword safely in its sheath. I realised it had been months since I'd made use of a weapon. Not to mention how unfit and out of practice I'd become. Muscle memory and adrenaline were likely to kick in if it came down to it, but I doubted that I'd be able to defend myself properly in a serious battle. At least not as well as I used to.

As if Alastor could read my mind, he asked, "Would you like to make use of this time in the training ring, Your Majesty?"

I looked towards the training grounds in the distance, where some of the palace guards were sparring, their laughter echoing from afar.

"I fear I won't be good competition," I told Alastor. "But now is as good a time as any to get back to it."

I couldn't avoid it for ever. I didn't want to see the mental image of Thatcher, and it would appear the moment I picked up a sword again. I needed to find a way to push past the memories.

Alastor nodded in understanding. Ever since we'd lost Jack, something had changed in the weapon keeper and second in command. Without being asked, he'd stepped up to take on Jack's responsibility as my head guard. I knew all of this must have weighed heavy on him as well. Jack was his friend, too. "We'll start off easy," he reassured me.

We made our way to the training grounds, where Alastor managed to borrow a sword for me. I wrapped my hand around the hilt and an image of Jack's body came into my mind.

"Have Your Majesties found out more about the diary?"

I knew what he was doing. Alastor was trying to distract me by talking about something else.

I shook my head and lifted the sword. "Unfortunately not."

With every day that passed, Aries was getting closer to what he was looking for, and it wouldn't be long before we had to face him. I thought about Elara's words. About how we had to find the objects before he did. After I'd found out about them, I'd thought the knowledge was best kept away from everyone and everything for as long as humanly possible. It was too much of a risk to meddle with something we did not understand or know how to control. And while I still believed that we were better off without going after them, it appeared we no longer had a choice. At least not while Aries was alive.

But Elara had a point. If we had the objects, we could find a way to hide them where Aries would never find them, or better yet, we could try to destroy them. We just needed to find that diary.

"I've been thinking," Alastor started. Which really could mean anything. Over the past few years, I'd learned that he wasn't much of a talker, but that his thoughts ran deeper than one would imagine. He swung his sword towards me.

"Yes?" I ducked away quickly.

"Aries is still some distance from the main city and Mistwood. Perhaps we would stand a better fighting chance if we were to take back the palace and fortify ourselves there."

"You want to take the fight to Aries?" I made a jab to Alastor's torso, and he stepped to the side, knocking my sword out of the way.

I'd known for a while that taking back Mistwood would be the first step in fighting Aries, but just the thought of stepping into that place, knowing that Thatcher was probably sitting on my throne with my family's blood on his hands, made my stomach drop and my blood run cold.

"It's risky." Then again, war always was. But I wasn't about to discredit Alastor's idea just yet. I was already a bit out of breath. The fact that we weren't in the sweltering heat of summer helped at least. Alastor feigned making a low swing before suddenly aiming his sword towards my chest, but I'd seen him make this move a thousand times before and I knew where to put my sword.

"It would be very risky, yes," Alastor agreed, letting out a huff as I nearly caught the material of his sleeve. "But Aries wouldn't expect it and it might be enough to take him off guard. At least until reinforcements arrive."

I let out a breath, lowering my sword for a moment. "I don't even know what is actually going on in my kingdom. Which aristocrats have cowardly taken Thatcher's side and who has remained loyal." There was no doubt that Norrandale would require Everness's army, but despite the fact that Elara was queen, it was not that simple.

Evernean law required all of the royal council to be in agreement and sign off on the army. Especially since, technically, Everness was not yet at war with Argon. Not to mention our alliance was only truly solidified once Elara and I got married. But anyone who believed Everness not to be Aries' next target was an absolute fool.

"Maybe we need to think beyond Everness's army," Alastor suggested. "Though I'm sure many in the kingdom are still loyal to you, Your Majesty, we all know that we need bigger numbers if we are to take on Aries."

I held up my sword, indicating I was ready to have another go. "What are you proposing?"

"With Your Majesties' permission, I could see about finding those reinforcements." I had no idea what Alastor had in mind or where he would even begin to look. This sort of thing could take months, months we did not have. But I also knew that, like Jack, Alastor was willing to give his life for the kingdom and that he would do anything to protect it. I trusted that if anyone could do this job, it was him.

This time, Alastor kept his swings quick and controlled, and I needed to focus in order to avoid the tip of his sword.

"You should take a few men with you at least. And you would need a letter with my seal on it," I added. Just in case anyone questioned the legitimacy of his intentions.

"It could be very dangerous, you know." His sword came from above and I had to lift mine above my head to defend myself. Metal clashed against metal and the muscles in my arms strained, but I continued to push against him.

Alastor had something close to a grin on his face. "I was sort of counting on it."

With all the strength I could muster, I forced his sword away from my head, and managed to knock it out of his hands. I watched in satisfaction as the weapon fell to the ground.

Chapter 14

Elara

The sunlight slowly started to fade out of the library as dusk approached. It wouldn't be long before I had to light a candle or two in order to find my way around.

The Palace of Levernia hosted a large library, something that didn't mean much to me considering my distaste for reading. Dark shelves not only lined the walls but stood prominently in one row after the other. On the left side of the library, from the entrance, there was a desk and a fireplace, which created a nice working area. There were also a few reading chairs within comfortable distance of the fireplace, making it the perfect reading spot. But other than that, and a few paintings, it was books as far as the eye could see.

It was hard to believe I'd been here all afternoon. But ever since Cai and I came across the king's letters that mentioned the diary, I couldn't help the feeling that this would be the best place to keep something like that safe. That was to say, if the diary still existed and hadn't been lost to time.

The royal library had thousands of books on hundreds of shelves and going through all of it alone would take months. I couldn't spend too much of my time on this task. Not when we had to ready all our forces to defend Everness in the event that Aries decided to attack. There were meetings to attend and documents to go through and sign. Which was why I had both Cai and Rhen help me by going through some parts of the library.

I had the entire afternoon to myself, so I opted to tackle the sections that Cai and Rhen had yet to look through. Cai had originally come across the writing about the diary in here, but there was nothing like a journal in any of those shelves. I flipped through the books, looking behind them at the wood of the shelves, until I started to squint because of the lack of light in the room. But I wasn't ready to give up on my search. I was surprisingly far from tired and had more than half of the library left to go.

A small light emerged from the door behind me, and I turned to see Rhen step into the room with a candle in his hand.

"I was wondering where you'd disappeared to."

I quickly stood up from where I'd been kneeling next to a shelf and dusted off my skirts.

"Is something wrong? Does someone require my presence?"

"No, thankfully. Anesta mentioned something about you being in here and I thought I'd come and check on your progress. I certainly haven't had much luck today in that area."

"I'm afraid I don't have any good news either."

Rhen stared at me for a moment with a curious expression.

"What?" I asked, looking down at my blue dress and back up at him.

"Just reminiscing, I suppose." He shrugged.

"About anything in particular?" I turned back to the shelf I had been looking through.

"It doesn't feel that long ago that you were just a thieving girl whom I chased across a rooftop, and yet, so much has changed. You went from a prisoner to a queen and now we're searching for the journal of the first king of Everness in the hopes that it could give us the information we need to go up against the King of Argon." Just hearing him say it out loud felt somewhat surreal.

"Probably because it wasn't that long ago," I reminded him.

"You might not believe me," he said, crossing his arms. "But I think the palace life suits you in some ways." It was undoubtable that the bandit in me would never truly leave. But I'd tried to take on this new role with all its responsibilities as best I could. I wanted to be the queen the kingdom actually needed.

"Well, the food is certainly a lot better."

Rhen ran his hands along one of the shelves, inspecting the books.

"You know, I've already tried looking there," I commented, but Rhen continued his search.

"Probably won't hurt to look a second time."

"I suppose not. Though it would be a very obvious place to hide it." I moved on to the next shelf.

"You might be surprised to find that not all kings are very creative," Rhen said, placing the candle on a nearby table.

"You're right. But do you really think it would just be lying around these books so randomly?"

"I don't know. It's very old. It would need to be more protected, if you ask me."

"More protected?" I mumbled to myself, scanning the library. "Where are the oldest books and the archives kept?"

"There." He pointed to the far back. "But Cai and I have already looked there."

I started making my way to the back shelves and Rhen followed behind, bringing the candle with him. We stopped in front of the shelves that lined the wall, and I eyed them with suspicion, not looking at any of the books specifically.

"What?" Rhen asked.

"Cai and I were looking through Magnus's rooms and he told me something interesting." I reached for one of the shelves and started pulling at it. "He mentioned the secret passageways in Mistwood Palace, and it's got me thinking." I yanked again and Rhen put the candle down.

"It's too heavy. Let me help." We both pulled at the wood, but it would not move.

"Not this one, then." I huffed and moved on to the next one. Rhen and I tried each of the shelves but none of them had a secret door hidden behind them.

"I really thought I was onto something for a moment there." I stepped back with a disappointed sigh.

"It was a clever idea," Rhen tried to reassure me. "With a palace as old as this one, it really isn't that far-fetched to think the library might have a secret room."

I scanned the walls again while biting the inside of my cheek. Most of the shelves went up quite high but there were some places where the walls were bare of books and had a painting or a piece of weaponry or armour displayed. My footsteps creaked over the wooden floor as I made my way back to the shelf in the corner. Next to it, steel armour had been erected to look like a knight standing there holding his sword. The wall behind it had some decorative panels and I let my fingers trace the edges. There was a small gap between the wall and the bookshelf, almost unnoticeable, but it was there.

I sucked in a breath and pressed both my hands to the wooden panel, and suddenly a door popped open. I looked over my shoulder at Rhen, whose eyebrows were a little raised.

"Well, I'll be damned." He helped me to pull open the secret door, and after some effort, we stepped into the secret little room. It was dark and dusty, with books and scrolls lying on shelves in disarray.

"All the kingdom's secrets must be locked away here," I said, more to myself than him.

"Too bad we don't have time for that." Rhen and I looked through all the written material, but nothing resembled a diary. I didn't want to believe that after all our effort this was just a dead end.

"I might have found something," Rhen said, just as I was beginning to feel all the hope inside me slip away.

"You found the diary?" I turned to face the shelf that he was looking through.

Not the diary, but a small cupboard in the wall behind the bookshelf. I was quick to yank on the handle, but it wouldn't budge.

"I suspect you need a key," Rhen replied with some sarcasm. "Unless, of course, your lock-picking skills haven't gone out of the window."

"I can still pick a lock." I gave him a flat expression over my shoulder after inspecting the lock. "But not one like this. These mechanisms are different, older."

"So, a key, then," Rhen said, and our momentum came to a halt. I decided to step back into the library, trying to think of any place where we might find a key. The desk near the fireplace caught my attention and I dashed over.

"What are you doing?" Rhen asked.

I felt under the desk and pulled open all the drawers. "Kings aren't very creative, remember?" Rhen watched as I fiddled under one of the desk drawers and pulled out a small metal object with a slight smirk.

"Surely it can't be that easy."

I wasn't going to wait to find out. We hurried back over to the secret room, and I bent down to unlock the little cupboard. There was a satisfying click as it unlocked.

Inside the cupboard was a small selection of books and scrolls, lying on each other in an unorganised fashion, as if someone had stacked them in there while in a mighty rush.

Rhen bent down and the two of us slowly started looking through each book and piece of paper.

"Looks like historical archives of the kingdom," I said while scanning. "Nothing about a diary yet, though it does mention King Evrin a few times."

Rhen looked up from the book in his hand. "Anything about treasure or Myrgonite stones?"

"Not yet."

"How many documents did you find that mentioned the old king's diary?" he asked.

"Three, technically."

Rhen thought about it for a second. "Everything that's led us here so far has not been in obvious sight." His eyes met mine and slowly we both looked to the cupboard.

"Could it be?" I said.

He carefully took out the remaining books and placed them on the floor next to us. I traced the back of the hidden cupboard until I felt a dent in the wood.

"Is there something?" I tugged on the wood until a little wooden box fell out, spluttering some dust into the air. We both sat staring at the box for a moment.

"What do you think the odds are that this is what we're looking for?" Rhen asked, and I reached for the old wooden box and gave it a little shake. Something rattled inside. Something that sounded an awful lot like it could be a book of some kind.

"I think the odds are looking pretty good right now."

Chapter 15

Elara

Evening had set in and after not being able to find Lance anywhere in the vicinity of the dining room, I knew there was only one place he was likely to be right now.

"Good evening, brother." I burst through his chamber doors. Only considering, after the fact, that I could have discovered Lance in some compromising position.

Luckily for me, he was only passed out, as I'd expected. The Prince of Everness lay draped over his expensive bedding, his face on the blankets.

When my initial burst didn't earn a response from him, I made an effort to close the doors extra hard behind me.

This time, I received a groan in return.

"I need to have a word with you." I stepped further into the room, expecting to find a mess, but it was surprisingly tidy. A servant must have recently been in to clean.

"Not now," came a grumble from the sheets.

"Should I ask the servants for a bucket of cold water, then?" This seemed to grab Lance's attention enough that he rolled over onto his back.

"Why do you hate me so?" he asked dramatically.

"We do not want to get on that boat right now." To say I wasn't fond of my brother would be an understatement. Especially considering the absolute rude idiot he could be at times. Though I would admit, in the months that we'd been living together, I could feel the elements of my distrust towards him begin to slip through the cracks. Instead of a threat, Lance had become more of an annoyance.

But that didn't mean he couldn't be helpful on occasion. Which was exactly why I was there.

"We found the diary," I said, crossing my arms.

"Good for you," Lance responded, with his eyes still closed.

"At least I think it's the diary. The problem is that it's locked in a box." After finding the wooden box, Rhen and I had searched the library from top to bottom for another key, including trying the one from the cupboard, but nothing could open the box. Out of desperation, I even tried to smash it, but it would not give. "And I can't get it open. I even tried to break it."

"That's because it's protected by magic." Lance slowly rolled onto his side and used the bedpost to pull himself into a sitting position. "You need a special key," he finished, and my eyes widened.

"I'm sorry, what did you just say?"

Lance opened his eyes after realising that he'd given himself away, but did not respond.

"Is there something you'd like to tell me?" I tried to push any growing anger down into the depths of myself. "Like how you know much more about the diary than you've let on?"

"And so, what if I do?" he said, with a nonchalance that only managed to spike my annoyance.

"Are you insane? You know how important this is!"

"Did you ever consider that maybe I was trying to save everyone from inevitable disappointment?" he said as I stomped over to him.

"Of course I didn't consider it," I responded harshly. "That would require you to think about someone other than yourself."

He gave me a look to suggest he didn't appreciate my sarcasm.

"That's not a nice thing to say to someone whose help you currently require."

I stared at him, not bothering to apologise. "Tell me what you know."

"Ah but it doesn't work that way." Lance sloppily lifted a finger. "You and I bargain for things, remember?"

"Lance." I scolded him like he was a child, especially because he was busy acting like one. "I know it might be hard for you to believe but this isn't about you. This is about all of us, and once upon a time you were willing to do a hell of a lot of damage to protect Everness."

"Yes, but that was before you lied to me." He tilted his head while I imagined hitting it with a particularly blunt object.

"What are you talking about?"

"You had me believe that I was crazy for going after the Myrgonite stones and those objects. You had me thinking I was truly losing it, and yet here we are, and suddenly you seem to know an awful lot about them."

"I did think you were insane back then," I told him truthfully. "But that was before I knew about all this, before Cai even knew."

"But you know about the three magical objects now, don't you? You know all about it. I bet you even know what they are."

"Don't be ridiculous." I felt my face grow hot. "If we knew that, then I wouldn't be looking for the diary, would I?"

Lance didn't look like he entirely believed me. I guessed it took a liar to know one.

"What do you want to bargain, then?" I needed this conversation to be over as quickly as possible. There was little use in trying to talk with Lance when he was in this state, but I feared we were running out of time.

"I want one of them," he said.

"You want what?"

"One of the Myrgonite objects. When this is over and you and Cai have collected your little jewels and saved the kingdom, I want what is rightfully mine."

The only reason Cai and I were now actively looking for the objects was so that we could prevent them from getting into the wrong hands, or from getting into anyone's hands ever again. And that list definitely included Lance. No one with that much attitude needed to have access to things containing ancient power that was beyond our comprehension.

"You're funny," I said sarcastically. "No."

"Come now, Elara. I daresay you even owe it to me. One for you, one for Cai and one for me. It's nice how it works out like that. It will be safe in our hands. Just like our ancestors probably would have wanted it. The objects will be out of harm's way and our kingdoms will be at peace. Everybody wins."

"If Cai and I should find those objects, the only thing we will be doing with them is destroying them."

"Destroy them?" Lance frowned. "Didn't you know that they cannot be destroyed?"

My expression told him I did not.

"I'm surprised that in all your research you had yet to discover this. The magic that was used on the stones also protects them. If

108

you should try to destroy any of the objects, it would kill you and anyone in the vicinity."

I suddenly felt foolish for believing that Cai and I would so easily be rid of the objects once we'd discovered them. Of course the stones couldn't just be destroyed, otherwise someone would have done it a long time ago. I tried to prevent the frustration reaching my face.

So many thoughts were running through my head, and combined with the many sleepless nights, I was no longer thinking straight.

Cai and I had our suspicions about what some of the objects could be. Both the heirloom necklace and the dagger he'd given me appeared to have small Myrgonite stones in them. But that didn't make them the magical objects that belonged to Queen Riona all those centuries ago. We needed the diary to be certain, and if we couldn't destroy them, then we had to find another way to keep them hidden from the world.

"All right, then," I reluctantly agreed, surprising both myself and Lance. "How do I get to the diary, then?"

"I don't know if the diary is in there for sure, but I know it can't be opened."

"You just said it could. All we need is the key."

His facial expression suggested I was being naive. "Don't you think that if it were that easy to get the key, we would have already had it by now?"

All the hope and excitement from earlier started to drift away from me. We'd come so far.

"It can't be that difficult." I placed my hands on my hips. "Where is it, then?"

"It's a story Mother once told me, when I was a child."

I was momentarily surprised. Lance had never spoken about our mother before.

"She used to love history and reading."

I wouldn't go so far as to say I was jealous of Lance knowing our mother before she died. Even after I'd gone through her things. It was difficult to miss someone I'd only seen in paintings. But I'd never heard Lance bring her up until now, so this had to be worth something.

He carefully got up, taking a moment to find his footing. Lance stumbled to the dressing table not too far from his bed and started drinking water from the pitcher that was meant for cleaning his face.

I avoided rolling my eyes, staying quiet so that he would keep talking.

"She knew so much about the kingdom. I don't know where she'd heard the tale or if it was just some made-up childhood story. But Mother believed the key to be in the centre of the forest." I couldn't help but gulp as soon as he'd said the words. The mere memory of that day created a knot in my stomach. The day I'd lost Ray. Cai and I walking through those misty woods, unsure if we would ever get out alive.

"Where in the centre of the forest?" I dared to ask.

"There's a large willow tree in the middle of it all, the oldest tree in the kingdom. Mother used to say that somewhere inside the tree, the key was hidden to all Everness's secrets."

That sounded promising.

"But it didn't come without a cost. You had to reach into the willow tree with your hand, and if the tree found you unworthy, it would kill you by taking your soul and then morph you into the tree itself." Well, that was a nice image to think about.

"If this is true, then why didn't King Magnus ever do something about it?"

Lance snorted, taking a seat on the bed again. "Father had no interest in that sort of thing. In fact, he was rather against it." For some reason, this didn't surprise me. Magnus never came across as the kind of king who would be in support of using magic. Although, looking back at all the trouble it had caused us, that may not have been entirely unreasonable.

"And what about you, then? You nearly caused a war with Norrandale trying to find out more about those Myrgonite stones." And here he was, still chasing after them.

"I found the box a long time ago and tried everything to open it. But I think it comes down to getting that key. I've sent men from the palace repeatedly, but none of them have come back alive."

Well, of course not. Not if the magical and deadly mist in the centre of the forest could help it. Cai and I hadn't told anyone about our experience in the mist. And I wasn't about to spill it to Lance either.

"So why didn't you just go into the forest and retrieve it yourself?"

He scoffed. "And get sucked in by a tree? No thank you." It may have been a cowardly answer, but if what Lance said was true and one had to be deemed worthy to retrieve the key, then we both knew there was no way he was getting it. The question remained: who would be deemed worthy?

"So basically, you've been no help to me at all."

"That's not true," Lance said. "I told you how to open the box."

"Yes, with some fabled key in the deadliest place in the forest, where some old tree is going to try and murder us."

"I never promised it would be easy."

I wanted to shake my head and scream and cry all at once. Every time it felt like we were making a little progress, we were forced to take a few steps back.

"No, you never did," I said truthfully, once again reminded why Lance didn't want to be king in the first place.

"Have you been to see Eloisa?"

My brother looked surprised at the sudden change of topic.

"Yes, why?"

"No reason. I just heard she asked for you a lot." I hadn't been visiting Eloisa much. Not that she ever responded to me when I was there, and according to her physician, she wasn't really getting better.

"Well, I'm just about the only family she knows."

I wasn't sure what Lance's intentions were behind his words.

"Magnus wasn't very fond of her, then?"

"I think it was easier for Father to pretend she didn't exist."

I wasn't surprised by this, though Lance stepping up to take any care of her at all did always make me wonder. Even though we were related, he definitely wasn't the most brotherly person I knew.

"Does she talk to you?" I ventured to ask, being at least a little curious as to exactly what kind of relationship he had with Eloisa.

"Not often," Lance confirmed. "But she looks at me sometimes and I know she knows who I am, even if she can't say it."

I wasn't sure how to respond. The topic had become rather personal, and at the risk of getting vulnerably intimate with the man who had bargained magic for information a few minutes ago, I took a step back.

"Well, I'd better get going, then. See what I can do about that key." The stars knew we had to find it, one way or another.

Chapter 16

Cai

I began my ascent of the wide staircase, making the familiar journey to my chambers. Even though I didn't have much of an appetite, I'd been hoping to join Elara for dinner, but I had found the dining room empty. I wanted to discuss what Alastor had told me and possible plans to take back Norrandale. I knew she would be happy, probably even eager, to talk about the topic considering my serious lack of interest in the past few months.

I wasn't entirely sure of my motives yet. Did I actually believe we stood a chance of taking back Mistwood, or was I delusional? Or did I feel overwhelmingly guilty for not even trying before?

I had asked a passing servant where they'd last seen her and had been directed to the library. Once I was certain she wasn't in the library either, I figured she'd probably gone to bed early and that I could join her for breakfast the next morning. Reluctantly, I had turned my steps towards my rooms.

I trudged over the carpet of the upper floors, walking past the many guest rooms. These hallways were filled with paintings, most of them depicting nature, especially the palace gardens and the wooded area surrounding it.

"Cai." Her voice came from behind me, and I turned around.

"There you are," I said as Elara hurried to catch up with me. "I've been looking for you."

"You were?" She seemed pleased at the idea.

"I wanted to talk to you about a discussion I had with Alastor about Norrandale."

"I need to talk to you as well." We walked beside each other through the hallway. We passed a servant lighting some lamps along the wall.

"I'm listening," I encouraged her.

"So, I think we may have found the diary."

"We?"

"Well, me and Rhen," she explained. "We were looking for it in the library this afternoon and then we came across this small wooden box."

"So we were right to spend all that time searching in the library."

Elara nodded. "It wasn't easy to find either. It was stashed in a locked cupboard that we found in a secret room hidden behind a wall panel. The only problem is that we can't open the box."

"You mean you can't break it or something?"

She shook her head. "Apparently it's protected by some kind of old magic, and we need the actual key to open it."

My heartbeat quickened a little at the use of the word *magic*. That wasn't a very good sign.

"And we don't know where the key is?"

"Actually, we do." She stepped closer and took hold of my upper arm as we walked. I wanted to pull her closer still. "It just won't be very easy to retrieve."

"How did you find out about all this? Did the box come with some kind of instructional scroll?"

My words caused the corner of her mouth to turn up a little.

"Of course not. Lance told me."

I was equally confused and surprised.

"Lance?"

Elara let out a very long sigh. "Yes, apparently he knew much more about the diary than he'd let on." This part did not shock me in any way. Of course Lance had been withholding information if it was to his benefit. The only question was how?

"But he also knew that the box couldn't be opened unless you used the key, which unfortunately happens to be in the centre of the forest."

"You mean … ?"

"In the mist? Yes." Her voice was filled with frustration. "Lance has sent people to get it in the past, none of whom came back, as could be expected. And, of course, Lance would never go and get it himself, so …" She trailed off.

There were many days that I would have given much to forget. And the time we were in that forest was one of them. When King Aries sent his men to Everness in another failed assassination attempt, Elara and I had accidentally ended up in the midst of Everness's fabled forest of mist. Where people wandered around trying to get out until they eventually died of hunger or thirst. And that was only if the wolves didn't get to them first. I remembered the story told at Camp Fairfrith one night, when the man had tried to scare the children with tales of the mist. He mentioned something about it only being royals who are able to get out of the forest. I didn't know if I believed him, but I knew Elara and I had somehow made it out of there alive and that I had no intention of going back, ever.

"Of all the places." I threw my head back in exasperation. "And how does Lance know all this?"

Elara's expression became unreadable. "He said it was something our mother used to believe in. Things she would tell him about when he was a child. For all we know, it's only a story and we're heading for another dead end." It certainly didn't feel like things were looking up for us yet.

"But we found that diary and that has to mean something. It has to lead somewhere or be opened somehow and it's hard to believe in all these things, but I don't know what else to believe anymore."

Her sadness forced a pang in my chest, and I wished I could do something to take it away, to make all of this just go away, but I couldn't.

"Did Lance give a reason for not sharing any of this before?" *Other than being something of a prick.*

"Well, you know Lance loves to drive a good bargain," Elara started with some uncertainty.

"What do you mean?" I had a feeling that I wasn't going to like whatever she was about to tell me.

"In exchange for the information, he wanted one of the three Myrgonite objects."

"Please do not tell me you agreed," I practically pleaded. "We need to destroy those things as soon as we can."

"I'm afraid they can't be destroyed. It would kill you and anyone close by."

"And I suppose Lance told you that? How do you know he wasn't lying?"

"Are you really willing to risk it?"

"I don't think we have a choice." I wanted to believe there was some way to destroy the objects without putting anyone in danger. But then I thought back to that book I'd come across in the library where I first read about the king's diary. It might have mentioned something about being unable to destroy the stones. Maybe I just didn't want to truly believe it.

"We need that key, and you know it. And since we can't just destroy the objects, we need to keep them separate and hidden. Lance suggested we each have possession of one."

I couldn't understand her reasoning. Did she still not realise how dangerous this was?

"Lara, the only reason we're looking for those objects in the first place is to keep them out of the wrong hands." The fact that he was her brother be damned. This was a lot bigger than bloodlines.

"Would you calm down?" Elara looked left and right, lowering her voice. She pushed me back into the nearest guestroom and closed the door behind her. Had it not been for the severity of the situation, I would have made some flirtatious joke.

"We're not actually going to give him anything," she explained, continuing to keep her voice low. "I just need him to believe it for now. I told you Lance knows a lot about the objects and the history of the realm. Even if we don't like it, we need his help. After all, he's been looking for them a lot longer than we have."

"Which is exactly why he shouldn't come anywhere near them." Never mind the fact that if someone as determined as Lance hadn't managed to find all of them, what hope did that give us?

"Look, we are the only two who suspect what at least two of the objects are. And we're going to keep it that way." She tried to reassure me. "All we need is the diary to confirm it and then hopefully it will lead us to the third."

"Then once Lance knows we have it, we still need to prevent him from getting it."

She frowned, not pleased with my words. "I already told you, I'm not going to come through on my promise."

"Do you honestly think he would just give up, especially knowing they are now within his reach? Why did you tell him about the objects anyway?" We mentioned nothing in the meeting apart from the gemstones.

"What do you mean?" she said, slightly defensively. "Lance has known about them for years."

"Yes, but by giving him that fake necklace at Woodsbrook, he seemed to give up on it a little at least. By agreeing to give him one of the objects, he knows we believe they exist and we wouldn't do so without reason."

"Are you seriously blaming me for this right now?"

"No, I'm saying we need to be careful. The more people know, the greater the risk."

"You think I don't know that?" She no longer bothered keeping her voice down and took a step back. "You still don't see me as a proper queen, do you? I'm still that naive girl who has no idea what she's doing."

"I did not say that."

"But you were thinking it," she threw back.

"Don't be ridiculous. I said we should be careful, not that you're incapable."

She shook her head and turned to the door. "Whatever, Cai. I'm going to try and get that key, and you can do whatever the hell you want."

"Whoa, whoa," I said, stepping towards her. "You're not actually going there yourself, are you?"

"Well, I don't see how we have much of a choice." She made for the door, and I took hold of her arm.

"Just think about this for a moment. We don't even know if it's there. This could all just be some story."

"My mother believed it," she responded with some offence, which was hard to argue with.

"It's too dangerous and I will not have you go back there."

She yanked her arm out of my grasp. "You don't get to decide that for me." Elara pulled open the door and I pressed my hand to the wood, closing it again. This conversation was not over.

"I'm just trying to protect you," I said more gently. "This could be deadly and I don't want you going alone."

"I'm King Evrin's descendant. I have to be the one to do it."

"Then could you at least give it some time? Until we figure out a plan on how to approach this?"

Elara considered it for a moment. "Fine." She pressed a kiss to my cheek before opening the door again. "Goodnight, Cai."

Chapter 17

Lance

I fastened the last of the buttons on my tunic and stood back to better inspect myself in the mirror. *Not too shabby, if I do say so myself.* I ruffled my dark hair a little and gave my reflection a satisfied nod.

My stomach let out a low growl and I left my room eager to reach the dining hall. I hoped they were serving a decent breakfast. For some reason, I was craving eggs.

The palace servants bowed as I passed them before going back to their duties. I flashed a grin at one of the maids, whose face immediately went red before she whispered something to the maid next to her.

By the time I reached the ground floor of the palace, I'd increased my pace. I couldn't remember the last time I was this hungry, and an enticing aroma drifted from the kitchens.

With anticipation at the prospect of breakfast, I opened the dining-room doors only to find that I was not the only one who'd had the idea to take my breakfast in here.

Gwen looked up from the book in her hands. "Good morning." Her tone wasn't cheerful but at least I'd managed to actually get a greeting from her.

"Morning," I replied, strolling over to a chair on the opposite side of the table and taking a seat. Apart from a tea set, some milk and some sugar, the table was still empty.

"Aren't you having breakfast?"

She nodded, eyes going back to her book. "In a minute. I'm having my tea first."

"All right, then." I reached for the teapot and a nearby cup and saucer.

"I didn't know you drank anything other than wine."

"No?" I looked at her, but Gwen continued to read. "I enjoy my tea in the morning as much as anyone. Most people prefer something like a black tea, but I find that I actually enjoy a good camomile." I was lying, of course. Though I'd heard these names many times before, I rarely drank tea, especially with the knowledge of what kind of tea it was. It all pretty much tasted the same to me.

Gwen could tell I wasn't being serious, and she finally lowered her book. "I'll wager my entire inheritance that you're lying and that you haven't had a cup of tea in years."

In all truth, she was too clever for her own good, but it made any conversation with her wonderfully entertaining.

"That's an awfully big wager." I took a sip of the tea. It definitely could use some more milk. Or perhaps something stronger. "Thankfully I don't need your money, Lady Gwen."

A servant entered the dining room and reached for the teapot. "Can I refill this for you, Your Highness?"

"Please, and would you also bring me some breakfast?"

"Of course, Your Highness. What would you like?"

I glanced at Gwen and back to the servant. "I'll have whatever she's having."

"Very good, Your Highness." He gave a short bow before leaving the room with the teapot.

"What are you reading?" I gestured to the book in her hands.

"A book," she replied, with a hint of both boredom and sarcasm, her eyes shooting left and right across the page.

"Not that I don't enjoy this little dance of banter between us, Lady Gwen." I took another sip of the tea and forced my face not to grimace. "But I'm afraid I must ask the reason for your hostility towards me."

She stared up at me from under her brow, her expression unimpressed.

"You know the longer you play this game of pretending to hate me, the more I'm going to try and make you like me," I continued when she didn't say anything. Gwen still didn't respond but I watched her swallow hard.

I was reaching for the flask in the pocket of my tunic when the servant entered carrying two plates, both with a silver cover. Deciding against pulling out my flask, I waited in anticipation for the servant to remove the cover, only to find two steaming scones on the plate, some butter and jam on the side. No eggs.

"This is what you ordered for breakfast?"

Gwen shrugged casually but I could see her trying to suppress a slight grin.

"Too much like cake for you, is it?"

"Not at all." I grimaced.

I used my knife to cut the warm scone in half and started spreading some butter on it, all the while thinking how stupid scones were and how much I'd rather have a proper breakfast.

Or at least some bacon, maybe. But my pride prevented me from calling back the servant.

"So do your plans entail staying inside and reading all day?" I couldn't blame her — the weather was miserable. There were constant bursts of rain, and if it wasn't raining, the wind blew something fierce.

"I wanted to go for a walk when the rain stopped, but you know." She gestured to the walking stick leaning on the chair next to her.

"Well, when you're feeling up to it, you should go and visit Windchaser. I'm sure he misses you." This piqued her interest, but she kept her expression nonchalant.

"He told you this himself, did he?"

"Of course." I took a big bite from the scone, my mouth filled with the buttery taste. "He's quite a talkative little foal."

"Hmph." She snorted at my response, putting her book down to start eating her breakfast.

"How long did the physician say you had to use the walking stick?"

"A few more weeks, though I don't know how much longer I can take it," Gwen complained, taking a teaspoon and scooping up a big dollop of cream. I watched her mouth as she licked it off the spoon, my own food temporarily forgotten.

"Does your ankle still hurt?" I quickly cleared my throat.

"A little. I don't think I should have walked on it after I got hurt."

"Probably not, no. Which is why I insisted you see a physician."

"Oh, you would just love to hear me say you were right."

I opened my mouth to respond that I wouldn't mind just that when the dining-room door opened, and Cai walked in.

His eyes landed on the two of us sitting across from each other.

"Having breakfast together?" If looks could kill, then I would have died. I wondered if Elara had told him about our conversation.

"Not on purpose," Gwen replied quickly. "Would you like to join us?"

"No thank you. I'm looking for Elara. Have you seen her?" He looked tired, like he hadn't been sleeping, and his expression suggested he wasn't looking for her so that they could share a cup of tea.

"I'm afraid not," I said before Gwen could respond. "Everything all right?"

The King of Norrandale continued to glare at me. "Everything's fine," he said through clenched teeth. "I just need to talk to her."

"Well, I'll let the queen know, should I run into her."

"At least join me for a cup of tea," Gwen pleaded, patting the table next to her.

Cai hesitated and I cleared my throat, wiping my mouth with a napkin. "I should get going anyway." The chair scraped over the floor as I got up from my seat.

"Lady Gwen." I bowed, then walked past Cai and out of the room.

It was the afternoon, as I lounged about in one of the parlours, when my sister walked in, a look of pure determination on her face.

"There you are," she said with a hint of annoyance.

"You were looking for me?" I didn't move from my comfortable position on one of the settees, one leg hanging off and touching the ground.

"Yes, I need you to show me something." She closed the door behind her, properly taking in me and the room. "What are you even doing in here?"

"Nothing actually," I admitted. "In fact, I'm rather bored."

Elara had a few rolled-up papers in her hands. She walked over to the settee and shoved my other leg off carelessly. "Come on, move over."

I let out a slight groan, sitting up. "Cai was looking for you earlier, by the way. I told him I'd pass on the message."

She didn't say anything, but her face told me enough.

"Did something happen between you two?" I asked as she unrolled the papers and placed them on the wooden table in front of us.

"No, everything's fine."

"You know, you used to be a better liar before you became queen."

I glanced at the many papers. They were all maps of Everness.

"I used to be a lot of things before I became queen," she mumbled, straightening out the last one. "Now, I need you to show me where the key is."

I looked at the table full of maps and then back to her. "Why?"

"Don't be stupid — so that we can go and get it."

"Who is 'we'? I'm definitely not going in there." I valued my life a little too much for that.

"We, me, it doesn't matter. Just tell me where it is."

"Where did you even get all this?" I started looking through the maps.

"In the library. They're older, so I figured they'd probably be more useful."

Most of the maps were too big, showing the entire kingdom and not the finer details that we needed. I shuffled through them until I found one that was more centred around the Evernean Forest.

"All right, see this creek here?" I pointed to a small line on the map.

"Yes."

"You want to follow it straight into the mist. That's where it gets tricky, because the creek ends and finding landmarks from there is damn near impossible."

"Great," she said sarcastically.

"It'll probably be quite a walk but eventually you want to reach a pool of water. Now, if you're coming from Levernia, you're likely to be on this side of the water." I showed her. "But the willow tree you're looking for is on the other side of the pool."

"How big is this pool of water?"

I stated the obvious: "I don't know. I've never seen it."

"Okay fine, there's a pool and a tree and then what?"

"Well, like I told you, the key is supposed to be inside the tree, according to what Mother said."

We both stared at the map intently. "Any chance she might have just been making it up?"

"She wasn't really the kind of person to make up stories. If anything, at the very least, she believed them herself."

"How do you know? You were a child."

"I heard her and Father argue over it often. He told her to stop filling my head with fairy tales and she told him they weren't fairy tales." I'd never told anyone that before. Never had a reason to.

"Mmmhh," Elara said, somewhat absentmindedly. "I guess I have no choice but to believe her, then." She picked up the map. "So, what, you stick your hand into the tree and if it deems you worthy it will relinquish the key?"

"Something like that. Who are you going to send?"

"No one." She didn't meet my eyes.

"At the risk of sounding like a concerned older brother, do you really think that's a good idea?"

"I don't think I have a choice. We need that diary." Elara carefully rolled up the map. "Whatever you do, don't tell Cai about this."

"Are you keeping things from your fiancé now? What's going on with you two?"

"Nothing." She stood up. "He's just being a little paranoid is all." That I could believe.

"Thanks for the help." She headed for the door, and I couldn't help but let out a laugh.

"What?"

"At one point you wanted to kill me and now you're actually saying thank you. Look how far we've come."

"Don't get cocky. I could always send you back to prison."

"I don't think so," I said, waving my hand. "It would be too boring in this place without my company."

Chapter 18

Elara

The moon was high in the night sky by the time I slid on my riding boots.

The fire in my room was slowly dying and bitter cold had enveloped me when I slipped out of my warm sheets. In that moment, I wanted nothing more than to crawl back to bed. But this needed to be done.

I plaited my hair away from my face and put on my warmest winter cloak. Pulling on my gloves, I headed for the doors to my chambers. I'd almost reached them before realising I'd forgotten my map, and so I turned back to grab it. This forced me to double-check my satchel again. Knife? Check. I reached for the sword mounted on the wall above the fireplace. It was too risky to go to the arsenal to retrieve any weapons, so I had to make do with what I could find in my rooms.

A small food supply and a flask of water, which I'd taken from the kitchens earlier? Check.

And now I had my map.

I carefully opened my doors, making sure there were no guards outside. I'd conveniently given both night guards the evening off.

Even as queen, it was surprisingly difficult to escape your own palace. I tiptoed down the corridors, avoiding all the main hallways, yet my boots continued to sound on the floors, and I could only hope no one would hear me.

I contemplated going through the servants' quarters, but I worried some of them might be awake, so instead I opted for the route Cordelia had shown me the first time I left the palace. When Lance had "hired" me to pretend to be Princess Eloisa and steal Cai's family heirloom. That time seemed a world away now.

It didn't take long for me to reach the door that would lead me to the stables.

The icy winter air hit me once more and I wished Aries could have picked a better time for all of this. It was unlikely that he would march all of his soldiers in the middle of winter — the risk was too great. But he was still in Norrandale, looking for the Myrgonite objects and the mine of stones, and my bet was that as soon as the snow melted, he would strike. Maybe even before that. Either way, I wasn't going to wait around to see it play out.

I pulled the hood of my cloak over my head and by the time I'd reached the stables, I could no longer feel my nose.

The horses rustled with unease at my disturbance in the middle of the night.

"Easy," I said with a soft voice. "It's just me."

I made a quick trip to the tack room before picking the horse nearest to the stable doors. By early tomorrow morning, when the stable boy walked in, it would be a matter of minutes before everyone knew I was gone.

I saddled the horse as best I could in the dark and led it out of the stables.

"I know it's cold." With my left foot in the stirrup, I swung my right leg over the horse and moved on the saddle until I found a comfortable seat. "But we have to do this before snowfall or it's only going to make it that much more difficult."

With only a little bit of moonlight to guide us, I steered the horse away from the stables and towards the woods in the distance. Despite wearing gloves, my hands felt cold and stiff, and I had trouble properly gripping the reins.

I could see the horse's breath and my own evaporating into the frigid air. It wasn't long before the palace grounds fell behind us and we reached the treeline. With the dark night looming, some part of me wished I hadn't done this alone. I thought about how much better and safer I would feel to have Cai by my side. But then I reminded myself that there was no way in hell he would have agreed to this.

I looked up at the inky shadows of the trees, breaking up the moonlight. Though I knew the forest could be a dangerous place to be alone in at night, I wanted to believe that the stories were true.

If the forest was really guarded by its natural elements and knew that I had no evil intent, maybe I would be lucky enough to receive protection instead of any kind of harm.

"You grew up in the forest," I told myself.

It had raised me and fed me and looked after me my whole life. Dare I see it as an old friend?

"You've been calling." My voice, a little shakier than I would have liked, slipped into the moonlit darkness.

"Well, here I am." The trees and the wind had been urging me back to the only home I had had for a very long time. I was no longer the Evernean queen. I was, once again, a bandit in the night.

* * *

The horse's hooves clopped over the forest floor and the tension in my shoulders told me we'd been riding for a few hours. Everyone at the palace was probably looking for me by now. I straightened my back, trying to better my posture and relieve some of the discomfort. So far the journey had been quiet and uneventful.

I'd stopped a few times to get a little sleep and give the horse some rest, but I knew we didn't have much time to lose, so I'd been travelling through the night. Though I was unable to shake the feeling that I was being watched with every step that I took, I told myself that it was only the eyes of the forest looking after me. There was nothing to fear here now.

An owl hooted somewhere in the distance, and I gave my horse's neck a little scratch.

"We'll stop soon, I promise."

I wasn't entirely sure how far I had to go, but I knew it couldn't be too much further away. Whether or not it was true, it almost always felt as if you didn't find the centre of the forest, but the centre of the forest had a way of finding you. And for the first time in my life, it could actually be helpful.

Clouds hid the moon's light, making it too dark to use the map, but I knew I had to find the creek, so I kept listening for any moving water.

When the darkness finally started to lift, I veered off the main forest path towards the middle of the forest. Here, the trees grew closer together, the branches and leaves crowding the way, and we had to walk slowly and carefully. Morning dew coated the greenery surrounding me, the sunlight slowly creeping into the dark forest.

After what felt like a very long time, I began to doubt if I was even going the right way. Maybe I'd taken a wrong turn somewhere in the dark. But then, finally, in the distance, water. Not a wide, gushing river but a small, crooked creek.

I stopped to let the horse drink and emptied my own flask before filling it up again. Even though I wasn't very thirsty, once I left the creek behind, who knew how long it would be until I found water again. I took an apple out of my satchel and bit into the crunchy fruit. While examining my map, I let the horse graze a bit on the small patches of surrounding grass here and there. If I continued to follow the creek, it wouldn't be long before I reached the mist.

After our little break, I mounted my horse again and continued our journey along the creek. While I was more certain that I was on the right path, I felt my nerves grow with every step as we got closer to the centre of the forest.

The morning sun brought a little warmth, and I could finally take off my gloves and flex my fingers. I felt tired and hungry despite my snack, but I had to conserve my food. There was no telling how long this might take.

The creek continued on and on, longer than any creek I'd followed before, twisting and turning in some places.

And then, out of nowhere, the light got bleaker. I looked up and it felt like a heavy cloud had come to rest above the trees. It grew more difficult to see into the far distance. My horse became slightly uneasy as the mist crept up on us. A warning, if nothing else.

"Easy," I said, trying to sound reassuring. But my heart was beginning to race, and I was no longer sure which one of us needed to be reassured more.

The white fog slithered like a snake between the trees, working its way over my horse's flanks towards my shoulders. Resisting the urge to turn back, I had to keep telling myself that I'd got out of here once and I would do it again.

Finally, the mist was all-consuming and I could only see a few short feet ahead of me. I halted the horse and slid out of the saddle. The creek was still next to us and I would follow it for as long as possible.

Each step I took was careful, as if the floor would suddenly fall away beneath me. But with the lack of vision, it wasn't entirely out of the question that I could accidentally fall into a ditch or something. I led the horse, staying close to the water and listening for anything that sounded out of the ordinary. Every so often, I would look around, deluding myself into thinking I could see into the distance. It might have only been a method of calming myself so that I could focus on the task at hand.

The creek came to an end through a crevice that allowed the water to flow underground. With no clear markers to lead the way, I might as well have been left in the dark. The only thing to do was to keep walking in as straight a line as possible.

Minutes passed. Hours passed. Days passed. It all blurred into one. Time had become a foreign concept in the mist that surrounded me.

Damn it, Lara, I thought. *Why couldn't you just have found a way to convince Cai to come with you?*

Because this is stupid, that's why. Because you might die in here. And then what good will that do?

I began to grow worried for everyone in the palace. At the very least, I was sure that Cai would find the note I'd left him. I didn't want them to send anyone after me. But I knew Cai would be upset that I'd left so suddenly, without a warning.

I trudged on and on and on. And when I got hungry again, we stopped. I rested against a tree trunk and drank from my water flask, giving the horse my last apple while simultaneously hoping that this wouldn't be the last meal either of us had.

At some point I must have fallen asleep, because I started to dream. Except I was aware that I was dreaming. The forest was still there and so was the mist, but there was something different about it. It didn't have the ominous presence of the mist in the centre of the forest. This was just regular morning mist.

I was not alone. There were two other people in the mist with me. One of them was a man, kneeling on the forest floor. In his arms, he held a woman in a white dress, her skin so pale it was difficult to tell the difference between her skin and the material of her dress. She wasn't moving and the man had tears streaming down his face. The woman was dead.

They didn't notice me. It was as if I didn't exist at all. I was merely here to watch. I thought about everything I knew regarding the forest. How, as a whole, it was like a living creature of its own. Something that had protected and guided me my whole life. And if the Evernean Forest was more than just trees and earth, was it possible that I was observing a memory of the forest, something that it wanted me to know or see?

The man held the woman to him and continued to cry. He began mumbling, but at first, I couldn't hear what he was saying. It took me some time to recognise the words. "*Why did you do it, Riona?*"

Riona?

But that would mean …

Recognition set in. The two people in front of me suddenly became more than words on paper. This was the first king and queen of Everness. The people whose history we'd been chasing, hoping to find answers. I marvelled at the forest again and what it was capable of. Was it possible that I was seeing something that took place centuries earlier?

King Evrin let Riona's body lie on the forest floor. Had she died here, or did he bring her here, and why? I'd always believed that Queen Riona was buried along with the other Evernean monarchs, but what if that was merely what King Evrin had everyone believe?

"It didn't have to come to this," Evrin said through his tears. "Why did you have to meddle with things beyond your power?"

I watched with surprise and confusion as he pulled a knife out of one of his pockets.

"Nothing in this place comes without a cost. You and I should have known better."

He wrapped both his hands around the hilt of the dagger and lifted it into the air. There was a small gemstone attached to the hilt of the dagger, making it look awfully familiar.

"May your body give protection to all those to come who will share your blood. May this place become a vessel of guidance and safety for those who need it. My darling Riona, I hope you rest in peace here for all eternity."

And then he plunged the Myrgonite dagger into her heart.

Chapter 19

Cai

I opened the window in my room, allowing the fresh morning air to seep in.

After getting dressed quickly, I headed for the dining room, hoping I would catch Elara for breakfast. It had been two days since we talked, and though I wasn't on track to agree with everything she said, I could no longer take the silence between us.

She'd been ignoring me the whole of yesterday and, partially, I did not blame her. Our conversation could have gone much better.

I hoped I wouldn't run into Lance like I had the day before. He was part of the reason we were arguing in the first place. I knew it wasn't likely that he had intentions of coming between us. He was, after all, the one who'd suggested she ask for my hand in marriage all those months ago. But it didn't mean I wanted to be his friend right now.

I walked into the dining room to find Gwen sitting there with her book.

"Two days in a row? You must really miss me," she said, slightly teasing, and I forced a smile her way.

"I wish I could join you but I'm looking for Elara again."

"Is something the matter with you two? You've been acting strange."

I sighed. "We had a fight, and I need to talk to her."

"I'm sorry," Gwen replied and shifted in her seat with some discomfort. It wasn't a wonder she took long breakfasts every morning with her reading material. It would be a while before she would be able to walk normally and go back to other leisurely activities. I bet she missed the archery range back home.

"How's your ankle feeling?"

"Still the same." She shrugged. "It's becoming quite a nuisance, I'll admit."

"Well, I'm sure it will feel better soon." I rubbed my hands together with some awkwardness, knowing I hadn't been a good brotherly figure to her in recent times. Knowing we both couldn't deal with what Thatcher had done and not knowing how to be there for her. Or how to even talk about it.

"Maybe you should try Her Majesty's chambers. It's still quite early, after all. She might be getting ready."

"Right." I nodded in thanks and headed back to Elara's rooms. I was surprised to find the doors standing wide open, with Anesta inside the room, her face as white as a sheet.

"What's going on?"

"I don't know," she breathed out. "I've asked Rhen to go and look for her. Maybe she's just gone out for an early ride without telling us."

"What do you mean Rhen is looking for her? Why would he be looking for her?"

Anesta looked at Elara's empty bed and then back to me. "She was acting strange all of last night. I thought maybe she just wasn't feeling well or something but now I don't know …"

"How do you know she's not just somewhere in the palace?"

"I looked through her trunk. Her cloak, her gloves, even her satchel weren't there. I think she's gone."

My heart sank from my chest all the way to my feet.

Gone?

"Gone where?"

"I don't know," Anesta said again, although I already had a few ideas in mind and none of them were good.

My eyes drifted to her sheets, the bed neatly made as she had left it. As I walked over to the bed, I spotted a folded piece of paper on a small table nearby. It was practically invisible between all the trinkets, but I spotted my name in her handwriting.

I quickly grabbed the paper and unfolded it. Letters from Elara were never a good sign.

Dear Cai,
Please don't be angry.

Well, it was a little too late for that.

We both know the importance of this key and the diary. I really believe it to be the answer to everything. Tell everyone that I'll be all right and not to send anyone looking for me. See you soon.

See you soon. Soon was too vague.

"What does it say?" Anesta asked.

"She's gone to look for a key to the diary. I don't know when she'll be back." I held out the letter towards her.

"Just like that?" She took the piece of paper from me. "She left just like that, without telling anyone?"

"She knew I thought it was too dangerous and that I would try and stop her," I admitted.

"But I doubt you would do so without good reason, Your Majesty."

"When has Elara ever listened to good reason though?"

She looked to the open bedroom doors behind me. "Should we alert the court?"

As much as I wanted to send the whole guard and every available man to look for her, letting the court know that the queen was missing could create chaos.

"Not yet," I told her. "Not until we absolutely need to. How long ago did you tell Rhen?"

"About two minutes before you walked into the room."

"Okay." I ran my hands through my hair. "As soon as he is back, we'll start devising some kind of plan. Maybe we can send out a search party or something."

"But Her Majesty specifically asked us not to—"

"Do you think I care?" I cried out, louder than intended, and Anesta's eyes widened a little.

"I'm sorry," I apologised quickly, rubbing my hand across my face. "I'm just worried about her."

"I know." Anesta looked to the empty bed again. "Me too."

Rhen walked into the room with a stone-like expression. He closed the doors behind him.

"I cannot find her."

"We know." Anesta handed him the letter. "She's gone to find the key to King Evrin's diary."

Rhen read the letter before looking back up at us. "I'll have to talk to the guards on shift, find out why no one saw her leave."

"She would have taken a horse. Maybe the stable boy saw something," Anesta added and Rhen gave a nod.

"I'll speak with him as well." He gave the piece of paper back to me.

"Her letter doesn't say where she went. Probably because she didn't want anyone going after her."

"I know where she went." And I would have placed my bets I wasn't the only one, if Lance had been the one to tell her where the key was in the first place. "We should probably gather a search party, but I don't know how far we'll get. Elara is not in the easiest place to reach."

"Where did she go?"

"The most dangerous place in Everness." I told him. "The centre of the forest."

Rhen's face fell. He'd been there the day Elara and I went missing in the mist. Some of Aries' men even died in there. He knew the horrors of the fabled mist in the middle of the Evernean Forest.

"Why the hell would she go there? And on her own, no less."

"Because that's where Lance told her the key was, and now she's going after it." I clenched my jaw. This was bad.

"I'll have to talk to him as well."

"Maybe you should leave that conversation to me." I imagined how much I would enjoy hitting Lance in the face. I'd never got to repay him for what happened at Woodsbrook Manor, after all.

"Are you sure that's a good idea?" Rhen raised an eyebrow. "We still need Lance alive after it."

"Do we?" I asked with some sarcasm, though I was so filled with anger at the fact that he knew what kind of danger Elara would be putting herself in and let her go anyway. Of course, he would be too cowardly to get it himself, but I bet Lance was eager for the answers in that diary just as much as we were.

"Well, let me go with the search party, then. I know how to get there."

Rhen seemed hesitant. "While your consultation would be appreciated, Your Majesty, you might need to stay at the palace."

"For goodness' sake, Rhen, how can I stay here and wait while she is out there somewhere, maybe hurt or lost or who knows what? The forest is dangerous regardless of the mist. She could be lost or hungry or something might have attacked her."

"I know," Rhen said with understanding. "Very well, Your Majesty. We will arrange a search party and leave as soon as possible."

Elara, how could you do this?

"Anything I can do to help?" Anesta crossed her arms shyly.

"If anyone asks, tell them the Queen is currently indisposed. I'll have someone stand at the doors and make sure that no one enters."

"Yes, Your Majesty."

Anesta gave a small curtsy before leaving the room.

"I'll need to find out exactly where she was heading," Rhen said, looking back to me.

"Well, I think we both know who we need to talk to about that."

We found Lance in the library, sitting in front of a chessboard.

"You have some explaining to do." I pointed at his face as Rhen and I walked into the room.

"Whoa, hey fellas." Lance put up his hands slightly defensively. "I'm already outnumbered, there's no need to crowd me."

"This is serious, Your Highness," Rhen responded. "We need your help with something."

"Well, of course." Lance dropped his hands and folded them together. "What can I help with?"

"Elara is missing." I cut to the chase. "And I think you know where she went."

He didn't respond at first and moved one of the chess pieces. Then he looked back to us and finally said, "I'm afraid I have no idea what you're talking about."

Something inside me snapped. I stormed over and tipped the chessboard off the table before grabbing Lance by his collar.

"Your Majesty!" Rhen called out but made no attempt to stop me.

"If you don't tell me where she is, I will not hesitate to beat you beyond recognition. I've been thinking about it for a while actually."

Lance didn't show any concern about my threat. He only looked at me with a blank expression.

"She made me promise," he said while I still gripped his collar. "Are you going to make me break a promise to her?"

Part of me had hoped that while Lance had put the idea in Elara's head, she had done the rest on her own. The fact that she had actually consulted him on this plan only hurt me more.

"This is her life we are talking about," I said, with no intention of lowering my voice. "She could die out there and you know it!"

"You have so little faith in her," he said softly, wickedly. "No wonder she didn't want to tell you."

I was about to strike him when Rhen was smart enough to step in and pull us apart. "Maybe I should continue with the questions," he suggested diplomatically.

"Fine," I spat out, not wanting to hear another word that came from Lance's mouth anyway.

* * *

I spent the morning walking up and down the palace grounds, trying not to think about all the things that could have gone wrong for Elara, while Rhen arranged our travel. I knew Rhen would give his life for Elara, so I had to trust that he would do his job. I didn't feel like having breakfast, but the air grew too cold to stay outside. I ventured back into the palace and found Gwen sitting in a drawing room. She had her injured leg stretched out in front of her and another book in her hand.

"Still reading." Her expression turned into a smile as I walked into the room and fell into one of the chairs. Heat radiated from the fireplace on the far wall. I watched the flames dance back and forth, my mind on an endless wander.

"Did you manage to speak to Her Majesty?"

Right, no one had told Gwen, yet.

"We have a problem on our hands."

She put the book down in her lap, giving me her full attention.

"Elara's missing."

"Missing?" she said a little too loud, looking to the open door and then back at me. "What do you mean missing?" she asked, in a softer tone this time.

"She's gone to find the key that will unlock the diary of the old Evernean king."

Gwen looked away with an expression of surprise. "And no one knows where she is?"

"We have some idea. Rhen and I are going to look for her. But we cannot let anyone know she's gone."

"Definitely not," Gwen agreed, her eyes lingering on me while the room was silent for a few moments. "I'm sure she's fine." She tried to reassure me. "She's not an easy person to take down."

I wanted to believe her, but my stomach turned with thoughts of the wood and all its dangers. Even if Elara did manage to make it out of the misty woods, there were so many other things that could befall her.

"We have to stay hopeful," Gwen continued, taking in my expression of dread.

A figure entered the drawing room and I turned to look, with the hope it was Rhen and that our search party was ready to leave. Somewhat surprisingly, it was Alastor who stood in front of me. "Your Majesty." He gave a bow, still dressed in his riding attire, as if he'd arrived at the palace and come straight to look for me.

"You've returned quickly." I stood up, awaiting any good news at this point.

"I've been in contact with the nobles of Norrandale. Many of them said that once you have a firm foot to stand on in the kingdom, they would be willing to go to battle with you. This, of course, includes any men they might be able to provide." That was entirely fair of them. I couldn't very well expect them to fight for me while I hid out in Everness. Our army needed a base. We needed a foothold.

"Something like taking back Mistwood Palace most likely."

"It would seem so, Your Majesty."

"Taking back the palace?" Gwen chirped, still seated on her chair. "Have you gone mad? That place is crawling with Argonian guards who would kill you without question."

"Naturally we wouldn't just walk in the front door," I argued before turning back to Alastor.

"This is something." I crossed my arms. "At the very least we can start devising some plans."

"There's more, Your Majesty."

"Oh?" Based on his tone, I couldn't tell if it would be good or bad.

"Though this is something we would probably need to discuss with Queen Elara. But on my way back here, I came across our old friends in the forest."

Old friends? Does he mean the bandits of Fairfrith?

"Olwin's men initially tried to attack me but when I informed them I knew their leader, they agreed to take me to him."

Olwin, of the Baruk clan. He was Elara's uncle's enemy and had turned on him during the rebellion.

"What happened?"

"I told him about matters in Norrandale and Everness, about the possibility of war. He said he would be open to some negotiations if the Queen wanted him and his men to fight in her army." Olwin's men were fierce and ruthless, a relentless clan of bandits with no concept of mercy. Having someone like him fight on our side could be very beneficial but there was no telling as to his loyalty or what he might want from Elara in return.

"Thank you for all your efforts, Alastor, I greatly appreciate it."

"Of course, Your Majesty."

Things were looking a little less dire than before. If we could raise an army and manage to find all three Myrgonite objects, we might stand a fighting chance against Argon.

Chapter 20

Elara

Around me, the forest was alive and breathing. A creature with a mind of its own. No wonder people got lost. It changed and shifted until they were uncertain of themselves, slowly luring them to their death.

But I wasn't just somebody. I was the rightful heir to the throne. I was the queen of Everness.

I was still shaken by the dream I'd had about King Evrin and Queen Riona. He'd buried her in the forest, with the Myrgonite dagger in her heart. The same dagger Cai had been given when he first entered Everness. And not only that, but Queen Riona had been part of some magical exchange beyond my comprehension. Was it her spirit residing in the forest that protected all the royal successors? Or did the forest take her as payment in exchange for protection? It was overwhelming to think about it all. And I still had a very important task at hand.

"I'm not doing this for myself, you know," I called out to the void, the sudden sound of my voice giving the horse a slight fright.

I stopped walking for a moment and looked left and right. There were so many trees, and they all looked the same.

"I'm trying to protect Everness and Norrandale from someone who is going to destroy them."

Stray hairs fell in front of my eyes, and I swatted them away, breathing heavily from all the walking. I had almost grown too hot for my cloak.

"I need to find that key." My voice was filled with desperation.

I'm actually starting to lose it, I thought. *You're talking to the damn trees, Elara.*

Taking in my surroundings, as far as I was able to see, I noticed something. Had that tree been there a minute ago? I looked left and right again and shook my head. Trees don't just get up and walk. *It's not like it could have moved.*

But as I took a few steps forward, I knew that my environment had changed. The trees were no longer where they'd been a moment before. Instead, a path had opened up between them, the trees lining the sides.

I rubbed my eyes. Maybe I was sleep-deprived.

Still, a voice in the back of my head urged me on, promising that what I was looking for would be at the other end of the path. And so, I followed it.

With a better sense of direction, I felt a bit of relief, and a little hope settled inside me.

All I knew was that I needed to find a pond and a tree.

What I did not expect was for the mist to slowly start clearing. I looked behind me. Had I gone the wrong way and now come out the other side or something? I could see light in the distance. It looked warm and inviting.

Unexpectedly, the mist gave way and, as if it had been a wall, I stepped through.

My breath got caught in my throat. There was sunshine and it was bright. In the middle of the mist, there was a bright clearing with green grass, and I could see far beyond me. But the wonder was short-lived.

My eyes drifted to the large body of water and then, in the centre of it all, the biggest willow I'd ever seen, perched on a small island.

"Lance, you idiot!" I could have screamed. This was not the body of water he had described. This was a lake.

I tied my horse to the nearest tree and stepped towards the water.

Dipping in my fingers, I tested the temperature. It wasn't as cold as I had expected. This place felt like some kind of magical spot where there was eternal summer.

Eyeing the willow in the distance, I made some calculations. It wasn't that far, and I'd probably be able to swim it.

I didn't give it much thought. I was hungry and tired and anxious to get back home.

So, I started to unlace my riding boots, exposing my feet to the soft grass beneath me.

I rolled up the cuffs of my breeches while my horse grazed lazily behind me.

"Okay." I shook out my hands as if it would shake the nerves away. I didn't even want to think about what would happen once I actually got to the tree.

I dropped my cloak and satchel on the ground, and slowly walked into the water. It was dark and slightly murky, and by the time it reached my knees, I could no longer see my feet.

My mind began to run wild with thoughts of what could be lurking beneath the surface. Suddenly the willow tree felt a lot further away than it had originally looked.

I tried to push the thoughts away but the deeper I got into the water, the more scared I became.

When the water reached my waist, I spotted something moving in the distance, breaking through the surface. Or maybe I'd only imagined it. I stopped walking, observing the water. I was definitely sleep-deprived, maybe even hallucinating. But no, I swore I could see something move beneath the water again. This time, I didn't hesitate. It might have only been a fish, but I wasn't going to wait around to find out.

I turned around and waded through the water as fast as I could. Looking back at the big old willow tree, I let out a few curses. Now what?

Pacing up and down the shoreline with my feet bare, I contemplated going back into the water. Scared as I was, I was also pretty desperate for that damned key. One thing was certain: I wasn't going back home empty-handed. Not when I had come so far.

I continued walking around the lake, seeing if there was any part where the swim might be shorter. But no, the tree had to be smack dab in the middle.

"Come on!" I cried out, looking back to the treeline where my horse still grazed happily on the unnaturally lush green grass. "You brought me all this way and now what? What am I supposed to do?"

With a huff, I continued to march along the shoreline, and like an answered prayer, I came across a little wooden rowing boat with two oars inside, casually beached where the water met the grass.

Though I was thankful, I wished the boat had decided to appear before I got all my clothes wet. I hurried over and pushed the little boat into the water, rowing until my arms grew sore from the movement. The island was small, but stepping onto it, I could finally take in just how big the tree really was.

It loomed large with thick branches and heavy leaves. They were all a dark shade of green. Its presence felt old, and I slowly walked closer. The tree looked like it had been there for hundreds of years, maybe even longer, watching. Waiting for someone as stupid as me to actually try to take something from it. But the thing that created a sense of dread in my stomach was that the lines within the bark seemed to have the shapes of different faces. Were these all people the tree had deemed unworthy?

It's just a tree. And the trees helped you before. They led you here. This tree is no different.

Except that if what Lance said was true, this tree had every intention of judging me, and if I didn't prove worthy, it would take my soul, absorbing me until I became a part of it.

I swallowed hard. It was looking for someone worthy. What did that even mean?

With my hand on the trunk, I walked around the tree until I came across a hollow. It was quite small, but it would be big enough to put my fist into.

I stood there, looking at the hollow while rubbing my right wrist. That key had better be in there. *I'm not here with selfish motives*, I reminded myself. *I'm here because I'm trying to find answers to protect my kingdom.*

Knowing that standing around and procrastinating wasn't going to make me feel better, I finally jammed my hand into the hollow of the old willow tree.

I immediately closed my eyes and turned my head away.

This was it. This was how I would die. Killed by a damn tree.

Expecting blinding pain, I held my breath, but nothing happened. After a few more seconds, I dared to open my eyes and move my fingers. They were definitely all still there. I let out the breath I'd been holding and started to feel around the hollow.

I couldn't control my relieved smile when I touched something metal, and I pulled out the old king's key. It was pure gold, and unlike any key I'd ever seen before. I tied it to a thin leather strap I'd been keeping in my pocket and hung the key around my neck. It was cold and heavy against my skin.

I looked up at the old willow tree, feeling grateful but too awkward to say thank you. I didn't understand the magic that surrounded the tree and this place, or why I was allowed to retrieve the key. But I wasn't going to wait around in case it changed its mind.

I stepped off the small island and back into the little boat, more than ready to go home.

Chapter 21

Elara

Tucked into the warmth of my winter cloak once more, I rode back to the palace. The only thing I could think about was a warm bath with a fire in my room, along with a dinner. I would have given anything for some warm stew, maybe a few slices of buttered bread and a steaming cup of tea.

Nightfall was around the corner, so I pushed the horse a little faster. There was rain in the air. I could practically smell it. The last thing I wanted to do was get stuck in a rainstorm at night while in the Evernean Forest.

With a gloved hand, I took hold of the key around my neck.

"You'd better have been worth all that trouble," I said, relieved that I had managed not only to find the key, but also to make it safely out of the mist. That diary held something important. I could feel it in my gut.

As the clouds continued to grey, I urged my horse on, galloping over the forest roads. We were near the outskirts of the woods when I noticed a group of soldiers on horseback in the distance. They all wore the Evernean uniform of the royal guards.

Of course they'd sent men looking for me. I could not have reasonably expected otherwise.

I squinted to try to spot Rhen, who was no doubt leading the party. When I saw him, I decided to call out. My voice immediately drew their attention, and I slowed my horse as Rhen came riding towards me.

"Your Majesty." His eyes were tired, telling of a lack of sleep, and I couldn't tell whether he was relieved or horrified.

"You're alive," he finally said, as if he was unable to say anything else.

"You have so little faith," I replied, trying to keep my tone cheery while knowing that I had no intention of going through everything I'd experienced over the past few days again.

Another horse came trotting over behind Rhen. It didn't take much to know that Cai was clearly displeased, though I could see some relief on his face. He didn't say anything but merely looked at me as if I'd betrayed him.

"We should get back to the palace." I gestured with my head towards the sky. "The rain is coming. And I'm freezing."

Cai and Rhen rode alongside me, the rest of the guards falling in behind us.

"I told you not to send anyone looking for me. I grew up in this forest, in case you forgot. I know my way around." No way I was telling them that I'd almost got lost.

"With all due respect, you're a fool if you believe that all of us would've just let you go," Rhen replied.

"I was fine, Rhen," I assured him. "I had the forest to look after me."

He frowned but didn't ask any further questions. Cai kept a straight face, looking ahead. Light rain began to fall as we made our way back through the palace gates. I handed my horse over to one of the nearby servants after dismounting. The key still hung heavy around my neck. The raindrops seemed to turn heavier until they were pelting down with every step I took towards the doors.

By the time I entered the palace, my clothes were soaked.

"Do we know where Her Majesty's guests are?" Rhen asked one of the servants by the door as he tried to stomp the mud off his boots.

"I believe they've taken an evening drink in the library," she responded.

I removed my gloves, and the servant girl stepped towards me. "Can I take this for you, Your Majesty?" she asked, gesturing to my cloak. I thanked her as she helped me remove it. It was a relief to get the heavy, wet piece of material off my back. Taking the key from around my neck, I clutched it tightly in my hand while making my way to the library, Rhen and Cai following close behind.

"Would you like me to announce you?" Rhen asked.

"No, thank you, Rhen." Some part of me was eager to see their faces when I held up the key. Was it truly terrible of me to want to feel like their queen and saviour?

Light from the library crept into the hallway from under the doors. I was so anxious to see everyone that I'd quickly forgotten about the bath and warm meal. They could wait.

With the rainwater still glistening on my clothes, I opened the library doors.

Many pairs of eyes looked up as I entered.

I let out a breath, only then realising how much I'd missed their familiar faces in the short time I'd been gone. How attached I'd become to all of them. Anesta was the first to jump up, her embroidery falling from her lap to the floor.

"Your Majesty!" she cried out. "You're back. You're safe." Ignoring all protocol, she ran over and gave me one of the tightest hugs I'd ever experienced. I didn't mind it at all. There was a part of me that relished the knowledge that I was wanted and missed.

"It's so nice and warm in here."

Gwen, unable to get up quickly, gave a little wave from the chair she was occupying.

Alastor gave a slight bow from where he stood at the hearth.

"Did you find it, Your Majesty?" Anesta asked in a hopeful tone.

I showed her the key in the palm of my hand. "If this doesn't open that damned box then I don't think anything will."

She took in my muddied boots and dirty riding clothes. "Shall I have the servants draw a bath for you, Your Majesty?"

"That would be wonderful, thank you."

She gave a quick curtsy and hurried out of the room.

"So, we've got the diary and a means to open it. Now we just have to hope there's some valuable information inside," Gwen said.

"If it should take this much effort to gain access to that diary, then there has to be something inside that King Evrin didn't want anyone to know." I had to believe that this would lead us somewhere and that it wasn't another dead end.

"We were quite worried about you, Your Majesty." Alastor spoke up before clearing his throat. "I'm glad to see you have returned safely."

"Yes, it was quite a journey," I admitted with a heavy breath. "But I'm quite capable of taking care of myself."

At this, Cai mumbled an "excuse me" and walked out of the library.

"What's his problem?" Gwen frowned at the door.

"He's upset because he didn't want me to go and find the key and I went anyway."

"But we needed the key. As you said, it wouldn't take this much to unlock the diary if it wasn't valuable."

"Try convincing him of that." I didn't like it when Cai and I were fighting, especially because we'd just got to a place where we were on good terms with each other.

Gwen flipped through the pages of the book she'd been reading. "I'm sure he'll come round, Your Majesty. He'll have to. Especially when we find out what's hiding in that diary."

"I hope so." I gave her half a smile before turning to Rhen.

"I have some things to take care of over the next few days, so I'm going to require your assistance with the diary."

As much as I wanted to scan every page of that old book, walking through the woods alone for so many hours had got me thinking about all the ways I still needed to protect Everness. While I trusted the diary would bring us certain answers, we needed men on the field to fight for us, or at the very least defend us. We had more soldiers stationed at the border and the kingdom was slowly preparing itself in the event of an attack. Buildings were being fortified, weapons made and food stored.

But I kept on worrying that it would not be enough. What if Aries still managed to break through our defences? I needed to invite the council members back to court so that we could have another council meeting.

Rhen looked a little surprised as he took the key from me. "Of course, Your Majesty." I knew I could trust him with this duty. That Rhen would not give up until he found what we were looking for.

"Now, if you'll excuse me." With the adrenaline fading, tiredness began to set in. I would ask for dinner to be brought up to my rooms. The first order of business would be taking a long, hot bath.

I contemplated going to Cai's rooms as I made my way up the stairs but then thought better of it.

It had been a long day and I was severely sleep-deprived. I knew both of us well enough to know the conversation would not be productive and only lead to us being more upset with each other. I hadn't meant to go behind Cai's back by leaving but I had to do what I believed was right, what I believed would help our kingdoms.

My rooms were lit with a few candles and the bathing chamber was filled with steam. Though Anesta was nowhere to be seen, there was a tray of food on one of the small tables in my room.

She probably knew I wanted some peace and privacy.

I took a bite from one of the bread rolls and began to undress, leaving my dirty clothes draped over a chair.

The warm water from the bath soothed my aching muscles. I lay back, slowly starting to relax as I snacked from my plate. I probably didn't look very ladylike as I devoured the juicy pieces of chicken, but I was too hungry to care.

When the water began to grow cold, I emerged from the bath, pulling on a white linen robe. My feet left wet prints on the floor, trailing from the bathing chambers to one of the chairs in front of the fireplace. I finished my dinner while my mind ran rampant with plans and ideas. Even though the key was a partial success, Aries had one of the biggest armies on the continent and he was already in Norrandale. We needed to find a way to fight back or soon there would be nothing left to fight for.

My train of thought was interrupted by a light knock on the door. Anesta must have come to check on me before going to bed.

"Come in."

The door creaked open and I looked over my shoulder, only to find Cai standing in my room.

I stood too, slightly surprised by his presence.

"Cai." No words came to mind. I would not apologise, so I hoped that was not the reason for his visit. "What are you doing here?"

"I wanted to see you." His words brought me some relief. While his face bore no semblance of joy, at least he wasn't avoiding me.

"You shouldn't have walked out like that," I said, referring to the library.

"I know." His eyes were on the floor, while he didn't make much of an attempt to move away from the door.

"Then why did you do it?"

Cai finally looked up. I could still see the disappointment in his eyes. "Because you make me furious sometimes."

I raised an eyebrow, inviting him to say more.

"I'd asked you not to go and you went anyway, without even telling me."

"I did tell you," I argued.

"I don't mean leaving me a short note telling me not to come and look for you. Do you have any idea how worried I was?"

This was the most emotion I'd seen from him in a while. Though it might not have been a positive reaction, it reminded me of the person he was before his best friend stabbed him in the back, before his family was murdered, before he was exiled from his kingdom. It reminded me of the Cai who would do anything to protect me, who didn't care for my impulsivity. The Cai who fought for the things he cared about.

"How many times do I have to say that I am capable of looking after myself? I was completely fine." More or less, anyway.

"You went into the most dangerous place in Everness, all by yourself with no assurance that you would come out alive," he said, walking over.

"Well, I'm fine now. I don't see why you're still so angry. Do you want me to say I'm sorry that I went? Because I won't."

"Do you have no care for your life?" His voice rose with every word. "You cannot disappear into the woods in the middle of the night. You have a responsibility to your kingdom."

"It's that responsibility I'm trying to keep. We need to open that diary, and the key is the only way we are going to do it." My frustration grew at his lack of reason. I stepped up to him and Cai towered over me, but I still glared up at him.

"It is not worth your life," he cried out, grabbing my upper arms. "Don't you see it?" His voice was laced with desperation. "I've lost everyone, Elara." His eyes bored into mine, the disappointment now replaced by deep worry. "I cannot bear to lose you too."

The way he said it caused my anger to dull. The pained look in his eyes that I'd grown used to in the past few months returned.

"You're not going to lose me, Cai," I said, softer now.

"You don't know that." He placed his forehead to mine. I closed my eyes and leaned into him, savouring the safety his presence always brought me. I missed this.

"I'm not going anywhere." It was a promise I hoped I could keep. "As long as I don't lose you either. I don't think I'll survive that." Despite our difference and conflicts, I loved Cai beyond my control and cared for him more than I'd ever cared for anyone. It was because of him that I'd found the will and strength to fight this upcoming war.

Cai placed his hands on my cheeks. "I will never leave you," he vowed, forcing me to look into those beautiful emerald eyes of his. Sadness or not, they were my home. "You saved my life once. You pulled me back from death. And I will go to hell and back to find you."

Cai pressed his mouth to mine in a loving kiss and I melted into him. Wrapping my arms around his shoulders, I urged him closer, allowing his hands to sweep over my body. I could feel the warmth of his hands through the material of my robe. Standing up on my toes, I deepened the kiss, pressing myself against him to eliminate any space between us. This was different from the kiss we'd shared in his room the other day. There was no pain now. There was only longing.

"I love you," I murmured against his mouth. I wanted all of him. Wanted him to know how much he mattered. I would do anything for him, regardless of the cost.

Cai pulled back, giving me a strange look.

"What?"

"You've never said that before," he responded, breathing heavily.

"What do you mean? Of course I have."

"No," he said slowly. "You've never told me you loved me before."

I thought back to previous interactions, to Cai confessing his love for me. I'd known I'd loved him for a while now. Ever since I got back from Norrandale the first time. But had I really never said it?

"Well, I mean it." My fingers curled in his golden locks. "I love you, Cai."

He looked at me with a wonder I'd never seen before. Then he was kissing me again.

How I had missed this closeness with him, this intimacy. The scent of him, the feeling of his hands on me. I could stay like this for ever, so enraptured by him, and to hell with the rest of the world.

Cai walked me backwards until I felt the bed touch the back of my legs. I pulled back for a second, gasping for air. My fingers moved to his torso of their own accord, untucking his linen shirt. I pushed my hands under the material, placing my fingers on his muscular abdomen. Cai grabbed the collar and pulled the shirt over his head in one swift motion, dropping it on the floor.

He took me back into his arms and hitched my legs around his waist while I kissed him with urgency. Then he carefully laid me on the bed, the silky sheets soft against my skin. Cai broke away, kissing my neck, and I tilted my head back. He took his time, letting his mouth trail over all the places his hands had been while I savoured the feeling of his lips.

I softened against him, allowing myself to forget about the past few days. This was what I needed. Cai and I did have our moments, but when it mattered most, we knew we could trust each other, be there for each other, and in some ways even heal each other. The two of us had enough pain to last us a lifetime, but when we were together, the walls that we surrounded ourselves with, for protection, shattered entirely. I could let myself go when I was with him.

I wrapped my legs around him, my fingers digging into his back as I pulled his mouth back to mine. His hand was splayed out over my ribcage, while soft sighs escaped me.

"Say it again." He said it so softly that I almost couldn't hear him. Cai's eyes were dark with need. It took me a moment to realise what he'd meant.

"I love you."

He groaned and undid the waistband of my robe, exposing me. I bit my lip as he trailed kisses from my collarbone to my navel.

"Again."

His mouth moved lower still. My heart pounded.

"I love you." My voice sounded ragged, caught somewhere between anguish and desperation.

Soon, I was gasping his name, my fingers buried in his hair, and the feel of it all was too much. I clutched the pillow, arching against him as I trembled in his arms. All I could think about was that I didn't want this to be over.

Cai moved back up and captured my cries with his mouth. His fingers dug into my thigh as he wrapped my leg around him.

"I love you, Elara." And I knew he did, with all his heart. Because I did too. I'd never really had anything in my life worth dying for … until now.

He moved painstakingly slowly at first and then deeper with more urgency. I felt like I could hardly breathe. Our fingers intertwined as he pressed my hand into the mattress above my head. Cai never stopped kissing me. I'd forgotten about Aries and about the Myrgonite objects. About war and council meetings and diaries and death. None of it mattered as long as I was in his arms, with his hands and his mouth on me.

I could die like this for all I cared.

Levernia was a big city, with a large market square and many houses, stacked onto one another. The cobblestone streets were decked in a thin layer of snow, disturbed by the tracks of people and horses.

I looked up at the tavern in front of us. It was secluded, hidden in a small alley away from the main streets.

Cai had been less than eager when I told him my idea of tracking down Uncle Arthur's old clan members and trying to convince them to fight on our side. After the rebellion, I tried to make sure everyone was safe and well looked after, but the people had split up and moved away. Some lived in the bigger cities, while others chose the serenity of the forest and living off the land.

I'd told Cai that they hadn't given me any kind of trouble thus far, and while there was the odd case of a carriage being robbed on a road somewhere, it wasn't anything like during Magnus's and Lance's rule.

I feared inviting them to the palace, for many reasons, so I settled for dressing in some plain clothes and going undercover. It took Rhen some time to find Donald and Murtag, both of whom were masters of the clan. Rhen had been spending most of his free time going through the diary but had yet to find anything of value.

According to him, Donald spent most of his early evenings at this little tavern.

I tied my horse to the post and made sure the hood of my cloak was secure. Not that anyone was likely to recognise me anyway.

Cai and Rhen followed, dressed in similar attire. The only way I could convince them of my plan was if they tagged along, and after the toll my recent disappearance had had on them both, I didn't have the heart to go rogue.

The wood creaked under my boots as I stepped into the tavern. A young barmaid leaned over the bar at the far end. She had a round face, tendrils of curly hair falling in front of her eyes, and a large stain of some kind on her apron. The rest of the room contained a few small tables and a fireplace in one of the corners.

I made my way to the bar while Cai and Rhen took a seat at one of the empty tables, close enough to jump in should any kind of danger befall me. I wasn't too worried, though. No one here had any idea who I was, and I patted my dress to make sure Cai's dagger was still in the pocket. Should anyone dare to come too close to me, they would regret it.

I hopped onto one of the wooden bar chairs and popped a coin onto the counter. Without even looking at me, the barmaid shoved the coin into her pocket and placed a pint of ale down in front of me. I supposed I couldn't expect much in terms of service from a place like this.

I slowly sipped the ale, not particularly enjoying the taste, while I scanned the room. Nobody looked familiar, though I could tell not all of the customers were of the same class of society. Some were clearly down to their very last coin while others looked more like merchants in need of a quiet evening. And some looked all too eager to drown their sorrows until they passed out somewhere.

It wouldn't have seemed like such a bad idea had I not detested the taste of this stuff.

The door to the tavern opened and I looked over my shoulder.

Donald looked exactly as I remembered him, tall and scrawny but not to be messed with. He was a serious danger with a dagger. Behind him were Murtag and Brosby. They didn't notice me staring at them at first, but as Donald made his way towards a table, our gazes met, and recognition settled on his face. He said something to the other two that I couldn't hear, presumably that he was going to get a drink, and made his way over to the bar.

I turned back, looking down at the cup in front of me.

"Never thought I'd see your face again." The voice came from my left as Donald took a seat next to me.

"You're a hard man to find, you know?"

"You've been looking for me?" He searched his coat pocket until he pulled out a coin and placed it on the bar top.

"Everyone seems to have scattered after the rebellion."

"I think many were surprised to find you on the throne. Especially after Arthur preached so much about ending the monarchy. I think they felt betrayed by him." We both kept our voices low, not making eye contact.

"So did I," I admitted. "Things might have turned out so differently if he'd just told me."

"A lot of the folks believe that you knew all along. That you and Arthur were just using them for your personal gain."

The barmaid walked up to us, took the coin and placed a cup in front of Donald. Some of the ale spilled over the edges.

"I promise you I didn't know."

"I did."

I couldn't keep my head from turning as I looked at him with surprise.

"Some of us had known your uncle since our time at the palace. We were the ones who helped him escape and fake his death." Of course. How did I not see it before? Uncle had known the masters of the clan for twenty years. Many of them used to work at the palace. And all of them hated my father, for whatever reasons they might have had.

"Arthur made us take an oath not to tell. And that we would fight with him to put you on the throne."

"Yes, so that he could use me as his puppet to rule as he pleased."

I took a sip from my cup out of frustration. The liquid tasted bitter.

"True as that may be, this kingdom was doing no good in the hands of your father or brother." I couldn't disagree with him, but it hardly felt as if we were faring much better now. "You've given back land taken by the Crown, lowered the unnecessary taxes. You try to look after the folk that weren't born with fancy titles, because you know what it's like to live like that. That's why most of us spread out. We could finally start building lives of our own. There was no need to steal."

"You don't understand," I said softly. "War is coming and unless we do something, too many innocent people are going to die."

"There's always another war coming." Donald took a big gulp of his beer and wiped his mouth with the back of his hand.

"The King of Argon is in Norrandale. His armies are slowly making their way north. If he reaches Everness, our army isn't big enough to fight back. We'll be lambs before the slaughter."

Donald didn't say anything but I could tell he was pondering my words.

"I need men to fight."

"I thought Everness had such a large army. King Magnus was always boasting about it."

"The king's guard suffered some major losses during the rebellion," I replied. "And while we do have a bigger army than Norrandale, it will not be enough compared to Argon's. The royal council don't see Aries for the threat he is yet, and while we might be able to hold up the kingdom's defences, we might need more men to go to Norrandale and fight. Argon has one of the largest armies on the continent. There are discussions of King Cai taking back Mistwood and it would take some time to gather all the loyalists. I need the people on my side too."

"And I suppose you're expecting I help you with this."

I turned in my chair now, no longer caring if we caught the attention of a few strangers in a tavern. "Not all the people see me as their queen yet. I am still in the first year of my reign and I haven't an heir to strengthen my claim. You helped my uncle raise a rebellion once, with enough people to overthrow the Crown. And I know Uncle had relations with some of the other bandit clans in the forest." True, Fairfrith might have been the biggest, but there were plenty of desperate people in the kingdom back then, willing to do anything just to live another day.

"With all due respect, that took twenty years, Your Majesty."

"I know you still have contacts in the clan. And I know you can gather people to fight. Maybe not enough to defeat an army but enough to stand a chance. I want to take the fight to Norrandale. To stop King Aries before he can set foot in Everness. I'm meeting with the royal council to gather their men but many of them aren't convinced he will turn to us next. There may have been no battles yet, but there will be, and they will be bloody and brutal."

"It will not be easy. As you said, many people don't acknowledge you as the true queen yet. And they don't want to live under the rule of a monarch anyway."

"Well, if Argon conquers Everness, there's no chance of a republic ever. This isn't just about me. This is about the kingdom and its future. We need the Everneans to fight for themselves."

Donald rubbed the scruff on his cheek. "I used to think Arthur was mad for thinking you could rule someday. But now I think he saw something in you that the rest of us didn't."

Or maybe he really was just mad. I didn't say it out loud.

"I promise that anyone who fights will not go unrewarded. I trust you and I trust the clan."

"I'll see what I can do, Your Majesty."

"You were loyal to my uncle for a very long time. And I don't expect the same from you. But I'm responsible for what happens to these people, and I will not go down without a fight."

"If you're willing to fight for the people, I'm sure there will be those who'd want to fight for you too."

I climbed down from the bar chair. "Send any news you have straight to the palace. I'll have the head of my guards deliver the messages to me personally."

Donald lifted his half-full cup. "To you then, Your Majesty."

Chapter 22

Cai

In the days that followed, Elara and I spent countless hours in meetings with her council discussing our preparations for reclaiming Mistwood and the possibility of sending Everness's army to Norrandale should it become necessary. The council members agreed that if I could take back Mistwood and round up the loyalists, there would be enough ground for us to stand on for a counterattack while still leaving enough soldiers in Everness to keep it defended. It would take some time to gather all the men and prepare for the journey.

In the meantime, a group of us would leave for Norrandale. I'd been in correspondence with Lord Burrow, a trusted member of my court, and we'd agreed to meet, along with all the men he could supply, on the way to Mistwood. He was in the process of convincing the other members of the council to also send men to join our cause. I could only hope that he would be successful.

It was a potentially treacherous journey to make in the winter. But the longer we waited, the more damage Aries might do. Most of his army had yet to arrive. Now was the time for us to strike.

The sun was just beginning to set and Elara lounged on one of the chairs in my rooms while I sharpened the sword my father had given me. I hadn't used it since the day we'd run from Norrandale. The thought of returning tied my stomach into knots but I couldn't live in exile for ever. Nor could we let Aries get away with what he'd done.

"I'm coming with you, you know," Elara said, breaking the silence in the room. I looked up from my sword. The thought of being separated from her nearly killed me, but knowing where we were about to go, and what we were about to do, I worried for her safety.

"I don't want to leave you here. But I also don't want to bring you into the middle of a battle." Elara had never experienced an easy life and had survived many atrocities but she was not trained for battle. And while she was capable of defending herself, this was different. This was war.

"I can't imagine you being a kingdom away while I have no idea whether or not you are safe."

Nor could I. As long as she was close by, I wouldn't live in the constant fear that something might have happened to her.

"If something should happen to me, how will I protect you? How will I make sure you stay safe?" These were the very thoughts that had kept me awake for the past few nights.

Elara sat up, meeting my eyes. "Don't say something like that."

I took a deep breath. "We both know I might not walk out of this battle alive." And I could live with that as long as I knew she was all right.

"No," she said, getting up from the chair and making her way towards me. She kneeled in front of me. "You are going to make it through this." Elara took my face in her hands. "Both of us are. And then years from now we will look back and this will all be a faint memory." For her sake, I very much hoped so.

I gave her a sad smile and she pressed a soft kiss to my lips.

"Does this mean you're leaving Lance in charge again?"

The corner of her mouth turned up a little. "I suppose it does."

The forest was cold and dark. Heavy clouds hung over the high tree branches, many devoid of their leaves. Our riding party was a long straight line of horses and men, slowly making their way down the half-frozen path.

Part of me couldn't believe we were really making the journey back to Norrandale. That we would attempt to take back the palace and hope none of us died in the process. But with all the information Alastor had gathered and a few allies awaiting our arrival, the best time to strike was now.

I worried about Elara's safety in coming with us but felt better when she was at my side, knowing I was unable to protect her if she remained in Everness. We had a few men with us, spared by the council. It wasn't enough to take on Aries' army, but if we could win back Mistwood Palace, it might give us the foothold we needed.

Gwen remained behind in Levernia, her ankle not yet healed enough for such a long journey. I would have preferred her not to stay back alone with Lance, but if there was anyone who could hold her own, it was Gwen.

I wondered, though, had she been able to travel, would she have been able to face her brother and his betrayal?

I didn't know how I was going to face Thatcher myself. According to Alastor's information, he'd been living at Mistwood as if he were the king. How would I look him in the eye and not wrap my hands around his neck, the man I once used to call brother?

My eyes searched for Elara riding ahead of me. It was easy to spot her burgundy cloak with her dark hair hanging in waves down her back.

Rhen rode next to her. I couldn't properly hear what they were saying, but it sounded like they were discussing King Evrin's diary. I nudged my horse forward, hoping to join the conversation.

"It's very difficult to read his handwriting and the pages are extremely fragile. I'm trying to be careful but it's going to take me some time to get through it."

"Anything of value yet?" Elara asked.

"Afraid not. He's mostly written about the responsibility of ruling the kingdom and how he's trying to assemble a proper council and so forth."

Initially I was worried that she would leave the diary in Rhen's hands, but I understood that while the old king's words were being dissected for information about ancient magic and powerful gemstones, Elara had to gather an army. If the diary proved to be useless, we needed men to fight. We needed men regardless of the Myrgonite objects.

She looked at him. "I can't say I'm surprised but let's hope you find something soon."

We made camp close to the Norrandish border that night, many fires lighting up the surrounding forest.

I sat on a log, staring into the flames in front of me, trying not to think of what was to come but knowing it was unavoidable.

There was a crunch of leaves behind me, and I looked over my shoulder, dagger already in hand.

"Sorry." Elara climbed over the log and took a seat next to me. "Didn't mean to startle you."

"It's okay." I slid the knife back into my boot. "I suppose I'm a little jumpy."

"I understand." She took a breath. "If I were you, I don't know how I would be able to go back."

I looked down at my nails, the dirt under my hands suddenly very interesting. "They haunt me," I said softly, but Elara heard me well enough.

"Who?"

"Thatcher, my family. I dream about them almost every night. It's why I don't sleep. Why I offer to take the night watch. Every time I close my eyes, I see him. I see him killing Jack, killing my family."

Elara interlocked our fingers and placed my hand in her lap. "I think you're brave for fighting and for going back."

I looked at her, the firelight reflecting in her eyes, and I found myself comforted by the way she looked at me. It was different compared to the way she used to look at me a few weeks ago. There was always so much hurt and desperation behind her gaze. But now, she looked at me like she wouldn't mind spending the rest of her life in my presence. Or maybe I was just projecting my own feelings onto her.

"I don't know what else to do," I admitted. "I don't know how to save my kingdom."

She rubbed her thumb across my hand. "Together. We do it together."

"Right." I pressed a long kiss to the back of her palm.

"How long do you think it will be before we reach Mistwood?"

"A few more days." I took in our campsite. The men were tired from days of travelling in the cold. "Let's hope the weather holds up."

The closer we got to the mountains, the colder it would get. She shivered slightly and I pulled her close to me.

"Do you think Anesta would mind sleeping alone in your tent tonight?"

Elara pressed a kiss to my cheek. "No, I don't think she would mind at all."

Chapter 23

Lance

The palace halls were quiet with the council and the court having returned to their own estates for the time being. The lamps cast a low light off the wooden panels of the walls and portraits as I made my way towards my sister's chambers.

I found Eloisa's nurse, Agatha, heading away from her rooms, most likely heading to the servants' quarters.

"Your Highness." The gentle old lady gave a curtsy.

"Is everything all right?"

"Of course, Your Highness. She is merely sleeping."

"Thank you, Agatha. Have a good evening." I dismissed her.

"You as well, Your Highness." She gave another curtsy and hurried off. I could imagine she was eager to have some time to herself.

I took the last few steps to Eloisa's bedroom and pried the door open as quietly as possible.

The room itself was dark apart from the moonlight shining in through the windows.

I closed the door behind me, spotting Eloisa's sleeping silhouette in her bed.

She seemed so at peace. These days, she spent more time sleeping than awake. The physician said her illness was slowly progressing and sadly there was nothing to be done.

I trod softly over the floor towards the chair next to her bed. The seat was still warm from where Agatha had likely been sitting only a few minutes before.

Eloisa's chest rose and fell, and had I not known better, I would have thought her perfectly healthy.

We were never particularly close as siblings, with Father sending her to live in the country for most of her life. Maybe he never forgave her for being the cause of Mother's death. But she always looked happy to see me when she was at court.

"It's strange to have you and Elara in this place together," I said, careful not to speak too loudly.

"She looks like you, and you kind of sound the same, but you're two completely different people."

Elara didn't often talk of Eloisa or come to see her. Discovering she had a long-lost sister was one thing, but to discover she had an identical twin was another. And Eloisa wasn't exactly communicative anymore. They couldn't talk or bond with each other. There was no hope for any kind of relationship, really. We all knew that Eloisa's health was slowly failing her and that eventually it would come down to a matter of days.

Elara may not have known our parents, but if she were in any way to become attached to Eloisa, it would only hurt so much more when the inevitable happened.

"Everyone's gone off to Norrandale now. They're going to try and get back Mistwood Palace."

The journey would be long and cold, and there was no guarantee that they would have any success.

"It was probably dangerous for Elara to go but it's not like she's going to leave Cai's side now." Whatever Elara might have said or done, Cai had gone from a grieving man, hiding in his room all day, to a king willing to fight for his right to the throne. I hoped they all made it out alive. Though I would never admit it. I worried about Aries and the power of his army. What he was capable of, especially when it came to the Myrgonite objects. Aries was not going to stop looking for them unless he was dead.

Cai and Elara knew more about the objects than they were willing to let on. But my sister had made a promise. I found myself wondering if she would keep it.

"Gwen is still here, though," I continued. "Her ankle hasn't healed enough to travel so far yet. She needs to stay off horses for a little while longer."

We didn't see too much of each other. Sometimes I would find her reading in the library or in the dining room. Gwen was a little less hostile than before. I think she missed the others and realised I was now the only company she had left.

The other day, as I was making my way to the stables, I found her walking in the garden with her stick. Light snow had fallen during the night, making the ground somewhat slippery. She nearly fell but did not want to accept my help to get her inside. She was more stubborn than the worst of the horses I'd ridden as a child.

She promised me that she would be off the walking stick soon anyway. I respectfully let her go but watched through the window as she slowly hobbled back inside the palace.

Once she was fully healed, she might want to go back to Norrandale. Or she might not be ready to face the brother who had betrayed her family. I wanted to sympathise with her situation, but I would be the first to admit that I could not call myself the best of brothers. Not that I carried regrets with me. I had my reasons, and Elara wasn't the sort who needed an older brother figure. She had spent her whole life taking care of herself. And now she had Cai to take care of her.

"Could you imagine the three of us growing up together?" I couldn't help but wonder. If Mother had not died and Elara had been raised in a palace. Everything would be different. Somehow, I still saw Elara ending up with Cai.

"Maybe I would not have been the black sheep of the family." With one sister on the throne and the other practically on her deathbed, it was difficult to know my place sometimes. I did not want to be king. Did not want the responsibility of the life that came with the title. I'd ruled as regent in my father's place for years and hated every second of it.

"Or maybe I would." It didn't really matter now. All I could hope was that Rhen found the answers somewhere in that old diary and that we wouldn't be damned to the mercy of Aries. I cared for our family name and the kingdom, but I would not be the one to save it.

Chapter 24

Elara

I opened the tent flap and stepped into the winter morning air of Norrandale.

So close to the mountains, the air felt much colder than in Everness, my fingertips numb despite my gloves. Our party had set up camp between Mistwood Palace and the mountains in the north. A few days later, Lord Burrow and his men arrived as promised by Alastor, who'd secured the alliance on behalf of Cai. The increase in our numbers brought me some comfort, but I still felt an ever-growing worry in my gut at the prospect of what was to come.

We were going to Mistwood with Cai leading the attack. There would be fighting and blood and death. And we could only hope that by the end of it, Cai would be back on his throne.

I wrapped my cloak around me in a futile attempt to keep out the cold and started making my way towards the main tent in the centre of our camp. There was a smell of smoke in the air from all the burnt-out fires from the night before. I could see my breath as I made my way past tents and soldiers sharpening their weapons.

The semi-frozen ground crunched under my riding boots, and I was grateful for wearing my breeches and a tunic again. Despite the fact that I'd grown quite fond of the beautiful dresses Anesta always put me in, they weren't practical for what we were about to do. Though I was certainly aware that all the layering in my skirts actually helped to keep my legs warm. Being so close to the mountains meant the weather would only get worse and the soldiers more unmotivated. We were all cold and tired, and if we wanted to take back Mistwood, we would have to do it soon.

Cai was already there as I entered the main tent. So were Alastor and Rhen. There was a large table in the middle, with maps and drawings of the landscape around Mistwood and the palace itself.

"Good morning." I tried to sound cheerful but there was a sense of dread in the air. Not just in the tent itself but all around the camp.

Cai gave me an attempt at a comforting smile, which we both knew to be fake, but I appreciated the gesture.

"Lord Burrow should be here any moment," Rhen said as I went to stand next to Cai.

"Good." I gazed over the maps, my eyes involuntarily going to the mountain ranges I knew to be filled with Myrgonite stones. Aries and his men were getting closer, and though it would be some time before they reached Mistwood, we needed to keep the front lines as far south as possible. Not only for the sake of the stones, but because the closer his men were to Everness, the bigger risk it was for my kingdom that they would invade.

The tent flap opened again, and Lord Burrow walked in, looking surprisingly awake and able compared to the rest of us.

"Your Majesties," he greeted us politely, looking over the table. "Do we have a plan for how we want to proceed?"

"I've sent word to Mannik and Stapleton, and they are willing to send all the men they can spare, but it will be a while still before the soldiers arrive. We do not have that much time to waste if we want to overthrow Mistwood. But we will need the men, regardless, for when the battle comes," Cai said.

"Will you be making Mistwood the fortress from where the army attacks?" Alastor asked. His long dark hair was tied up and he appeared to carry a weapon on just about every part of his body. Should I have been his enemy, I would not want to come across him in the middle of the night.

"I would prefer to keep the fighting as far away from my ancestral home as possible," Cai replied. "But it might be a good place for us to gather before we march on the Argonian army."

Not to mention that if Cai reclaimed his throne by taking Mistwood, it might persuade the people to turn back to their exiled king. As it was, we needed every able-bodied person to fight on our side.

"Are we to attack them directly? Force our way into the palace?" Lord Burrow questioned.

"No, I want the element of surprise. Alastor, do you have the numbers for the Argonian soldiers currently residing at Mistwood?"

"We're looking at a few hundred, Your Majesty. Enough to keep the palace under their control against civilians or small loyalist groups."

"With our numbers, surely, we are looking at an easy victory."

"With all due respect, Lord Burrow," I interjected. "You must keep in mind that Argonian soldiers are not like our men. They've been trained in different ways, and based on what I've seen of them, it would take at least two or three of our men to take an Argonian down."

"She's right," Cai affirmed. "These men are ruthless, and we must be prepared for every possible outcome. Aries cannot easily be outsmarted."

"What about civilians?" Lord Burrow asked. "Is there any risk of court members getting in the middle of it?"

"I doubt it," Alastor responded. "The court had been sent back to their estates before the Argonians arrived. Apparently, we are not the only ones who want to fortify the palace. And then, apart from the soldiers, Lord Thatcher is there, of course, in charge of all of them."

I felt Cai tense up next to me at the mention of Thatcher.

"Thatcher's a puppet," I said to no one in particular. "He has no real power. Aries is only using him for his inside knowledge of Norrandale."

We continued the meeting, looking at all the possible entrances to the palace, where the guards were likely to be stationed and how we would go about infiltrating the building. Once we had more or less established a plan, Lord Burrow departed the tent with Rhen and Alastor following to meet with the soldiers.

I looked over the drawings of Mistwood again.

"What are these?" I asked Cai, pointing to lines drawn beneath the building.

"The catacombs that run under the palace."

"Anything interesting down there?"

"It's mostly just my ancestors who are buried there. Maybe an heirloom or two." He shrugged.

"Do you think it could be used as another way for us to enter undetected?"

"There are so many tunnels down there, it would be easy to get lost. Not even I know the way."

"Once we've taken back the palace, what happens next?" The winter wind sang outside the tent. It was to be another dreadfully cold day.

"We wait for the rest of our army to arrive, and then we start planning where and how to attack Aries."

Even as he said it, I could see the hesitance on his face. He'd have had it any other way if possible. So would I.

I might have lived through a rebel uprising. But it would be nothing compared to facing the armies of Argon on the battlefield. Still, we had no choice but to try to save our kingdoms.

"Speaking of which," I cleared my throat, "Rhen might have found something in the diary."

At this, Cai's expression changed to interest. I'd wanted to tell him last night, but Cai fell asleep so early and I didn't want to disturb the little rest he managed to get these days.

"He said that he found the entries where King Evrin wrote about the Myrgonite mines and how Queen Riona had taken three of the stones and had a goldsmith forge the objects for her. The king didn't know what kind of magic was used yet he'd warned Riona not to meddle with ancient magic. But she wouldn't listen. She wanted to be the most powerful queen history had ever seen. Initially the objects seemed to give her protection and immense luck. But the good effects were soon overcome by something much darker. Magic that old could not be used freely and without consequence. The king described it as if the magic was taking away from her soul. She became obsessed with gaining more power and using the objects, no matter what was at risk. The more powerful she became, the less she was herself."

"So, it's as bad as we thought, then." He ran his hand through his golden hair, which had grown much since we'd last been in Norrandale.

"Does the king mention anything about what the objects were or was even his diary not privileged with that information?"

"No, he did say what two of the objects were."

Cai looked at me expectantly.

"Queen Riona was very fond of wearing a certain necklace. One laced with many jewels and that contained a Myrgonite stone in the middle."

Cai pulled the nearest chair closer and slowly took a seat. "Well, I guess that answers that question, then." He rubbed his jaw where a few days' worth of stubble coated his face.

"And the other?"

"Apparently she never had any kind of weapons when it came to exerting her power, apart from one very specific dagger." I pulled out the knife Cai had gifted to me on my birthday.

"One with gold detailing on the hilt." I rubbed my thumb over the small jewel encrusted in the dagger before placing it on the table.

"Where did you get this again?"

Cai leaned over the table, picked up the dagger and inspected it. "On the day I first entered Everness, there was an old woman in the woods. She looked like some kind of pedlar. She gifted me the dagger because we'd given her some water to drink."

I remembered the dream I had while in the forest. King Evrin had buried Riona with the dagger.

"Do you think at some point it was stolen?"

"Maybe," Cai said in contemplation. "But there was something strange about her." I didn't reply, silently urging him to continue. "She knew I was the prince despite the fact that we weren't dressed in any uniforms or royal attire. She had no way of knowing my title."

"That is strange," I agreed.

"And she told me to go to this pool where I would see my future. I didn't believe her at first but then I saw a silhouette in the water."

"You've never told me about this."

"It was a silhouette of you," he said, meeting my gaze. "On the day of the rebellion, when you came back."

I pressed my lips together. "Do you think she gave you that dagger on purpose, knowing what it is?"

"Maybe. I don't know." He handed the dagger back to me and I slid it into the pocket of my breeches. Suddenly it felt heavier, making it impossible not to be aware of the knife and whatever ancient power it might possess.

"So, it doesn't say anything about what the third object could be?"

"The king himself doesn't sound certain in his writing. But he seemed to believe that the other two objects and their power were connected to the third somehow."

"Does it, by any chance, mention that the stones can't be destroyed?" he asked.

"I don't know yet," I said, stepping closer to him. "But Rhen will keep looking."

"Do you think it's safe for him to know all this?"

Cai wrapped his arm around my waist, pulling me against him.

"Rhen only knows it could be a dagger and a necklace. I don't think he suspects your family's necklace that you gifted to Eloisa without knowing what it was. The necklace is safe with my belongings and nobody knows about the dagger."

He rested his head against my stomach, appearing tired and worried. I held on to his shoulders, savouring this quiet moment before we would step out of the tent and be surrounded by soldiers and preparations to attack.

"Aries doesn't know what the Myrgonite stones look like yet, neither does anyone else. If he doesn't find the mines, he'll put all his energy into looking for the objects."

"What if we used it against him?"

"What do you mean?" Cai moved his head so he could look up at me.

"I mean, what if we somehow used the objects against Aries to stop him?"

He was taken aback, as if he could not believe the words that had just left my mouth.

"We've talked about this, Elara." Briefly, when we were heading to Argon and still didn't know what the objects were. I'd made the suggestion of using them in the future and Cai shut me down, claiming it was too dangerous.

"Why not? It's going to be difficult if not impossible to beat him as it is. This way we could save thousands of men from dying for the sake of nothing."

He pulled back from me. "Did you not hear everything you've just told me about Queen Riona and what the magic did to her?"

I stepped away from him. "Only because she became greedy and overused the objects for her own power and gain. This is for a noble cause. To stop someone from doing the same thing Riona tried to do."

"We have no way of knowing what the consequences would be for something like that." He stood up. "I am not prepared to risk your life to find out."

"But maybe if we used them together—"

"Promise me." He took hold of my wrists, looking into my eyes with a serious expression. "Promise me that you will not try and use the objects in any way."

His eyes were pleading. Begging me.

"Fine. I promise." But I wasn't sure I meant it.

Chapter 25

Gwen

My stomach rumbled as I made my way to the dining room.

The walking stick made the process feel achingly slow, especially because I was also carrying a book with me. I wanted to return it to the library after dinner and didn't want to hobble back all the way to my rooms to retrieve it, doubling the distance I would have to walk.

According to the physician, it was for only one more week that I needed to keep off the ankle.

I missed my morning rides. But the winter mornings were now so cold, it probably wouldn't have been very pleasant anyway.

The palace was awfully quiet and there was a constant feeling of emptiness. Apart from the odd servant here and there, I hardly spoke to or saw anyone. I wondered how the others were faring. They would have reached Norrandale by now. Would be close to Mistwood.

I didn't want to spend too much time thinking about what likely lay ahead for them. Though I hated the discomfort of my injury, some days I was thankful that it prevented me from going with them.

I knew I couldn't avoid it for ever and that I would have to return home sometime. But I didn't know if I was ready to face my brother, who was a traitor to the Crown and would likely be executed for treason. Even less did I want to consider what might happen if Elara and Cai did not succeed.

I entered the dining room and found Prince Lance lounging in a chair, at the head of the table, with a cup in his hands. There was some food on the table in front of him, but it didn't look like he'd eaten much yet. The wine jug, on the other hand, was almost empty.

"Lady Gwen." He didn't look surprised to see me, but in the state he was in, I doubted anything would surprise him.

"Your Highness." I wouldn't outright admit that I'd been avoiding him, but I'd mostly kept to my rooms or sometimes the library during the hours I knew he wasn't likely to frequent it.

Lance hardly ever came to eat dinner in the dining hall, much less at this early hour. Though I was more than used to seeing him with a cup in his hands, I had a feeling that something had driven him to drown himself in wine.

"I was just on my way to the library," I blurted out.

"Did you get lost, then?"

"Of course not. Why would you ask that?"

"As you can see—" he gestured to the room — "this is not the library."

I felt my face heat a little. Damn his arrogance.

"I know that." I glared at him from across the room. "I just wanted to grab something to snack on while I read." It was, of course, a blatant lie. I was starving.

"But I shan't disturb you," I continued, making to turn, which was a lot slower than I would have liked with the walking stick.

"Won't you join me?"

"What?" I looked over my shoulder.

Lance used his leg to push out the chair next to him. "Won't you join me for dinner, Lady Gwen?"

My stomach let out another rumble and I hoped he couldn't hear it.

"I'm actually really not that hungry." I continued to lie, hoping I could ask one of the servants to bring me some dinner in the library. "Enjoy your evening, then." I gave him the politest nod I could offer before slowly making my way to the library with much annoyance and having no one to blame but myself.

Thankfully there was a fire lit in the library, warming up the room to a comfortable temperature. I returned the book to the shelf where I'd found it before scanning for something I'd yet to read. If my circumstances did not change soon, I would be through the entire royal collection before spring. I was growing tired of having nothing better to do than read, but with the weather and my injury being what they were, it did not appear that I had many other options.

After a few more minutes of hunting through the shelves, I managed to find something that looked somewhat interesting, and I decided to scan through the first few pages to see if it was worth reading.

The fire crackled as I took in the words, slowly becoming more invested after every line.

"There you are."

It was an effort not to jump at the sudden sound of a voice at the door.

"Of course I'm here." I didn't look at Lance and instead kept my eyes glued to the book in front of me, half leaning against a shelf to keep my balance. "It's where I said I would be, isn't it?"

When Lance didn't respond, I looked up to where he stood halfway in the door of the library. He was smirking, his eyes a little lazy.

"If you came to check on my well-being, I can assure you I'm perfectly fine, thank you." I didn't know what else to say to break the silence.

"That's not why I'm here."

I swallowed, the book still in my hands, urging me to turn my attention back to it.

Lance stepped into the library, carrying a plate. "I brought you something to eat."

He placed it on a small table next to one of the reading chairs. The plate was filled with bread and cheeses and dark purple grapes, a particular favourite of mine. My stomach rumbled at the sight of it.

"That's uncommonly kind of you," I responded with some hesitance.

"You think me incapable of kindness?" he asked, his expression suggesting it was a serious question.

I continued to look longingly at the food, contemplating.

"Do you really want me to answer that?"

In his other hand, Lance held a cup of wine from which he took a big swig.

"Maybe not," he said after a moment. Was it only my imagination or did he look a little hurt? But then I reminded myself that my opinion could never matter to someone like him.

"Thank you for the food." I turned the page in my book. "Have a good evening, Your Highness."

Lance didn't move. I lost the sentence I'd last read and frowned.

"Why are you avoiding me, Lady Gwen?"

I gave a shrug, still scanning the page. "I'm not avoiding you."

"Yes, you are." In my peripheral vision, I saw him taking a step closer. "You think I haven't noticed that you do everything in your power to avoid us running into each other in the palace?"

How *did* he know?

Lance took another step and another, slowly closing the distance to the shelf I stood by.

"Am I truly such a terrible host, then?"

"No, you're not." It was getting more difficult to pretend I was reading. Especially as the Prince of Everness came to a standstill in front of me while I was against the shelf, with no ability to back away from him.

"Then what is it?" His eyes were so blue, as I remembered them being from the first time we'd met in Norrandale. There was an iciness to them that unnerved me.

My book was now forgotten but I took hold of my walking stick.

"Nothing," I insisted. I would never allow him to know the truth. There would be no point in it.

"I think you're lying." He didn't appear upset now but rather intrigued. It only managed to annoy me more.

"I'm just not a very sociable person." I continued to look up at him, not wanting to appear intimidated in any way.

"Now I know you're lying." In hindsight, it might not have been my best choice of words.

"Is it because you find me so attractive that every time you lay your eyes on me, you are at a complete loss for words?"

It was an effort not to bark out a laugh. "You wish." I gave his chest a light smack with my book and then realised it could be seen as an act of flirtation.

"I think that's exactly what it is. You're simply besotted with me." He had to be much more drunk than I'd initially thought. Although he'd always come across as rather arrogant, he'd never spoken to me like this before.

"I am not besotted with you, Prince Lance. In fact, I might just despise you."

"Oh, despise me?" he said with raised eyebrows. "Is that what you tell yourself when you go to bed at night and dream of me?"

"You're ridiculous." I refrained from rolling my eyes at him.

"Kiss me," he said, still looking down at me.

"What?" I blurted out.

"You heard me." There was a challenge in his voice. "Kiss me."

"I am not going to kiss you," I responded quickly, looking at him as if he'd lost his mind.

"Why?" His twinkling eyes accompanied a devilish smile. "Afraid you'll like it?"

I was at a loss for words, completely dumbfounded.

"No," I said in an attempt to gather myself. "Because you're drunk, Lance."

His expression changed suddenly, as if he was taken aback.

"Because you're always drunk."

With the book uncomfortably lodged under my arm, I stepped away from him.

"And because I'm not some kind of concubine or courtesan for you to play with because you're bored."

"I never said—"

"You treat me as if I'm here for your personal amusement. But I can assure you, had it not been for my injury, I would have left with the others without hesitation." It wasn't completely true, but I was angry with him. I wanted to hurt him.

Lance pressed his lips into a line and nodded slowly. "Right," he said, blowing out a breath. "Right, of course." He started to retreat towards the door. "I apologise for having offended you, miss."

He pulled the library door shut behind him and I fell down into the reading chair.

I grabbed a roll from the plate next to me and bit into it angrily.

He was the one who had barged in here, completely under the influence of wine and making inappropriate conversation. I would not feel guilty for what I'd said.

And yet …

The look on his face as he'd left. It would keep me up for the rest of the night, wrestling with my sheets.

Chapter 26

Cai

My horse was uneasy beneath me.

She refused to stand still, ears pulled back, huffing out cold air. Perhaps she sensed the bloodbath that was to come, the clashing of swords and dead soldiers coating the floors of Mistwood.

It was in the early hours of the morning and the sun had yet to rise.

The air was deathly quiet, almost as if in expectation.

We were a few hundred men outside the palace walls. The air was filled with mist, concealing us from any possible watchmen on the palace towers. Luck might have just been on our side.

Never in my life had I imagined I would have to break into my own palace. To attempt to win back the home I'd grown up in. The palace I was born to rule from. I dismounted and gave the mare a small pat on the neck.

"Are you all right, Your Majesty?" Alastor was by my side, multiple weapons in hand and strapped to his body.

"I'm not sure," I confessed. "Am I wrong to wish that it hadn't come to this?"

"Of course not, Your Majesty. I believe all of us wish the same."

I looked to the soldiers standing behind us, as far as the mist would allow me to see. They were all here for my kingdom's sake. Because they believed that I could lead them to something better.

As if sensing my worry, Elara jumped off her horse and stepped up next to me. She took my hand in hers.

"I'd rather you stay behind," I told her. "But I know you well enough to know there's no chance of that happening."

She gave me half a smile. "I'll be fine. And besides, Rhen has my back."

"It's time, Your Majesty," Alastor said. I gave a nod and unsheathed my knife.

We crept towards the palace courtyard through the mist. The process was achingly slow as we tried not to make a sound, but we wanted the element of surprise to avoid suffering damage from the archers in the towers.

We would not all go at once but instead sneak into the palace, using the darkness to our advantage until we were too many for them to fight off.

There were a few guards in the courtyard, as could be expected. Alastor went up behind one, soft as a mouse, and I held a breath as he sliced the man's neck open, blood spilling onto his Argonian armour. It was done quietly, but enough noise was made to cause the Argonian closest to me to look over, ready to inspect the source of the scuffle. I didn't give him the chance before impaling him through the chest. He gasped in surprise, falling forward.

One by one, we picked off the guards in the courtyard, hiding in the shadows and moving with quiet coordination.

I kept close to the walls until I reached the window of the study on the lower floor. The latch had been broken for as long as I could remember, and I'd never got round to telling anyone to fix it. I could not have expected it would come in handy much later.

I jammed my knife between the window and frame and moved the hilt. It opened with relative ease, but the cold weather and rain caused it to creak, and I flinched, grabbing the wooden frame.

I looked around to see if there were any movements out of the ordinary, anyone possibly approaching me. But the darkness remained quiet.

I hoisted my body up onto the thick window ledge and climbed inside the study. After a few moments, Alastor followed. With his dark clothes, he was almost impossible to see, the mist covering any stars and blocking the moonlight that might have given us away.

My eyes drifted to the desk with a few papers strewn about. Many of them contained my signature.

Alastor and I made our way to the open study door and peered out into the hall. No guards were about. We looked at each other and nodded before going in opposite directions.

Outside, Lord Burrow's men were surrounding the palace and the courtyard as well as attempting to sneak in on the other side of the palace. We would close in on the Argonians before they knew what had hit them.

A few lamps lit the hallway, and I listened carefully for anyone that could possibly be approaching from either side. I rounded the corner of the hall that would eventually lead me to the throne room and unsheathed my sword. Behind me, I heard someone yell, "Hey!" As if he'd come out of nowhere, the Argonian was on me in a second. Did he know who I was? Or did he suspect me to be just another intruder, a loyalist?

He carried a broad sword with a slightly curved blade, the symbols of Argon engraved in the metal. The guard took a swing towards me and then another. It was an effort to defend myself.

I struck low, managing to cut his leg, weakening him. After that it was easier to counterattack, until eventually the soldier was on the ground, clutching his bleeding wounds. I was running now, my footsteps loud across the floor. I could hear commotion closer to the other side of the palace. The Argonians must have spotted Lord Burrow's men and all flooded in that direction.

I reached the throne room. It was entirely devoid of life and sound.

Did Thatcher know I was here? Had he been alerted to our presence and was he now hiding like the coward I knew him to be?

"Where are you?" I mumbled to myself, sword ready to strike at any moment. If Thatcher wasn't here, he could be anywhere in the palace.

My eyes found the throne at the end of the room. The throne my father had once sat on. The throne Thatcher had placed himself on after killing Jack in front of our eyes. A shudder went through me. I could still picture Jack's blood on the floor, the dead guards surrounding us and Thatcher confessing to the murder of my family. My palms began to sweat against the hilt of my sword. I could feel my heart beating in my throat.

He was around here somewhere. I could feel it.

From somewhere in the distance, I heard a scream and the sound of swords clashing. I could only hope our men were holding their ground against the Argonian guards.

Another scream sounded, closer now, and this time it was female and heartbreakingly familiar.

Chapter 27

Elara

It was strange to be back in Mistwood.

The memories of our last time here were still very fresh. As I slowly made my way through the halls, I could see us running back to our horses, fleeing for our lives as we were outnumbered by Thatcher and the Argonian guards. But not this time. This time we were prepared. This time we surrounded them.

That didn't mean the Argonians weren't dangerous, though. My hands clenched around the hilt of my sword, strengthening my grip. It felt cold and unfamiliar in my hands. It had been too long since I'd properly wielded a weapon.

I wondered where Cai was by now. Was he injured? Had he crossed paths with Thatcher? And what would he do if he did?

I entered another hallway and saw a body lying on the floor, unmoving. My breath caught in my throat for a moment but then I noticed he wore Argonian armour.

I kept my steps as light as possible while approaching the dead guard.

From the other side of the palace, I could hear fighting. They'd probably been alerted to our presence by now.

I'd lost Rhen somehow as we'd entered. The darkness and having to keep quiet stopped us from communicating. I would have felt better with him by my side, but finding Cai was the most important thing now.

I peered around every corner, making sure I was alone and moving slowly through the palace. There were a few lamps that created a dim light in some of the hallways, at least enough to see where I was going. The further I was from the servants' quarters, the louder the fighting became. I decided to avoid the worst of it and headed left, in the direction of the throne room.

My heart beat so loudly I was afraid someone nearby might hear it, but then I reminded myself that Rhen and I had practised my sword fighting. All those hours in the training yard hadn't been for nothing. I was stronger than I'd been before, and I wouldn't go down without defending myself.

"Cai," I whispered, knowing it was possibly foolish and wanting desperately to find him all the same. Or Rhen or even Alastor. I felt too exposed here on my own. This was dangerous.

"Cai," I whispered again. This time there was a noise behind me. I turned just in time to see an Argonian coming at me.

The man was quite a few years older, with a dark beard, hate flaring in his eyes. Despite it being winter, he wore a uniform with no sleeves, showcasing his powerful arms and the sword that was coming right at my chest.

I held up my sword to block the hit and my wrists strained at the impact. He was strong, there was no doubt about it. Argonians didn't need much skill when they could simply use brute force. Even so, he was quick, attacking me left and right, and my muscles burned as I attempted to hold off each swing. I was merely defending, completely unable to attack.

With each move, I had to take a step back. How was I going to get out of this alive? Although I had a desperate need to survive, I struggled to imagine a scenario where I would walk away from this fight.

I couldn't help but let out a yelp of pain as he managed to cut my arm, causing a burning sensation as blood quickly stained the ripped material of my white shirt.

He made another swing, for my neck this time, and I held my sword upright, stopping him only inches from my face. Sparks flew as the metal clashed. He held me there, pushing harder. My arm wasn't strong enough and I clenched my teeth in pain, not wanting to give up.

The Argonian pulled back before aiming another hit at me. With a sickening clang, my sword hit the floor. I was as good as dead.

I looked up at the soldier in panic. He jabbed at my torso, and I barely dodged. I contemplated running but knew he would catch up with me.

I couldn't die now. Not like this.

The Argonian's eyes suddenly filled with surprise and then pain as a knife lodged in his shoulder. I looked around, never before so grateful to see the King of Norrandale, bloodied and breathing hard, but he was there for me.

I watched as the Argonian regained his composure and pulled the knife from his shoulder, not appearing to care about the wound or the stream of blood.

His eyes were locked on Cai, a new target acquired, who looked as ready as ever to take him on. They stormed towards each other, the hallway filled with the sound of male grunts. I watched them fight with worry in my chest, feeling slightly helpless.

But Cai could not easily be overcome. He'd had years of practice, not only with a broadsword — he'd faced many Argonians in his life. He knew the kind of style they fought with. He knew where to look for weaknesses.

He was quick, despite looking tired, and he not only defended against the Argonian easily but pushed him back with attacking swings.

I looked for my own sword. It lay on the floor, but the moment I tried to pick it up, my arm protested in pain, and I feared I would not be able to take a swing with the heavy weapon.

Cai let out a sound, catching my attention. The guard had managed to knock him to the ground. With one big swing, he knocked Cai's sword out of his hand, and it slid over the tiled floor, away from him.

I was already up and moving towards them. He knocked Cai's head against the tiles before wrapping his hands around his neck. This wasn't about defending anything anymore. This was cold-blooded murder.

He was so focused on Cai and his thirst for blood that he seemed to forget I was also there.

I didn't think. Not as I watched Cai fight for his life.

He was going to kill him.

I came up behind the guard, pulling the dagger with the Myrgonite stone from my pocket.

I wouldn't allow him to kill Cai. And so I didn't hesitate.

Blood spattered as I jammed the dagger into the Argonian's neck, both of my hands wrapped around the hilt and the stone. I felt something surge inside me. The guard tried to grab the dagger to pull it out, but I wouldn't let him. I was overcome with a strength beyond me, and I tried to push it further, his deep red blood soaking my fingers as I finally twisted.

Cai managed to get out from under him, eyes wide.

I pulled the dagger out, which took more effort than I would have imagined, and the guard dropped like a stone.

My chest heaved, as if I'd been holding my breath this whole time.

I didn't hesitate to run over to Cai, not caring about the dead guard and the fact that it was like the dagger had sucked the life out of him.

"Are you all right?" I asked, kneeling in front of Cai. He had marks on his neck.

"What did you do?" He breathed out. He didn't look angry, but he didn't look relieved either. "What did you do?" he asked again as I inspected him for more wounds.

"It doesn't matter now." I tried to reassure both of us, placing a bloodied hand on his shoulder.

His eyes finally travelled to my bleeding arm. "You're hurt." His voice was hoarse.

The pain in my arm was growing and I could feel the blood trickling down my skin.

Cai didn't hesitate before ripping a piece of his shirt and wrapping it around the wound.

"I'll be fine," I insisted. "The only thing that matters is that you're still alive." Still, I bit my lip to keep a sound of pain from escaping me as he tied the material around my arm.

His eyes wouldn't meet mine as he helped me up.

"Yes, but at what cost?" he muttered under his breath.

I stared at the back of his head as he retrieved his sword and made his way further down the hall. I was quickly on his heels, grabbing my own sword along the way. I held it with my uninjured arm. My hands and the Myrgonite dagger were covered with the Argonian's blood. It felt sticky against my skin. I quickly shoved the dagger back into its sheath, blood and all.

At what cost?

"At what cost?" I whispered loud enough for him to hear once we'd reached the end of the hall. "When it comes to your life, it doesn't matter the cost."

Cai looked around to make sure there were no other guards nearby.

"I told you, Elara — in fact, I begged you — not to use that damned stone."

"He was going to kill you, Cai, all right! I wasn't thinking. My only thought was to save you."

I wasn't thinking. I should have used my sword or anything else. But it was too heavy, and I was so overcome with fear that Cai would lose his life that all sense went out of me. In that moment, I would have done anything to save him. And I would do it again.

I couldn't understand Cai's worry. This wasn't me trying to make use of the Myrgonite stones for my own power or greed. This was about saving the person that I cared about most in this world. How could I be punished for protecting the ones I loved?

Regardless, I didn't have much time to consider the repercussions, because Cai and I walked into the throne room.

And on the dais, Thatcher was waiting.

Chapter 28

Cai

There he was.

I finally laid eyes on the man who'd taken nearly everything from me.

I would have attacked him immediately had it not been for the young man who was with him.

I didn't know what had happened to Conner after we'd left for Argon. He'd stayed behind at Mistwood to continue his training and I'd had no way of knowing if he'd survived the initial attack of Argon's guards.

But there he was, still alive and breathing … for now.

Conner's face was pale as Thatcher used his body to shield himself. My biggest concern was the knife he held to Conner's throat.

The young boy's eyes met mine, wide with panic and pleading for me to do something.

I'd thought about this moment so many times. About what I would do when I saw Thatcher again. But I should have known it wouldn't be as simple as a duel. Thatcher was a coward after all.

"Let him go." I held up my sword. Elara was close by my side. "He has nothing to do with this."

"Maybe not." Thatcher held the knife dangerously close to Conner's skin. The boy swallowed hard, the apple of his throat bobbing against the steel. "But he's the only reason you're not coming at me with that sword right now."

"Afraid to face me like a man? And yet you always insisted you were better than me at fighting."

"In hand-to-hand combat, maybe, but I also know when I'm outnumbered."

"That's right, we have this whole place surrounded," Elara said. I didn't remember the last time I'd seen her face filled with so much anger. "Accept it, Thatcher, you've lost."

"Maybe I have, maybe I haven't." He gestured with his head to Conner. "I could always still kill him."

He braced himself as if to slice open Conner's throat, and I shouted out, "No!"

Thatcher eyed me from the dais, inviting me to make the next move.

"Let him go, and I'll put my sword down."

I was going to murder him but not until I was sure both Conner and Elara were completely safe.

"How do I know I can trust you?" He kept eyeing Elara as if she would pounce on him with that sword at any moment. Had it not been for Conner, I believed she might have, despite her injured arm.

"Have I ever lied to you, Thatch?" I used his old nickname in the hope he would let his guard down.

This palace was filled with endless memories for the two of us, from a very young age. We would chase each other around with wooden swords, sneak into parties we were too young to attend, climb the trees in the gardens and practise fighting. He had gone and thrown it all away, and for what?

"I suppose not."

"I'll put my weapon down and you let Conner go, and then we can fight this out, man to man."

"Are you sure about this?" Elara said softly.

"I know what I'm doing." I didn't want to be angry with her, but I was overcome with feelings of disappointment and worry. She'd used the Myrgonite dagger after I begged her not to, and now neither of us knew what the consequence might be.

"All right." I was thankful he agreed. "Man to man, then."

I slowly lowered my sword until it lay on the floor next to me.

He gave Conner a hard shove, pushing him in Elara's direction. She pulled the boy to her and retreated with him, putting them both out of our way.

Thatcher still had the knife in his hand, and I doubted he would be willing to let go of it. I would simply have to take my chances.

I balled my hands into fists, readying my arms in the right position.

Thatcher didn't hesitate. He came straight at me, with the knife pointing towards my chest.

I dodged left and knocked his arm as hard as I could manage. He let out a grunt of discomfort, running one hand through his hair to get it out of his face.

He swiped at me again and I kept the muscles in my arms rigid as I gave him another hit, this time at his elbow.

One more good hit to his wrist or lower arm and I might be able to rid him of the knife.

I'd been sparring with Thatcher for as long as I could remember. And though I'd never had the intention of actually hurting him until now, I knew all his moves and his weaknesses.

Thatcher often forgot to keep his face guarded, and so before he could anticipate it, my fist collided with his nose, knocking his head back. Before he could recover, I gave him another hit for good measure.

He let out a grunt of pain or anger, maybe both. *Just you wait, bastard. I'm only getting started.*

He started to circle me, blood running down to his mouth. Conner was gone, but Elara still stood by the door, knowing that no matter how much she wanted to protect me, this was my fight, and I would have to see it through. I wondered if I would have been able to do the same, had our positions been swapped. Would I be able to stand and watch as she risked her life, fighting the person who'd taken almost everything from her? Her family and her kingdom. A fight that we all knew could only end in death.

I eyed Thatcher, waiting for him to make a move.

"Well, come on then," he spat out. "I know you want to kill me."

Damn right I did.

"You betrayed everyone, Thatcher. Your king, your kingdom, your family. Did you even think about Gwen in any of this?" His poor younger sister, whose life would never be the same. She'd not only lost her brother, but also her home, and she would be labelled as the sister of a traitor for the rest of history.

"I am not her keeper." He went to stab me again, this time in my stomach, but I turned, and the knife caught in my tunic and ripped the material. I used the opportunity to grab Thatcher's arm and come down on it with my elbow.

He groaned in anguish, letting go of the knife and pulling his arm back.

"You killed my family. The people who treated you as if you were their own," I cried out, still hoping, somehow, that after everything, Thatcher might say that he was sorry, that he regretted it.

"You don't even know the half of it," Thatcher stated with proud arrogance.

"Who do you think poisoned your father?" The words hit me harder than I would have liked. It was the equivalent of standing on a frozen lake and having the ice break beneath your feet. That initial moment when you're submerged in the icy water and it feels as though your heart is going to stop. "Who do you think gave the servant the poison for your wine? Who do you think let Argon's guards into the palace? It was right in front of you the entire time and you were too blind to see it."

I'd thought and wondered about it for a long time, but hearing him say it, and hearing him confess to my father's murder, was more than I could bear.

"You were never my king, Cai." He managed to land a punch to my jaw. The pain shot through my face. "And you never will be." Every word was like another blow.

I tried to go for his face again, but Thatcher was more prepared this time, blocking me. The only downside to my knowing all his moves when he fought was that he knew mine as well. And he had no qualms about taking advantage of my weak spots.

Another hit to my side, which I reciprocated. There was no version where this ended well.

"Believe me, it wasn't easy killing your mother."

I defended against his blow and hit him straight in the eye, causing Thatcher to stagger back a little.

"Right until the end she cried out for you." It was as if all my nightmares had come alive before me. I could see my mother's face in my dreams. Hear her voice. Hear her call out for me to help her before Thatcher slashed her throat. I would do anything, pay any price, if I could erase the mental images of Thatcher murdering my family. The people who treated him as their own son. My fists were up again, ready to strike once more.

"She seemed particularly attached to this." I watched as he pulled a ring from his pocket. The ring my father had given my mother on their wedding day. The ring she never took off. After he passed, I would often find her sitting staring at it. Like it connected her to him, even in death.

"That doesn't belong to you." Fury surged through my veins.

"Doesn't it?" he challenged. "I figured I own everything in the royal household, since I basically rule this part of the kingdom now."

"You're a fool if you think Aries will allow you any power. He's using you."

Thatcher twirled the ring in his hands as if to taunt me that he'd pried it off my mother's corpse.

"That belongs to my wife," I said through clenched teeth.

"Your wife?" He raised an eyebrow, sparing a quick glance at Elara. "I didn't realise congratulations were in order." I had no doubts in my mind. Elara was the only person I wanted to spend the rest of my life with.

"I believe Aries wouldn't be opposed to the idea of an alliance with Everness. But only the marital sort, of course. Perhaps if he decides he doesn't want her, I can take my turn to play with your toy."

I lost it.

I tackled Thatcher to the ground with all the strength I possessed. We both hit the floor hard, knocking over some decorative armour in the process. I saw my mother's ring skid across the throne-room floor.

Thatcher was quick to throw a punch to my side, hitting my ribs. He knocked me on the side of my head, causing the world around me to spin for a moment as stars entered my vision. It gave him enough time to shift our positions so that he was pinning me down.

Thatcher managed another blow to the side of my head, and I tried to keep my eyes focused on him, but every hit was more painful than the previous one and my sight grew blurry.

As my head rolled to the side, I noticed Elara pick up the ring. Her eyes were filled with fear. Maybe she was calling my name. I couldn't be sure.

"Thatcher, please! You'll kill him."

If I died now, I would be leaving her to fight all of this alone. Thatcher and Aries could get to her, hurt her or, worse, kill her.

I couldn't give up on her. Not when she was the only thing worth fighting for.

My arm reached out and took hold of the metal helmet that we'd knocked over. Thatcher didn't have time to react before I hit him, as hard as I could manage, on the side of his head.

The armour was heavy enough to cause damage, and a small trail of blood started to drip from his temple. He pressed his hand to his head, coating his fingers in blood. I took the chance to kick at his legs and roll him over so that he was under me again.

"You're never going to beat him, you know." Thatcher attempted to hit me again, but he missed, slightly disoriented. "Aries is too powerful. He will destroy you and everything you love."

Though I would not want to admit that Thatcher could be right, Aries was already halfway there.

"He will end you and Elara. Both of you will be dead, just like your mother and your father, and the only thing left of your legacy will be two empty thrones."

I didn't care anymore. I brought the armour down on his face again and again.

Blood spattered across my face and the floor. I heard Elara call to me, but the noise was drowned out by the ringing in my ears. All I could see was Thatcher driving his sword through Jack. My father on his deathbed, my mother and grandmother dying at Thatcher's hand. I saw Elara in Aries' clutches. All the people I loved either dead or hurt. I was helpless to save them once and I would not be again.

Thatcher let out moans of pain, unable to fight back. I hit him over and over, and eventually he didn't move anymore, but I didn't stop.

He'd taken my family, my throne and my kingdom, and all I could see was red. Fire might as well have blazed in front of my eyes. Anger like I'd never felt before overcame me until hatred was all I could feel.

I only stopped when I was completely out of breath, unable to move my arms any longer. I sat back on the floor, heaving. Thatcher's face was barely recognisable, and I realised I'd murdered my best friend.

Chapter 29

Cai

There was blood on my hands.

They were sticky with it and there was a metallic taste on my tongue. The reflection that greeted me in the mirror was not a pleasant one. Red coated my face and hair, staining it with evidence of what I'd done. Who I'd killed.

I was back in my old rooms. A place that I'd enjoyed spending my afternoons in, with a large fireplace, comfortable bed and beautiful view from all the windows. Now it felt empty and sombre.

Shortly after my fight with Thatcher, the palace had filled with all the loyalist soldiers celebrating our victory. I should have been celebrating too. But I did not feel victorious, despite having won back Mistwood.

I'd lost Elara in the chaos of it all. I'd heard her screaming. But was she screaming because she was afraid or because she wanted me to stop butchering Thatcher? I couldn't have stopped. I was overcome by something stronger than myself. Something beyond my control. I was possessed by anger and pain and fear … or something much darker.

It could not have pleased Elara to watch such a scene play out before her. To witness me in such a way. I was certain she had to be upset by the matter. I remembered the way her voice sounded as she'd called my name.

There was a basin in my room, which I filled from a pitcher. I dipped my hands into the cold water, watching as red swirls of blood changed the colour.

Soap. I needed soap.

I started to scrub my hands, but the blood was everywhere, under my nails, in the creases of my fingers. I scrubbed until my hands felt raw, but still, somehow, they weren't clean enough. My jacket and shirt dropped to the floor as I ripped them off.

The cold day caused goosebumps to form on my arms, but I didn't care. I poured more clean water from the pitcher and washed my face before moving on to my hair. So much blood.

I didn't want to think about what had happened, but the image was as clear as ever in my mind. I could still hear Thatcher's voice and the last words he'd spoken. The way he'd spoken of my mother and Elara angered me still. The only thing I could see as I smashed the armour into him was the image of him driving his sword through Jack. I watched it over and over again in my head.

We'd been forced to leave Jack's body behind and it haunted me. Perhaps it would continue to haunt me the same way today probably would.

There was a time in my life that I thought I'd never stop dreaming of Argon and that battlefield. But in recent months, every time I'd closed my eyes I could only see Thatcher murdering my family. I worried that the nightmare would morph into something new and much worse. Would my slumbers be disturbed by visions of me killing

Thatcher over and over again? Watching as the life disappeared from his eyes and his face became unrecognisable. I was not sorry that I had ended his life. Not after everything he'd done.

But I was not myself. Something more than anger had taken possession of me. And I had no way of resisting it.

The thought worried me immensely.

Once I was sure most of the blood had been washed off, I had to find Elara.

I hurried out the door as I was putting on a new, clean shirt.

The palace hallways were filled with soldiers. They carried crates of food and weapons into the building, everything we'd brought along with us from the camp. Many of them bowed their heads as I passed.

Somehow, I felt as though I should be the one bowing to them. Had it not been for their sacrifice and loyalty, I would not be walking the halls of my home once again.

I made my way towards the guest chambers Elara had occupied on her previous stay. She would probably want to clean up as well.

The morning sunlight peeked in through the windows. Had so many hours already passed since we'd arrived? We had yet to eat today, it being too early when we left the camp. Elara was probably hungry too. As soon as we'd talked, we would need to find something to eat, and then I needed to start getting matters back into order in the palace. But my first priority was her.

Part of me knew that the conversation to come would not be full of pleasantries. I had asked her not to use the dagger and she did anyway, and she had seen me brutally murder someone we both knew and used to care for.

I didn't want to believe that the magic of the objects was somehow involved but I could not help but suspect it. Not after everything that had happened today and the way we'd defeated the Argonians. As much as I wanted to believe we were building a strong army, I did not want to be naive.

As I walked at a brisk pace towards Elara's old chambers, I thought back to the way the dagger glinted in her hands before she'd killed the soldier. The way she'd been in possession of the necklace as we'd escaped Woodsbrook and all throughout the rebellion. How we'd escaped death time and time again, despite the circumstances. And if the objects had something to do with it, what would be the cost?

That, perhaps, scared me most of all, even more than having to face Aries in battle again. Whatever had happened today, Elara and I needed to talk about it urgently.

Or maybe I was looking for an excuse not to blame myself for taking another life. The life of someone I used to call brother. Maybe I did not like the person I was becoming.

I wrestled with all the thoughts in my mind, wondering if it had been the dagger, or if I'd just lost a part of myself that I would never find again.

Chapter 30

Gwen

The Evernean winter had graced us with a day of sunshine, and though it was still quite cold, there wasn't a cloud in the sky. My ankle was feeling much better. I couldn't run or ride yet, but it was a significant improvement over having to hobble along everywhere.

I took advantage of the nicer weather by having my morning tea out on the veranda, overlooking the gardens. I poured myself a fresh cup of the herbal tea and held it in my hands, hoping that it would warm my fingertips.

The taste of the tea was soothing, and I took frequent sips while paging through the latest book I'd borrowed from the library. This particular book was a romance, and while I preferred my tales to be more on the adventure side, it was a nice change of pace. Although I always found it frustrating when the two main characters took such a long time to get together when it was so obvious they belonged with each other.

The door to the veranda opened behind me and I dropped the book in my lap, looking back.

Lance looked equally surprised to see me.

"Pardon me." He let out a cough. "I didn't realise you'd be here."

We hadn't spoken since our last conversation in the library, when Lance had been extremely drunk, and I'd insulted him beyond reprimand. For the first time since I'd come to live at the Palace of Levernia, it felt as though he'd been avoiding me.

Not that I had much to complain about. But it was strange to see Lance so out of sorts. I almost wanted him to go back to normal so I could stop the pressing sensation that I should feel guilty for the way I'd acted.

"Just having some tea." I held up my cup somewhat awkwardly.

"All right then." It was clear he'd been planning to sit outside as well. "I shan't bother you anymore."

"No." I used the table to pull myself up. "This is your palace. I shall get out of your way."

"Technically it's Elara's palace," he said with a hint of a smile as I grabbed my book.

"Still, you've lived here your whole life. It's your home as much as it is hers."

"I suppose."

I left my teacup on the table, not being able to walk with more than my cane and book. Lance was still standing in the door as I passed him. As I stepped inside, he took hold of my arm, urging me to look back.

There was a moment of silence as his eyes searched me, as if he were looking for the right words.

"I don't want you to hate me."

I certainly couldn't have anticipated him saying that.

"I don't hate you." I strongly disliked him and his manners, but I didn't think I'd ever truly hated anyone.

"Yes, you do," he insisted. "You don't talk to me. You don't want to be in the same room as me. You can hardly look me in the eye."

I let out a sigh. "That doesn't mean I hate you."

"Then what does it mean?" he pressed.

I thought about what to say and how to say it, but the words did not come easily.

"It just means I don't want to talk to you."

I tried to pull my hand away, still clutching the book, but Lance did not let go.

"Why not?"

"Because I don't want to, Lance. Isn't that reason enough?"

"No, it's not." Damn him and his persistence. I was starting to grow agitated. Part of me feared that if he pushed me far enough, we'd only have a repeat of our conversation in the library. And then he would look at me like a dog who'd just been kicked. I wanted to despise him for it. For everything.

"What did I do, Gwen?"

"Nothing." I had no interest in continuing this conversation with him in the least bit.

"Well, I must have done something because I'm the only person around here that you treat with so much resentment."

How could I not when he clearly thought so little of me that he remembered nothing at all?

"Why do you care anyway? I don't want to talk about this."

"To hell with what you want. I'm not leaving until you tell me."

"Well, if you're not leaving, then I am." I pulled my arm hard enough that Lance wouldn't be able to hold on without hurting me and started to walk away.

Of course, this did nothing to prevent the spoiled prince from following me.

Naturally, I wasn't able to walk very fast and so he easily stepped in front of me, blocking my way.

I let out a groan of frustration, contemplating hitting him with the walking stick.

"Do you want me to beg, is that it?"

"No," I cried out. "I want you to leave me alone."

"I will if you tell me what's the matter. Why do you detest me?"

And I was so desperate to get away from him that before I could think better of it, I blurted out, "Because, you incompetent, selfish bastard, you stole my first kiss."

I was sixteen years old when I last saw the Prince of Everness. He was tall for his age back then, with sharp features to accompany his midnight hair. We were all gathered in the throne room of Mistwood when King Magnus and Prince Lance came to visit Norrandale. I wasn't privy to the reason for their visit, but I believed it was regarding some political matter.

The heat from the fireplace was warm against my back as I watched the prince saunter in with his father. His eyes met mine as they passed, and I quickly looked away.

I had always sensed he was trouble in one way or another, but I did not know better than to avoid it.

Lance didn't show much interest in spending time with Cai or Thatcher, or even with his father and the royal council. It was as if he'd been forced to tag along on this trip and he'd rather be anywhere else instead. Until the day he'd caught me dancing alone in the ballroom.

My dance teacher had left an hour before, but I had yet to get the steps right and I refused to stop until I did so.

I turned about the room until my eye suddenly caught a figure standing by the door.

Mid-step, with my arms still up in the air, I stopped to take in the unwelcome viewer.

"Can I help you?" He was a mere guest at the palace while I practically lived there. If anyone was intruding, it most definitely was him.

"What are you doing?" he asked curiously.

"What does it look like I'm doing, I'm practising my dancing." My intention wasn't to be rude to the Prince of Everness, but I'd felt quite embarrassed at being caught dancing alone. Besides, he'd made no effort to be polite to anyone here at court.

"You're doing it wrong."

"Well, if I could do it right, I wouldn't need to practise now, would I?" Did he intend to leave or just keep standing there and invading my privacy?

To my disappointment, he stepped into the ballroom.

"You do know who I am, don't you?"

"Of course," I scoffed. "You're the future king of Everness."

"And did they not teach you that people of my birth rank should be addressed by their titles?" What an entitled jerk. He clearly got most of his traits from his father.

"They did," I responded. "But if you insist on me using your title, then I must insist you do the same." And then I added, "Your Highness."

"Which is?"

I realised that instead of chasing him away, I was aiding him to continue our conversation.

"You may call me Lady Gwen." I gave a small curtsy only because I had to. "My father is a close friend of the King."

"Pleased to make your acquaintance then, Lady Gwen." He'd drawn out my name.

"Well then, I'd better be getting back to my practice."

"I could show you how to do it, if you'd like?"

The idea of suddenly dancing alone with the prince unnerved me. Butterflies fluttered in my stomach as I replied, "Well, I can hardly say no to the future king."

Prince Lance had stepped in front of me. His arm wrapped around my waist while his free hand took mine.

My dancing practice was to prepare me for when I would come out to society, and I'd never actually danced with a boy before. I had to look up to meet his eyes. They were the lightest shade of blue I'd ever seen.

"So first, you're going to step back with your right foot."

"I know that."

He looked down at me with amusement and something in my stomach fluttered.

Lance started to count the steps. One back, one right, two front, two left.

Then came a turn, and this was the part where I usually messed up the number of steps I had to take.

"Now step out with your right foot so you can rest your weight on your left."

I tried as he suggested while he spun me around, and surprisingly, for the first time, I did not lose my balance.

I was too satisfied not to give the slightest smile. Our steps echoed across the quiet ballroom accompanied by the sound of Lance's counting.

The more we danced, the easier it became for me to keep up with him. When we finished the last turn of the dance, Lance surprised me by suddenly dipping me, his arm still wrapped around my waist while I clung to his shoulder for fear that he would accidentally drop me.

He quickly pulled me back up, as if I weighed nothing, and it took me a moment to catch my breath. I was unsure if it was because of the dancing or our proximity.

"Thank you," I said, quickly taking a step away from him to a more appropriate distance. "For helping me."

"You're very welcome, Lady Gwen."

"Well, I'd best be going or I'm going to be late for my riding lesson." I curtsied before hurrying out of the room, but not before looking back as I crossed the threshold. Lance was still standing in the middle of the ballroom, the right corner of his mouth turned up in a slight smile.

From then on, I saw Lance more frequently in the palace — at dinners, a royal picnic and court gatherings.

One night, the King held a musical event in the ballroom. All the finest musicians in the kingdom had been invited to perform. The atmosphere was lively as the melodies filled the large hall.

As I was not yet old enough to attend such events, I would usually sneak out to one of the small balconies that overlooked the ballroom. Back in the day of Cai's grandfather, the ballroom would be used for operas very often and the most important guests would sit and watch from their private balconies.

I was careful to hide behind the wall as I observed the beautiful dresses of the women and the fine tunics and jackets of the gentlemen, glittering with gold stitching and medallions.

My parents were down there as well, in conversation with the King and Queen. I also spotted Thatcher and Cai, observing the amiable young women around them.

"I was wondering where you were."

The sound of his voice made me jump.

Once again, I felt like he'd caught me doing something I wasn't supposed to.

"What are you doing up here?" Lance asked.

How did he even find me?

"I'm just watching the party."

"I can see that. But why aren't you down there with the other guests?"

"Not old enough." I shrugged. "Mother says I will make my debut next year."

"Ah, I see." Even though Lance wasn't much older than me, I was suddenly very much aware that I was up there alone with a boy, no chaperone in sight. How did I keep getting myself into these situations?

Lance had a cup of wine in his hands, which he offered to me. "Would you like some?"

"I've never had wine before." Mother said it was improper for a lady to drink wine before she was out in society.

"I promise one sip won't kill you."

I didn't know whether I was trying to prove something to him or to myself, but I grabbed the cup and took a big gulp.

It was nothing like the grape juice I'd had before. Instead, it had more of a sour and bitter taste as it ran down my throat.

My expression must have given away my distaste. Lance chuckled as I handed back the cup and wiped my mouth.

"How do people get drunk on that stuff?"

"Easy," Lance said. "The more you have, the easier it is to drink."

"How many cups have you had?"

"Two." He looked down at the cup. "Maybe three."

The musicians below started a new tune, and a few people gathered to dance. I pressed myself against the wall to avoid being spotted by the guests.

Lance stood next to me, with his shoulder leaning against the wall, allowing him to look as casual and unfazed as he always did.

"How long are you and your father to stay here in Norrandale?"

"We are leaving tomorrow actually."

"So soon?" I attempted not to sound disappointed.

"I'm afraid we've received news that my sister is unwell. We must return to Levernia immediately."

"I'm sorry to hear that."

"Why? Are you going to miss me?" The guests were temporarily forgotten. I could think only of his close presence.

"No." I was surprised by his bluntness. "I meant your sister."

"So, you won't miss me, then?" He was teasing me now, I could tell. And I didn't know how to respond. Had never had a boy speak to me like that.

I decided to try to focus on the party again, but I could feel his eyes lingering on me.

"You should come to Everness one day."

"Why?" Was he suggesting that I visit him or did he simply believe himself to live in the superior kingdom?

"The library," he said, clearing his throat. "You like reading, don't you? The palace at Levernia has a very fine library."

The second, then.

"Perhaps one day I will. Though I doubt my mother would allow me to leave the kingdom. Not unless she found me an Evernean husband, and even then, I think she is too much of a loyalist to do that."

When Lance didn't say anything, I looked back up at him. A strand of dark hair had fallen across his eyes, and before I could stop myself, I brushed it out of the way. We stared at each other for a moment, as if both having realised what I'd just done.

Then Lance lowered his head and pressed his lips to mine in a kiss. It only lasted for a moment, but I could have sworn I was no longer breathing. I didn't know if I wanted to slap him for having the audacity or ask him to do it again.

Instead, my mouth fell open with no words coming out and I stood there like an absolute idiot.

"I'm afraid I must go, or my father will start to look for me."

Anything. Say anything.

"I bid you goodnight, Lady Gwen."

It was the last time I saw the Prince of Everness until I walked into the Palace of Levernia a few months ago. By the time I'd risen the following morning, Lance and King Magnus had already departed. I knew it was foolish of me to hope I would hear from him and yet … Was it entirely deluded of me, as a young girl, to hope that he might have liked me?

But there was nothing. As the weeks passed, I came to realise that the spoiled prince did not care for me in any way. Instead, he was simply bored and looking for something to pass the time. I promised myself I would never fall victim to a prince like that again.

"What?" Lance asked, full of surprise.

"You," I said, jabbing a finger at his chest. "Stole. My. First. Kiss."

He took a moment to respond. "When?"

Of course, he couldn't remember.

"When you and your father last visited Norrandale. That night at the party when you found me spying on the guests."

"I—" He hesitated. "That was? You mean to tell me you hadn't kissed anyone before that?"

"I was sixteen," I reminded him. "And I wasn't out in society. And I'd like to think myself a lady who doesn't just go around kissing random boys."

"So, you—" Lance pressed his fingers to the bridge of his nose as if still trying to process the information. "You're angry with me because I kissed you once, a very long time ago?"

"Yes," I huffed. "Well, no." I groaned in frustration, unable to believe that I was actually having this conversation with him.

"I'm angry because you made me believe that you cared for me in some way, showing me how to dance and following me around the palace all the damned time. And then you had the audacity to kiss me without a chaperone around and leave without a word. My reputation could have been ruined, and I never heard from you again."

Saying it out loud felt a little ridiculous. Of course, my mother would have had a fit if she'd known I was kissing boys while hiding away from parties, but as no one was likely to discover us up there and I would never breathe a word of my encounters with Lance, it was unlikely my reputation would have suffered from the matter. And yet somehow, against my will, my heart did. I was hurt by him in a way I'd never been hurt before, even if it was over such a small thing.

"I was a kid, Gwen." Lance tried to defend himself. "And I was probably already tipsy on wine."

"I know," I said abruptly. "I just thought our acquaintance mattered to you in some way, even if it was just as friends. But I know better now. I realised that you were just a selfish ass who wanted to play with my feelings to pass the time until you found another way to entertain yourself." I made to move past him, but he took hold of my upper arms.

"That's not fair. I didn't even know that you wanted me to write. I thought you didn't care."

I didn't want him to say anything that could possibly change the way I felt about him in that moment.

"You're right. It was a very long time ago. And I'm glad you didn't write. It's for the better."

"If that was the case then why are you still upset with me?"

I wanted this to end. I wanted to go back to my rooms and crawl under the covers and wait until I was well enough to leave this damn place and its damn prince.

"Because," I said, pulling myself away from him. "Because it meant nothing to you. Because *I* meant nothing to you."

And with that I finally walked away.

Chapter 31

Gwen

I took a deep breath and steadied myself on the horse.

In hindsight, it might not have been the best idea, but I'd been cooped up in that damned palace for days, and if I did not get out, I was afraid I would go mad somehow.

The weather had been miserable for the past week and today was the first day I could actually see the sun again.

I could walk almost completely normally with the cane but riding a horse was another thing. Then again, I wasn't planning on doing anything drastic. I was simply going to take Bessie for a walk around the palace grounds.

Her hoof had healed nicely over the past few weeks, and she'd looked quite pleased to see me in the stables this morning. Although she was probably more interested in the apple in my hand.

I allowed my foot to dangle out of the stirrup, not wanting to put any extra pressure on it.

All the rain had turned the world into a brown, muddy mess and it was difficult to navigate our way in some places.

My fingers were stiff and cold despite the leather gloves I wore. I longed for spring, with its temperate days and flowers blooming everywhere. There were few things I detested more than the cold.

I wouldn't go as far as the forest, so I made sure to turn Bessie around long before we'd reached the treeline. She seemed to be enjoying the little walk, sometimes stopping to sniff something on the ground.

Though I was not eager to admit it, I would miss her once I returned to Norrandale, something I knew was inevitable now that my injury had mostly healed, and I would be ready to travel soon. I wondered how the others were faring. Had they taken Mistwood ? Had the army arrived? And what of my brother? Had he been taken prisoner? I had a sinking feeling in my chest that whatever was going on at Mistwood, it was not pleasant.

Part of me felt guilty for not being there with the others, but I was a liability with my injury, and so I told myself that I would only leave for Norrandale once King Cai had sent word that it was safe.

As Bessie and I made our way back to the palace, I contemplated using the good weather for some archery practice. There was no range, but surely I could have a servant set up a target of some sort, and there had to be a bow and arrow lying around somewhere.

I wished I'd thought of it sooner, but it was only recently that I had been able to stand on both legs. After all this time that had passed since we'd left Norrandale, I was sure to be out of practice. But it was something to do, to make the time go by.

As the stables came into view, it was impossible to miss the horse galloping towards us, much less its rider and his raven-black hair.

What the hell was Lance doing out here on horseback? He was the last person I'd wanted to talk to, and I figured he knew as much since we had hardly seen anything of each other in the past few days.

I still felt mortified after that conversation and my confession to him. Why had I stupidly blurted out something so humiliating to the Prince of Everness?

Cai had better send news fast, because the sooner I could leave, the better.

"Lady Gwen." He sounded out of breath and even his horse let out a huff.

Prince Lance looked dishevelled, his hair windblown and his cape wrapped around him awkwardly. But his riding breeches clung to his strong thighs, which I'd never noticed until now, or the way his dark jacket fitted him so perfectly.

"Your Highness." I dipped my head in greeting.

"Are you certain you are well enough to be out riding like this? Have you consulted the physician?"

Though the doctor hadn't directly said I could be riding again, he did say I should slowly increase the use of my ankle, exercising it little by little.

"Quite certain, Your Highness. I'm hardly using it at all." I moved my ankle, where it dangled next to the stirrup, as if to prove my point.

"Well, I'm sure Bess is happy to be out and about again." Initially I was uncertain about taking her out now that I knew she was his horse. But she was the only horse in the stable I'd grown accustomed to riding and I didn't want to risk another injury by getting on a different mare or stallion that might be unpredictable.

"I'm glad her hoof is in better condition."

There was a moment of silence between us, Bess having ducked her head to sniff around for any green blades of grass that she could find.

"Are you also out enjoying the weather, Your Highness?" If he said yes, then I could bid him a good morning and be on my way back again. But something in his expression told me I was not going to hear what I wanted to.

"No, I was looking for you, actually."

"How can I be of service, Your Highness?" My grip tightened on the reins.

"Please don't call me that. I think we're well enough acquainted by now that you can call me by my first name."

"You were the one who insisted upon using titles," and then I added, "Your Highness."

"I was just trying to tease you that day. You came into the library and looked so upset upon seeing me that I couldn't help myself." That seemed to be a recurring problem with him, but I didn't say it out loud.

"Is that what you came all this way to tell me, that I should call you by your birth name?"

"No, of course not."

"Then pray tell, Your Highness, what is the reason you have graced me with your presence?" I would not give him the satisfaction of getting what he wanted.

"Enough, Gwen," he said, louder than I'd expected. "It cannot go on like this."

"I see no reason why not." I lifted Bess's head and urged her to start walking again, passing Lance and his horse.

"I'm sorry, all right. Is that what you want from me, an apology?" his voice came from behind.

"No," I called over my shoulder.

"I'm sorry I misread the situation and that you never heard from me again."

"You pressured me for an answer, and I gave you one. That's all. It's in the past now." It was in the past. I had no reason to hold the grudge all these years. In fact, I had pretty much forgotten about him until we arrived in Everness and he'd taken to taunting me so often. If he'd only stayed out of my way, then none of this would have happened.

Lance and his horse had almost caught up to us despite our brisk pace.

"If it's in the past like you say, then why are you still upset about it?"

"I'm not upset," I said too quickly.

Bessie reared her head as Lance suddenly ran his horse in front of us, forcing me to stop.

"It meant something to me too."

"What?" I barked out more harshly than intended.

"I know what you think of me and all the reasons I didn't reach out to you again. But whatever had happened between us on that trip to Norrandale, I liked your company, Gwen, and it was never my intention to hurt you."

"You don't have to explain yourself to me." I shook my head, still pretending not to care.

"Yes, I do," he insisted. "I don't want you to walk through the palace halls avoiding me every day. I'd like for us to be friends."

Well now, there was a sentence I'd never thought I'd hear from the Prince of Everness.

"Friends?" I asked with surprise.

"Yes, you know. When two people are more than mere acquaintances but less than lovers."

"I know what friends means, Lance," I retorted.

"Just checking." He put up his hands slightly defensively. "You didn't seem entirely familiar with the concept is all."

"Don't be facetious." I pressed my leg into Bessie's side, getting her to walk again. "Maybe I'm just surprised that you're capable of having a friendship." It was a mean thing to say. But then again, I hadn't seen anyone around the palace, in all the time I stayed there, come to visit Lance. Nor had I ever heard him refer to anyone as his friend.

"It isn't easy to make true friends as a royal. Not when people only want something from you most of the time."

"You're right," I finally agreed, thinking back to my life at Norrandale and the people I'd left behind. "True friendship at court is a rare thing."

"So, friends then?"

"Very well," I agreed. "Friends." If it meant putting the past entirely behind us and turning over a new leaf, I supposed no serious harm could come from being friends with the Prince of Everness. As long as Lance behaved himself. Which wasn't exactly something I was counting on.

Chapter 32

Elara

My hands were shaking when I stepped through the doors of my room.

After our men had properly taken charge of the palace, I went back to the old rooms I'd stayed in before running to Everness. Everything looked as it had before, apart from a bit of dust gathering here and there and no wood in the fireplace.

I hadn't seen Cai since what happened in the throne room. I needed to find him and make sure he was all right, but I was covered in blood and dirt, and I wanted to get rid of the worst of it before I did anything else.

I'd handed Conner over to one of our guards to make sure he was safe, but I couldn't pull myself away from the fight between Cai and Thatcher. Nor could I unsee the way Cai brutally took Thatcher's life. I couldn't say it was undeserved, but seeing Cai's pain and anger take control of him like that made me realise once again how much of a toll this had all taken on him.

Part of me worried about the way he was filled with blind rage at that moment. How he'd changed into someone I barely recognised.

Was this one of the many reasons Cai dreaded war so much? Because he was afraid of the person it might change him into? Jack had once told me, long ago, that the first war with Argon had changed Cai in ways he never recovered from. I didn't know the Cai he was before Argon, but I didn't want to lose the one I'd come to know in the last few months. What if this war changed all of us in ways we could not imagine? What if we became strangers to ourselves?

All I knew was that I needed to talk to Cai as soon as possible.

My clothes were spattered in blood and my boots covered in dirt from trekking to Mistwood through the muddied earth.

I started by removing my shirt. My arm burned with every movement. Luckily, I'd worn a sleeveless top under my linen shirt to keep me warm. I wouldn't have to get changed before cleaning the wound.

I made my way to the bathing chamber, noticing in the mirror how pale my face looked. The water was cold as I pressed a wet cloth to my skin. At least the bleeding had mostly stopped, but it might still require some stitches. Now I would have a scar on each arm. One from the rebel girl who'd tried to assassinate me in my own throne room a few months earlier, and one from the Argonian soldier today. Not that it mattered much at this point. I was pretty much covered in them anyway.

After rummaging through a few of the drawers, I found a needle and some thread. The cut was at a bit of an awkward angle, so it wasn't going to be very easy.

Before the needle could pierce my skin, there was a knock on the door, and I jumped up from where I'd been sitting on the bed. I hurried over to the door and braced myself before opening it.

Cai stood there with his hair dishevelled, and his pupils still dilated, but he was no longer covered in Thatcher's blood.

"I was just on my way to see you," I said, leaving the door open so that he could step inside. "I just wanted to put on some clean clothes and get all this blood off me." I shuddered again at the memory of stabbing the Argonian soldier.

Cai's eyes travelled to the red gash on my arm. "How's your wound?"

"It's just a scratch." I shrugged it off, picking up the threaded needle once more.

"Shouldn't we call for a physician of some kind? I'm sure one has already been sent for to look after all the men who sustained injuries."

I gave him a look that suggested he should know me better by now.

Cai took a seat next to me on the bed. "Would you let me help you at least?"

Reluctantly I handed him the needle and turned so that he could easily reach the cut on my upper arm.

"I hope you know what you're doing," I muttered under my breath before clenching my jaw as the needle broke through my skin. I'd forgotten how much I disliked this.

"Of course I do. We've done this before, remember?" I did remember. Back at Fairfrith camp after we'd escaped Lance at Woodsbrook I'd had a nasty cut on my leg, which Cai did an impressive job of stitching up.

"I could really use a strong drink right about now," I said, not looking for any particular kind of answer.

"Me too," he said under his breath.

"Are you okay?" I asked carefully, trying not to look as he made the stitches.

"I'm still alive," Cai said without much emotion. "I'm more worried about you."

"I'm fine." Which we both knew was only half the truth. I probably would have been dead had Cai not shown up to save me. Despite my hours of training and sparring with Rhen, my only comparison to this event was the day of the rebellion. I didn't have the kind of training and experience that all the other soldiers and Cai had.

Cai finished stitching the wound and broke off the remaining thread.

"Are you sure you're all right, though? It got pretty intense back there."

"I suppose so, yes." He stood up and looked around the room until he found a piece of bedlinen. I watched him rip the linen into a long bandage before taking a seat next to me again.

"To witness and be part of so much death can have an effect on a person, you know? It's perfectly understandable to be having a hard time right now."

He started to wrap the bandage carefully around my arm.

"Thatcher betrayed you in the worst way possible. I can't imagine what that must have felt like." I suddenly felt like crying and I wasn't even sure why. All the events of the day must have taken their toll on me.

"I'm sorry you had to see it."

True, Cai didn't merely drive a sword through Thatcher but beat him to death and continued beating him after he was no longer alive. I would be lying if I said it wasn't gruesome to watch. But I was more afraid that this would somehow break Cai beyond repair and that I would never get him back.

I placed my hand on his arm. "Cai, I don't care about what happened in the throne room. I just want to make sure you're okay."

He didn't reply, merely looked at the floor, which was answer enough. I slipped my hand into the pocket of my breeches and pulled out Cai's mother's ring.

"I believe this is yours," I said softly, opening his hand so that I could place the ring inside.

Cai looked at the ring in his palm and his eyes slowly started to water. I knew he was seeing her in his mind. The kind and soft-spoken woman who raised him to be the man he was today. Her memory would haunt him for the rest of his life, and I knew he blamed himself for her death. I just wished there was something I could say to him to make him realise that it wasn't his fault.

"It was her wedding ring," he said, his voice a little hoarse. "She loved this ring that my father gave her." He held it up between his fingers. "She never took it off." A single tear rolled down his cheek. "She used to joke that if someone wanted that ring, they would have to pry it off her cold, dead hand."

A sob escaped him, and my heart felt like it was shattering. I used my thumb to wipe the tear from his cheek and pulled him into my embrace. Cai held on to me tightly, and in that moment, I would have done anything if it meant he would stop hurting.

I let him cry on my shoulder, willing to sit there for the rest of the day if it would make him feel better. "I know you miss your mum." I tried to soothe him, rubbing circles on his back. "But I promise you she is looking over you right now and she is proud of the man you are and what you're doing for your kingdom." Cai sobbed against me, and I only pulled him closer.

"I know this will probably be the hardest thing either of us ever has to do." My neck was wet from Cai's tears, but I didn't want to pull away. "But you and I are going to make it through this." I turned my head to press a kiss to his cheek. "Together."

Chapter 33

Cai

I sat with Elara holding me for a few minutes before pulling back and wiping the tears from my face, attempting to pull myself together again.

"I have to go and find Lord Burrow," I said, clearing my throat. "We need to have a discussion about today and our plans for moving forward."

I stood up from the bed and Elara was quick to follow. "Do you really think that's a good idea after everything that has happened today?"

I was already making my way towards her bedroom door, my mind occupied with too many thoughts at once. Today was a big victory and I should have been happy. But there were also losses, and the road that lay ahead of us was still a very long and treacherous one. This was only the beginning. I was an exiled king in the process of reclaiming my throne. But I needed more than a palace and a throne. I needed loyal soldiers and battle plans.

"Maybe you should just take the rest of the day for yourself. All these things can wait till tomorrow."

"It can't wait," I replied, reaching the door. "Every minute we don't do something is a minute that Aries comes closer to destroying us."

I stepped out of her room, thinking about our next steps and of all the things I had to take care of in the upcoming days. The news that we'd reclaimed Mistwood wouldn't take long to reach Aries, and I had no doubts that he would retaliate.

"Cai, you just experienced something horrible and traumatising. You can't just sweep it under the carpet and pretend it didn't happen."

I turned around to face her. "I don't have a choice." I'd spent endless weeks mourning and grieving. But if I didn't refocus all my efforts now, I was going to lose my kingdom. "Kings at war do not have the luxury of falling apart." Something had happened to me in that throne room. It felt as though I'd been woken up from a long and hazy dream. I knew as I sat in Elara's room that it would be the last time I cried for my mother for a while. "I have a responsibility towards Norrandale now."

"And I'm not asking you to shy away from any of your responsibilities," she said. "I'm asking you to look after yourself. To not shut me out again. I want you to confide in me, Cai." I didn't want to shut her out at all. But I had a tunnel vision of my goal, and my personal well-being was not a priority anymore. "Please don't do anything unnecessary."

"Unnecessary?" I asked. "You think me fearing for our lives is unnecessary? You do know you could have died today?"

Even saying the words out loud created an ache in my chest. I could not describe the fear I'd felt when I saw the Argonian guard attack her. Didn't want to consider what might have happened if I'd shown up only a few moments later. Losing her would be a fate worse than death. Did she not understand that?

"Don't you think I know that? And I'm not the only one, Cai. I almost watched you lose your life more than once today."

"Is that why you used the Myrgonite dagger?" The words flew out of my mouth before I could stop them.

"So that's what this is actually about," she said, placing her hands on her hips. "You're upset about that damned stone."

I only noticed then how loud our conversation had grown and that anyone passing at the end of the hallway would be able to hear every word.

There was a parlour a little further down the hall and so I pulled Elara inside.

"Of course I'm upset," I said, closing the door behind me. "You know how dangerous it is."

"He was going to kill you, Cai. Don't pretend you wouldn't have done the same for me."

I thought back to the moment I heard Elara scream. Of course I would have done the same. I would have burned down my kingdom and the rest of the world along with it if it meant saving her life.

I should have told her as much. I wanted to. But then I thought back to all the things we'd read about Queen Riona and what the magic had done to her. We were messing with something we didn't understand and I feared the consequences. "We shouldn't be carrying that thing around in the first place."

"Where else did you want me to put it? It wasn't safe to leave at the camp. Or would you rather I'd have left it back in Everness for Lance to find and use as he pleases?"

It was a valid question. We'd been so focused on finding all of the objects, but we hadn't decided where to hide the two we'd already found as we looked for the third. Not to mention we still needed to find a way to destroy them without killing anyone.

"Where's the necklace?"

"I left it with Anesta. She doesn't know what it is, but I know she will keep it safe along with my other things, and I didn't want to keep the two objects together in case someone should find them." It was probably the smarter thing to do but that didn't put me at ease in any way.

"Maybe we shouldn't have Rhen working on the diary anymore. He already knows too much."

"You don't trust him?"

"It's not that. The more people know about this, the more dangerous it becomes. And even if we find the third object, we don't know how to destroy them yet."

"Rhen has a much better knowledge and understanding of Evernean history. He's the right person to do this and I asked him to help for a reason. You and I are too busy gathering armies against Aries. Our first objective is preparing for the battle we know is to come," she argued.

"Rhen already knows what two of the objects are. That's dangerous information, the kind that some people would kill for. If Aries should find out in any way, who's to say he won't take Rhen hostage and torture him until he tells Aries everything he wants to know?"

"Rhen would rather die than betray us."

"And is that the kind of sacrifice you're willing to make?" The words sank in and momentarily silenced her.

"Maybe I should take the dagger." I held out my hand and Elara looked up at me as if I'd just lost my mind.

"What?"

"The Myrgonite dagger. I need you to give it to me so I can put it somewhere safe."

She looked taken aback. "You don't trust me with it?"

"No, I think it's dangerous and it needs to be hidden. We'll have to find somewhere for the necklace as well. At least until we figure out what the third object is."

Elara pressed her lips into a line, clearly reluctant.

I could not forget her facial expression as she drove the dagger into the Argonian. I imagined it was quite similar to mine when I'd killed Thatcher. Whatever kind of magic that stone held, it was a dangerous weapon. It was already starting to have some kind of effect on us.

"We're going up against one of the greatest armies on the continent, Cai. We are at every disadvantage, and we have very little time."

"I know that," I said, clenching my teeth. "But there were other weapons in that hallway. You should not have used the dagger." *You don't know what the cost might be.*

"I killed someone for you!" she cried out. "And you're angry about what weapon I used to save your life?"

"Did you not see what happened in the throne room? Did you not see what I did? Something, some force that is bigger than us, has more power than we realise, and if we're not careful, it could be the end of everything you and I hold dear. It's not worth it!"

She continued to stare up at me, contemplating my words. "Please just give me the dagger," I asked again, hoping that she could understand. I was just trying to protect everyone.

"After everything we've been through, I'd think you'd trust me better."

It was intended to be hurtful, and she'd managed to hit her mark.

"You and I have been carrying the Myrgonite objects around with us for a very long time. I have no doubt that the stones protected us at times and we did not even realise. But magic requires balance, and we don't know the price."

She didn't answer me, simply shook her head in dismay and walked out of the room.

We had been in so many life-threatening situations since we'd met, and yet, in many ways, it appeared as if luck was on our side. At the very least, we always walked out alive. But for everything the stones gave, they were going to take, too.

And I had a sickening feeling that it was time to pay up.

Chapter 34

Gwen

A gust of wind blew one of the windows in my bedroom shut and I jumped a little in my seat.

I'd been sitting next to the fire, trying to write a letter to my family, but after many failed attempts, it seemed futile.

This morning, a messenger arrived with a letter from Cai. He said that they'd won back Mistwood Palace and that war plans were in progress as they gathered more men. He didn't say anything about Thatcher, which disappointed me a little, though I wasn't entirely sure why. What my brother had done was unforgiveable. And yet, I still wanted to know.

I could go back to Norrandale if the weather allowed, something which wasn't looking very promising at the moment, not to mention the impending war. Norrandale was no longer my sanctuary, but Everness was not my home, and I felt torn. From where I sat, I could see grey clouds gathering in the distance, and every room in the palace felt cold despite having all the fireplaces lit.

According to news from Mistwood, my parents had gone into hiding after what Thatcher did.

Either they were humiliated by his betrayal or they feared for their own lives. Perhaps both.

I thought that maybe I could send a letter to our estate, hoping they would eventually get it, but once I actually started to write, the words would not come to me.

I scrunched up the piece of paper and tossed it into the fire. Writing letters would have to wait.

It would be evening soon, and I needed some new reading material for dinner. Despite our newfound friendship, I hadn't been seeing Lance around the dinner table much. But, according to a servant, he'd been spending most of his time in Eloisa's room, which was entirely understandable with her declining health. Not that I minded my own company at all. A slight pitter-patter sang against the window. Lovely, now it was raining too.

I got up and left my rooms, heading in the direction of the library. With the high ceilings of the palace, it was difficult to hear the rain on the roof, but the world outside the windows I passed was grey and dreary, growing ever darker.

I walked slowly, still trying to be careful of my ankle, when I heard a cry in the distance. As I rounded the corner, I saw a figure, glass bottle in hand, before he suddenly turned and threw the bottle against the wall. Glass shattered everywhere, the amber liquid spilling across the floor.

Lance hadn't noticed my presence at the end of the hallway. He leaned back against the wall and slid down to the floor with his head in his hands.

Whatever was going on, this was a deeply personal moment, and I was intruding. I doubted Lance would want me to see this, and yet, as I turned to leave, I heard the soft muffles of him crying and my gut twisted into knots.

Something was clearly very wrong if he was in such a state. If it had been anyone else, I would have rushed over without a thought and tried to comfort them.

But this was Lance.

I had no idea how to react.

I shifted my weight and the damned wooden floor creaked. Lance's eyes shot straight in my direction. He looked surprised and anguished all at once.

"Are you all right?" I managed to croak out.

I started to approach, though carefully. He might still chase me away, not wanting to be seen in such a state.

Lance's head hung low. As I reached him, he looked up, his eyes bloodshot from crying.

"She's dead," he said softly. "Eloisa's dead."

The youngest Evernean princess, with an illness of the mind, had always been hidden from the world. I had no idea what her and Lance's relationship was like, but based on how much time he'd been spending sitting by her bed the last few weeks, it was clear he had cared for her in some way. Not to mention his current reaction on her passing.

"I'm so sorry." I crouched down so that I could be at his level, broken glass crunching under my shoes. "Was she in a lot of pain?"

He shook his head, looking down at the floor.

"The physician said she shouldn't really have felt anything, she was in such a deep sleep by then."

I didn't know entirely what to say. Didn't know how to give my condolences.

"I'm really sorry, Lance." I wished I could say I understood but our circumstances were vastly different when it came to our siblings.

"She was the last of my family. Now I have no one left." His mother had died when he was a little boy, his father only a few months ago, and now his younger sister.

"You still have Elara." I gently placed my hand on his bent knee.

"Please," Lance said, wiping a rebellious tear from his cheek as if he'd not been crying. "She wouldn't give a damn if I died, just like the rest of you."

"That's not true. You may not be Elara's favourite person in the world, but I know she doesn't want you to die. Even though she would probably never admit it, I think that deep down she cares for you in a way she cannot necessarily explain. If she didn't, then you would still be in prison."

"After everything I've done, I wouldn't be surprised if she hated me. She has every right to. I'm selfish and reckless and I know it."

Well, at least he was self-aware. That had to count for something, right?

"Sometimes we care for the people we are bound to by blood, even when we shouldn't." I wasn't sure if I was referring to him and Elara or me and Thatcher.

"Well, she is a much better ruler than I could ever be."

"Eh." I shrugged, trying to make light of the situation. "Nobody's perfect."

He tried to push himself up but let out a hiss as some of the shattered glass pressed into his skin.

"Did it cut you?"

Without waiting for him to respond, I pulled his hand towards me. It was a very small cut, and I could easily pick out the glass.

"What a waste," he murmured, giving another sniff. "That was a damned good bottle of whisky."

I couldn't help but let out a snort as I made sure there was no more glass in his hand. I felt Lance's eyes linger on me. For some reason, it made my stomach flutter.

"There, it should be fine." I let go of his hand, which had a small trace of blood left on it but nothing serious.

Lance rubbed his face with his good hand. His eyes were still red from crying, and I could tell he was holding back a little. Perhaps he needed privacy to cry by himself. I wouldn't blame him. His sister had just died.

A loud booming noise erupted from outside.

"Thunder," I noted. "It seems like there is a bit of a storm coming."

"Mmhh," Lance agreed absentmindedly. We sat in silence for a few moments before the thunder sounded again.

I looked out of the nearest window as movement from outside caught my eye.

"The horses," I said. "The horses are still in the paddock."

Lance's eyes grew wide, and he shot up into a standing position.

"They'll never get them all in in time," I continued without hesitation, already on the move. Lance and I hurried through the palace until we reached the door that would lead us to the stables and paddocks. Before we could open the door, a strong gust of wind blew it open, the curtains flapping about.

Outside, it was now pouring rain, the sky completely covered with a dark grey blanket.

"You should stay inside. You can't go out in this weather." To tell me that I couldn't do something was probably the surest way to get me to do it.

"Like hell I can't." I was out of the door before he could stop me. The royal stables had many horses, so it would take a while to get them all inside, even if we took two at a time. When we reached the paddock, the servants were already at work while the stable master's voice was carried away by the wind as he tried to give orders.

There was another crack of thunder and one of the horses took fright and reared. Without intending to do so, I looked for Bessie. I found her in the field furthest from the stables, calling to one of the other horses that was being led away by the stable boy. Poor thing, she probably didn't want to be left alone there.

I made my way over to her as Lance grabbed some rope and took hold of one of the other horses.

I pulled her leather halter over her nose, but it took me a minute because she was tossing her head so much. "Come on, girl," I pleaded with her. "I'm trying to help you." Eventually I managed to lead her to her stable, both of us soaked to the bone. I made sure to close her stall door tightly. She seemed a little more at ease now that she was next to her friend.

I was back outside quickly, trying not to shudder at the loud thunder. Lightning flashed close by.

The problem with horses was that they were herd animals and if one was frightened, it got all the others worked up. Lance had a horse in each hand, walking past me as I made my way to the nearest stallion. Not bothering to search for other halters, I took Bessie's and slipped it over his head before we made our way to the stable. My ankle was starting to hurt from all the quick walking, but I didn't care.

"Where is Windchaser and his mother?" I asked with concern, noting that I hadn't seen them yet.

"Don't worry, they were the first to be taken to the stables. They're all tucked in, warm and cosy," he assured me.

There was another flash of lightning. It was getting closer.

The stable boy and the servants brought in four more horses. "That's all of them, Your Highness."

"Thank you. I think we'd all best get inside." Nobody had to ask me twice. Now that I was certain all the horses were safe and warm, I wanted to hurry myself to a fire as quickly as possible.

Lance walked ahead of me, and I ran to catch up with him, but pain shot through my ankle. That was what I got for running around the palace grounds in the rain.

I tried to step on my injured foot but only managed to let out a cry of discomfort as I attempted to walk. The sound made Lance look over his shoulder.

Before either of us could move any further, there was an earth-shattering sound next to me. Lightning struck a nearby tree, breaking the trunk. I braced myself in case it was going to fall my way but luckily, because of the way the lightning had struck, it missed me.

And then Lance was there, and before I could protest, he had picked me up in his arms.

"What are you doing?"

"Preventing you from getting yourself killed." The rain was so heavy now that I could barely see a few feet in front of us.

There was another loud crack of thunder, and I jumped a little in Lance's arms.

He carried me inside and put me down in the nearest room, which happened to be the library.

Both of us were completely soaked. My hair and clothes felt heavy with all the water.

Lance had placed me right in front of the fireplace and I scooted closer, hoping to feel more warmth. My entire body shivered so much, even my teeth clattered.

I watched Lance remove his jacket and then his shirt, draping them over a nearby chair. His stomach muscles were more defined than I would have imagined for someone who so frequently gazed upon the bottom of a bottle. I looked away, clearing my throat.

Lance added a few more logs to the fire, the flames surging in the hearth.

"You shouldn't have gone out in that weather." His voice carried the tone of *I told you so*.

"You don't know me at all if you think I'm going to leave horses out in a storm like that."

"You've probably made your injury worse now." My ankle did hurt a little, but I wasn't going to give him the satisfaction of agreeing with him.

"Here, let me look at it."

"My ankle is quite fine, thank you." I moved it as if to prove my point and then flinched in pain.

"Why do you always have to be so stubborn?"

He got on his knees and started to undo the lacings of my shoe, which was covered with mud and soaked from the rain. I couldn't move away unless I kicked him, which, though it would have given me pleasure, didn't feel like the kind thing to do now that we'd agreed to be friends.

He quickly pulled off my stocking, appearing very focused on the task at hand. When his cold hands touched my ankle, a shiver went through me, which I blamed on the fact that my clothes were wet all the way through to my shift.

Lance carefully inspected my ankle, fingers delicately tracing over my skin.

"It's a little swollen but it should be fine."

"See." I pulled my foot away. "Told you it was fine."

"You could be lying on the ground, bleeding to death, and you'd probably still say you were fine just to spite me."

I gave him a look that suggested I was annoyed but that he wasn't wrong.

"You're shaking. We need to get you out of those wet clothes."

"Ha." I barked out a laugh. "And how many girls have fallen for that one? Plenty, probably, is my guess."

"Fine, die of the cold. What do I care?"

I was shaking. And my wet hair wasn't much help.

"Do you think you could get me a towel?" And then after a second, I added, "Please?" The servants were running about the palace, closing windows and curtains making sure all the rooms were lit and warm. No one had seen us as we came in through the garden door.

I could see that Lance was burning to make some kind of comment about the towel, but he was smart enough to simply get up and leave the room in search of one.

I started by removing my other shoe and stocking, my feet absolutely frozen.

The dress was a little more complicated. The outer skirt I could loosen and slowly wriggle out of, and the top of my dress was easy enough to undo at the front. Then there was another skirt for warmth. I tossed all the layers on the ground, already feeling better now that the icy material was no longer sticking to me. The corset was a different problem.

The library doors opened and closed, with Lance carrying the much-needed towel.

I was surprised that he did not bring one for himself, as droplets of rain were still on his face, tendrils of his dark hair sticking to his forehead.

"Thank you." I immediately went about pressing my hair with the towel, trying to remove as much of the water as possible. I longed for a hot bath and the warmth of my bed. Thunder rattled the windows, and I winced a little.

"Not a big fan, are you?"

"I'm not overly fond of the loud noise and deadly lightning, no."

I reached behind me to start undoing my corset, but it was laced all the way up my back, and I could only reach so far. Perhaps I should have gone up to my room to undress and change, but something kept me in front of the fire, with him.

"Need some help with that?"

"No."

He continued to stare at me, challenging me to admit defeat.

"Yes," I sighed. I would have been happy to leave the corset as it was had it not been for the fact that it was also soaked through. I was so tired of this wretched weather.

Lance took a seat behind me, moving my hair so that it lay over one shoulder. He must have seen my hesitation as he started to undo the knot of the corset strings.

"Don't tell me I'm the first man to take off your corset too." It was intended to be a joke, but I had no idea how to respond. A slightly awkward silence fell over the room. The fact that I didn't immediately laugh it off with denial caused Lance to curse under his breath. Every second felt like an eternity as he pulled at the strings.

Despite the pouring rain and rolling thunder, the room suddenly felt too quiet, the air too dense. A tension hung in the atmosphere, though I struggled to identify why. Most likely because of our some-what compromising position. If Mother had seen me like this, she would have had a complete and utter fit. In fact, the knowledge alone would be enough to put her to bed rest for at least a week. Maybe she would have been right.

Despite it being a merely circumstantial matter, I had no business sitting on a library floor with the Prince of Everness while he was unlacing my corset.

I felt his hands through the material of my shift as Lance loosened every string one by one. Perhaps I was only imagining it, but it felt as though his breathing quickened. I could feel it against the back of my neck. His breath was warm against my cold skin.

When the corset was finally undone, I pulled it off and wrapped the towel around my shoulders to better cover myself.

"Is your ankle still in pain?" Lance shifted so that he was facing me again.

"Not much." Maybe I was simply too cold to feel the pain.

"Still, you should probably keep it elevated." Before I could offer any comment, he'd pulled a pillow off one of the nearby chairs and propped my ankle on it.

"Why are you being so nice to me?" I muttered, unsure what to make of all his kind acts.

"We're friends, aren't we?" he said it softly, gazing into the hearth as the flames created a warm glow about the room.

"Yes, we're friends." Still, I was seeing a different side to him from the cruel, partying prince with his lack of empathy and responsibility. I mean, it was still there, but underneath it all, there was more to him. It reminded me of the boy I had met in Norrandale all those years ago. Someone I thought was long gone.

His lashes were coated with water as he stared into the fire. It took me a moment to realise that it wasn't just the rain, but that Lance was crying again, given away by the fact that a tear escaped his eye, which he quickly wiped away.

Now that the adrenaline rush of getting everyone and everything safely inside was over, the undeniable truth had settled over him again, covering him in his grief. Eloisa was still dead, and nothing was going to change that.

"We'll make sure she gets a proper burial in the family crypt, even if everyone else isn't here," I reassured him. We'd have to send a messenger to Norrandale with word of the princess's death as soon as possible. Queen Elara needed to know too.

"So few people truly knew her." His forehead crinkled a little, forming a frown. "Father wanted it that way."

"I'm sorry I didn't get to know her better." It felt like the right thing to say.

"I think she would have liked you." For some reason the words made me smile, until I saw Lance's expression, as if he were mentally wrestling with himself.

"It's all right to mourn her, you know? You *should* feel sad, you should cry and scream and throw bottles if that's what you want." I couldn't even begin to say how much I'd wanted to do all of that since news had reached me of Thatcher's betrayal. But I didn't let any of it out. Didn't want to feel like more of a burden.

"I suppose. Though I don't know how I feel about having an audience." I was right about Lance not wanting to show his pain to anyone. And I could understand and respect that.

"You mean you've never let anyone else see you cry?"

"I don't make a habit of it, no," he said through his teeth.

"Good to know I was your first then." I wiggled my eyebrows slightly suggestively, making a joke about the fact that he had taken two of my firsts. Something I struggled to be mad about now.

Lance's gaze softened a little as he gave me a side-eye but there was still much sadness lingering behind his gaze.

"I could leave if you like. I should probably retire to my rooms anyway." Putting on some dry and clean clothes sounded like the best thing in the world.

"No, it's all right. I'd like for you to stay."

I moved, while being careful with my ankle, and took a seat next to him so that our shoulders touched as we sat in front of the fire.

"Then I'll stay."

We both stared into the burning flames until Lance spoke up again. "Tell me something to take my mind off everything."

He didn't move his arm away from mine and, somehow, I found myself enjoying the feeling of being this close to him.

"You mean like a story?"

"My mother used to tell me stories before I went to sleep. I only remember some of them. But I used to love listening to the sound of her voice." He looked at me then, with the saddest smile I'd ever seen a boy wear. "Tell me a story, Gwen."

"Okay," I said hesitantly, feeling a bit of pressure at having to live up to the old queen's stories. This was the second time Lance had told me of his mother. He was only a little boy when she died but it had clearly left its mark on him. I could tell by the way he spoke of her that they were close.

"Oh, wait, I have one." I readjusted myself and pulled the towel a little tighter around my shoulders.

"When I was very young, probably four or five, Thatcher and I were playing outside one day. It was one of the few times our family stayed at the country estate to get a little break from court. The estate was surrounded by hills, especially this one really big one. Thatcher had dared me to roll down the hill from the highest point, all the way to the bottom. It was a long way down and I knew I probably shouldn't do it."

"I'm assuming you did anyway," Lance interrupted.

"Thatcher said I was too scared, and I was going to prove him wrong."

The corner of Lance's mouth curled up. "Of course you were."

"So anyway, I rolled down the hill until I felt completely sick. But that wasn't the worst of it. I'd knocked my head really hard on the way down and it wouldn't stop aching. Probably gave myself a concussion."

That made Lance snort.

"But as I lay there at the bottom the hill, in a lot of pain, I found myself in a patch of wild mariposa lilies. They were so bright and beautiful, and I decided then and there that they would be my favourite flower. Whenever they were in bloom, I would go and cut some and put them in a vase in my room. Especially when I was feeling sad. Mariposa lilies always made me feel better."

"And what was your brother doing during all of this?" Lance asked.

"Oh, you know Thatch." I shrugged. "He was standing at the top of the hill, laughing his head off as I tumbled down."

"Bastard."

"I should have seen him back then for what he was." I spent most of my days trying not to think too much about my brother or what he did, for my own sanity. But despite being a kingdom away, it was like he was following me everywhere. Lingering in my thoughts like an unwanted ghost.

"Your brother doesn't deserve you," Lance said in a more serious tone. "He shouldn't have done what he did anyway, but he especially shouldn't have done it because of you." Because of what it would do to me. How much Thatcher's betrayal would hurt me.

"Yeah, he shouldn't have," I replied softly, feeling a new wave of grief wash over me for the brother I no longer knew. "But he did it anyway."

"If it makes you feel any better," Lance looked at me, "I never liked him." It was a poor attempt at cheering me up, but I appreciated the effort.

"Not even when you first met him?"

"You mean on that trip I took to Norrandale with my father?"

I nodded.

"I remember him following Cai around like some kind of lost puppy. But apart from that I don't remember much."

"Oh I know that."

He gave me a look. "I do remember kissing you, Gwen."

"Really?" I faked surprise. "I'm surprised you do."

"We've had this conversation before." Yes, we had. And he'd told me it meant something to him too, but what exactly, I didn't know.

"Not that it matters," I said a little dramatically. "It wasn't that good a kiss anyway."

"Now I know you're lying."

"Am not," I insisted. "Why? Has no one ever told you that you have mediocre kissing skills, Prince?"

He ran his tongue across his teeth, drawing my attention to his mouth.

"No." He tried to hide a grin. "They have not."

"Well, good thing I told you, then. Since we're friends and all, I suppose it is now my responsibility to keep you humble and so forth. Can't have you walking around with any delusions about yourself."

His mouth fell slightly open, and I couldn't say I didn't relish the fact that I'd caught him off guard at least a little bit.

Lance's eyes narrowed. "If it was such a bad kiss, then why did it have you swooning over me for months after?"

Oh, I'd walked right into that one, hadn't I?

"I didn't say it was bad, I said it was mediocre," I corrected him, though still not entirely helping myself.

"Then why'd you hold a grudge for literal years?"

I needed to change the subject fast, before I made a fool of myself.

"You're so full of it," I replied with derision.

"Oh, am I?" Lance asked with a mocking tone, looking down into my eyes. He clearly enjoyed teasing me and some part of me enjoyed the attention.

"Yes," I replied. "You most definitely are."

His face was closer now and I didn't dare break the eye contact and give him the upper hand. I didn't want to let him know that despite everything, despite all the years, he still got to me.

"Then you must not be doing a very good job of humbling me, after all." His gaze travelled to my lips and then back up to my eyes.

"Well, your ego is so big, it's going to take a while to bring you back down to earth."

Lance was so close to me now that we practically shared a breath. I could feel my heart beating in anxious anticipation.

"Gwen." He tucked a strand of hair behind my ear. I forgot how to breathe.

"Yes?"

"Tell me if this is mediocre."

And then his lips were on mine.

Lance kissed me slowly but with certainty. Like he meant it. Like he'd been thinking about doing it for some time now. I didn't pull back, even though I knew I should. Nothing good could come from kissing the Prince of Everness. And yet …

I savoured the feeling of his mouth moving against mine. It was like the first drop of rain after an endless drought. Something I didn't realise I craved until I had a taste. And now I wanted more.

Lance's hand cupped my jaw, tilting my head so that he could kiss me even harder. The world around us disappeared, and there was only me and Lance in the library and the scent of him, which reminded me of Norrandale on an icy winter morning combined with something minty.

I placed my hand on his wrist, and he hesitated for a moment as if he thought I was going to pull away from him, but on the contrary, I wanted him closer. Yet I was out of my mind with fear. Was this only happening because we were trying to distract ourselves from our grief? Were we placeholders until something better came along to fill the void? I didn't want to consider it.

The kiss grew more urgent, as if neither of us could afford to take our time anymore. The string between us had been pulled taut until it finally snapped, and I feared I might drown in this moment and in him.

Lance breathed something that sounded like my name when thunder suddenly rumbled outside. The noise was loud enough that the windows rattled, and it caused us both to jump.

I tried to catch my breath while my mind slipped back to reality.

"I really hate the thunder," I muttered, brushing my hair away from my face. My cheeks were flushed, and I felt both hot and freezing all over my body.

"Come on." Lance stood up, looking a little dazed himself. "I'll help you to your rooms." He pulled me into a standing position.

This was a bad idea. As much as I'd enjoyed kissing Lance, I knew it couldn't happen again. I didn't want to be another one of Lance's games. Both of us had too many things that we needed to deal with. And most of all, I didn't want to give him the opportunity to break my heart.

Chapter 35

Elara

"I don't know what to do."

I paced up and down my rooms, rubbing my hands together to keep my fingers from freezing.

"What do you mean, Your Majesty?" Anesta was sitting in a chair close to the fire. I'd invited her to join me for dinner, hoping that her company would bring me ease. I had picked at my plate for a few minutes while Anesta ate but grew too sick to my stomach to finish the meal. Not after everything that had happened today.

"I'm talking about Cai and how he is being completely irrational and paranoid."

Each footstep sounded loudly on the hardwood floors, and I realised I had yet to change out of my dirtied clothes and boots. I was deep in thought when I returned to my rooms, mentally going over my conversation with Cai. Wondering how everything between us had gone so wrong so quickly. He'd wanted me to give back the Myrgonite dagger, not trusting me to keep it safe.

The woollen vest was no longer doing enough to keep me

warm despite the fire, and my muddy boots were leaving traces of dirt everywhere.

"I see, Your Majesty," Anesta said diplomatically.

I kicked off my boots and started looking through my trunk of clothes for something clean to wear. Our trunks had arrived a few hours ago, the palace quickly settling back into its previous state. With the exception of all the court members being replaced by soldiers, of course.

"I have been Queen of Everness longer than he has been King of Norrandale, if you want to be technical about it, and he still treats me like I'm an infant who knows nothing and is likely to cause our doom because of it."

As I said the words out loud, I realised what was behind my frustration. After everything we'd been through, it felt as though Cai had no faith in me. Not as a ruler and not even as a betrothed. I wanted to understand his reasoning, to see his perspective, but I could not comprehend this irrational behaviour of his.

I scrubbed at my face and neck, removing any trace of dirt or blood, as if I could wash away the day's events along with it.

"Maybe His Majesty is only having a bad reaction after everything that has happened today. It might have brought back a lot of bad memories for him."

"That doesn't excuse his behaviour." I wished I could tell her about the dagger and how Cai had insisted I give it back to him. But it was better to keep Anesta out of it as much as possible. If Cai was right about one thing, it was that the more people knew about the Myrgonite objects, the more dangerous it was for all of us.

"Then again, I don't think I'll ever be able to unsee it. To forget what he did to Thatcher." I dropped onto the bed, my body aching all over. I desperately needed a good night's rest.

"I heard it was pretty bad."

"Thatcher deserved it. I know he did." I reconsidered Anesta's words and my conversation with Cai. Maybe I was overreacting. Maybe we both were. And even if I was a little upset with him, I still worried about him.

"I'm quite relieved that I don't have to be part of the fighting," Anesta admitted. "Though as the queen of Everness and future queen of Norrandale, you ought to be careful as well, Your Majesty."

"Don't you get started on me too, Anesta."

Her mouth curved into a slight smile, but it didn't meet her eyes. "Maybe His Majesty isn't being entirely paranoid. If you get killed, who is going to rule Everness? The kingdom cannot afford to lose you."

"Nobody is going to lose me," I assured her, "I'm tougher than I look."

Anesta took a seat on the bed next to me. "You're the toughest person I know, that's for sure."

I gave her a hug from the side. "Thanks for believing in me. And for everything you do all the time. I know I don't thank you enough."

"Of course, Your Majesty. You have given me one of the highest positions at court. I could never repay you for that."

"I don't expect you to repay me at all. Having you as my friend is more than enough."

There was a knock at the door and Anesta quickly jumped up from the bed to answer.

I heard her speak to one of the servants for a moment before she turned around with a piece of paper in her hands.

"A letter for you, Your Majesty. It's from Everness."

I shot up from the bed, grabbing the envelope.

"It's definitely Lance's handwriting." I could easily recognise it by now, and it was accompanied by the royal seal. I ripped open the paper and began to scan through his words.

"What's the matter, Your Majesty?" Anesta asked, reading my expression. "Is something wrong?"

"It's the princess." I swallowed hard. "She's dead."

Chapter 36

Lance

I took a bite of my pastry, glad that I'd requested the cook make something savoury instead of some chocolaty doughy business. I was in a hurry to get to Gwen's rooms, but my rumbling stomach had to be prioritised. It was the first day of relatively pleasant weather after many days of rain and storms. I thought it would be a good idea to go out for a ride.

I'd enquired with the stable boy and he informed me Gwen had been spending some time down at the stables again. Apparently, Windchaser was growing quite fond of her because of all the carrots and sugar cubes she'd been feeding him.

When I knocked on her door, nobody responded. I wondered if she was inside and simply didn't want to see me. I knew she wasn't in the library or the dining room as I'd made sure to check both places on my way from the kitchens.

"Gwen," I called out. "Are you there?" Still there was no response.

I reached for the door handle, fearing she was purposely avoiding me. Perhaps it was ungentlemanly to burst into a lady's room, but I didn't care if Gwen didn't want to see me. I couldn't go back to the way things were before, with her ignoring me again.

Her bedroom door opened with a squeak, but I found the room void of life. I couldn't see her cloak or riding boots anywhere. Maybe I was too late, and she'd already gone out riding. I could always try to catch up with her, but I had no idea in which direction she'd gone. Last time I went riding after Gwen, it took me more than an hour to find her.

I found a servant cleaning in one of the hallways.

"Have you perhaps seen Lady Gwen anywhere?"

"Your Highness." The girl did a quick bow. "I believe I saw her making her way towards the stables." I was right. She'd used the opportunity of the fine weather to get some fresh air. *Great minds think alike, I suppose.*

"And was that long ago?"

"Not at all, Your Highness." The girl shook her head. "It was only a few minutes ago." She couldn't be very far, then. If I was quick, I might still catch her on her way out. I hurried down to the stable yard, beyond which the horses grazed in their paddocks. After all the rain, there were many large patches of mud. I would have to remind the grooms to keep an eye on the horses' hooves so that they didn't get infected.

"Your Highness." The stable boy was in the midst of cleaning some tack. He looked a little surprised to see me.

"I'm looking for Lady Gwen. Has she gone out already?"

"She has gone out, Your Highness," he confirmed, with a bit of a stutter. "But I don't think she's coming back."

"What do you mean, she's not coming back?"

"She, uh." He hesitated. "I overheard her talking to Bessie as she was tacking up. She mentioned something about Norrandale, and she had a satchel with her, which looked quite full."

I didn't respond to him. I merely ran out of the stables as fast as my legs could carry me. She couldn't be gone. She just couldn't be.

A flash of her light hair, which glinted with a bit of red in the sun, came into view. She stood in the courtyard with a servant who held on to Bessie as Gwen fastened her cloak.

"Have you gone mad?" I called out loud enough for Bessie to get a bit of a fright. Gwen looked up with surprise.

"Lance. What are you doing here?"

"What am I doing here? Why are you stealing my horse and leaving for Norrandale without so much as a word?" I didn't know if I was angry or sad or both.

"I'm not stealing your horse, I'm just borrowing her." Gwen corrected me. "And I was going to say goodbye."

"When?" I asked with exasperation.

"Well." She looked down at the ground, somewhat ashamed. "I left a letter with one of your servants. I'm guessing it's probably in your room somewhere."

"You were going to say goodbye in a letter? After you hated me for years because of what happened in Norrandale. Now who's the hypocrite?"

"That was different."

"How was that different?"

Gwen looked away with a sigh. "I just didn't know how to say goodbye, all right?"

Something in her tone softened the anger inside me.

"It's the middle of winter. You don't know the way. You'll die out there."

"I've made the journey once before. And the weather has finally turned enough for me to travel. I can't wait any longer."

"What about your things?" I asked. "You hardly have anything with you."

"I'll send for them once I've arrived at Mistwood."

This girl was insane.

She took the reins from the servant, and I grabbed them from her.

"Go and fetch my carriage." The servant boy gave a silent bow and scurried off.

"Lance, what are you doing?" Gwen turned to face me with a scowl.

"I'm coming with you," I said with determination.

"You can't come with me to Norrandale."

"Well, I can't send a group of guards with you. I need every able-bodied man here to protect the palace in case things go awry with Argon."

"That's exactly why you need to stay," Gwen argued.

"I'll have the council summoned again. They will keep things under control until I can return." With war on the rise, I knew I was not the right person to protect this kingdom. Even if I cared about the monarchy and our family line. This was Elara's battle.

But the thought of living in the Palace of Levernia on my own again … Before I knew Elara was still alive or any of this stuff happened, I was used to Eloisa spending much time in the country, my father always being occupied in his study before he got ill, and the little company I had were the few people who lived, on and off, at court. None of them were truly my friends in any sort of sense, as any time they spent with me was because I was the heir to the throne and then, for a short time, their monarch. And then Elara was there with a small army of people who all cared about her. They were noisy and often a little obnoxious, but they looked after each other, and even though I couldn't particularly say I liked all of them, I'd grown accustomed to their presence.

And then they all left, and it was quiet again. Except for Gwen. Even if she was often ignoring me, at least she was there. I couldn't go back to the way it was before. I wouldn't.

"I won't let you go alone, Gwen." I stared her down as she looked into my eyes with equal determination.

After a few moments of bitter silence, she finally conceded.

"Fine, I guess you can tag along."

The earth crunched under the wheels of the carriage, every bump and rock causing it to sway a little. Gwen had her cloak wrapped around her like a blanket as she looked out of the carriage window. I couldn't help but watch her from the opposite seat. Her expression was full of worry.

Her brother was a traitor, her kingdom was under attack and her family was hiding out somewhere with no way of reaching her. I realised then how alone she must have been feeling. Something which I, unfortunately, identified with very well.

"Here." I held out the small flask to her.

She looked at me with her nose slightly turned up. "No thank you."

"It's not what you think it is and you're practically shivering. This will help to warm you up a little." When she didn't respond, I added, for my own personal amusement, "Unless you'd rather have me warm you up."

I'd never seen anyone grab a flask so quickly. She tilted her head back, gulping down a big sip. Her surprised expression as she swallowed the tea I'd put in the flask was quite amusing.

"It's tea." She handed back the flask. "I thought you didn't really like tea."

"I don't," I replied, taking a sip for myself, and I immediately felt a little bit warmer. "But you do."

She looked uncertain but her eyes remained on me.

"Are you looking forward to going back to Mistwood?" It was truly none of my business, but I did find myself curious. It was still her home, after all, even if her family was no longer there.

"I don't know." She shrugged. "I'd never left Norrandale before. I didn't know anything apart from Mistwood and our country estate. And now ..." Gwen let out a sigh heavy with sadness. "Now I don't think it will ever be the same again. I feel as though I'm returning to a strange place that I no longer recognise."

"And what about your brother?" Family was a complicated thing. I didn't know a family dynamic that wasn't problematic. But even though I didn't like Thatcher during his stay at Levernia, from my understanding they were quite close, even if they often bickered like little children.

"Well, if we're going to start talking about that then I'm going to need something stronger than that." She pointed to the flask in my hand.

"That bad?" I held out the flask to her and our fingers brushed as she took it from me, her skin warm against mine despite the cool temperature outside.

"You know what he did," she responded rhetorically.

"He's still your brother. You're still allowed to love him. Even if you're angry."

She contemplated my words. "I don't know what I feel for him. Don't know where he is or if he's even alive. Cai didn't mention anything about Thatcher in his letter."

"Do you think Cai would hurt him? He was his best friend."

"Thatcher killed the queen mother," she said sorrowfully. As if it brought her pain merely to say the words out loud. "Cai's never going to forgive him for that." She took a sip from the flask. "And I don't know if I can either."

I didn't know how to respond or what words of comfort might be appropriate. The word *comfort* wasn't exactly part of my father's vocabulary.

I peered out of the carriage window, watching the light as it slowly diminished.

"It will be dusk soon. I think we'll stop at the next town and find some accommodation for the evening if that suits you."

Gwen nodded but her mind was clearly someplace else. She didn't return my flask, and I didn't ask for it back.

Chapter 37

Gwen

The carriage rolled along the forest road as the afternoon sun slowly began to set. The air was already starting to feel colder, and I nestled deeper into my cloak to prevent myself from shivering. Despite all my layers of clothes, I never felt warm. Spring couldn't come soon enough.

Lance sat on the opposite seat. He'd been sleeping for a while, and though I wished I could do the same, my mind was too restless to allow my body to sleep.

I put my head out of the carriage window to see how far we were from the nearest town. There were a few lights and some smoke in the distance. Not too long now and I'd have a warm bed and a meal.

"Lance," I called out to him, but he didn't react. "Wake up, would you? We're almost there."

The only response I received was a few incoherent mumblings.

"Lance," I said, louder this time, and when there was still no response, I opted to give him a little kick in the shin.

He immediately sat up. "Ow, what the hell was that for?"

"You wouldn't wake up."

"Well, I'm awake now," he grumbled, running his hands through his dark hair.

A slight breeze entered through the carriage window, and I shivered a little.

"Are you cold?" Lance asked.

"Mostly just my hands. I can't believe I forgot to put on gloves this morning." I tucked my hands into my lap but my fingers were starting to feel numb.

"Here." Lance moved to sit next to me. "Give me your hands." I didn't see a reason not to.

He took both my hands and held them up to his mouth before blowing his warm breath onto my palms. Then he rubbed my hands with his, trying to create a little warmth. The act was so gentle and sweet that it took me by surprise.

"Can I tell you something, Lance?" I didn't give him a chance to respond. "I'm glad you're coming with me to Norrandale." This journey frightened me more than I wanted to admit. I didn't mind travelling so far without company, but it was whatever awaited me on the other side that I feared. It was nice to know I was not alone.

Lance stopped warming my hands for a moment and looked up at me, his expression once again unreadable.

"Really?"

"Yes."

"Even though I'm a selfish narcissist with mediocre kissing skills?"

I pressed my tongue to my cheek. "You're not going to let me forget that anytime soon, are you?"

"Let you forget?" he asked with a raised eyebrow. "How do you think I'm supposed to feel?"

"I already told you," I said with as much confidence as I could muster while his warm hands covered mine. "I'm merely keeping you humble, Prince."

A mischievous look crossed his face, and I knew I was in trouble.

"Is that so?"

"Yes," I said with certainty.

"Is that so?" he asked again, his voice having dropped a little lower as he leaned towards me.

"Yes."

Our noses almost touched. His hands still cradled mine. Those cold blue eyes stared right through me, and it felt as if my heart had stopped beating altogether.

"Do you want me to kiss you, Gwen?"

"*Yes.*"

The word had left my mouth before I could think better of it, and just as well, because the moment Lance's mouth was on mine, I forgot all the reasons I shouldn't be kissing him. My lips parted of their own accord and there were warnings going off in my head, but I ignored them all.

Lance pulled me closer, filling the air around me until there was only him, and I was breathing him in like fresh air.

His hand was in my hair and his tongue slid into my mouth, teasing me, challenging me.

I sank into him, reaching for his arm and wanting to pull him closer. But Lance was ahead of me, his hands shifting to my waist, and he pulled me onto his lap. I let out a small gasp and then his mouth was on my neck, and the cold I'd felt before was long forgotten as heat surged through every part of my body. His fingers travelled the length of my back, tracing my curves, before he pressed me against his chest.

Lance undid my cloak, letting it fall to the carriage floor, and the buttons of my collar were next. It was ice and scorching fire merged together, and then he pushed the sleeve of my dress off my shoulder. His lips were on my throat and my collarbone, and every part of my skin that was exposed. I was dizzy and aching for him and wanting to run away all at the same time.

I clung to him, flushed with heat while silently wishing that this would never end.

"This is a bad idea," I finally managed to get out, because I feared being used and I feared that he didn't care as much as I wanted him to.

"Do you want me to stop?" He was breathing hard but so was I.

I let my hands cup his face, a day's worth of stubble on his cheeks. I replied by kissing him again, because apparently, I had no self-control, and Lance had some kind of hold on me that I just couldn't shake off.

His fingers dug into my waist, and I wondered what his hands would feel like on my bare skin. I moved my hips against his and a low groan erupted from the back of his throat. My lips pressed kisses to his defined jawline and down his neck until he pulled my mouth back to his. Despite my instincts warning me about getting entangled with the Prince of Everness, something about kissing him just felt right. And there was nothing mediocre about it.

We reached the town and found a beautiful little inn with a few rooms to spare for the night. Seeing as Lance was royal, the owner made sure we got the best of service and the nicest of rooms.

I fell onto my bed with a sigh, tired from sitting in the carriage all day, although I had to admit it was better than doing the trip on horseback.

The room had a plush red carpet to match the curtains that covered the window, which looked out onto the street. Outside, the town had a lively atmosphere despite the colder weather. I could hear people in the streets, walking and laughing. There was also a tavern a few houses down, from which there came a lot of noise. Someone played a violin somewhere and the music caused me suddenly to miss Norrandale.

But not the Norrandale I would return to now. I wanted the home I'd left behind. Not the kingdom in the grasp of war and filled with treachery.

I had dinner in my rooms and proceeded to take a bath in the porcelain tub in the corner of the room. My nightgown didn't do much to keep me warm, so I got under my covers as quickly as possible. I thought about blowing out the candle next to my bed but I was not feeling sleepy yet. Then I remembered the two books I'd brought with me from Levernia, so I hopped out of bed and hurried over to my trunk to retrieve one.

After twenty or so pages, my eyes slowly started to droop, but I was mentally invested in the story and had a hard time putting it down. I decided that I would finish the chapter and then go to sleep as we had a long day of travelling ahead of us tomorrow.

My thoughts drifted to the prince in the room next door. I wondered if he was still awake. I'd let myself slip up earlier in the carriage when I kissed him. I knew better than to fall for the charms of a boy who had made me no promises and wasn't likely to either.

I turned the page of my book but suddenly found myself unable to concentrate on the story any longer. My mind was too occupied with midnight hair and warm hands trailing my icy skin.

This was ridiculous.

I needed to go to sleep and forget about all of it. There were more important things to worry about. Like whatever was going on at Mistwood Palace.

A bang against my door nearly had me jumping out of my skin. The door handle rattled, but I'd locked the door earlier. A curse sounded on the other side, allowing me to recognise the perpetrator and filling me with some relief.

Lance tried the door handle again, but of course it would not budge. With a huff, I slipped out from the covers and made my way over to the door.

"What on earth do you think you're doing?" I cried out, turning the key. The door had barely unlocked before Lance pushed it open and leaned in the doorway.

"Gwen darling," he said with a lopsided smile, looking pleasantly surprised. "What are you doing in my rooms?"

"*Your* rooms?" I questioned. "This is my room, Lance."

He looked into the hallway and back into the room, swaying a little.

"Nope, pretty sure this is my room."

He didn't have a cup in his hand, but I remembered the tavern down the road from the inn.

"Goodnight, Lance."

I started to close the door, but he was already walking into the room and then he shut the door behind him.

"Don't worry, I know why you're here."

He removed his gloves and jacket and tossed them onto the nearest chair.

"You do now, do you?"

"Yes, of course," he replied with a serious tone. "You're here for this." He gestured to himself and I had to press my lips into a line to keep from chuckling.

"I'm really not," I promised him. "In fact, I would really like to go to bed now, so if you could just show yourself out—"

"Let me guess what happened." He took a seat on the edge of the bed before starting to remove his boots. "You were dreaming about me and now you can't fall asleep again."

"You're right. You are the only thing I think about night and day. I can't seem to help myself," I replied in a very sarcastic tone.

"I knew it," he said, more to himself than me, and then his mouth spread into a grin. "I bet I wasn't wearing any clothes in your dream either."

"Okay, mister, it's time for you to go now." I made my way towards the bed, ready to push him out of the room if I had to.

"It's okay, Gwen." Lance had no intention of leaving. Instead, he took hold of my wrists and pulled me between his legs. His expression grew more serious. "I think about you too."

I looked down at him. "You do?" My throat had gone a little dry.

"Of course I do."

He lifted my hand to his mouth and pressed a featherlight kiss to my palm. I couldn't move away.

"Don't leave me, Gwen." There was a look of desperation behind those eyes. One I'd never seen there before.

"Promise me you'll stay," he pleaded, and his entreaty tugged at my heart strings even though I wished it didn't.

When I didn't reply he asked again. "Promise?"

I sighed with the knowledge that I probably wasn't going to win this fight.

"I'll stay."

Lance moved back and plopped his head onto the pillow. He didn't even bother getting under the covers. I stood and watched the scene, unsure of how to react when he patted the spot beside him.

"I promise to keep my hands to myself." Lance's eyes were already shut, and I suspected he was going to fall asleep any minute.

I was not going to get the prince to leave my bed, and I didn't want to stand and freeze any longer, which left me with few options, so I lifted the covers and got into the other side of the bed. The room was silent for a minute and I thought Lance had fallen asleep when he said, "You're so kind, Gwen."

His eyes were still closed, and he was lying on his stomach.

"Am not." Especially not to him. I'd treated him with a lot of hostility when I first arrived at the Palace of Levernia.

"Yes, you are," Lance mumbled into his pillow. "You just don't always let people see it."

I didn't know how to respond.

"And you're very pretty." I wanted to smile at his choice of words, knowing he would probably never say such a thing had he been entirely sober, but I felt flattered all the same.

"I am?"

Lance slowly opened his eyes and reached over, brushing his thumb over my cheek.

"You're the prettiest girl I've ever seen." His eyes closed again, as if he couldn't keep them open any longer.

"Well thank you, I suppose." I blew out the candle on the bedside table and lay back on the pillow, closing my eyes in an attempt to go to sleep.

After several minutes, I turned on my side, hoping to get more comfortable, but the tiredness I had felt before had decided to disappear, much to my annoyance.

An arm came around me, and above the blanket, Lance moved himself so that he was lying behind my back. He found my hand and entangled our fingers. I fell asleep to the sound of him breathing.

Chapter 38

Elara

I bit the inside of my cheek as I stared out of the council-room window. Where the hell was Cai? Alastor had said this was urgent.

He'd been spending the past week or two arranging scouting groups for the surrounding area and towns, as well as finding more loyalists to join the cause. The Norrandish army was slowly growing but it wasn't enough to defeat Aries yet. I'd sent word to Everness, reporting our success at Mistwood to the council and requesting they send any men that we could spare to march to Norrandale.

A few minutes ago, Alastor had arrived back at the palace, out of breath and with the look of death in his eyes. Whatever he had to tell me and Cai, it couldn't be good.

The door to the council room opened and Cai rushed in, his face white as a sheet. "You called for me?"

"Yes, Your Majesties." Alastor cleared his throat. "I rode through the night to get here. I thought it best you both hear this as soon as possible."

Cai and I made eye contact. I hated when there was tension between us. We'd been through a lot in these past few months and we needed each other now more than ever.

I braced myself for what was to come.

"Aries is coming. His army has arrived."

It was always coming, and we knew it. But for some reason that didn't lessen the blow.

"So, he's decided to stop searching for the Myrgonite stones." It was more of a statement than a question.

"With Thatcher no longer giving him free rein to do what he pleases, he knows we're going to oppose him. He also knows it's better to strike now while he has the upper hand," Cai responded, before looking to Alastor. "How far away is he?"

"His soldiers are still raiding farms and villages as they move, so he's not going to need supplies for a while. If the weather holds up like this, I'd probably say two weeks, maybe a month given they have to travel through the mountains."

That was not enough time for all of Norrandale's army to get here, never mind Everness's. I could tell Cai and Alastor were thinking the same thing. Travel during the winter was hard enough as it was, and armies moved slowly.

"It would take a blizzard to hold them back now," I said, while knowing better than to trust my fate to the weather.

I would never be able to put into words the amount of fear written on Cai's face. It was as if he could see everything and everyone he cared about disappearing before his eyes, taken from him in the most horrid of ways. This was a nightmare. And none of us could wake up and make it stop.

"If Aries is coming, we need to do everything in our power to stop him," Cai said as calmly as possible. "We'll need to gather a lot in a very short amount of time."

He pulled a map from one of the shelves and rolled it open on the table.

"Alastor, I want you to send messengers in every direction." He pointed to all the major cities that surrounded Mistwood. "I'll write letters, stamped with my seal. We'll make the threat known to our people and call on all the loyalists to start marching. If Aries wants to catch us off guard, we need to be a step ahead of him. I don't want him to reach Mistwood at all. So, we're going to have to meet him in the field."

Cai placed his finger where all the mountains were drawn. "There's a valley here, close to the old mines. We can find a way to ambush his army there while keeping the high ground."

"I agree, Your Majesty," Alastor said. "We should use the terrain to our advantage. I'll make sure the reinforcements march in that direction."

"I'll send word to Everness," I added. "To try and gather any forces I can. But at this rate, they'll never make it on time."

"I suppose it's worth a try, though. Every sword is going to count now." Cai didn't look at me as he said it, his eyes boring into the map as he contemplated the possibility of losing his kingdom.

"Alastor, I want you to alert everyone in the palace. Let them know we are preparing for battle. I'll get you those letters by the end of the day."

Alastor bowed and left to fulfil his duties. As soon as the door was shut behind him, Cai fell into the nearest chair, full of dismay. My heart ached to see him in such a state. But it was clouded by my own worry for what we would have to face, combined with our unresolved argument.

"It's going to be all right." It was the only thing I could think to say.

"Is it?" He ran a hand through his golden hair.

Probably not. We were all likely to die before this was over and if it wasn't at the hands of Aries, it would be from those damned stones that started this whole thing.

"If we don't make it out of this alive," I started, "then we need to make sure Aries never gets his hands on any of the Myrgonite objects. And the only way to truly ensure that is if we find another way to destroy them or hide them somewhere they can never be found."

"Is it even possible to do that?"

"I honestly don't know."

"So Rhen hasn't found anything in the diary yet?" he asked.

"I don't think so. We haven't spoken much in the last few days. I'm sure if he's found something he would tell me immediately. And even if he doesn't," I stepped a little closer to Cai, "I'm not going to stop looking until it's found." It was a promise I would make to myself, to him and to our kingdoms.

"We should probably get to work, then." He didn't say it hopefully but at least he was willing to fight, and I would take that any day over the state he was in when he was in exile.

"I'll see you at dinner then."

As I made my way towards my rooms, I spotted Rhen coming down the hall.

"I've been looking for you. But first, we have guests, Your Majesty."

"Guests?" I frowned. "Who?"

"Come and see for yourself." I relied on the fact that Rhen appeared quite calm to reassure myself that these were not unwanted guests at least.

I followed him towards the courtyard and spotted a familiar carriage from the window.

"Gwen," I cried out happily as I rushed to the door.

She climbed out of the carriage, looking tired and a little weary, but as her eyes fell on me, she looked happy to see me.

I pulled her into a hug, comforted by her familiar face. "We've all missed you. How was your journey?"

"I won't lie, I'm quite tired from travelling."

"We'd best get you inside where it's much warmer." I was about to link my elbow with hers to lead her inside when another figure emerged from the carriage.

Lance was dressed in some of his finest clothing, with his hair neat and his face shaved. He didn't look like he'd been travelling at all. This must have been what Rhen meant when he said "guests", as in more than one.

"What are you doing here?" I asked in surprise. If anything, I would have believed Lance would stay as far away from the fighting as possible. My eyes slowly travelled to Gwen and then back to him.

"Well," he said, removing his gloves. "I wasn't going to let you have all the fun without me."

I wasn't sure what to make of it but I couldn't let the thought linger for too long. We had too many other important things to worry about.

"It's good to see you," I said to Gwen, taking her arm. "But Aries' armies are now marching this way. We are readying ourselves for battle. It would have been safer if you'd stayed in Everness." Cai would also worry about Gwen being here and how we would keep her protected when none of us knew if we were making it out of this alive.

We stepped into the palace where people were already starting to bustle about in preparation.

"Have all the men arrived?" Her face was full of concern, her eyes scanning the inside of the palace, like she was looking for something. Someone? How were we going to tell her?

"Not yet. And the Evernean army probably won't reach us in time either."

"What about Everness itself?" Lance asked, trailing behind us. "Should things go bad here in Norrandale, we are going to need all our forces in Everness, because it will become a refuge for the people of Norrandale as well as all of us." Everness was the fall-back plan. But we needed those men. My heart sank. The cause seemed lost either way.

I gave him a nod. Eloisa was gone but Lance didn't even appear to be in mourning. I wanted to say I was sorry for his loss, or was it our loss? She was still family after all. This was too complicated.

"What of my brother?" Gwen asked suddenly and I swallowed hard, meeting Rhen's eyes over her shoulder. He slowly shook his head. Now was not the time.

"You should talk to Cai. I'm sure he's been told of your arrival. First, let's get you to your rooms."

Rhen offered to take her as I called for a servant to bring her luggage.

Lance fell into step beside me. "He's dead, isn't he? And based on the look on your face, it was probably Cai who killed him."

"Not a word," I said under my breath.

"You said you wanted to speak to me?" I asked Rhen once Gwen and Lance had been settled.

"Yes, I do, but we should probably go somewhere more private." Rhen looked over his shoulder as if someone might be listening to us.

"Is it about the diary?" I asked in a hushed tone, and he nodded.

"All right, let's find somewhere we can talk without interruption." We walked side by side in silence, heading towards the nearest study. My stomach rumbled, not loud enough for anyone to hear but enough to indicate that I was, in fact, quite hungry. I stopped a servant who passed us, asking if they would bring some food and something warm to drink for me and Rhen.

It wasn't Cai's personal study but a much smaller one. Outside the window, I saw the last traces of snow on the palace ground that had yet to melt away. The study was cold and dark with no fire to warm the room. Neither Rhen nor I took a seat.

"So, I think there might be a link between the objects," Rhen said once he'd closed the door. He hardly wore his uniform these days, spending most of his time in the library or a study, poring over the pages of the old king's diary. He was desperate for an answer, like the rest of us.

"King Evrin made an entry about the queen's slow descent into madness and how she grew more hungry for power and violence. The king decided to track down the goldsmith who'd forged the objects in the first place, since he was the only one who knew what kind of magic was used."

Of course, in all of this no one had really given the goldsmith much thought, even though he was the one who'd made it all possible.

"Turns out the goldsmith hailed from a line of magic wielders who came from the continent. But because of their abilities, they were often persecuted. At this point, there was no one left from their legacy apart from the goldsmith and his family. The magic he'd been taught by his forefathers was so ancient and rare that no one knew it even existed anymore."

"So did the king find him?" I rubbed my hands together, trying to create some warmth.

"Well kind of. It took some time to track down the goldsmith, but when they found him, he'd killed himself and his family had disappeared."

"So, it was just another dead end?"

"Not entirely." Rhen rubbed his hand over his face, where a little stubble had grown. "The smithy was covered in scribblings, most of it incomprehensible, but the king and his men did find a little information with regards to the stones."

There was a light knock on the door before the servant girl entered, carrying a tray.

"Thank you," I told her as she set the tray down on the nearest table. There were two cups of warm cider and a plate of small pies, steaming in the cold room.

The servant girl nodded again, and I caught her looking at Rhen admiringly before leaving the room. I could hardly blame her. Rhen was a tall man with a strong jawline and deep brown eyes. It was understandable that girls would find him attractive. Not to mention that he was a captain of the royal guard.

I grabbed the cup of cider nearest to me, holding it with both hands so I could warm them.

"So, you were saying about the information they found," I encouraged him to continue, taking a long sip of the cider, revelling in the way it warmed me.

"Yes." Rhen cleared his throat, trying to remember the last thing he'd said. "Right, so when the smith had placed the magic within the objects, he'd linked them all together."

I reached for one of the small pies. Biting into it, I found it to be minced meat, the pastry crunchy in my mouth. It might just have been the best thing I'd ever eaten. Either that or I was really starved. Both options seemed likely.

"A link? That's interesting. What does that mean for us?" The thought gave me the slightest bit of hope that we stood a chance of finding the third object. Especially now, when it mattered more than ever.

"I can't be a hundred per cent certain. I think even the king was making assumptions at this point. But he believed that one object might be used to find the other. I'm not exactly sure how, but there is a possibility at least," Rhen said, drinking his cider.

Luckily, we had not just one but two of the other objects, and if what Rhen said was true and we could somehow use them to find the third, this significantly increased our chances.

"This is good news. Thank you for all your trouble. I'm sure Cai will be happy to hear we have a new lead, as well."

"Speaking of which." He put the empty cup back on the tray. "Is everything all right between you two?"

The question was too personal for someone who was merely the captain of my guard. But for the most part, I viewed Rhen more like a friend than just somebody who was obligated to protect me with their life.

"Things are fine. Cai is under a lot of stress. I mean, we all are. There is a lot at stake here." Of all things, I didn't care to have this particular conversation with Rhen. Not when there were so many more important things to worry about, especially with his new information about the stones. Once I'd sent for the armies of Everness, finding the third object would be my top priority.

"You and Cai will make it through this, just like you've made it through everything else," Rhen reassured me.

For both our sakes, I hoped he was right.

Chapter 39

Gwen

I lowered the bow as I inspected the target in the distance.

Considering how long it had been since I'd had proper practice, I expected my aim to be worse. The arrow impaled the target on the edge of the centre dot. I contemplated pulling every arrow out and starting again but my arms ached.

Based on the way the light had changed, I had to have been out there for hours already. My face felt numb, and I could hardly feel my fingers anymore.

I begrudgingly stalked over to the target and started removing the arrows, one by one, before placing them in my quiver.

My footsteps echoed over the quiet gardens when I walked up the stone steps. I entered the palace with the sole intent of going to my rooms and taking a long, hot bath. I requested dinner in my room as well, like I'd been having every evening for the past few days.

I wasn't sure if anyone took their dinners together in the dining hall. I suspected, at the very least, some of the soldiers might, now that the palace was being turned into a fortress. But I didn't quite feel like facing everyone just yet.

There were soldiers everywhere on the lower floors. It was strange to see the palace in such a state. Everyone felt on edge. I was grateful for the more silent hallways as I reached the upper floors, where the royal family's rooms and guest chambers were. Thankfully, I got to keep my old room with all my things. It was as if my bedroom was the only thing that hadn't changed in all the time that had passed.

A bedroom door opened to my right, and I nearly jumped at the sudden sound.

Lance looked a little surprised to see me. We hadn't spoken much since arriving at the palace, mostly because I'd been trying my best to avoid people altogether. And because I wasn't entirely sure where I stood with Lance yet — nor did I have the mental capacity for such a conversation.

"Gwen." His eyes travelled to the bow and quiver in my hands. "I see you've been out?"

"I just needed to get my mind off … everything, I guess."

He leaned against his doorframe, wearing a black shirt and matching black trousers, his hair neatly combed.

"Have you talked to Cai again recently?"

I nodded silently.

"Are you still angry with him?" Lance asked carefully. I could tell by his expression that he wasn't trying to stir anything up but that he was honestly wondering.

"No," I said at first, and then, "I mean, I don't think so. What Thatcher did was unforgiveable." Still, he was my brother.

"I still think you're allowed to be sad about it."

"Am I?" I clenched my teeth, not particularly wanting to feel vulnerable in front of him right now. Not him. Not anyone. I didn't like people seeing me cry.

"You watched me sob my eyes out when Eloisa passed away," Lance reminded me.

"But that was different. She didn't stab your whole family in the back." Mourning him made me feel like I was a traitor myself. And yet … there was so much pain inside my chest that sometimes it was hard to breathe.

"He was still your brother, Gwen. And you loved him." Lance stepped away from the threshold, approaching me. "And despite what he did, you're allowed to grieve for him."

"Maybe." I didn't have the energy to try to disagree.

"Is that why you've been hiding out in your rooms these last few days?"

I nodded slowly. "Why, did you think I was avoiding you again?"

The corner of Lance's mouth turned up slightly. "Maybe a little."

"Don't worry. You haven't done anything to anger me. At least not that I know of."

Lance's expression was playful, but concern lingered behind it.

"I'm not sure I know how to grieve for him," I admitted.

"I would suggest you do it my way, but I don't think you'll like it." It didn't take much to understand his meaning.

"I don't think getting drunk is going to make me feel better."

"That just means you haven't had enough," Lance replied, somewhat convincingly.

It made me laugh despite the fact that I wanted to break down.

He took another step towards me and placed his hands on my upper arms. "I think you need to allow yourself to be sad and to be angry. At him and at everyone. You need to allow yourself to sit in that pain so that it doesn't consume you."

I didn't know if Lance was talking from experience. He'd suffered more loss than most people I knew.

Tears began to fill my eyes and, without meaning to, I started to spill all the thoughts that had been running through my mind the past couple of days.

"My brother is dead. I don't know if I'll ever see my family again. My kingdom is in turmoil and I just ..." I sucked in a breath. "I feel so alone."

Lance's icy-blue eyes gazed into mine. "You're right," he breathed out, like he was trying to get a grip on himself. "Things are less than ideal for you right now and it feels like the whole world is going to hell. But you're wrong about one thing."

He leaned down a little. I'd never seen Lance look so serious before. "You are not alone."

Without thinking, I closed the distance between us. I had no idea why I did it. Maybe I wanted to distract myself. Maybe I wanted some form of comfort. Maybe I just needed him in ways I wasn't ready to admit.

Lance didn't hesitate. He grabbed my waist, and I immediately dropped the bow and arrows onto the ground with a thump. His lips moved reverently against mine but there was a hunger behind his kisses, as if he'd been holding himself back. I held on to him, my fingers digging into his shirt. I ached for some form of touch or comfort. I ached to be closer. To have more of him.

Lance started walking us backwards until my back pressed against the wall. My face had been red from the cold, but it now felt flushed for a completely different reason.

He raked his hand through my hair, tilting my head up to gain better access to my mouth.

I leaned into him. Part of my mind screamed at what the hell I was doing while the other loved the taste of him.

Lance smiled against my mouth. "I'd forgotten how much I liked doing that." He took my lip between his teeth and shivers ran up and down every inch of my body. I wrapped my leg around him and Lance took hold of my thigh, pressing himself up against me.

His lips brushed over mine and I could almost have deluded myself into thinking that a sense of longing lingered there. Lance kissed me as if he could devour me right there and then in the hallway.

With my eyes closed, I could melt into him and forget about everything that was wrong and unfair in the world. I knew I shouldn't be doing this. But I knew I wasn't strong enough to stop myself either.

I didn't need to, because in the midst of our heated kiss, Lance was suddenly ripped away from me.

"You bastard!" Cai's voice boomed through the hallway. Lance barely had time to register what was going on before Cai punched him square on his jaw. "She's as good as my sister. You have no right to lay your hands on her!"

Lance's head whipped back as Cai made a hit to his nose and then another to his stomach. The impact was enough to make him fall backwards onto the floor.

"Cai!" I cried out, afraid to jump between the two of them. I'd never seen Cai filled with so much rage.

He was on top of Lance in an instant, landing one blow after the other. Lance used his hands to try to defend himself a little, but he was making no attempt to fight Cai, and I doubted it was because he didn't know how.

"You come into my house, uninvited, after everything you've done, and this is how you treat her?"

"It's not him, Cai. It was my doing." But he wouldn't listen. He continued to punch Lance, who had blood dripping from his nose.

I couldn't bear to watch it any longer and I tried to pry Cai away from Lance, but he was too strong and too determined.

"Cai, that's enough!"

I was afraid that if he didn't stop soon, he might kill him.

It was Elara's sudden scream at the end of the hall that made Cai freeze.

"Cai." Her voice was shaky, almost desperate. "Please."

I realised then that she'd seen him do it. She'd seen him kill my brother, and based on the look in her eyes, it haunted her.

Cai sat back, both him and Lance breathing heavily. He took hold of Lance's collar, pulling his head up from the floor before leaning down to whisper into his face. "If you ever so much as hurt a hair on her head, I will end you."

"I have no such intentions," Lance huffed out before Cai let him go, his eyes quickly shooting to Elara as she stormed away. He was up in a moment, chasing after her and leaving me and Lance alone in the hallway.

I kneeled by his side and helped him sit up slowly.

"We need to get you cleaned up." His lip was split and his nose was bleeding. "I've never seen Cai like that."

Lance pressed his fingers to his nose and flinched. "Can't say I didn't deserve it a little."

"Still, he shouldn't have done that to you for kissing me."

Lance gave me a wide smirk before saying, "It was entirely worth it."

We sat on Lance's bed while I helped nurse the wounds Cai had inflicted.

I knew the two of them had a bit of history and Cai had never exactly taken a liking to Lance, but his outburst had been rather intense. Though I suspected that it only partly had to do with Lance kissing me, and it was more because of everything that had happened since his return to Mistwood.

While I was saddened by my brother's death, I knew how close he and Cai had been. It must have shattered something in Cai that was now beyond repair.

I'd asked a servant to bring a bowl of water and some cloth and ointments. Lance lay back on a few stacked pillows, holding a piece of the cloth to his nose.

"I'm sorry for what happened," I said. "I think Cai's overwhelmed with everything that's happening and seeing us made him snap."

I took another piece of cloth and sank it into the bowl of lukewarm water before wringing it out.

"He shouldn't have taken it out on you, though."

Lance wiped the last of the blood away from his nose. "I probably would have done the same if I had been in his position."

"You mean you've never caught Cai and Lara kissing?"

"That's not what I meant." He sat up with a frown. "And I'd rather not think about that, to be honest."

"You know, they've probably done a lot more than kissing—"

"Okay," he said. "You can stop talking, please."

I gently pressed the damp cloth to his lip, and he flinched. "I have to say, he got you pretty good."

"That's only because I wasn't hitting back."

True. Lance had let Cai hit him without defending himself.

"Right, because he wouldn't have stood a chance, I'm sure," I teased. While Lance might have been strong, Cai was a trained soldier.

"Hey, I would at least have given him a black eye or something."

"Sure. Sure."

He reached towards me and playfully pinched my leg. "Thanks for taking care of me, though."

"Well, I did get you into trouble with the King of Norrandale after all."

"Who knew you could be a bad influence?"

I used my finger to scrape some ointment out of the little pot before taking hold of Lance's chin. "Hold still now."

I dabbed a bit of the ointment on his lips and placed the pot on the table next to his bed. "You can put this on every day. It should feel better within a couple of days."

I handed him a small bottle of tonic. "And sip this slowly. It will help with the pain."

Lance pulled out the little cork and downed the entire bottle of pain medicine.

"I said sip. That stuff will make you sleepy."

He cringed at the bitter taste.

"You're pretty good at this, you know?"

"What, nursing?" Lance gave a nod.

"Thatcher would get himself into trouble sometimes and it was usually me and Cai who looked after him."

"Well, if I should be getting into any more fights, you'll be the first person I call on."

"I'd prefer if you didn't get in any fights at all." I started gathering the bloody cloths and bowl.

"That's true. I can't risk my looks. It's the only thing I've got going for me."

This made me look up at him. "That's not true."

"No?" He lay back on the bed with a groan. "You think I'm more than just a pretty face?"

"Yes," I said, after a breath.

"Right, of course, I'm a selfish and conceited prince with bad habits and low morals."

"Sometimes," I replied with honesty, because I hated lying. "But you also care a lot for your family and your kingdom. You're very smart, maybe even too clever for your own good. You're good with animals and you've been a good friend to me."

"I hadn't realised you've been paying so much attention to me." He was trying to be witty, but I saw in his eyes that I'd struck something.

"Don't flatter yourself." I patted his leg. "We can't have your ego getting any bigger than it already is."

His eyes were slowly starting to close, the tonic taking its effect. It would probably knock him out for a couple of hours but at least he would feel better when he woke up.

"You should get some rest." He turned to his side, and I took a nearby blanket and draped it over him.

Lance gave a low hum in reply, nestling into his pillows.

I stood up from the bed, making sure that nothing was lying around.

When I turned to leave, Lance's hand shot out and took hold of my wrist. His eyes were still closed.

"Gwen, there's something I need to tell you," he said in a sleepy tone.

"Yes?"

"I don't want to just be your friend."

I wanted to believe he meant it, but I wasn't sure if it was just the pain medicine talking. So, I bent down and brushed a few locks of hair away from his face before pressing a kiss to his forehead.

"Feel better, okay? I'll see you later." Lance was fast asleep when I left the room.

Chapter 40

Elara

I stormed to my rooms with my fists clenched.

Cai called after me but I ignored him, proceeding in a fury.

I accidentally stepped on the hem of my long skirts and nearly toppled over. Cai's footsteps were behind me. He managed to catch up with me before I could slam my bedroom door in his face.

"Lara." Cai's fingers wrapped around the door, and he stepped inside.

"How could you?" I cried out.

"You did not see the state I found them in." His knuckles were red and split. Some of it from beating up Lance just now and some of it a reminder of what he did to Thatcher.

"Was Gwen screaming for help?" I asked, pouring some water into the basin.

"What?" He frowned.

"Was Gwen in trouble? Was Lance hurting her?"

"Well, I …" He hesitated. I dipped a washcloth into the water and wrung it out.

"Gwen is a grown woman, Cai. And I know you view her as your little sister. But she can make her own choices."

"Even if that choice is Lance? I won't allow it."

"I didn't say it was a good choice." I took a seat on one of the chairs in front of the fireplace, gesturing for Cai to do the same. Even if I was furious with him, I didn't want to see him hurt.

"What's he even doing here?" Cai reluctantly fell into the chair opposite me.

"Does it matter?" We had so much more to be worried about. I took Cai's hand, pressing the wet cloth to his skin.

He sucked his teeth and tried to pull back, but I had a firm grip on his hand.

I noticed Cai staring at me, his expression almost that of a young boy being caught doing something he shouldn't.

 - "We cannot go on like this. I cannot go on like this."

"What do you mean?" He was trying not to flinch as I cleaned his hands.

"I mean, I can't keep fighting with you like this. We're supposed to be on each other's side, now more than ever."

He looked down at my hand holding his. "I don't want to fight with you either."

"Well, for starters, that means you can't just beat up my brother, no matter how much of a selfish bastard he can be."

"It's not like he didn't deserve it at least a little bit." After everything Lance had done to Cai, he might have deserved worse. But I meant it that we couldn't be fighting among ourselves right now.

"Fine," I agreed with him. "Maybe a little bit."

I carefully inspected all the fine cuts on his knuckles and where small bruises had formed.

We were both clearly thinking the same thing. Knowing what Cai had done to earn those bruises.

"You shouldn't have been witness to that," he said after a few moments of silence. I didn't have to ask what he'd meant.

"Do you regret killing him?"

"I wish that it hadn't come down to it. I wish he'd never stabbed us all in the back. I wish he'd never killed Jack or murdered my family. But he did. And no matter how I try to play it out in my head, it always ends the same. I kill Thatcher every time."

I dropped the cloth onto one of the little side tables, but my other hand still held Cai's.

"Just because he deserved to die doesn't make it any easier now that he's gone."

"He haunts me," Cai said, wearing a grave expression. "Every time I close my eyes, I see him in front of me, taunting me still."

I didn't know what words could comfort him. Cai was going to have to live with what he had done for the rest of his life. And I feared nothing would make it easier.

"Elara, I want you to know something." He folded his other hand over mine. "What happened in that throne room." He looked away, as if searching for the right words. "I don't know how to explain it but it's like I wasn't myself. Or like I wasn't fully in control of myself. And maybe I was just so overcome with anger and hatred but …"

"You think it had something to do with the dagger and that guard I killed?"

"Maybe. I feel like I don't know anything anymore."

"I think you might be right." I reached into the pocket of my dress and pulled out the Myrgonite dagger. I wasn't the kind of person to easily admit I was wrong, but there was too much danger to be prideful now. "Whatever kind of weapon or magic this is, we don't understand it. I agree with you that this should be hidden until we can find a way to destroy it." I handed the dagger to Cai, who inspected it in his lap.

"There was something more in the diary," I added.

"The king found writings from the goldsmith who'd forged the objects, and he believed that the objects were linked by the magic. And therefore, they could be used to find each other."

He pondered my words, eyes still focused on the dagger.

"So, you're saying we can use the necklace and the dagger to find the third object?"

"Maybe. I suppose anything is worth a try at this point."

"I think you should keep it." Cai used his free hand to hold the dagger out to me. "I'll do everything I can to make sure we have an army to fight Aries, and you can put all your efforts into finding another way to destroy the objects. I don't think you should use either of them, even if it is to find the third one."

After everything we'd been through, I could not deny that the objects must have had some effect on us. There were too many things that Cai and I could not explain. The way that he killed Thatcher. The unnerving feeling that came over me every time I was close to either of the Myrgonite objects. Not to mention that it was affecting the mental state of the two of us, causing tensions between us that we actively had to fight to resolve. "I promise to keep them safe."

His thumb stroked my hand. "If anyone is capable of saving us, it's you, Elara."

"But what if I can't?" I asked so softly, I wasn't sure if Cai could hear. I'd spent most of the past few months searching for answers and trying to find solutions. I didn't want to allow myself to consider the possibility of failure because I feared it would make me lose hope entirely. But now it felt as though there was an impending doom drawing near, in the same way storm clouds do. And I couldn't help but worry that, despite all our efforts, we would not come out victorious.

Cai placed his hand on my cheek, forcing me to look at him. "Then I'd be happy to die by your side, if it means I get to spend the afterlife with you."

I turned my face into his hand, pressing a kiss to his palm.

"I don't think I'd mind spending eternity with you either."

There were much worse fates, after all.

I looked down at the dagger in my lap again. "You should keep this." The metal of the hilt was cold between my fingers as I handed it back to Cai. "I have the necklace, which I can try and use to find the third object. You were right. It would be too dangerous to have them all together. Especially if there is some kind of link. I think we need to keep them separated. I trust you'll know where to keep this safe."

"I have a few places in mind."

"Good." I stood up from the chair, brushing invisible flecks of dust from my skirts. "Well, I should probably get to it, then."

Cai also stood, dagger in hand. "I should follow up on news regarding our armies."

"And while you're at it, try not to kill my brother if you can."

He gave me half a smile. "I can't make any promises." He pressed a kiss to my temple, sparing me a last glance before leaving the room. We'd managed to reconcile and yet I still felt unnerved. Like there was something between us, unresolved. A lingering force that nagged at my subconscious, except I couldn't tell what it wanted. Only that it was not to be ignored.

* * *

The library was deathly quiet apart from the peaceful crackling of the fire and the turning of pages.

Mistwood's library had endless rows of shelves, filled with countless books. Dust hung in the air, suggesting the library hadn't been cleaned or used very often in the past few months. There was a large wooden table close to the fireplace where I had King Evrin's diary laid out in front of me.

Candles decorated the rest of the table, to provide better light for reading in the dark. The sun set early in winter and there weren't many hours in the day when one could read by sunlight.

I stood up from the table to add another few logs to the fire, suspecting that I was going to be there for a good few more hours. The wooden chair creaked under me as I returned to my seat, forcing my eyes to focus on the diary in front of me. I'd had little sleep in the last few days and my eyes strained with every word that I read. But this was important. Rhen had worked through much of the diary and made lots of notes, but I had a few hours free tonight and could go through a bit of it myself. See if I could find anything that perhaps he might have missed.

The pages of the diary were old and delicate, and I winced every time I had to turn a page, praying that I wouldn't damage it somehow. In some parts, the ink was faded and barely readable. It took an insurmountable amount of time to make any decent progress.

At the very least we now suspected the objects were all linked to each other. But I found myself worrying about what could happen when and if we did manage to have all three Myrgonite objects in our possession. If they truly were as dangerous as the king said, we needed to stay as far away from them as possible. But in doing that we also needed to keep them far away from King Aries. I carefully turned a page. It was the start of a new entry, after the king had searched the goldsmith's forge.

I miss her terribly some days. But then I remember the person she was in the end. No longer the woman I had married but a monster, corrupted by the dark magic of the stones. I've been going through more of the writings we'd found in the goldsmith's forge. Most of it is incomprehensible, scribblings and sentences that make no sense and have no order. Perhaps the use of so much magic had caught up to the goldsmith himself, driving him mad in the end. I used to think he'd killed himself for fear of what I might do to him once I found him. Now I wonder if maybe he simply wasn't able to live with himself after what he'd done.

Riona was a clever woman, and she knew I would eventually figure out that two of the stones were in her necklace and dagger. She'd always been too fond of carrying them around, refusing to take them off for fear of being parted from her precious objects. She knew I would try and stop her if I had all three objects, so I suspect she's hidden the third Myrgonite stone somewhere I'll never think to look. It has to be in the palace somewhere. Riona could never be parted from the stones. She'd want it somewhere she'd be able to keep an eye on it.

I found something interesting among the notes of the goldsmith. Not only could the magic be a link between the objects, but if that is the case, the objects can be used to destroy each other. Destroy one and you destroy them all. But the objects need to be in close range of each other to achieve this. And then there was still the destruction it would cause if someone tried to destroy it.

I looked up from the page, eyes wide. This was something. The objects could be used not only to find each other but also to destroy each other. But we still didn't have a safe way of destroying one of them, not without killing anyone, at least. I delicately turned the page to start reading the next entry.

I'd warned her that she was meddling with something which she did not understand. But nothing was ever enough for Riona. Nothing could satisfy her endless greed. And it cost her life. I mourn the girl who was once my wife, a very long time ago. But she has been gone for a while now. I fear it is a stranger that I buried in the forest. I had hidden the necklace with all the other royal jewels, undetectable and not to be used for a long time, as there is no queen. The dagger I buried in the forest with her, and I hope that time will continue to keep it hidden. But the third object is yet to be uncovered. It is close to me. I can feel it. It whispers to me like a voice in my head. It calls to me in the middle of the night, urging me to retrieve the dagger and the necklace. To use them in order to find the last Myrgonite object.

Months ago, I would have jumped at the chance. But now, I do not think myself safe from the effects of the magic. I want to think of myself as a virtuous man, but temptation is a strong motivator, and once I have all three objects, I might not have the strength to destroy them. This kind of magic sows destruction. And once it has you in its clutches, you can never be free. Destroying the objects will not come without sacrifice and I believe it would have to be the ultimate price. As king to my people, I cannot risk it. I can only hope that if

I continue to keep the objects far away from each other, the magic will fall into a slumber, and all will grow forgetful that it even existed at all.

It was a lot to take in. The king was clearly fighting an internal battle, which meant the third object had to be among his royal possessions. But after so much time, there was no way of knowing if the object was even in the palace. If the necklace had managed to travel from Everness into the hands of Norrandale, then the third object could be anywhere. Whatever grasp it had on him, the king understood the danger of the objects, and not only that, but that there would be a consequence to trying to destroy the magic. I closed the diary knowing I had to inform the others of my latest find sooner rather than later, but it wasn't exactly the hopeful news I wanted to bring. I knew it wouldn't be easy. But this war and these stones had already cost everyone so much. What did we have left to sacrifice?

Chapter 41

Lance

"With the men we've gathered so far, we have enough archers to create a strong line of attack."

A map had been laid out on the table in the council room and Alastor gestured to the valley where the battle would be taking place.

"The hills are going to be a massive advantage to us during the initial attack." Cai stood next to Alastor, explaining his battle plans to everyone in the room. I wasn't entirely sure what I was doing there but I suspected it had something to do with Elara. For whatever reason, she seemed to trust my opinion when it came to certain things.

Taking on the throne after a rebellion was a massive responsibility, but Elara had risen to the occasion and grown into a very good queen, if I had to say so myself. But the truth remained that she had not grown up at court, and I thought she sometimes doubted herself. It helped to have someone around to guide her every now and then. And I was happy to do it. Her over me in that position any day.

"If Mannik's and Ryker's men arrive on time, we can put some of them on the left and right flanks to try and split up Aries' army," Cai continued.

"You've been in contact with Olwin and Donald. How are numbers looking over there?" Elara asked Alastor.

"I haven't heard much recently but our last correspondence consisted of their reports on their growing numbers. They've roped in a few of the other bandit groups in Everness, but this means nothing if we cannot get them to Norrandale in time," Alastor replied.

I saw the look of worry on Elara's face. We needed the men, and every person counted. But more importantly we needed them here on time, and this seemed to be our biggest problem.

The meeting continued for another hour as plans were discussed, and more plans in case those plans didn't work. Relief flooded me when it finally came to an end. Just the topic of discussing war was incredibly morbid when all of us in the room knew the costs and sacrifices that were going to be made. People were going to die out there, and no matter what Elara and Cai did, neither of them could stop it.

I left the council room, eager to get my mind off the matter. And I knew exactly what I needed.

My feet carried me through the hallways to the other side of the palace. I gently knocked on Gwen's door until I heard her call out, "Come in." She sat in a comfortable-looking chair with a thick book in her lap.

Gwen looked up and a smile crossed her face as she took in my figure. "Hey, you. Aren't you supposed to be in some meeting?"

"It just finished." I shrugged. "I want to find out if you'd like to join me for a cup of tea." My eyes travelled to the teacup on the side table next to her. "But I see you already have one."

Gwen looked at the teacup before lifting it to her lips and finishing the contents. The cup clattered a little as she placed it back on the saucer.

"Looks like I'm all out."

I couldn't help but grin as she stood up and left her book on the chair. She linked her arm with mine as we started to walk. I didn't know exactly where we were heading. I didn't have much of a plan other than wanting to be in her presence.

"Your face is looking much better," she commented. The bruising had pretty much faded, and Cai and I had come to some sort of unspoken understanding where we tolerated each other with as much gentlemanliness as either of us could muster.

"Only thanks to your skills as a healer."

"I'm the furthest thing from a healer," she scoffed. "But I'm glad I could help."

We made our way to the main stairwell and naturally gravitated towards the library. On our way there, we passed a servant, and I requested she bring us a pot of tea and some refreshments. We stepped inside and Gwen took a seat. I added a log to the fire in the fireplace before joining her.

"How did the meeting go?" she asked.

"Much as you would expect. Cai and Elara are considering all their options and there is a lot to think about. I guess it all comes down to gathering enough men in time."

She nodded, but her expression told me that her mind was somewhere else.

"Have you heard anything from your parents?" I remembered her sending them a letter soon after arriving, but I didn't know if she'd heard anything back.

"They're out in the country. My mother wants me to go to them as she feels it's safer for me there."

Her mother was right. Gwen would be safer there than here, where every day the risk to our safety only grew.

"Are you going?"

She met my gaze with determination. "Of course not. My real family is here and I'm not leaving any of you." Part of me was relieved to have her around. I didn't want her to go but I also didn't want her in the middle of all the fighting. But at the end of the day, it was her choice and hers alone. If she wanted to stay, then I would make sure nothing happened to her.

"They've disowned Thatcher, you know." Also understandable after everything he'd done. But that didn't make the matter any easier for Gwen to digest. Her family had been torn apart, and I didn't know how to make her feel better.

"And he won't have a proper burial because he was a traitor. His body is lying in some shallow grave with all the prisoners and criminals." She sucked in a breath.

"I'm sorry." It was the only thing I could think of saying. "Would you like for him to be buried somewhere else?"

"No. I don't know." She brushed her hair out of her face with frustration. "I don't know how to feel about any of this anymore." Which for someone like Gwen, who always knew exactly what she wanted, had to be quite challenging.

"I don't think there's a right way to feel about it." I tried to reassure her. "It's a lot for anyone to go through. You shouldn't be so hard on yourself."

Gwen pressed her lips into a line in contemplation. "I just can't wait for all of this to be over." Her and everyone else.

"It will be soon." Which wouldn't necessarily be a good thing. There was no guarantee that we would be walking out of this victorious. There was a light knock on the door before the servant girl entered with a tray. She placed the teacups and teapot on the table along with a few finger sandwiches, mini scones and cream.

"Anything else, Your Highness?" she asked once she'd poured some tea into both cups.

"No, thank you."

The servant left the library, and I added a bit of cream to Gwen's tea before handing her the cup. Our fingers grazed when she took the cup from me, and she let them linger there for a moment.

"Why are we drinking tea anyway? You don't even like tea." She was eager to change the subject, and I was happy to oblige.

"No, I don't. But I like you."

A blush crept into her cheeks, and she hid a smile behind her cup. I brought the steaming cup to my mouth, taking a sip of my tea while enjoying the fact that I had this effect on her.

"What book were you reading back there?"

"Since when do you care about books?" she asked with a raised eyebrow.

"Would you rather talk about Aries and the impending battle where thousands of people are going to die and there is no guarantee that we won't be defeated?" It was rather grim to think about.

"Well, when you put it like that, then yes, I suppose I'd rather talk about books."

"I bet you're reading a romance."

"Why? Because I'm a woman?" Gwen was quick to be on the offensive and I revelled in the fact that I could so easily tease her.

"No, because you're you."

She frowned. "What's that supposed to mean?"

"It means I think you're more of a romantic than you want people to think."

"Oh, you reckon?" Her seriousness began to slip away as we fell into our usual back and forth.

"I do." I took another sip of my tea, not particularly enjoying the taste but enjoying the company.

"And what made you come to this conclusion?"

"Well, you see, Lady Gwen, you like to read books but I'm very good at reading people."

"A useful trait, I should think."

"It can be," I replied, tilting my head. I'd always known how people felt about me — how much they disliked me. I couldn't say it was always a pleasure but at least I always knew where I stood.

"And what else have you noticed about me since you're such a good observer?"

"You're smart," I said. "A lot smarter than people give you credit for. And you're witty." I did enjoy her sense of humour.

"Keep going," Gwen insisted, clearly enjoying the compliments.

"You're one of the strongest and most caring people I know." Gwen would do anything for the people she loved, that much was obvious by now.

"You really think that?"

"I know that."

"Sometimes you're a lot kinder than you realise." Her words took me by surprise. I wasn't used to having someone say something nice about me. In fact, the whole thing felt quite foreign, making me unsure how to react.

"There isn't a lot of room to be kind when you're a monarch."

"Is that what your father taught you?" she asked carefully. We'd never discussed my father before. I didn't care to talk about him.

"I can't say my father was a very kind man. I suppose it must have passed on to me."

"I don't believe that," she replied. "I don't think we're just born with all our characteristics and that's how we are for the rest of our lives. We have a choice in the way we want to act with others. Elara decided to take on the duty of being queen, my brother made a choice to betray his kingdom. It comes down to who you decide you want to be."

"I suppose you're right." I gave her a knowing smile. "See, I told you that you're smart."

"It must be all the reading I'm doing." She chuckled. "Who knew that books could make you smart?"

Chapter 42

Elara

There was a knock on my door as I put in my earrings.

"Come in," I called out, expecting it to be Cai, who had said he would escort me to dinner.

The door to my bedroom opened in the reflection of my mirror and I watched the captain of my guard step into the room.

"Oh, Rhen. It's you."

"Expecting someone else?"

I turned to him with a smile plastered on my face. "Do you have any news, updates?"

He cleared his throat and placed his hands behind his back. "I wanted to talk to you about something, yes."

I looked at him expectantly and watched his eyes travel to Anesta, who was in the corner of the room, polishing my crown. She rubbed the cloth across the gemstones with so much vigour, I was almost surprised one of them didn't fall out.

"Go ahead." I trusted that whatever he was about to say, Anesta would keep confidential. In all her time as my lady-in-waiting, she had never given me a reason to doubt her.

Rhen opened his mouth to speak, but the door to my bedroom creaked and all heads turned in that direction.

Cai seemed a little surprised to see so many faces looking at him upon entering the room.

"Oh, my apologies. I didn't mean to interrupt."

"Not at all." I walked over to Anesta and took my crown from her hands. "Rhen was just here to escort Lady Anesta to dinner."

"He was?" Anesta looked up at me with surprise and her cheeks grew a little red.

"Yes, he was." I gave a slight smirk while she fixed a few of my stray hairs, making sure that the crown sat perfectly atop my head.

Whatever Rhen had to say could probably wait an hour or two until after dinner. Right now, we had a slightly more important matter at hand, and that was the matter of family. With tensions being as high as they were between all of us, and not to mention our possible impending doom, if not at the hands of the Argonians, then by some magical stones, I figured we could all use one final dinner together as friends and family.

One night where we didn't quarrel or worry about what was to come. One night where we all wore our finest things and had good food and expensive wine and laughed about silly matters.

Rhen held out his arm to escort Anesta and she took it, a slight tint forming on her cheeks. Both of us had put on our most lavish gowns — hers a pale pink satin with empire sleeves and silver stitching, and mine a golden dress with swirling patterns on the skirt and a square neckline. Small strings of pearls were draped across the bodice and they perfectly accompanied my necklace and crown. For the first time in a long time, I felt like the kind of queen I used to imagine as a child. Not one who worried about politics and enemies plotting, but someone who had endless beautiful things to magnify her own beauty and presence.

"You look breathtaking," Cai murmured as I tucked my hand into the crook of his elbow.

"This old thing?" His words still managed to stir something in my stomach and I felt a wave of happiness settle over me as the four of us made our way from my rooms to the dining hall.

The entire room had been decorated with candlelight as far as the eye could see. A long table stood in the centre of the room, filled with silver dishes and cutlery. Steam rose from the warm plates of food. Gwen and Lance were already seated at the table. And so was Alastor. It wasn't part of the usual protocol to have those without titles at the dinner table, but tonight was a special occasion and I saw it as only fitting that the captain of our guards joined us. Lord Burrow was there and so was Lord Stapleton, who'd arrived earlier that day with his men.

Everyone stood as Cai and I entered the room. He was looking very dashing himself, in a white doublet with his gold crown atop his head. We matched quite well, without intention.

Cai took a seat at the head of the table, and I joined him on his right-hand side.

"Thank you for accepting my invitation." I addressed everyone around the table. Servants with wine jugs poured the dark red liquid into glasses. "I'd like to make a toast." I lifted my glass into the air. "To friends and family."

"*To friends and family,*" everyone echoed before taking a seat.

Lance and Gwen sat next to each other and Cai spent the majority of the evening trying not to stare daggers at my brother from across the table. For the most part Lance behaved himself fairly well. The food was probably the best food I'd ever had in my life. The roasted pig had been glazed with a honey sauce, and steaming potatoes and vegetables were piled onto my plate. There was chocolate dessert with whipped cream and endless glasses of red wine, and by the end of it I felt so stuffed that my dress sat too tight. Cai held my hand atop the table and gave me a smile whenever we made eye contact. The conversation flowed easily, with Lord Burrow telling stories of some of the old parties and dances that were held at Mistwood, with someone getting drunk and making a fool of himself or not being able to dance. There was laughter and it was pleasant, and by the end of it, I was tired enough to yawn.

After dinner, I contemplated going back to my rooms and falling asleep immediately, but I couldn't get what Rhen had said about the stones the other day out of my mind. I was wearing the necklace, and if the stones were linked, there was a chance it could help me find the third Myrgonite object. I'd tried looking quite a few times over the past few days without making use of the other two objects, as Cai had asked, but my search was unsuccessful. However, there were still a few places in the palace I had yet to look.

As I made my way back to my room, I recalled old conversations with Cai. He'd spoken about secret tunnels in Mistwood. If they were in the king's chambers and the throne room, there had to be more around the palace. I merely had to find them. I took a lamp from a nearby table in the hallway.

The best place to start would probably be the throne room. There was a secret hallway that could be used as an escape route for the king and queen. I hadn't got far the last time I was in there, when the soldiers of Argon attacked. I'd heard Cai calling out to me and turned around to look for him. But it had to lead somewhere, and maybe there were other tunnels connected to it. It was somewhere to start at least.

With the candle in my hand, I walked across the throne room, my shoes clicking on the floor. Images flashed before my eyes. I walked over the spot where Thatcher's corpse had lain, his blood spilled across the floor. It was now polished and clean, as if the blood had never been there at all.

My eyes scanned the wall close to the thrones. Now, I just had to find the right spot, as the secret door was quite well concealed. I let my hand trace across the stone wall until I felt a change in the texture, and then I pushed. There was a clicking sound, and the door popped open. Well, that was easy enough. An eerie feeling crept over me. Cai's words were still in my mind, of him asking me not to make use of the objects to find the last remaining one. But they were like a foggy memory now, drowned out by a strong urge to explore the tunnels. Was the third object calling out to me?

I didn't remember deciding to step inside the dark hallway. It was so pitch-black that I could not see the end of it despite the small lamp I carried with me. The same stone had been used to make the walls and floor, and it was clearly very old, the feel of it rough against my hands. I decided to leave the door open, not wanting to risk the chance of getting stuck in there.

The hallway was deathly quiet and so every step I took echoed into the dark void. Holding the lamp up above my head, I tried not to let my imagination run wild. It was just a hallway. There was nothing to be afraid of.

When I reached the end of the hall, there were two ways to go. One was another tunnel, and the other was a small flight of stairs leading down. It might have been my imagination, but I swore I could feel a very light draught coming from the tunnel on the left. If my suspicions were correct, that was the escape route that led out of Mistwood. Which meant the stairs had to lead down to the catacombs. At least I hoped they did, and I wouldn't end up in some tunnel maze that I wouldn't be able to get out of.

I slowly took the stairs, one by one, until I reached the bottom. There were a few torches lining the walls, so I removed the glass from my lamp and used the candle to light the torches. They illuminated my surroundings rapidly.

The walls here were much older than the ones above ground, clearly built when Mistwood Palace was first erected, before all the changes had been made throughout the centuries. The tunnels were a little bit wider and the arched ceiling higher.

Here and there the walls were carved out, with stone coffins lying in them. Cai's ancestors. I tried to read some of the names as I passed by: Jaehaera, Maegelle, Espen, Remington. The others were unrecognisable, worn away by age.

I moved further on, away from the torchlight and into the depths of the catacombs.

If there was anywhere in the palace to hide something valuable, this would be it.

I was making my way past a burial chamber when something scurried over my foot and I jumped, nearly letting out a scream. It was most probably a rat, but being alone in the dark put me on edge.

I reached a vast chamber where the ceiling was even higher, and six pillars stood along the centre. There were a few sarcophagi around the room, the marble carefully etched with the figures of the old kings and queens.

I looked down at the necklace lying heavy on my neck. What if the third object had been buried inside one of these coffins with one of the old rulers? There was no way that I would be able to remove the stone tops myself.

In the darkness, the Myrgonite stone on the necklace seemed almost to glow. So small and delicate, hidden well between all the other gems, looking entirely insignificant and yet being able to carry so much power.

If the stones were linked, had the voice in my head purposefully led me down here? Was the tug I felt towards this place something more than a gut feeling? My fingers reached for the gemstone. It was slightly warm to the touch. Maybe it had truly wanted me to come down here. Maybe it was calling out to the third Myrgonite object like one calls out to a long-lost sister.

I suddenly got the eerie feeling that there was a presence down here apart from my own. Could it be the last object, pulling me towards it? Or was it something much darker and more sinister? Part of me wanted to leave, to return to the stairs and escape tunnel, but my feet were firmly planted.

Where are you? It had to be close. I knew it had to be. But it was as if I could no longer trust my thoughts or feelings. As if the stone was playing tricks on my mind.

I walked over to the nearest sarcophagus. To my surprise, it had the name Erik carved into the stone. My breath caught in my throat. This was Cai's father. I reached out to place my hand on it, but as soon as I touched the stone, it wasn't King Erik's coffin before me but Cai's. His body was inside, dressed in his royal armour, his soft golden locks framing his face. But the rest of him was covered in blood.

Dead.

Cai was dead, his soul departed, and I could do nothing to bring him back to me.

I quickly pulled my hand back, looking around me, but I was still alone. I didn't know what this place was, but a fear was beginning to grow inside me. I stepped away from the sarcophagus, turning to leave. I needed to find Cai. It would be better to do this together. All the while, I tried not to think of the horrible image of him being dead. Were the stones trying to give me some kind of warning or were they making a promise? I was almost at the base of the stairs when a voice came from the darkness.

"Leaving so soon, Your Majesty?"

Something hit the back of my head and the world around me was enveloped in darkness.

Chapter 43

Elara

I woke up to the smell of meat roasting over a fire. My eyes took a moment to adjust to the light.

I was in a tent. This much I could tell. Warm blankets of fur covered my body while a piercing ache erupted in my head.

I sat up, the blankets falling down and exposing me to the cold air. I still wore the dress I'd worn to dinner, but my crown and the necklace were gone. A sinking feeling went through me. Not the necklace.

I looked around the tent. There was the small cot I was lying on, a chest and a small table. Loud noises came from outside.

I stood up, which made my head spin and caused me to sway.

Focus, Elara. You need to get out of here.

My legs felt weak and shaky. How long had I been out?

I reached for the tent flap, pulling it back.

We were at the base of a mountain. A valley stretched out before me. I immediately recognised it from the time Cai had brought me here to show me the Myrgonite mines.

Almost the entire valley was filled with tents and campfires. Thousands upon thousands of Argonian soldiers were going about their business, preparing for battle. Some were training, while others prepared food or talked around the fires, laughing with each other.

It was as if my heart had stopped beating. I knew Aries' army was large, but this was unlike anything I'd ever seen. My gaze shifted to the mountain where hundreds of Aries' men were digging, searching for the Myrgonite stones.

This was so much worse than I'd imagined. Aries was getting closer and closer to the old Myrgonite mines, and against an army of this size, our people would be slaughtered. Our only potential advantage was using the high ground of the valley as Cai had planned, but with our lack of numbers, there was no guarantee that even that would work.

My chest ached at the thought of Cai. They'd probably discovered I was gone by now. He must be worried beyond his mind. Were they on their way? We'd been preparing for battle, but would everyone arrive before it was too late?

I looked back inside the tent. There was a pair of boots next to the bed.

They hadn't tied me up or put a guard to watch over me. Did they not expect me to try to escape?

Mistwood was only a few hours' ride away. But maybe Aries didn't think I would be foolish enough to attempt it in this cold, with no supplies and no horse.

I put on the boots and stepped out of the tent, the cold air hitting my face once more. Goosebumps covered my skin. The evening gown wasn't nearly warm enough.

I started to walk through the camp, not entirely sure where I was going but not willing to sit and wait around either. I had to find my necklace before Aries discovered what it was. Unless, of course, he already had.

I could feel the gaze of some of the soldiers as I passed, though I couldn't blame them. I was walking around an army camp in a dress that was hardly appropriate for the occasion. I wished I'd been carrying a weapon of some kind. I doubted it would make much of a difference but at the very least I would feel a little better.

"Your Majesty."

I turned at the sound of a soldier's voice. His attire was more formal than the others and he carried a spear in his hand. I'd seen him before when we were in Argon. He must have been one of Aries' personal guards.

"Yes?"

"If you would allow me to escort you. His Majesty requires your presence." The polite way he asked reassured me a little, but this was still Aries, and they had still brought me here against my will.

I squared my shoulders. "Very well."

The guard led me through the tents along the base of the mountain. Aries' tent was a little higher than the others and also significantly bigger, as could be expected. Two guards were stationed outside his tent, both with spears by their sides.

"Please inform His Majesty that Queen Elara has awakened."

"You can let her in, Frederick." A masculine voice came from inside the tent. I didn't realise how afraid I was until I heard him speak.

Frederick held the tent flap open and I stepped out of the bright morning light.

The scent of grapefruit hit my nostrils, and my eyes fell to Aries, who was seated at a table, a plate of grapefruit in front of him, which he ate with a golden fork.

He wore no armour, lounging quite casually and not as if he was preparing for battle.

"Elara." His cruel silver eyes looked up from his plate and I shuddered. "I'm glad to see you're up and about again."

"Me too. Considering how hard your goons knocked me on my head."

"I must plead your forgiveness for my guards' methods." Aries dabbed the corners of his mouth with a cloth. "I feared if I'd merely sent an invitation, you wouldn't come."

He gestured to the chair across from him. "Please, have a seat."

"No, thank you." I needed to find a way to get out of there or at least some sort of weapon to protect myself with.

"There really isn't a need for any hostility between us." When I didn't move, his eyes caught one of the guards behind me, who forced me into the chair.

"You and I want the same things, after all."

"Oh, do we now?"

Aries looked at me with a devilish smirk and I remembered how Cai told me he'd killed his own father. He was enjoying this, toying with me.

"Of course," he said after a moment. "We both want our kingdoms to thrive. And we want those we'd cared about avenged." Cai had killed Aries' younger brother on the battlefield and Aries was never going to forgive him for it. Although we both knew this was about so much more than avenging his brother. This was about Aries' unending greed for power.

"Which is why I would like you to reconsider my offer of marriage. Together we could rule Everness, Norrandale and Argon. You'd be one of the most powerful queens on the continent."

329

The mere thought of being wed to a man like him sent shivers up my spine.

"Thank you for your proposal but I'd rather be impaled on a pike."

That devilish smirk fell away. He didn't take kindly to being insulted.

"That is not entirely out of the question."

"Well, go on, then." I placed my hands on the arms of the chair. "If that's what you plan to do, then why don't you just kill me now?"

It was a risk to call his bluff, but I figured if he wanted me dead, then Aries' guards would have killed me. This served some other purpose.

"I don't want to kill you, Elara." Aries relaxed back into his chair, still eyeing me. "The way I see it, you have two choices."

I had a bad feeling about where this was going.

"First, you align yourself and your kingdom with Argon and help me find the Myrgonite objects, and then you and I can rule together, and our kingdoms can flourish."

That was what this was about. Aries rightfully suspected I knew where the Myrgonite mines were, along with the magical objects.

"And my second option?"

"Your second option is that you help me find the Myrgonite stones anyway and then you get to sit and watch as I kill everyone you love."

I leaned forward, laying my arms on the table. "And why the hell would I help you find a single damn stone?"

"You wouldn't," he replied curtly. "Which is why I've taken measures to ensure your cooperation."

My stomach dropped.

"What did you do?"

"Just a little bit of insurance is all." He casually flicked his hand in a gesture to one of the guards, who bowed his head before disappearing out of the tent.

"What did you do?" I asked again, my voice laced with more panic this time. Whatever it was, Aries knew it would be enough to get me to cave and give up the biggest secret in the kingdom.

"Now, don't think I take any pleasure in doing this. But seeing as you refuse to listen to reason, I'm afraid more drastic measures must be taken."

My hands clenched the arms of the chair.

There was a sound behind me and I looked towards the opening of the tent.

No.

Not this.

Cordelia's face was streaked with tears and a cloth had been tied around her mouth to prevent her from letting out anything but small cries. The Argonian guard held her firmly despite her hands being tied behind her back. Her expression was filled with terror.

I shot out of the chair.

Aries' guards had their weapons ready and held out towards me.

"Don't think about doing anything stupid," Aries said, almost sounding bored.

He was right. I had nothing on me to defend myself, not to mention fighting off a group of his guards to free Cordelia.

"You monster," I cried out.

Aries must have sent a group of his men to Everness to find her. He'd had this planned all along. His soldiers had been hiding in the catacombs of the palace just waiting for the right moment and I had walked right into his trap.

"As I understand, she is a close friend of yours." Aries walked around the table, making his way to Cordelia. "It would be a terrible shame for her to get hurt."

"If you so much as lay a hand on her."

I didn't know what to do. Didn't know how to get myself out of this or how I would save the both of us.

"If you don't help me find the Myrgonite stones, then I'll have no choice but to use your little friend here to convince you."

He trailed a finger up her neck and to her jawline. Cordelia tried to pull away but the guard's grip on her remained firm. It took everything in me not to launch myself at Aries.

"And what if I don't know where the stones are?"

In a second, Aries was upon me, his hand wrapped around my throat.

"Do you take me for a fool?" he ground out. I clawed at his arm.

"You're a smart girl. And we both know that you have all the answers I'm looking for."

Air, I needed air. My nails dug into his wrist so hard I almost drew blood.

"So, it's time to stop playing your childish little games and do your duty as queen."

His calloused hand released my throat, and I gasped and coughed, not being able to fill my lungs up fast enough.

I was hunched forward, with my hands on my knees as I tried to return my breathing to normal.

"So, do we have a deal, Queen of Everness?"

He would kill Cordelia, and if I continued to refuse him, he would only keep finding more people I cared about, until I was surrounded by the corpses of my friends and family. This had to end. I had to find a way to stop him.

"Yes," I said through ragged breaths, glaring up at him. "We have a deal."

Chapter 44

Cai

I hadn't been in the armoury of the palace since the last time we'd prepared to leave for battle against Argon. The room had a low ceiling, every inch of the walls lined with swords, knives and other sharp weapons. There were a few shields with my family's crest embellished on the steel, all specially made for the royal family. At the far end of the room, the armour pieces were stored on racks.

The armoury didn't have any windows, so I had no idea what time of day it was or how many hours had passed since I'd come down here.

The low-burning candles suggested it had been a while. In a few hours, we would march to the valley and face Aries and the Argonian army. My people were relying on me to lead them to victory, to free us from the clutches of Argon. Instead, it felt as though I was leading them all to their deaths. We would walk into a massacre, entirely outnumbered.

Our impending doom lay like a heavy weight on my chest, outweighing the strongest armour. I picked up my sword from the table in the middle of the room. It had been sharpened and cleaned, ready for battle. The steel glinted in the candlelight as I turned it in my hands. My father had gifted me the sword when I was much younger. It had been everywhere with me, to Argon and to Everness. He'd told me that I would do great things with it someday.

What I would give to have him here now. He always knew the right thing to say.

I'd come to the armoury in search of some privacy, a moment of peace as I tried to ready myself for what was to come.

We had run out of options. Aries had Elara now. There was no time to wait for more reinforcements or answers about the Myrgonite objects.

The mere thought of the woman I loved in the clutches of that man made me sick to my stomach. Aries had known perfectly well what he was doing all along. Had known that Elara would be enough to lure me out onto the battlefield where he could finish me once and for all. I didn't allow myself to think of the possibility of him hurting her. She was alive. I knew she had to be, and I would find her. That was all that mattered now.

I clutched the sword and made my way towards the stairs that led back up to the lower floor of the palace.

My footsteps were heavy on the stone, echoing the dread inside my chest.

I wasn't in the hallway for long before Alastor was at my side, clad in his Norrandish armour while still strapping more small weapons to himself.

"How are the preparations coming along?" I asked as he fell into step beside me.

"Quite well, Your Majesty. The horses are almost ready and so are Lord Burrow's men."

"Good. I want us ready to leave soon." We would be travelling in the dark, hoping that it would keep us undetected until we reached the battlefield. If our army pushed through the cold weather fast enough, we might be able to strike around dawn.

"I'll inform the men, Your Majesty."

It had taken us more than a day to prepare. My mind was constantly on Elara, wondering whether or not she was still safe in the clutches of the Argonian king.

She was one of the bravest people I knew, stubborn and fearless. But Aries had ways to make even the strongest bend at the knee and I had no doubt that he would use Elara to try to gain everything he'd been going after.

With every minute that passed, Elara and Norrandale were at greater risk.

"Alastor." I stopped walking, turning to face him.

"Yes, Your Majesty?"

"I know things haven't been the same without Jack." The mere thought of him made me clutch the hilt of my sword even tighter. "But I want to thank you for stepping up. You've been a great help to me in the past few months."

"Nothing will ever be the same without him," Alastor admitted. "But it's been a pleasure to serve you, Your Majesty." He gave a slight bow and hurried off to continue his duties, but his words haunted me. The way he said it made it feel like a goodbye. It was one of the many hard truths of what we were about to face. Alastor and I could step onto that battlefield tomorrow morning and neither of us walk away alive.

I'd almost reached the throne room when a servant came running up to me.

"A message for you, Your Majesty," he huffed, out of breath.

I took the note and unfolded it with urgency. Based on how fast the servant had been running, it had to be something serious.

Meet me in the library as soon as possible.
— Rhen

He wasn't the first person I wanted to talk to. Not when there were so many important matters at hand. But if Rhen wanted to see me then it must have had something to do with the Myrgonite objects.

I thanked the servant and started towards the library. According to Elara, Rhen had been spending most of his nights in there, reading and rereading the old Evernean king's diary. It was able to confirm what Elara and I had long suspected two of the objects were. But it left the third and most important one unidentified.

I figured if there was anything else noteworthy in the diary, we would have found it by now. But if Rhen was seeking my presence, maybe there was some important information after all. Something we'd missed before.

Elara believed that destroying the magic was the answer to everything for us. And true as that might have been, right now I was more concerned with a few thousand Argonian soldiers camped in the mountains of Norrandale, who were keeping her as prisoner. For all I knew, Aries was torturing her for information.

The thought made me feel sick. I quickened my pace.

The library was quiet in comparison to the hustle and bustle of soldiers and servants in the rest of the palace. No one was bothered about books when we were about to march into battle.

Rhen stood by the table, half-burnt candles surrounding the books and pages before him. He was rolling up a scroll when he noticed my presence.

"You're here quicker than I thought you'd be, Your Majesty."

"Your note suggested this was important?" I kept my voice calm and cool. Whatever he had dragged me all the way here for, it had better be worth it.

"Yes, Your Majesty." He picked up King Evrin's diary, binding it with a leather strap before he placed it inside a satchel.

"King Evrin died before he could discover what the third object was."

I'd figured as much a long time ago.

"So, I started looking into Queen Riona. Based on the king's writing and numerous other accounts of people who'd met her, it got me thinking about the kind of person she was."

I stepped further into the room. "Elara told me that according to the king, she changed once she'd started adorning herself with the objects."

"Exactly. But so did the king." Rhen placed the satchel over his shoulder and started to clear the rest of the table. He had yet to put on his uniform.

"As the diary continued, his writing grew more paranoid and unhinged. As if the king were slowly losing his mental capabilities. He believed Queen Riona was keeping the third object close. But I realised it wouldn't have made sense for her to keep the object hidden. It doesn't fit her personality, not when she so openly carried the other two."

It made sense, based on everything Elara had told me about what Rhen had uncovered thus far.

"You think she hid it in plain sight? Somewhere or something rather obvious."

"Your Majesty." Rhen cleared his throat. "I think I know what the third Myrgonite object is."

Chapter 45

Elara

An icy wind swept across the valley like a whisper of warning.

War was coming.

In fact, it was already here. With thousands of Argonian soldiers camped out and ready to fight. One battle to end it all.

Frederick had been instructed to bind my hands behind my back before taking me to the caves. I nearly tripped over a rock trying to keep up with his brisk pace as he pulled me along.

"Apologies, Your Majesty, but we really mustn't keep King Aries waiting."

"You can tell your king—" I tried to blow a stray hair out of my face — "that if he wants me at a certain destination quickly, he will have to stop putting me in ridiculous shoes and clothes."

Not only had Aries managed to kidnap me from the palace with relative ease, but he'd also had trunks of clothing and accessories brought from the nearest town. I had no doubt they were stolen, and I didn't want to consider what the Argonians had done to the people they had taken them from. Most likely a noble family, if

I had to guess by the quality of the dresses.

Of course, Aries took it as his opportunity to dress me in some of the finest clothes and jewellery, often placing me in the seat next to him as he made his plans, talked with his men and overlooked the camp. I knew he wanted to keep an eye on me. But this dressing up and parading me next to him was to show me off as a trophy. If I would not succumb and marry him, he would get every other possible use out of me.

Which was why Frederick and I were currently making our way to the Myrgonite mines.

When Aries had placed the map in front of me last night, I contemplated every possible way I could get out of it. But as we stood in Aries' tent, Cordelia was still bound and watching as I held her life in my hands.

I tried to lie at first, hoping it might send Aries and his men on a wild goose chase until I could figure out a way to free Cordelia. If only she managed to escape, that would be enough. But I was not the first person who had tried lying to the King of Argon, though I suspected most of my predecessors didn't live to see the light of day after that.

I didn't know how he knew, if it was my eyes or the tone of my voice that gave me away. I used to be a good liar. But there was too much at stake this time, and when Aries threatened Cordelia's life again, I finally showed him where the Myrgonite mines were.

The best I could hope for was that this would distract him and his men until Cai and the Norrandish armies arrived, whatever men Cai had managed to gather. We would probably still be outnumbered, but at the very least it gave us a fighting chance.

Frederick led me down the path that I had ridden with Cai several months ago. How different things had been then. Before we knew what the Myrgonite objects were, before Thatcher had betrayed us and Cai was exiled. What I would have given to be back there now. When did things become so dire?

I struggled on after Frederick until we reached the entrance of the cave. Aries and a few of his men were already inside, torches lit, some of them gawking. Cordelia was there too. One of the men held her bound figure. Her eyes fell to mine. They were swollen from crying. She looked so tired and weak. What had they been doing to her? Where were they holding her? I wished I could knock Frederick out of the way, somehow free myself from the ropes that bound my own hands, and I would fight every one of those Argonian men if it meant I could set her free. She didn't deserve any of this. The love of her life had been murdered and now she was being held captive because of me.

Time. I needed more time.

"I knew you would be worth it somehow." Aries' silver eyes lingered on me, on my clothes, and I shuddered.

The cave loomed above us in all its glory, Myrgonite glinting in the light of their torches.

Aries ran his hand along one of the rocky walls, inspecting his new prize. This would make him richer than any of the other kings on the continent. And money had a power all of its own.

"This was more than I expected," he admitted with glee.

Where are you, Cai? I needed him. Things were already bad before and they were becoming increasingly worse.

"We had a deal," I reminded Aries. "I tell you where the caves are, you free Lady Cordelia." If Cordelia was let go, she could make her way to Mistwood. She could tell the others what she saw of the camp and that Aries knew the location of the mines.

"Funny." He scratched the stubble on his cheeks. "I don't remember agreeing to that."

My heart dropped.

No.

"You liar!" I called out, yanking myself away from Frederick, but his grip held firm. "You told me you'd let her go!"

Of course I shouldn't have trusted him. Why did I for a second believe that he would actually free Cordelia? Nothing about Aries suggested he was a man of his word, unless, of course, it came to his love for violence.

"She serves no purpose here. She doesn't have anything to do with this and you got what you wanted," I said, with a voice full of panic. "Let her go." And then I added, "Please." I would beg for her life if it meant he didn't hurt her.

Aries slowly walked over to Cordelia. I watched with disgust as he cupped her cheek, forcing her to look up at him. His thumb slowly brushed her jaw, soft whimpers escaping her.

"You're right."

I hadn't seen him pull out the knife.

"She doesn't serve a purpose anymore."

Bright red blood spilled from her neck.

My screams echoed through the cave.

I watched Cordelia's body drop to the ground, the life slowly slipping from her eyes.

Blood began to pool around her.

"I'll kill you!"

Frederick's grip tightened on me.

"I'll kill you for this!"

"Now now." Aries tried to hush me, wiping the bloody blade on the sleeve of a nearby guard. Her life and the lives of all those he took meant nothing to him. He truly was a monster. "There's no need for that."

He came to a standstill in front of me. Cordelia's blood had spattered onto his face. I was going to be sick.

"I gave you the option, remember. I told you that I would kill everyone you loved, and you chose not to listen to me." His tone was that of a parent lecturing a child.

Aries flinched only slightly when I spat in his face.

The world around us seemed to go quiet for a moment, anticipating what he would do next.

Pain erupted in my cheek as his hand collided with my face. The force of his strike was strong enough that it wrenched me out of Frederick's grasp, and I fell onto the cave floor.

"I'm growing rather tired of your temper tantrums, Queen Elara," Aries said in warning.

I tried to catch my breath, my ears practically ringing from the impact of his hand.

"It doesn't matter if you know where the cave is. Cai and his army are coming for you and you will not live to see the end of the battle," I said through deep breaths, thinking about all the ways I wanted to end his life.

Aries sank down to his haunches next to me. "Even if Cai is foolish enough to try and kill me, we both know he would never succeed. Nor would the Norrandish army."

He brushed a tendril of hair out of my face like he hadn't just hit me, and I flinched away.

"You will never find those Myrgonite objects, you know."

My skin still stung. I didn't want to turn my head to look at him. I found myself staring at his boots instead.

"I don't need to find them." Aries stood back up, dusted off his hands. He gestured to Frederick to pull me back into a standing position. My legs felt numb. My eyes went to Cordelia's body lying only a few metres away. I'd failed to save her. She died because of me. My cheeks were wet but I didn't remember crying.

"I only need to keep you alive until Cai gets here and he will lead me straight to them. He would never risk your life, not even if the fate of his kingdom depended upon it."

His gaze became more sinister, if that was even possible. "And then nothing, or no one, will stand against me ever again."

Chapter 46

Cai

Moving an army across mountainous terrain was usually challenging enough by itself. Doing so in winter felt damn near impossible.

My horse shuddered beneath me, as if to say, "Why the hell are you making me walk on rocky ground while an icy wind beats against us?"

Had my kingdom and the woman I loved not depended on it, I might have said, "Fair point."

We moved slowly and stealthily, allowing the light of the full moon to guide us so that we wouldn't have to use as many torches. Soon, the moon's light would disappear, and dawn would spread over the kingdom of Norrandale. A feud that had been going on for hundreds of years would finally come to an end.

Our cavalry marched ahead, archers following, and the foot soldiers behind. Everyone was cold and uncomfortable, trudging through the dreary weather and making tracks in the thin layer of snow that coated the ground. The very last of winter leaving its marks before spring arrived soon. Luckily there had been no snowfall overnight or it would have made our journey much more treacherous.

What had felt like a fairly comfortable journey in the past now seemed to drag on for ever. We finally stopped close to the path that led up the mountain and into the valley. We stayed hidden in the coverage of the forest, hoping that the scouts Aries had no doubt sent out would not be able to spot us. The path itself was too narrow for our entire army to get through comfortably, not to mention we still needed to travel uphill before we reached the valley where Aries was camped. We were going to have to divide and hope that the uphill advantage would be enough to help us.

I mounted my horse again after having relieved myself behind a nearby tree.

"Your Majesty." Alastor's whisper came from behind me. We'd ordered the entire army to be as quiet as possible, not wanting to give away our location.

"Yes?"

"There's a messenger here for you."

The young soldier stepped up to my horse, his face covered in dirt, his eyes wide with adrenaline.

I took the note from him and squinted as I tried to read the scribblings in the dark.

"What does it say?" Alastor asked, having mounted his own horse.

"Men," I said, suddenly feeling a little breathless, and even a morsel of relief. "Mannik and Ryker. Their men have arrived." The noble men my father had entrusted to run his council had come through for me. Loyal to the Crown, to the end.

There was a slight laugh from Alastor. Almost nervous. He wasn't the sort of person who got nervous easily, but war will do strange things to a person. "Just in the nick of time, then."

"Yes," I said, thinking about Elara. Wondering what she was doing, if she was safe. If only I could tell her that I was on my way. That I would see her soon. And as the first light began to appear over the horizon, I felt something I hadn't been feeling for a while ... hope.

My legs ached by the time we'd reached the top of the slope. I had dismounted and I was peering over the brow of the hill that we would soon descend. My archers were spread out next to me, waiting for my order. I carefully observed the camp. Endless tents and small burnt-out fires. It wasn't too difficult to find Aries' tent on the far side of the valley. My eyes travelled to the Myrgonite caves in the distance. It was obvious that Aries had discovered them now. I waited for that sinking feeling I was certain would come. But I realised that after today, it wouldn't matter anymore. One way or another. And where was Elara? Aries would keep her close, which meant I needed to find a way to get to his tent.

"On my signal," I said, lifting my arm. Row upon row of bowstrings were pulled taut, flaming arrows waiting to be released. I waited a second. Thought of my father. Of the king that he was and the man he wanted me to be. Today I would live up to his legacy, or end it.

Let me make you proud. I dropped my hand.

The sky turned yellow as the burning arrows made their way up into the air before dropping back down. Time seemed to slow as I watched the camp catch fire.

"Good morning, Aries. I hope you like surprises."

"Get ready to strike again!" Alastor shouted behind me.

Tents were on fire — soldiers were screaming, running around without their armour. The Argonian army had fallen into chaos, but

I knew it wouldn't be long before they coordinated themselves again. Already a few of them had their shields ready for the next assault.

"Now," I told Alastor, and he gave the signal to the archers. Once again, the arrows rained down on the Argonians, killing some, wounding more.

In the next few minutes their archers started to respond, managing to hit a few of our own. When they finally got into battle formation, I began to ready the cavalry.

My horse stomped nervously, knowing that whatever was about to come would not be good. I tightened my grip on the reins, searching the crowds until my eyes landed on one very particular figure.

Aries stood at the back of the army, close to his tent, armed and ready for blood. Though it was quite a distance, it was as if something in my gut knew he was watching me, daring me to come for him.

The cavalry descended, meeting the Argonian forces midway up the hill. There were so many of them. Men on horses, foot soldiers, some with spears. I needed to find a way through all of them if I wanted to get to Aries, but more importantly, to Elara.

Mannik and Stapleton's men flanked us, coming from the left and right as we tried to cage in the army. Swords, horses and men collided. I could practically taste the blood in the air.

For a second, I was pulled outside my body as I witnessed the carnage before me. I was the young prince again, on the battlefields of Argon. Panic surged up inside me. Every choice I'd made, everything I'd done was to try to avoid this situation, so I would not find myself back in this position.

I shook my head, trying to regain focus. This was inevitable. This was always going to happen. I merely had to accept it. Today would be the day that I finally faced my demons.

And then all I could think about was Elara. And there was something to fight for. Something more important than my own survival.

I headed to the right, where our men appeared to have the upper hand. The battle became a blur. I swung my sword in every direction, every soldier having become an obstacle between me and Elara.

At some point, someone knocked me off my horse and I hit the ground with a hard thud. It was an effort to get air into my lungs again. A sword came down hard on my armour.

I took out a knife that had been strapped to me and stabbed the soldier in the leg, giving me enough time to grab hold of my sword and run him through.

And then I found the next soldier and the next, killing them one by one. And with each soldier, I got closer to the large tent that loomed at the base of the mountain. Only I could no longer see Aries himself. He had to be somewhere in the fighting. I had no doubt he would find me again.

I made my way along the side of the battleground, trying to avoid the centre where the fighting was thickest. Alastor was close behind me, constantly having my back. We fought together until I could finally reach Aries' tent. There was no one outside to guard it. I couldn't even be sure she was in there, but I didn't know where else to look.

Alastor and I sneaked around the back of the tent, and I carefully lifted the canvas.

"You keep watch, I'll go inside."

Alastor gave a nod and held up his sword, ready to strike.

I climbed into the back of the tent, trying to make as little noise as possible, should someone be ready to chop my head off.

My eyes fell on her silhouette. She was seated in a chair, hands clutching the armrests as she looked out onto the battlefield.

I stood up straight. "Elara."

Her head turned. She was out of the chair immediately, running towards me. I caught her in my arms, pressing my face into her neck, taking in the scent of her.

"You're alive." She breathed out with relief. "You're still alive."

I pulled back to inspect her for wounds, but she appeared unharmed.

Her eyes widened as she took in the state of me. "Are you hurt?"

I had to have been covered in blood from head to toe by now.

"No, I'm fine." A little worse for wear, maybe, but still alive.

"I don't know where Aries is. I lost sight of him in the battle."

I placed my hands on both her cheeks. "Elara, I want you to listen to me very carefully."

Her hands were clutching my arms as if she were afraid I would disappear if she let go.

"I need you to stay here for now." She looked up at me with surprise. "Our army is on the other side of the valley, and I can't get both of us through there, not until the fighting has eased a little."

I pulled the Myrgonite dagger from my boot and pressed it into her hand. "Keep this with you. I know it will protect you."

"What about you?" she asked, eyes full of worry. "Who's going to protect you?"

"Alastor is right by my side," I assured her. "I just wanted to make sure you were safe. I promise I'm coming back to get you."

"Okay," she said after a moment.

I kissed the side of her head, not wanting to let go of her either. Just a little longer. We only had to hold out a little longer.

"I love you," I whispered into her hair.

"I love you too. Please be safe."

I forced myself to pull away from her. A stray tear rolled down her cheek and she quickly wiped it away, still trying to be the strong one.

With a parting nod, I stepped out of the tent, sword in my hand. I looked around for Aries. It was time to end this once and for all.

Chapter 47

Lance

I was freezing.

My entire body shivered as I rode through the Norrandish forest, following the path that led to the mountains. I could no longer feel my fingers or my toes and every part of me yearned to turn around. To go back to Mistwood, where there was a warm fire and some ale. But I knew I couldn't. I knew I had to find her.

When I'd walked into Gwen's room last night, she was packing a small bag.

"What are you doing?" I asked her.

"Just gathering a few supplies. I'm not actually sure what one needs for this sort of thing."

I closed her bedroom door behind me, leaning against the frame with my arms crossed. "What sort of thing?"

"You know, battle." Gwen looked nervous and excited at the same time.

It took me a moment to realise what she meant.

"Gwen," I said slowly. "Tell me you don't plan on leaving with the army in a few hours."

She stopped what she was doing and looked at me. "Well, I'm not just going to sit here and wait for better days."

I didn't know if it was meant to be a jab at me. At the fact that I wasn't going with Cai's men. But it was not my fight. And I wasn't trained to be a soldier. If something went wrong on that battlefield the next morning, I would need to flee back to Everness to warn the council, to decide our next steps and how we were going to protect Everness if Aries was coming.

"This isn't about waiting around for better days. With all due respect, you have never seen real war before. You have no idea what you're walking into."

"I'm not as fragile as you think."

I dropped my hands and walked over to her bed, where she'd resumed her packing.

"I don't think you're fragile." My choice of words seemed to please her momentarily, until I added, "I think you're being stupid."

"Well, I'd rather be stupid than a coward." That one definitely felt directed at me.

"Sometimes being alive is better than being brave."

Gwen sighed, dropping her bag. "It's not like I plan on walking into the middle of a battle. I'll stay far behind, take my bow and arrows with me."

"Staying alive doesn't make you a coward." I tried to reason with her. "Those soldiers have been training for years. They know what to expect. They know what they're doing. To walk into a battle with no experience of that sort of thing is to have a death wish. You'd be no help to anyone."

"You don't understand." Her expression grew weary. "My friends and family are out there, and I cannot patiently sit here and wait for the worst to happen."

"It's my family too," I reminded her. "But we're needed here, Gwen. Someone has to hold down the fort. You have an entire infirmary to run."

She didn't respond, looking down at the things splayed out on her bed.

"Promise me." I stepped in front of her and lifted her chin. "Promise me you won't go."

She looked at me, eyes full of worry and pain and everything in between.

"Promise me," I said again, when she hesitated.

"Fine, I promise." There was no sincerity in her voice, yet I had no choice but to believe her.

I couldn't sleep after that, plagued by an unsettling feeling in my chest. I got dressed and made my way to Gwen's room, hoping she might be awake too. Perhaps she would be willing to join me for something to drink. Even if it had to be tea. Anything to avoid rolling around in my bed for another few hours.

She didn't answer when I knocked, and when I stepped inside the room, there was no trace of her. The bed made, that bag she was packing earlier gone.

I let out a string of curses, running back out into the hall.

Horse. I needed a horse and a weapon of some kind, although I didn't know how far it would get me. The Norrandish army had left hours ago. I had no idea how long it would take for me to catch up. If I was lucky, I would reach them before the battle started. I could stop Gwen from doing something reckless and life-threatening.

I didn't bother with proper winter riding attire, which was my first mistake. The only horse I could manage to find was an old mare with absolutely no interest in walking the woods in the dead of night.

It was nearing dawn now, light slowly emerging before the sunrise. I couldn't be too far away. If I stopped the horse and listened carefully, I was almost certain I could hear fighting in the distance.

I gave the poor old mare a good kick in the sides, alerting her that we needed to get a move on. She surprisingly obliged, speeding up to a slow canter. It wasn't quite the gallop I needed but it was better than walking.

Low-hanging tree branches scratched me as we passed, and slowly the sounds of war became clearer. The screaming and the fighting got louder until I reached the hill that would lead into the valley of the Norrandish mountains.

Most of the soldiers appeared to be down there in the midst of a bloody battle, apart from a few stray archers who remained at the top of the hill, aiming at potential targets. It would be a lot more challenging to wound or kill an Argonian now. They were no longer able to send arrows flying randomly into the air, as that risked hitting the Norrandish soldiers too.

I dismounted the horse and tied her to a nearby tree, my eyes scanning for a familiar face. She wasn't among any of them. I wouldn't allow myself to consider the possibility that she was already dead, or worse, taken by one of the Argonian soldiers.

Where are you, Gwen?

As if my silent prayer had been answered, I finally saw her on the far side of the hill, bow and arrow in hand. She aimed into the valley before sending the arrow flying. I didn't hesitate. I ran to her as quickly as my legs would carry me.

"Gwen!"

She didn't hear me at first. It was hard to hear anything above the fighting.

"Gwen!"

She turned then, at the sound of my voice, and lowered her bow.

"Lance?" Her eyes were wide with surprise.

I reached her, out of breath, tired and muscles burning.

"What are you doing here?"

I was so relieved to see her still alive, I didn't know if I wanted to kiss her or grab her by the shoulders to try to shake some sense into her.

"What am *I* doing here? What are *you* doing here?"

Her bow continued to hang loosely at her side, but her posture looked defeated.

"Look, I'm sorry, but I told you. I couldn't just sit there and wait. Not while the people I care about are out here fighting for their lives."

"And what about me?" I cried out with a tone of desperation. "What if I need you alive and safe?"

She slowly seemed to register the importance that she held. "My brother," she said with a whimper. "I just felt like if I was here, then maybe ..." She trailed off, a single tear rolling down her cheek.

I took her face in my hands, wiping the tear away with my thumb. "Gwen, you don't have to atone for your brother. He made his choices. Now I'm asking you to make yours."

I pressed my forehead to hers, the world around us momentarily forgotten. "Come with me."

Don't ever leave me again was what I didn't say out loud.

I pulled back a little, looking towards the valley below, to all the bloodshed taking place.

"Come back with me, and whatever happens out here today, we will find a way to face it."

Gwen didn't see the archer on the side of the battlefield, bowstring taut, arrow aimed directly at her. Before she could answer, I pulled her into me, turning us so that I could cover my body with hers. I looked down at her, my breathing ragged.

Gwen turned pale instantly, sucking in a breath. We both let our eyes slowly fall to the arrow now in my lower side.

Pain sliced through me a moment later, as if it took my body a few seconds to register what had happened.

"Lance," Gwen said, with panic in her voice. She grabbed me as the world began to sway. I didn't remember falling to the ground but suddenly I was there, looking up at Gwen and the dark winter clouds above her.

"No, no no."

Blood soaked my jacket, and she pressed her hand to the wound. *Bleeding out from an arrow*, I thought. *What a crappy way to die.*

"Stay with me, Lance. You're going to be fine."

Dark spots filled my vision, and I felt Gwen grab my chin, blood transferring from her hands to my face. "Look at me," she ordered. Were those tears in her eyes? "Stay with me."

Yes, I wanted to say, but I felt so heavy, it was too difficult to form words.

"Please, Lance."

My eyelids grew heavier.

Gwen continued to press her hand to the wound, trying to stop the blood. "Please stay with me." It was the last thing I heard before the world went completely dark.

Chapter 48

Elara

The world around me had erupted into chaos.

Everywhere I looked, men lay dying, crying for mercy, most of them Norrandish.

But Cai was here, and he was still alive, and so I did as he asked and stayed put in Aries' tent, the dagger he'd given me buried in the pocket of my dress.

I tried to search for him among the faces but there were so many soldiers that they practically merged together.

After what felt like hours but must have been only minutes, I saw Aries emerge from the fighting. His face was coated in blood, the morning light reflecting off his armour.

Aries made his way up to the tent where I sat, careful to keep my expression neutral.

He barged into the tent, grabbed the nearest jug of wine and drank straight from it.

Only once his thirst had been satiated did he look at me.

My stomach twisted.

"You look a little pale," was the only thing he said.

I cleared my throat, looking out of the tent again. "It's not a pretty view."

Aries let out a snort. "Too delicate for your fragile little heart?"

I didn't reply, knowing that whatever I said would probably get me killed.

"Though I must disagree with you." He grabbed a nearby piece of cloth and wiped the blood from his face. "I think this is the perfect view."

My fists clenched in my lap.

"And I must say, your dress is quite exquisite." Of course he would think so. He'd picked it out. "But I do feel as though something is missing. If you're going to be seated by my side, then you must look like a true queen."

I didn't know what he'd meant until I suddenly felt him behind me. I tensed up, preparing to defend myself, when I felt the cool gemstones being laid against my skin. Aries had one of the Myrgonite objects with him all this time and he didn't even know it. With the necklace so close, the dagger felt heavy in my pocket. Two Myrgonite objects. Big mistake, Aries.

I watched as he placed the Argonian crown atop his head before taking my crown out from a nearby trunk. I'd been wearing it the night his men kidnapped me. Aries must have kept it for this very purpose, like this was all some sick and twisted game to him. He placed it on my head and let his hands travel to my shoulders, fingers resting on my collarbone, and I tried not to shudder.

"Now we can watch."

He took a seat on the chair next to me, wine jug in his hand. This was what he'd promised. That I could be sitting there as his wife and the queen of Argon, observing our victory, or that I would be next to him anyway, as his dolled-up trophy, watching as he destroyed everything I cared about.

The Norrandish lines were starting to fall, our men thinning out as the sheer force of the Argonians overpowered them. It was easy to believe they'd originally hailed from an ancient warrior people — brutal and fearless, they used the battlefield as their dancefloor.

We'd always known it was a long shot to take on Aries' army, which was why we'd tried to avoid it until it was impossible. But to witness the atrocity with my own eyes. To know we were going to lose it all. Not to mention Aries now knowing where the Myrgonite mines were.

But he didn't have the three Myrgonite objects yet.

My hand found the dagger inside my pocket. It was practically buzzing with magic.

If I had anything to do with it, he would never find the objects.

I had a choice to make. I could let Aries get what he wanted, let him win. Or I could fight.

Old instincts kicked in. I pulled the dagger out and went for Aries' neck. But being the warrior he was, he must have sensed my movement, and he jerked away fast enough that I only managed to scratch him.

"Bitch." Aries pressed a hand to his neck, and I used the opportunity to jam the dagger into his shin. He tried to grab it, but I was quicker this time, pulling it out before he could reach it.

I moved to the other side of the tent, putting the table between me and Aries to give me a moment to regain my composure and focus. With little effort, Aries overturned the table, spilling wine and platters of food.

I looked for the object closest to me, which happened to be a candlestick, and threw it at Aries' head with all my might.

Unfortunately, I missed, and Aries let out a laugh that made my blood turn cold. I grabbed another candlestick and hurled it at him. This time, it hit him right between his eyes. Aries was startled for a second, pressing his fingers to the newly formed mark on his head that was now bleeding.

I backed out of the tent, my heart beating rapidly. But there was something else, something more.

The magic of the Myrgonite seemed to flow through my veins. I felt stronger than I had before, braver. Something surged through me, inexplicable as if it had a mind of its own, and for the first time, I understood the danger of this power, how easily it could consume you.

I didn't have much time to consider it before Aries was out of the tent. Luckily, he hadn't grabbed a weapon, probably thinking he wouldn't need one.

Aries came at me like a wolf ready to pounce but I was prepared this time.

I sliced through the air, knowing that if I wasn't going to get in a lethal cut or stab, I could wound him until he couldn't fight me anymore. I would make him bleed.

Aries dodged me left and right, his leg and his neck still bleeding.

He almost managed to grab my wrist but I was quicker, cutting his hand. As he pulled back, I aimed for his arm, and more blood seeped out from his skin.

"You're a fool if you think this is going to end well for you," he said.

I made to stab him again, but Aries grabbed my arm, and I struggled against him until we fell to the ground. With his weight, he could easily overpower me, pinning me down. Our hands fought over the dagger, but I refused to let go. Aries' hands covered mine over the hilt, and with brute strength he managed to turn the blade around so that it was facing down at me. It wouldn't take too much for him to plunge the knife into my heart.

Fear spiked in my chest. There was a horrid smile on Aries' face, like I was already dead. We both knew I didn't have the strength to keep him from using the knife to kill me. The need for survival overtook every thought and instinct. I couldn't prevent him from stabbing me. I could only direct his aim. Knowing there was no other way out, I moved our hands, no longer resisting.

Maybe I was a fool trying to take on the King of Argon. But I was also many other things. I was a thief. I was a girl raised among bandits in the forest, who pretended to be a princess in order to steal from a prince. I was the girl bound to the King of Norrandale by a force stronger than any ancient magic. I was the daughter of King Magnus and Queen Estella, and I was the Queen of Everness. The Myrgonite dagger sank into my left shoulder and I let out a scream. But the movement was enough for Aries to lose his balance.

My right arm found a rock on the ground next to me, and I used the remainder of my strength to hit Aries on the side of his head. I managed to hit him hard enough that he fell to the side, bleeding now from his forehead and his temple. While he was disoriented, I scurried out from under him and braced myself before pulling the dagger from my shoulder. Immediately more pain shot through my body, and I clenched my teeth to hold back a cry of pain. I forced myself not to look at the blood that trickled down my left arm.

"I told you I would kill you," I shouted over the battle happening around us. "You have taken enough from this world, Aries." Aries tried to grab me again, but I cut the dagger straight across his stomach. He let out a cry of both anger and pain. It was no longer me who was fighting. It was a force beyond me, stronger and more powerful than anything I'd ever experienced.

"And it's time to pay up."

I finally understood Cai's anger in that moment. The hatred he felt for Thatcher after he took everything from him. I understood because I felt it too. I buried the dagger deep into his chest, twisting as I thought about every life that had ended because of him.

I stepped back, blood dripping from the dagger onto my dress. Blood filled Aries' mouth, and he fell to his knees.

I don't know why I expected him to look more fearful as he lay at death's door. Instead, he was smiling.

"Even if you kill me, your army will never survive this. Nor will anyone stop coming after the Myrgonite objects."

Before I could reply, a sword cut through Aries' neck, beheading him.

I looked up to see Cai standing behind him, out of breath and tired but alive. He looked like he was in shock, not quite believing what he'd just done.

Aries was gone, his head now separated from his body, both on the ground before me.

But the battle was still going on at full force, the Argonians trained never to surrender even if their king was dead.

Cai was by my side. "You're bleeding."

"It's just my shoulder." I didn't know who I was trying to make feel better because I was in a lot of pain.

Cai used his sword to cut a piece of my dress and pressed the material to my wound.

"We need to get out of here."

I nodded, but I spotted something on the hill in the distance, a large group of people who wore no uniform or official armour. They were not Argonian or Norrandish.

"Look." I pointed to them. "It's Uncle Arthur's men and the Baruk clan."

"There's more," Cai said, and slowly more and more men trickled in after Donald and Olwin's men. Not only had they managed to gather all the bandits, but they'd made it in time.

"They came." Cai sounded just as surprised as I was. The merged group of bandits stormed down the hill and into the fight. We were still outnumbered, but if we were to go down, it would not be without trying.

Cai took my hand, leading as we tried to fight our way through the mass of soldiers. I tried to hold on to him with all my might, but we got separated, and I lost sight of him in the crowd.

One of the Argonians came at me with a sword, which I dodged in the nick of time. But he struck again, and I only had the dagger to hold off the blow. My shoulder was still bleeding, and if it had been any other dagger, I wouldn't have stood a chance. But the Myrgonite glowed when it hit the steel of the sword, nearly denting the blade.

The soldier didn't hesitate to come at me again. I grabbed the hilt of the dagger with both hands and forced the sword away from me, before turning quickly enough that I landed the dagger in the soldier's neck.

Blood spattered as I pulled away and he grasped at the flowing blood. Another life gone by my hands. I didn't have time to consider it. This was about survival.

I looked around, trying to find Cai once more.

Where are you?

I was nearing the hill when someone bumped into me — a fighting soldier, a falling body, I wasn't certain. The force was enough to knock me off my feet, causing my crown to fall off and slide across the icy ground.

My fingers dug into the mixture of blood and dirt as I attempted to push myself up, but the ground was slippery, and my dress was by no means helping.

"Here, I got you." Two arms wrapped around me, pulling me into a standing position.

"Rhen, you're alive." I let out a breath of relief at his familiar face. And then I saw the dark eyes he shared with Cordelia and her dead body in a nearby cave. How would I tell him she was gone?

Before he could reply, an Argonian soldier came at him, but Rhen dodged and pulled me out of the way. When he tried to come towards us again, one of Uncle Arthur's men stabbed him with a sword, but that didn't stop the Argonian from fighting.

"You need to get out of here," Rhen said, trying to pull me to safety.

"You think?" I cried out, still clutching the dagger, but the crown was left behind.

"I mean it." Rhen's grip on mine tightened. "We need to retreat."

"Retreat?" I called out with surprise. "I know we're not exactly holding the high ground right now but—"

He stopped to look me in the eye. "I need you to trust me, Elara."

Of course I trusted him, but that didn't mean I understood.

I continued to look at him with confusion when Rhen spotted someone behind me.

"Your Majesty," he called out. I looked over my shoulder to see Cai running towards us. Relief flooded his eyes when he confirmed I was still okay. I didn't know how much more of this I could take.

"I have a plan," Rhen informed him. "But I need you to retreat with your men." At first Cai appeared sceptical. But then something flickered in his eyes, as if in understanding.

He gave a brief nod and started calling for the retreat, helping me back up the hill behind him.

"What's going on?" I asked. "Why are we retreating?"

Cai didn't answer me, still calling out for his men to follow him. The Argonians seemed pleased at this, some of them killing our men even as they were running away. I looked for Rhen, until I spotted him not coming with us but running straight towards the middle of the fighting.

We made it to the top of the hill, out of breath and covered in blood. The archers formed a defensive line, keeping the Argonians from coming up the hill after us. My eyes stayed on Rhen. He was looking for something, jumping over the corpses to get there.

And then I saw it.

The Evernean crown in the middle of it all, its gemstones reflecting the weak morning sunlight.

"No," I breathed out.

All this time. It couldn't have been there all this time.

Rhen was still running, sword in hand, and I finally understood what he was about to do.

"No, he can't," I said, grabbing Cai's arm. "It's going to kill him."

Cai looked at me with sad eyes.

Rhen had almost reached the crown. The third Myrgonite object.

"No, no, no." I managed to take a few steps down the hill before Cai grabbed me, pulling me back.

"No!" I gave out a cry.

Rhen stopped in front of the crown as it lay on its side in the middle of the valley. He lifted his sword high above his head and then he plunged it down.

At first there was only a piercing light, so bright that I had to turn my face into Cai's chest not to be blinded. There was a loud noise and then I heard the anguished cries from the Argonian men. Cries of pain and torture. Cries of death. I couldn't watch.

The light began to fade, pulling back into the Myrgonite crown. When the light returned to normal, the crown was still there but broken. Rhen's bloodied and battered body lay next to it. It wouldn't take a physician to know he was no longer breathing. But all around him, Argonian corpses covered the ground, too many to count. Just about the entire army had been brought down by the last magic that erupted from the Myrgonite stone. The royal crown. My crown.

All around it was deathly quiet, apart from a cool winter breeze and the cries of a few circling crows, already there to feast on the flesh of dead soldiers. No one knew quite what to do. No one knew what exactly had just happened, what they'd borne witness to.

And then the air began to hum.

It was a soft buzzing at first, and in a few seconds, it became louder.

The ground beneath my feet began to shake and I grabbed Cai for support.

"The mountain," Cai said under his breath. I looked to see what he meant. Rocks were beginning to crumble at the top of the mountain. Snow peaks cascading into rivers of snow.

"It's the caves." I wiped a tear-stained cheek, or maybe it was blood. I was no longer sure. "They're collapsing."

The wave of magic sent out from Rhen destroying the crown must have caused structural damage to the Myrgonite mines. The ground beneath shook harder and it became an effort to keep standing.

The remainder of the Norrandish army watched as the mountain with the Myrgonite mines collapsed into itself, created dust and rocks and rubble, reshaping the earth as if the Myrgonite stones had never been there at all.

Chapter 49

Lance

One thing I could be certain about was that getting shot with an arrow was a pain in the arse.

Or a pain in the lower side, in my case. I didn't remember the arrow being removed or the wound being stitched up.

All I remembered was waking up in the new infirmary with Elara sitting next to my cot.

Everything hurt. My body felt as though it had been trampled by a herd of horses.

"Look who's still alive," she joked.

"Barely," I croaked out with a groan. I tried to sit up, but a pain shot through my side, rendering me immobile.

"I wouldn't move too much, if I were you. Physician said you're lucky to be alive. You lost a lot of blood."

"Where's Gwen?" She'd kneeled by my side when it happened. She'd begged me not to leave her. I'd heard her cry, fearing that I would die in front of her.

"I told her to go and get some rest. She hasn't left your side since it happened, though I don't know what the two of you were doing there in the first place."

"It's a long story." Something I didn't have the energy to go into at that moment. Despite just waking up, I felt tired. I could have used a drink, but I suspected I wasn't going to get one anytime soon.

Elara leaned a little closer, her expression curious. "What exactly is going on between the two of you anyway?"

"When did we become the kind of siblings to discuss this sort of thing?" Elara and I had never been close, probably never would be, and reasonably so. The fact that we got along at all was more than enough.

"Way to evade the question." But she didn't press me further.

I looked around the infirmary at the wounded soldiers that surrounded me. Some asleep, some reading, some still moaning in pain.

"So, when can I be moved to my rooms?"

"Soon. We're a little understaffed, with most of the servants helping here in the infirmary." Elara crossed her legs, sitting on a chair next to me. She wasn't wearing a dress, looking quite comfortable in her riding breeches and a white shirt, the cut of it slightly feminine.

"Are you going to tell me how the hell you managed to defeat Aries and the entire Argonian army?"

She was here, making idle conversation, so I had to assume that Cai was still alive. That while there were probably many casualties, somehow, for some reason and by some miracle, we had come out victorious.

"It's a long story." Elara threw my own words back at me. It was hard to argue with that kind of logic.

She reached into the pocket of her breeches and pulled out something small before holding it out to me.

"Is that what I think it is?"

"Before you get too excited, it doesn't possess any magical powers, and it never will. It's a pretty little gemstone and that's it."

I turned the small Myrgonite stone in my hand, inspecting it. It appeared very delicate, with a rosy hue, though not quite conforming to one colour. But like Elara said, it didn't feel special or magical in any way.

"It's not what you were hoping for, I know. But I kept my promise in a way."

"I can't believe you actually destroyed the Myrgonite objects."

"I didn't actually." A look of sadness crossed her face. "Rhen did."

"Rhen?"

She nodded, her expression saying enough about what the price of destroying those objects was.

I cleared my throat. "Rhen was a good soldier." Despite the fact that he'd betrayed me. He'd always been loyal to Elara. I had to respect that.

I clutched the stone in my fist. "Thank you." I knew that, to her, it meant something. An extension of her trust and the hope that perhaps we could move forward. She gave me a small smile in return.

Gwen looked pleased when she entered my room a few days later. I was still on bedrest, but this didn't stop her from visiting me every day, bringing me updates and gossip on everything that was going on in the palace. About the Argonians who were still alive being captured and locked up in the Mistwood prison. About Cai and Elara's plans for Argon and the international relations of their two kingdoms with the kingdoms on the continent. I didn't really care to hear any of it, but for her I would sit and listen patiently.

We hadn't talked about what happened on the battlefield, mostly because Gwen kept the conversation light. I wasn't sure if it was because she was trying to distract herself after all the loss and horror she'd experienced or if she was trying to avoid the topic altogether.

She pulled open one of the curtains allowing the morning sun to illuminate the room.

"I never thanked you."

She turned to face me. "Thank me for what?"

"For trying to keep me from bleeding to death out there." Silence fell over the room and Gwen froze, curtains still in hand.

She pressed her mouth into a line, choosing her next words. "You know there's a time I would've probably let you bleed out."

"I don't doubt it."

"You shouldn't have come after me." She strode over and took a seat on the bed.

"You shouldn't have been there in the first place," I reminded her. She'd broken her promise that she would stay behind. But after everything that had happened, it didn't feel worth it to bring it up anymore.

Without looking at me, Gwen placed her hand on top of mine. Her skin was soft, and I suddenly craved holding so much more than just her hand. "Thanks for coming after me."

"Thanks for saving my life."

She looked up then, wilful eyes gazing into mine. "Technically you saved mine."

I gave her a wink, settling back against my pillow. "We'll call it even, then."

Gwen shook her head, but she was wearing a smile. I realised that I longed to see that smile when it wasn't there.

"I have a gift for you."

"It's not my birthday."

"It's not a birthday present," I countered, pointing to the drawer next to my bed. "But I need you to help me get it out." I was still too weak to reach that far.

Gwen opened the drawer. I could tell she was at least a little curious, maybe even excited.

"It's in the little box."

She picked up the small wooden box, removing the lid. Her eyes widened at the sight of the small ring with a mariposa lily made of silver..

"Before you get excited, it's not that kind of a ring."

She looked at me with a raised eyebrow. "You expected me to say yes if it were?"

I wasn't sure what to reply, so I took the box from her and pulled out the little silver ring with the rosy gemstone placed in the centre of her favourite flower.

"This stone has a very special history," I said, taking her hand and sliding the ring onto her finger. Realisation seemed to set in, and she looked at me with surprise.

"Lance, where did you get this?"

"I have my ways." It was too soon to make any kind of serious vows or commitments. We needed to get to know each other without the threat of war looming over our heads, without the intervention of our families and our past. We needed a clean slate. I wanted to get to know her more, to spend time with her. I knew there was more to her than she let most people see. I'd caught glimpses of it in the past few months.

"I'm going back to Everness once I'm recovered."

Gwen looked disappointed, and I wondered if she thought this was some kind of parting gift.

"I want you to come with me," I added quickly. I wasn't sure what she would say, but I'd thought about it for days, and I knew it would kill me if I didn't at least ask her.

The corner of her mouth tugged up. "You mean you're not just leaving without a word this time?"

"Well, we can't have you holding a grudge for another few years. It seems like an awful waste of time."

She admired the ring on her finger. The Myrgonite stone, something that was once the only thing I truly cared about, the only thing I wanted.

And now, it had been replaced.

"I'll come on one condition."

"Is that condition that I kiss you again, on the hidden balcony of the ballroom?" I couldn't help but tease her. She swatted my arm and I grabbed her hand.

"I'm listening."

"You set up a shooting range at the Levernian palace." The fact that this was her only request made me chuckle.

"As you wish."

Chapter 50

Elara

I found Cai sitting in the library.

It was another cold winter night, and the fireplace warmed up the room, making it more comfortable than the icy hallways.

"There you are." The door closed behind me with a soft thud.

Cai looked over his shoulder from one of the reading chairs. "Were you looking for me?" He appeared pleased at the thought.

"Indeed." I walked over to the reading chair and placed my arm around his shoulders. "I wanted to see how you were doing after the council meeting today?"

Cai had formed a new council composed of the loyalist aristocrats who had stood by his side during exile and provided men to fight in the battle against Argon. He'd also met with some representatives from Argon and diplomats from other kingdoms, Cedia and Briarstead, on the continent, to discuss the future of Argon. Truth be told, I didn't care much what happened to the kingdom now without its king or any legal heirs. I only cared that we'd made it out alive and that Cai and I could finally start building a future together, focusing on our own kingdoms.

It felt like I was able to breathe properly for the first time in a while.

"I'm fine, thanks." He closed the book that was in his hands. "Just tired." He shut his eyes and leaned into me.

"Me too." Even now that it was all over, I still found it hard to sleep through the night. The only thing that helped was having Cai close to me.

I pulled away from Cai and removed the satchel I'd been carrying over my shoulder.

"I did have another purpose in coming here, though."

Anesta had come to me a few days ago, with the satchel in hand. Apparently Rhen had given it to her before he'd left for battle.

"What's inside?"

"King Evrin's diary." I pulled out the old book, dropping the satchel on the carpet in front of the fireplace. "Rhen gave it to Anesta, and she thought it was best that I have it back."

"You did go through an awful lot of trouble to find it," Cai reminded me.

"Yeah." I traced my fingers over the old leather spine, delicate pages carrying centuries-old secrets inside. "I suppose it was worth it in the end." If it had not been for the diary, we might never have discovered what the Myrgonite objects were. And if not for Rhen's sacrifice, that dangerous magic would still exist. King Evrin was right. Some things were better left buried.

"King Aries and his men who knew about the Myrgonite stones are gone, and we know that our friends and family who know about this are trustworthy."

"I'm not sure if I would use that exact word for Lance but it's close enough."

I gave him a knowing look, unable to hide my smile. "I just feel like this book was so well hidden for a reason, and while it's pretty much impossible to get to those stones now, I don't want to risk anyone finding out about it, even after we're gone."

"So, what are you saying? That we should hide it somewhere?"

I shook my head. "No, I think we should destroy it. Just like everything else about the magic was destroyed."

Cai put down the book he'd been reading and folded his hands. "Maybe you're right. Maybe everyone will be better off if we destroy everything."

I kneeled in front of the fireplace and slowly started to tear the pages from King Evrin's diary. It didn't take much effort since the paper was so old and fragile. One by one, I tossed them into the burning flames, watching as the words were turned into ash, slowly destroying history.

When it was gone, I tossed the leather binding in, for good measure, and finally stepped away from the heat of the flames. Cai came to stand behind me, wrapping his arms around my waist.

"Feel better?" he asked, pressing a kiss to my temple. I nodded, eyes still boring into the flames. "Now we can only hope that Queen Riona didn't also keep a journal."

I let out a snort and turned around so that I could face him, letting my hands rest around his neck. Cai's hands drew lazy circles on my back.

"Let's not do all that again for a long time," I said, referring to everything we'd been through in the past few months.

"I'd be perfectly happy if we never have to do that again ever."

I could not agree more.

"I'm sorry about Rhen." Neither of us had brought up his name since the day of the battle. Rhen sacrificed everything for us, for our kingdoms, for me. "And I'm sorry about Cordelia." Most of my nightmares consisted of watching Aries kill her over and over again, and I could never save her.

"I'd like to think they're all together now. Her and Jack and Rhen." Everyone we'd lost to this bloody and brutal war.

"Yeah." A sad smile crossed his face. Everything felt a little more broken than it had been before, including us. But at least we still had each other.

"It's almost strange not to have the palace full of soldiers anymore." The court was slowly returning to its previous state. I let my fingers tangle in the hair at the nape of his neck. "Everything's been so crazy, it almost feels too quiet. Like I don't know what I'm supposed to do with myself."

Cai got a sneaky look in his eye, his hands tightening around my waist. "I might have a few ideas in mind."

"Is that so?" I feigned ignorance as he pulled me into him, pressing slow kisses to my neck. "You know what, you might be right. We need to revise all the borderlines for the nobility's lands. So much paperwork."

Cai let out a low growl against my skin before grabbing my hips and throwing me over his shoulder. I let out a yelp in surprise.

"What exactly do you think you're doing, Your Majesty?"

His free hand trailed under the skirts of my dress, brushing against my calf. "All the things I have in mind."

I took a deep breath, trying to calm my nerves.

"I don't know if I can do this, Anesta."

She tied a ribbon into my hair, and I met her eyes in the mirror.

"You'll be fine, I promise." She looked back to the task at hand, and I wished I could share her calmness. "You've fought kings of enemy kingdoms, dealt with magical gemstones and enchanted forests. I know you can do this."

"I'm not supposed to be this nervous. Why am I freaking out like this?"

Anesta stood back to admire her handiwork.

"It is perfectly normal for any bride to be nervous on her wedding day."

"Are you sure?"

I took in my reflection. My wedding gown consisted of white and gold material and a long skirt that trailed on the ground behind me. Anesta had used ribbons to tie the top of my hair away from my face and completed the look with a pair of delicate golden earrings. I'd never felt so beautiful in my entire life.

"I am completely sure. You are the most wonderful-looking bride I've ever seen. I can't wait to see the look on Cai's face when he sees you for the first time."

Cai, who would be waiting for me at the end of the aisle. I was incredibly nervous and excited at the same time.

"This is all thanks to you," I replied, gesturing to my attire. "I never could have done any of this without you."

"Are you kidding?" Anesta chuckled. "I don't think anyone had more fun helping to plan the wedding than I did." That was true. When I told Anesta that I needed her help with all the preparations, she practically jumped out of her skin with excitement. She'd spent hours on end making all the arrangements for flowers and food and music. She found the seamstress who made my dress and took care of all the invitations. I couldn't have been more grateful to her.

"Okay," Anesta said, clasping her hands together. "Are you ready?"

I took another steadying breath. "Yes, I think so."

I'd never seen Anesta smile so wide. "Wonderful. Come on, let's get you to the ceremony."

Despite it being a royal wedding, Cai and I had decided to keep the entire affair as intimate and personal as possible. The ceremony would take place in the gardens and the reception in the great hall.

Anesta handed me a bouquet of flowers, and I followed her down the stairs towards the entrance to the garden.

Lance waited for me by the doors. He looked impeccably dressed, with his hair combed back. A smile crossed his face as I came into view.

"Never thought this day would finally come," he said, holding out his arm.

"For a while there, me neither," I responded, taking his arm. Musicians started to play as Anesta walked out in front of us, also with a bouquet of flowers.

"Thanks for walking me down the aisle."

Lance looked down at me and smiled again. "Anytime."

Spring was in full bloom and the gardens looked like a painting full of colour. There were beautiful decorations everywhere. Grand arrangements of flowers were placed on top of pillars to section off the area where the ceremony would take place. White ribbons had been tied to the backs of all the chairs while the ground was scattered with rose petals. At the end of the aisle was an arch also covered in different flowers from the garden. All the guests stood as we stopped at the entrance to the aisle.

But there, at the end, was Cai, and he was waiting for me, and in that moment, I felt more happiness than I'd ever thought possible.

Lance and I walked to the music until we reached Cai, and Alastor, who would be officiating.

Cai took my hand and gave it a squeeze, giving me all the comfort and reassurance I needed. Looking at him, I'd never felt more sure of anything in my entire life.

The great hall had been decorated with expensive tablecloths and floral centrepieces. Trestles laden with food were set out and servants walked the room serving wine.

Cai and I sat close to each other at our table, taking in all our guests and the party around us.

"Well, it certainly looks like everyone's enjoying themselves." Cai had hardly let go of my hand the whole day and I wouldn't have had it any other way.

"Especially Donald and Olwin." I gestured to the bandits making the most of the free wine. "It's nice to see them getting along after all these years."

"I was surprised that you'd decided to invite Brett and Creston." The two were enjoying their meals next to some of the other council members.

"I wanted the entire royal council here. And I have to admit, since the war, I feel like I actually managed to gain some respect from Brett and Creston." My council had finally fully accepted me as their queen and ruler.

Gwen and Lance were on the dancefloor, slowly swaying to the music.

"Gwen looks so beautiful in that dress," I commented, taking a sip of my wine. She wore an emerald gown and her whole face practically glowed as she smiled up at Lance.

"I'll admit, I never thought I would see Lance in love."

Some days it still took me by surprise to see how much he cared for Gwen. But I was happy for them.

"Me neither." I doubted Cai and Lance would ever be friends, given their past, but they'd come to some sort of mutual understanding and treated each other as respectfully as possible.

"She's good for him," he said, gesturing to Gwen. "And I'm glad someone is looking after her. She deserves to be happy."

"Yeah." I smiled and squeezed his hand. "What about you? Are you happy?"

"Incredibly happy."

I gave him a kiss before resting my head on his shoulder and admiring my wedding ring. It was the beautiful one that had belonged to his mother. I couldn't have asked for anything more special.

We had conquered war and death, deadly forests and ancient magic. I didn't believe there was anything that could come our way that we could not handle or work through together. For now, I would enjoy the peace we could finally experience and focus on the life that we wanted to build together. I didn't know what the future held, only that he was in it and that he always would be.

And while our names would be etched together in history, we were held together by something much stronger than ink on paper or alliances or treaties.

He was a part of my soul now, and I was a part of his. And it would stay that way, until the end of time.

Epilogue

6 years later

There were few things I loved in the world as much as the Evernean Forest on a spring morning. Sunbeams casting light through the canopy of trees, birds singing their melodies to one another, the smell of the wildflowers and the sound of flowing water from a nearby creek.

I readjusted myself on the blanket we'd laid out over a small patch of grass. It was the first sunny day since winter, and we'd decided to come out here and have a little picnic. Gwen was sprawled out on her stomach next to me, a book in her hands.

"The novel not quite interesting enough?" she asked, and I eyed the closed book lying next to me.

"You know how I feel about reading." I shrugged and she smiled, closing her own book. "Don't stop on my account, though."

"No, I prefer your company." She moved so she could sit next to me. "Besides, you're only here for a few more days. I want to spend as much time with you as possible."

As much as I wanted to stay in Everness for a little while longer, Cai and I had a few matters that required our presence back in Norrandale.

"We'll be back before spring is over and then we're going to spend the entire summer in Everness," I reassured her.

"I know. I just miss your company when you're gone."

I watched Cai in the distance and the little boy by his side. A smile made its way across my face, accompanied by the feeling of pure contentment. I almost wished we could stay for ever.

"You could always come to Norrandale," I suggested, already knowing what her answer would be. Since Gwen had moved to Levernia, she hadn't been back to Mistwood or Norrandale once. She'd made a life for herself here in Everness and I believed her to be quite happy.

"You're right. It's just that Mistwood doesn't feel like home anymore. And it's a long distance to travel with Philip. I mean, have you ever had to sit in a carriage with a four-year-old for hours on end?"

We both looked to where the little boy played with Cai. Dark tendrils of hair framed his face and he had icy-blue eyes. He looked so much like his father. But he definitely had Gwen's temperament. No one could doubt it.

"Good point. Although we do spend as much time here as possible." It was hard to travel between the two kingdoms sometimes. Cai and I both heavily relied on our councils to keep things running while we were gone, but we tried to balance our time between the two palaces. In the years that had passed, I'd grown quite fond of both my homes. But that didn't mean I didn't spend as much time in the forest as possible, whenever we were in Levernia. In a way, the forest would always be my home too. A part of me would always be there. The place that had raised me and protected me. The forest with monstrous wolves, deadly mists, and trees that listened and kept watch. The Myrgonite magic might have been destroyed long ago, but this would always be the magic that remained to me. The real magic.

"Aunty Lara! Aunty Lara!" Philip came running over while Cai walked behind him with a grin on his face. "Look what Uncle Cai found!"

My nephew ran towards me with outstretched hands, and I caught him in my arms. "What did you two find? Show me."

He opened his hand to reveal a pinkish pebble inside. Probably picked up from the creek.

"What a pretty stone that is, Philip."

"Can I keep it?" He looked to Gwen.

"Of course you can." She chuckled. With a satisfied expression, he made himself comfortable on the blanket, admiring his new prize. It didn't take much to impress at that age.

I reached for a blueberry tart as Cai sat down next to me, wrapping his arm around me.

"At least leave one for me, please."

I'd already had about five of them, but I couldn't help it — they were too delicious. I held out the half-eaten tart to him and Cai bent his head to take a bite.

"These are not bad."

"They're not as good as Brutus's, though."

"Oh, I miss Brutus's cooking and baking," Gwen chirped in. "I mean, the food here is great. But that man makes the best cakes in the world."

"That's true," I agreed.

"Speaking of which." She clapped her hands and looked at Philip. "Are you ready to go, little man? It's almost time for lunch." And no doubt Lance was expecting us back at the palace.

"Not yet." The boy shook his head, black curls swishing left and right.

Cai's hand splayed out over my stomach and its small bump. I covered his hand with mine, smiling as Gwen tried to argue with her child about lunch times.

"How about I tell you a story and then we go?" This sparked little Philip's interest. Whenever Cai and I stayed here, he would often request his Aunt Lara put him to bed with a story. I'd never thought myself much of a storyteller, but it turned out, if you were a queen long enough, there was always something interesting to tell. One thing was certain about my life as Queen of Everness and Norrandale, there was never a dull moment.

"Are you going to tell the one about the princess locked away in the kingdom across the sea again?" Philip had really taken a liking to that one for some reason.

"Not today." I patted my lap so that he would come and sit. The little boy didn't hesitate. "Then what story are you going to tell, Aunty Lara?"

I thought about it for a moment before a smile crept onto my face.

"I'm going to tell you a story about a girl who was a thief."

THE END

Acknowledgements

I've come to find that writing the acknowledgements of a book is both a satisfying and slightly emotional process. Writing a book is no easy task (any author can tell you that) and so it feels nice to be able to turn the last page, knowing you have completed something new. Something which probably took months if not years of work and had you concerned for your mental health a few times. No book is ever going to be perfect. But every book is still its own accomplishment. At the same time, writing the acknowledgements means saying goodbye. This thing, this world, these characters that you have spent so much time with, becomes something of the past.

Lara and her story have been a part of my life since I was eighteen years old. I am now a completely different person, and my life looks vastly different compared to when I started this series. But these books and this story was always there. I can admit that I am a little sad to know that Lara and Cai's story is over and that I probably won't write about them again. This series has seen me at all my low points and highlights. This world has become more than an escape but like a place of comfort or something that brings you nostalgia. The Twisted Crown Trilogy will always have a very special place in my heart. And this journey would not have been possible without so many people.

First, to my editor, Jasmine. Working with you has been such a pleasure and an honour. You made one of my biggest dreams, to be a published author, come true and I could not be more grateful. Thank you for taking a chance on me. Thank you for helping me improve my craft and challenging me as a writer so that I could become better. Thank you for the many hours of work you put into my novels to deliver the best possible story. I wouldn't be here without you. To the other editors and proofreaders, Laurel, Hannah and Kim. Your comments and suggestions were always so helpful and insightful. You tied up all the details in the books perfectly, every single time. I really appreciated all your edits and notes.

Mom and Dad, you have supported my writing for as long as I can remember. Thank you for being there every step of the way and encouraging me not to give up and keep pursuing the things I love. To my friends, I love each and every one of you more than words can say. Your support not just in my career but in every aspect of my life means the world. You are the most wonderful, kind and loving people I know and I'm so grateful to have all of you in my life.

To the entire team at Joffe. I feel so blessed to have you as my publisher. Thank you for all the work and effort you have put into this series. I will always be eternally grateful. To my wonderful readers. I hope you have loved this story as much as I have loved writing it. Thank you for reading my books and sharing my work and leaving me nice comments. I write novels because I love to, because I don't know how not to. But I also write because I know what a book can mean to a reader. I hope this story meant something to you in one way or another. I hope I can continue to write books that you will love.

The prospect of a new series is intimidating and exciting and I hope it will live up to your expectations. But for now, we greet this world. I am happy to know it will always be a part of me. Even though it's the end of a series, this isn't goodbye for us. It's only see you soon.

Love Leané

The Joffe Books Story

We began in 2014 when Jasper agreed to publish his mum's much-rejected romance novel and it became a bestseller.

Since then we've grown into the largest independent publisher in the UK. We're extremely proud to publish some of the very best writers in the world, including Joy Ellis, Faith Martin, Caro Ramsay, Helen Forrester, Simon Brett and Robert Goddard. Everyone at Joffe Books loves reading and we never forget that it all begins with the magic of an author telling a story.

We are proud to publish talented first-time authors, as well as established writers whose books we love introducing to a new generation of readers.

We won Trade Publisher of the Year at the Independent Publishing Awards in 2023. We have been shortlisted for Independent Publisher of the Year at the British Book Awards for the last four years, and were shortlisted for the Diversity and Inclusivity Award at the 2022 Independent Publishing Awards. In 2023 we were shortlisted for Publisher of the Year at the RNA Industry Awards.

We built this company with your help, and we love to hear from you, so please email us about absolutely anything bookish at: feedback@joffebooks.com.

If you want to receive free books every Friday and hear about all our new releases, join our mailing list here.

And when you tell your friends about us, just remember: it's pronounced Joffe as in coffee or toffee!